OFFSIDE ANGEL

PHOENIX ANGELS HOCKEY
BOOK 2

MARIAH WOLFE

OFFSIDE ANGEL

PHOENIX ANGELS HOCKEY BOOK 1

Zane Whitaker ruined my life the first time he kissed me.

Ruined me for other men.

Ruined me for any hope of a happy future that didn't involve him.

In return, I almost ruined everything he's ever worked for.

I left before that could happen.

I ran.

And if I had it my way, I'd keep on running.

But Zane sees things differently.

And now that he's found me again...

He's intent on convincing me of his perspective.

One.

Night.

At.

A.

Time.

OFFSIDE ANGEL is the second book in the Phoenix Angels Hockey duet. The story begins in Book 1 of the series, OFFSIDE DEVIL.

1

ZANE

Finding her looked different in my head.

In my head, I never followed Mira through the water-stained hallways of some pay-by-the hour motel.

In my head, she is already at home with me, and two horrible weeks haven't passed, and we're tangled in my sheets, fucking for the hundredth time like the darker parts of life don't even exist.

But this isn't happening in my head.

This is real.

The private investigator I hired woke me up with a phone call at two in the morning to tell me he had a lead. "Sunshine Ray's, room 315."

"You're sure?" I asked, already sliding out of bed and pulling on the jeans I shucked off a few measly hours ago. Sunshine Ray's—that's a motel just outside the city. I can be there in half an hour. "You laid eyes on her this time?"

"Black hair, legs for days. It's your woman."

Forgive me for having my doubts, but *"my woman"* has allegedly been spotted in southern California, Utah, New Mexico, even as far east as Austin, Texas. None of them panned out. No matter how fast I ran there or how long I searched, I never found her.

Aiden has been at Jace's or Reeves's house more than he's been at home. I've missed more practices in the last two weeks than in the last six years combined. I'm running on fucking fumes and clinging to every tiny lead.

But this time is different.

This time... *I saw her.*

It was a glimpse from the motel parking lot—silky black hair whipping around a corner with an ice bucket under her arm—but it's the closest I've been to Mira in two weeks.

I stalk down the hallway, studying every room number. They're not in any kind of order, as far as I can tell. By the looks of the rust brown stains on the carpet and the patched-over holes in the walls, the front office has good reason to make the layout as confusing as possible. If all of their best clients get arrested in what I have to assume are frequent raids, they'd go out of business.

Room 629... Room 428... Room 135.

I'm about to turn around and force the gangly man behind the front desk to take me to Room 315 himself... when, suddenly, there it is.

It's at the end of the second floor, wedged between a maintenance closet and the back stairs down to the parking lot. The window is closed tight, but there are muffled voices coming through the thin door.

I press my ear to the warped wood.

There are shuffling noises, heavy breathing. Then a hard, quick slapping sound.

"Stop fighting," a man growls. "Let me choke you."

Mira is supposed to be alone. In the few emails she's sent to Taylor, she hasn't mentioned being with anyone else.

But I don't think. Don't hesitate.

I just step back, lower my shoulder, and plow through the cheap door. It's there one second, gone the next, replaced by a view of the queen-sized motel bed through the shattered frame.

A woman is on her back along the end of the bed, her head tipped over the side, mouth open, a cheap polyester dress twisted up high over her hips. A naked man is standing over her, with a dick not capable of choking anyone clutched in his tight fist.

"Who the hell are you?!" he gasps, twisting away to give me a full view of his pale, pimpled ass. "If you're the police, you have to announce yourself first!"

I ignore the moron and—oh, fucking hell. Her hair is red.

Her hair is red.

Copper-colored tresses cascade over the side of the bed to the threadbare carpet as the woman gawks at me from upside down. There's a massive tattoo along the woman's thigh and over her hip.

It's not Mira.

"Where is she?" I growl. Hope is curdling in my chest, but I ignore it. I have to.

The guy flings a hand at the woman in front of him. "She's right fucking here. What do you mean? Who are you—"

"Dark hair," I spit. "A woman with long, dark hair. She was staying here."

He frowns for a fraction of a second. Then there's recognition. His eyes go wide. "I didn't touch her. She wasn't here for me. She left as soon as we got here."

When I saw Mira from the parking lot, I thought she was walking back to her room. She was moving this direction…

I don't wait for more of an explanation—I hurtle through the gaping door and turn for the stairs.

I pound down the metal staircase and leap from the fourth step, landing hard on the concrete. Jace would yell at me to be careful. I've been flaky the last couple weeks; the last thing I need is to tear my ACL and let Carson finish out this season on a high. He'd win the captain spot for sure.

Not that I give an ounce of a flying fuck about that now.

I sprint down the length of the building and take a hard right towards the front office.

And there she is.

She's standing under the glowing security light stationed next to the front door. It's the only working light in the entire lot. She might as well be on a stage. Her back is to me, but it's her. Dark hair, long legs. Just like the P.I. said.

My woman.

Taylor told me Mira would come back if she wanted to. "She disappears and pops back up all the time. Just give her some space."

"Or you can let her go," Daniel suggested once Taylor was out of earshot. "You have Aiden and yourself to think about. No one would blame you for moving on."

How about option three?

I angle across the parking lot at a breakneck pace.

She hears the gravel under my feet and starts to turn as I grab her shoulder and whip her around.

"I found you," I pant, at the exact same time that this woman I definitely do not know screams in my face.

"Get off of me!" she shrieks, flailing until I let go and stumble back. "Don't fucking touch me!"

Her hair is dark, but up close, it's thin and greasy and tangled. She's either lived a hard life or she's twenty years older than Mira, at least. Probably both.

It's not her and I should've known from several football fields away, but I saw what I wanted to see.

I saw Mira.

"I-I'm sorry." I hold up my hands in surrender, but quickly lower them when she flinches away. "I thought you were—"

The woman is shaking. The man behind the front desk is staring out at us, his hand resting on the phone.

I could explain myself, but it doesn't matter. I just turn around and walk away.

~

As soon as I come through the door, Daniel is there. He doesn't ask, but I feel the question burning inside of him.

"It wasn't her," I grumble, shuffling to the fridge. "Obviously."

I've spent so many hours on the road the last two weeks that the fridge is almost empty. Jemma offered to pick Aiden and Jalen up from preschool and take them back to her house. Most days, she feeds Aiden dinner, too.

I haven't eaten anything that wasn't a protein shake or from a takeout container in weeks.

I slam the fridge closed and pour myself a glass of water from the tap instead.

Daniel sighs. "Have you considered—I mean, the P.I. you're working with is legit, right? If she was out there to be found, he would've found her. Maybe she isn't... Maybe she's..."

"Dead?" I snap, whipping around to face him. "You can say it. It's not like I haven't thought it a thousand fucking times. Mira could be dead."

Her apartment was ransacked.

The window was open.

No one else knows about Mira's dad or her brother. Taylor thinks the apartment was probably broken into while Mira was living with me. A run-of-the-mill robbery.

I'd be inclined to believe her... if I didn't know better.

I assumed she escaped, but maybe her sadistic brother caught up to her. Or maybe he dragged her away from the open window and hauled her back to his car.

I've considered every possibility, theories constantly running through my head while I'm in the shower and lying in bed and strapping on my skates. But the only one I can allow myself to think about is the one where Mira got away. Where she's safe, but on the run.

The only theory I can stomach is the one where she comes home to me.

Daniel leans on his elbows. "You know I don't want that to be true. Not even just for you. For Taylor, too. She doesn't show it, but she's been a wreck since Mira left. But I hate seeing you like this." He droops. "But the team—Coach, especially— is worried."

I narrow my eyes. "I don't give a shit about how I'm playing. Mira is missing. That's more important than hockey. If Coach wants to bench me, then he—"

"They're worried about *you*," Daniel cuts in. "I am, too. We want to find Mira, but we also want *you* to be okay if, at the end of this, that doesn't happen."

I sag back against the fridge, suddenly exhausted. "It's not me I'm worried about."

As if on cue, a small voice echoes down the hallway.

It's my son.

"He hasn't woken up once since I got here," Daniel says. "Do you want me to go talk to him or do you—?"

"I got it." I wave him towards the door. "Thanks for coming over so late. I appreciate it."

Daniel smiles. "What are best friends if not middle-of-the-night babysitters? I was just doing my job."

I let him out and set the alarm. I've trusted the building's security since I moved in a couple years ago, but with everything that has happened, an additional security system seemed like a good idea. I would've up and moved Aiden by now—got us somewhere outside the city center, somewhere with a yard—but if Mira comes back, I want her to know where to find us.

I lean against the wall for just a second as a new wave of disappointment craters my chest, hollowing me out. I need to sleep and eat a real meal. Everyone around me is right to be a little worried. I feel like I'm barely holding it together.

Then I shove off the wall and walk to Aiden's room.

The closer I get, the louder his voice is. When I crack open the door, his room is still dark, but I can hear him… singing?

It takes me a few seconds to place the song. To realize the words he's sniffling through are Italian.

It's the song Mira taught him. The Italian lullaby.

My skin feels sticky from just stepping foot in that seedy motel, but I drop down onto the bed next to Aiden's lump in the middle.

His voice cuts off. A second later, he pokes his head out of the top of his covers. His eyes are red-rimmed and glassy. "I had a bad dream."

"Do you want to talk about it?"

He frowns, considering it. He blinks back more tears. "We were at the park. Mira was there. She went down the slide with me."

A few weeks before Mira moved out, we all went to the park. Aiden convinced Mira to go down the tall metal slide with him over and over again. When they were finished, we crowded onto a blanket and ate sandwiches Mira made for us.

It was a good day.

I smooth his hair back from his forehead. Shit, it's getting shaggy. He needs a haircut. "That doesn't sound scary."

"Not scary." He scooches closer to me, his head pillowed on my knee. "But I woked up. I didn't want to, but I did."

My breath catches in my chest. I can't believe I thought for even a second that Aiden would be better off without Mira around.

He sniffles, burrowing deeper into my side. "When is she coming back? Where is she?"

"I don't know," I mutter, stroking his unruly hair the way I so often saw Mira doing. "But I'm going to find out."

2

MIRA

It takes everything in me not to run to him.

Zane's golden hair is glowing in the moonlight. He looks like some mythical creature who crash-landed in this depressing reality. No one like *him* should be *here*.

The first few nights I spent on musty motel mattresses and showering in cloudy motel water, I thought the same thing about myself: *I shouldn't be here.* I spent months in a fairy tale with Zane and Aiden and it made me soft, made me forget the rules of running.

But two incredibly long weeks later, I'm almost back to form. I can now brush a roach off the motel pillow and still sleep like a baby.

A baby who startles at every sound and wakes up screaming from nightmares, that is.

If it's not roaches and mysterious stains testing my sleep, it's dreams of blood and knives and mindless screaming. Every night, I wake up panting and gasping for air. I can never remember if I was the person with the knife or the person running.

Just like in real life, I'm probably both.

Zane cuts across the dark parking lot and jogs up the stairs. Twenty seconds later, I see him on the second floor walkway.

I have no idea how he found me. I thought I was being careful. But here he is.

Again.

The first time he caught up to me was at a truck stop just outside of Albuquerque. I thought I was seeing things. It had been over twenty-four hours since I'd eaten anything and I was standing in line to pay a quarter for a Styrofoam cup I could fill with water from the soda fountain. When I saw him walk past the windows, heading for the bathrooms around back, I thought I was delirious.

But it was really Zane.

It was Zane in Albuquerque and again in Flagstaff. He even picked up my trail in Mesa Verde.

It makes no sense. I use public libraries to read my email, I haven't used my card since I cashed the final check Zane handed me, and I don't stay anywhere for longer than a day.

So I have no idea how Zane is following me so closely.

All I know is I'm grateful Dante isn't as resourceful as Zane. If he was, I'd already be dead.

And if Zane would finally give up, maybe I could bring myself to run farther away. I could put this part of the country and my name in my rearview mirror and never look back. I could forget about my brother's crusade for revenge —for a little while, at least.

As it is, I live for these little glimpses of Zane. Even though I know he's running himself ragged chasing after me. Even though I know I should want him to move on and find some nice, normal girl without a literal skeleton in her closet.

I don't know what I'll do when he stops chasing me.

Zane disappears around the side of the building and I sink deeper into the driver's seat of the clunker I bought with the little bit of cash I still have. I'm parked in a used car lot across the street from the motel. I was on my way out of town when I saw Zane's Ferrari roar past me. I should have kept going, but I couldn't help myself.

Especially after the night I had.

I've taken to sleeping during the day and driving at night. Fewer eyes on me means fewer chances of being recognized. But today, I overslept. I should've checked out of the room a little after five. Instead, I woke up at one in the morning to pounding on my door.

Before I could wake up enough to be terrified, they announced themselves. "I'm with the front desk. You missed check-out. If you don't come out, I'll call the cops."

I must have slept for twelve hours. Maybe more.

It was nice…

Until it wasn't.

I stumbled to the door and the man from the front desk sighed with relief. "You didn't kill yourself. Great. I did not want to deal with that kind of mess again. This room has a history."

When I grabbed my single duffel bag and left, a balding man with a big gut and a redhead in a polyester dress were waiting nearby. They shuffled in right after me, apparently not worried about a change of sheets.

It's probably their door Zane is banging down right now. It doesn't take much imagination to figure out what they're doing in there.

If it wasn't so fucking depressing, I could almost smile at the full circleness of them being interrupted by aggressive knocking. If Zane knocks, that is. Somehow, I doubt it. It's not really his style.

My eyes snap to the corner of the building as a woman ambles towards the main office. She sways back and forth as she walks like she's in imminent danger of falling over. Under the yellow light, she leans against the wall and lights a cigarette.

She's only been there a few seconds when Zane comes tearing around the building where she just came from. He's running like his life depends on it.

I jolt up, hand poised on my keys in the ignition.

Is he being chased? Is he in trouble?

Fuck my cover. I'd blow it in a second if it meant mowing down anyone trying to hurt Zane.

But he's not running *from* anyone.

He's running *towards* someone.

More specifically, towards the woman with long, dark hair standing under the only light on the entire street.

My stomach drops. I realize what's happening a second before Zane grabs the woman and spins her around. She screams and Zane stumbles back, hands raised and the look on his face says it all.

He thought she was me.

He was running like his life depended on it because he thought he'd found *me.*

Guilt slices through me as Zane walks back to his car, head hung low. I live for these little glimpses of Zane, but I don't need to be any closer than I am right now to see the truth: this is killing him.

While he's been chasing me all around the southwestern US, who has been watching Aiden? I sprang for the premium TV package in a motel room the other night to catch the Angels game, but Zane was benched. He didn't play a single minute.

How much longer can this go on before it breaks him?

How many more almost run-ins can we have before our paths finally cross? And then what?

I drop my face into my hands, taking deep, even breaths to keep the tears at bay. Because I know the truth. I've known it since the moment I laid eyes on Zane Whitaker. Since the moment I felt that magnetic draw towards him.

No matter what happens, I can never be with him.

Even if he catches up to me, I'll still have to leave him.

After a few minutes, his car starts.

A few minutes later, he drives away.

I watch until his tail lights disappear behind the horizon.

Then I start my engine and drive in the opposite direction.

3

ZANE

Madonna is blaring from the showers—Jace's choice, and he'll beat the brakes off anyone who tries to protest—and Davis is chanting something I can't make out. A few of the guys join in, their voices echoing off the wet tile.

The atmosphere before a big game used to be my favorite. The zing of anticipation in my chest. The blind optimism that settles over the entire team. Tunnel vision: win or die.

I used to pop out of bed on game days and count down the hours until I could get to the arena. Until I could strap into my skates and be where I belonged. Where I'd always belonged.

Tonight, I'd rather be anywhere else.

"You gonna take a shower, Z?" Reeves drops down on the bench across from me, a towel wrapped around his neck.

"I wait until *after* I've played to take a shower," I mumble.

"Then you're missing out on a competitive edge." Jace runs a hand down his freshly-shaven face. "I'm more aerodynamic now… according to Davis."

In another version of this conversation, I'd laugh. Maybe I'd even get up and go shave the stubble I've let grow into what's becoming a raggedy beard.

In this version, I drop back against the wall and sigh.

Reeves snorts. "Has Davis ever heard of a helmet? I don't think aerodynamics cares about the hair on my chin when I'm wearing forty pounds of pads and a two-inch-thick helmet."

"Davis has probably never heard of 'aerodynamics' before whatever clickbait article he read this tip from." Jace shrugs. "But it's fun. As captain, I deem this team bonding. It's important. Which is why Zane should get his hairy ass to the showers and shave."

He shoves my shoulder, but I shake him off. "I'm good."

Reeves pushes from the other side. "Come on, Z. Put on your game face. Since you didn't try to punch Carson in the face this week, Coach is going to let you play tonight."

I should regret getting benched last week, but watching Carson's eyes go wide when I swung at him is the closest thing I've felt to joy in two weeks. I'm not even sure what he said since he was too scared to say it above a whisper, but it was something about Mira.

Suffice it to say, he deserved it.

"More aerodynamic or not, the beard is not a good look." Jace wrinkles his nose. "Rachelle said it makes it look like you don't have a neck and now, I can't unsee it. I'll shave you myself."

"Are we finally talking about the depression beard?" Daniel leaves his equipment cart in the walkway and slides onto the bench next to me. "I get it. I grew a beard any lumberjack would've been proud of when I lost my leg. But all glorious things must come to an end."

I slap Daniel's hand away from my face. "I don't give a fuck what I look like."

"Obviously," he drawls. "But Taylor has mentioned the beard, too. Now feels like as good a time as any for an intervention."

"I don't need a fucking intervention!" I shove off the bench. "I don't care about shaving or aerodynamics or whether we beat the Firebirds tonight. None of this bullshit fucking matters!"

My voice is still echoing in the now-silent locker room when my phone rings.

I recognize the ringtone and lunge for my locker. I answer it, breathless. "What do you have?"

"She's still in town," the P.I. says. "Desert Lodge, Room 224."

If she ever was here, I figured she would've bolted by now. If she was really trying to run, she'd be half a country away.

Maybe that means she isn't *trying to run.*

"You're sure?"

I ask every time, even though all it would take is an inkling for me to break down every door in the entire building.

"I saw her myself. I'm posted outside and she's still in the room."

She's still there. Right now.

"Don't leave," I growl. "I'm on my way."

I pocket my phone and turn around to find half the team staring back at me.

Before I can start to explain myself—why I have to go, why I won't make it to the game—they start talking.

"Aiden is already at our house with Rachelle, so we can keep him overnight." Jace points to Reeves. "But we're leaving town tomorrow morning to see Rachelle's parents. Can you and Jemma—"

"We'll pick him up first thing in the morning," Reeves agrees before Jace can even finish. "We can keep him all day and for the night if we need to."

Daniel throws up a hand. "Taylor and I are free, too. If Aiden would rather be at home, we can bunk with him at Chateau Whitaker."

I stare at them all blankly. "What about the game?"

Jace raises an amused eyebrow. "I thought 'none of this fucking matters'?" When I can't find the words to answer, he nods and juts a chin toward the door. "Finding Mira is important. I know you think the sun shines out of your ass, but believe it or not, we *can* win without you on the ice. So get the fuck outta here. We'll hold down the fort."

Say less.

I shuck off my warm-up jersey and toss my pads and skates in the locker.

"Leave it all," Daniel orders. "We'll clean it up. You gotta go."

"Go where?" I whirl around as Coach Popov comes to a stop

behind me. He takes in the scene slowly. "We have a game to play, men."

My teammates were emotionally behind me one hundred percent five seconds ago. Now, they're literally behind me. Not one of them pipes up to explain things to Coach.

I don't even blame them. This is my fight; not theirs.

I pull on my T-shirt and sit down to lace up my sneakers. "I have to go."

"Whitaker, this game is big for you," Coach says. "It's your first game back after the shit you pulled last week."

"It's only big because every reporter wants to know why I was benched," I spit. "But I don't care what they think. Carson was an asshole. He ran his mouth about my family. I handled it."

I'm aware that Carson is probably back in the showers, listening to all of this like everyone else.

I'm also aware that I should probably look like I learned some valuable lesson about teamwork or some shit after my punishment, at least in front of Coach. But I don't have the energy to pretend for anyone anymore.

Coach narrows his eyes. "Carson may have some room to mature, but he's focused. He's been here at every practice. He *wants* to be here."

"Then make him captain!" I slam my locker closed and whirl around. "If Carson's the better choice, then have at it. Make him captain. But I'm not going to put this job before my family. Not anymore."

I look around at my teammates—my friends. My brothers. "I love this team, but I have to have a life outside of this arena. I have a family who has to come first." I run a hand through my hair. "They should have always come first."

Maybe I just threw captain away.

Maybe I just handed the title to Carson.

But it doesn't matter. Whether it was right now or six months from now, I was always going to come to this conclusion.

I turn back to Coach Popov. "This team has given me so much. It was all I had to live for there for a while. But now... my priorities are straightened out. I know what matters most. And I'm not going to let it slip away."

4

MIRA

I shouldn't be here.

I should be halfway to Oregon by now. I even stopped at a library today and looked up *"Things to do in Portland"* on the public computer. As if I'm on a sightseeing trip instead of running from my deranged brother.

But as I scrolled through the list, I couldn't help but wonder what Aiden would make of a ride on the aerial tram or which books he'd choose from Powell's. I imagined holding hands with Zane while we walked along the waterfront.

Now, I'm alone in another shitty motel on the outskirts of Phoenix because I don't have the heart to face any of that alone. I can't even imagine being further from Zane and Aiden than I am right now.

Which is a problem.

"I just have to go," I mutter, testing out my voice for the first time today. The most interaction I've had in weeks is the motel clerk who told me he was glad I hadn't killed myself.

It could've been worse, but it could also be…

Well, actually, I don't think it will get better than the life I was building here in Phoenix.

"There's nothing for me here," I say more forcefully, trying to drill that reality into my own head.

I can't be with the people I want to be with, and the longer I stay, the more danger I'm in.

The more danger *they* are in.

So I shove the few items of clothing I have into my duffel bag and get ready for check-out.

This time, I'm going to leave.

This time, I'm really going to start over.

I sling my bag over my shoulder and walk to the door. But as I'm reaching for the handle, someone pounds on the other side of it.

I barely manage to bite back a yelp as I throw myself away from the door.

I wait for them to announce themselves—maintenance or housekeeping or room service to the wrong unit. I wait for my sign that I'm just being paranoid and this isn't the nightmare I've been running from for the last six years.

But there's nothing. Only an eerie, all-consuming silence.

My heart is in my throat, but I quickly grab my bag and retreat to the bathroom. Running is a finely-tuned instinct. I don't need to think about it.

As soon as I checked in late morning, I tested to make sure the bathroom window opened. I can use the trash can for a boost and climb over the sill. It'll dump me behind the building. I can run into the ravine behind the motel and hide there until I can get to my car.

Or ditch the car.

If Dante is here, he might know what I'm driving. But there's a Greyhound station not far up the road. I can take a bus and—

Something heavy thuds against the door, and I jolt so hard, my shoulder bashes against the bathroom door frame.

This is it. He's found me.

I push through the panic and lift the windowsill, but it catches. The stupid thing slid open like a dream earlier, but now, the glass is off-centered in the paint-crusted frame. It's wedged in tight.

"Open," I beg, pounding the palm of my hand against the metal, trying to straighten it out. "For God's sake, open."

There's another thud behind me. The walls are shaking and tears are pooling in my eyes.

"Please," I whimper, jockeying the window back and forth to try to loosen it. "I don't want to die."

The words are barely out of my mouth when the door explodes open.

I scream and drop to the floor. *This is how it ends*, I think. *In the fetal position in a motel bathroom. This is how I die.*

"Mira?"

I look up and there he is.

Zane.

Every cell in my body sighs with relief. Not just that I'm not going to die tonight, but that he's here. *Finally.*

Zane's blue eyes scrape over the room, a frantic edge to his every movement. Then he sees me.

I see the same relief I'm feeling reflected back at me. His mouth falls open and he moves towards me like a man possessed.

I'm still shaking from the adrenaline dump, and I want nothing more than to curl against Zane's chest. I want to fall asleep to the steady thrum of his heartbeat and breathe in the wintergreen scent of him. I want to give myself everything I know I can't have.

Then my mind flashes back to Zane walking, dejected, across that parking lot the other night.

I hold out a hand. "Wait."

He slams to a stop in the doorway. His jaw flexes. "Are you hurt?"

I'm aching right now. Every lovesick part of me is dying to close the distance between us.

"You have a game," I breathe. "Tonight. You should be—"

"Are. You. Hurt?" he grits out.

He takes another step towards me, but I fling out my arm. "Don't! Please."

It's been so long since I've seen him this close. I drink in every micro-emotion that flickers across his face. The pinch of his brows, the flattening of his lips.

"I've been chasing you down for weeks, Mira." His breath catches on my name, a hint at how much the search has cost him. "Let me fucking touch you."

"You can't, Zane. We—I have to leave."

"Fuck that!" he snarls. "No. You're staying. You're not going anywhere."

I press the heels of my hands to my eyes. Part of me wants to remove them and realize that I'm in an empty bathroom. That Zane was never here and this was all a dream.

A much bigger, more selfish part of me wants Zane to ignore my boundaries and wrap his arms around me.

I drag my hands down my face and he's still there. Still oscillating his eyes over me like I might not be real. "Nothing has changed. I'm not good for you and Aiden."

"You're the best thing that's ever happened to either of us." He spits the words angrily, but they're tender and vulnerable.

I shake my head. "I'm not going to be the reason that Aiden gets taken from you. Or the reason that you two get hurt. My brother is still coming after me. He *will* find me."

"When he does, I'll be there to kill him." Zane stands tall and I'm positive he can do it. If anyone could end the nightmare I've been living in, it's Zane. He could kill Dante.

But it would come with a price.

"You can't be there for Aiden from prison," I say softly. "I'm not going to let you risk everything for me."

Zane crosses the bathroom in two steps. He raises his hands to touch me and then drops them, a low growl vibrating through his chest. "I never should have asked you to leave."

"I understand why you did." I drop my eyes. "You were looking out for your son."

Suddenly, his finger catches my chin. It's the barest brush of skin against mine, but all of my nerve endings converge there. I feel like I've been operating at half power for weeks and Zane just gave me a jump start.

"I should have been looking out for you, too." He's close enough that I feel his breath on my skin. I feel the heat radiating off of him. "None of this is your fault, Mira. You've been running for so long, and it's time to stop."

My throat bobs against his hand. A racking sob bursts out of me, and Zane swipes his thumb over my bottom lip. It's more physical touch than I've had in so long. It's overwhelming. He's barely touching me, but I feel it everywhere.

"I want to agree with you," I whisper. "But I can't. Not if it's going to put you and Aiden at risk."

"We're already at risk. Aiden is crying himself to sleep at night thinking about you. He wakes up from dreams of you singing the lullabies you taught him. He asks about you *every single day*, and I have to—" Zane drags a hand over his beard. It's longer than I've ever seen it. It makes him look older. More tired. He meets my eyes. "I can't watch my son miss you another day. I won't do it. You need to come home."

Home.

The word radiates through me, settling like water in all of my deepest, most broken places.

I realize all at once that I've never had a home before I met this man. Zane and Aiden gave me a home for the first time in my life, and I want to go back there more than anything.

Tears burn in my eyes. I try to blink them back, but they won't stop. They pour down my face until I can't see. Until I can't breathe.

"Let me touch you," Zane growls. His finger shakes against my chin. "Let me hold you."

The last little bit of restraint I had is gone. I collapse against Zane, and he lowers us both gently to the floor. He curls me against his chest and soothes a warm hand down my spine.

He kisses the side of my head. "You're not leaving again. I'm not letting you leave."

I saw Zane the night he thought he'd found me. He ran towards that woman with everything he had. The same way he's holding me right now—with everything he has.

He told me before that being an addict means he doesn't do things halfway. And I know he'll sacrifice absolutely everything to protect me.

Which is why I *have* to leave.

For good this time.

No more shitty motels twenty minutes from his condo. No more sitting by and watching him try to chase me down.

I'm going to disappear for good: new name, new start. I'm going to give Zane and Aiden the clean break they deserve.

But first...

I lift my face and stroke a trembling hand down Zane's cheek. "Okay."

His eyes go wide. I feel his hand tighten on my back, pulling me closer. "Okay?"

"I'll stay. I'll come home."

The relief that breaks across his face would bring me to my knees if I wasn't already there. He's happy, and I hate that I'm going to take it all away in just a little while.

Then Zane's mouth is on mine, and I can't think about anything.

5

MIRA

He curls his hand around the back of my neck and parts my lips with his tongue. He tastes me slowly and deeply.

I'm not sure how anyone survives without this. I've been drowning and touching him is like taking my first real breath in way too long.

Will we be able to walk away from this?

"We can't," Zane pants against my mouth.

Did I say that out loud?

"What?"

He hitches me around his waist and stands up. We stumble forward and I'm sandwiched between the wall and the hard press of his erection against my stomach. I instinctively shift closer, and Zane's teeth scrape over my neck in a growl.

"We can't do this in here." He says it with obvious regret in his voice.

I need this to happen *here*. If we leave—if he takes me back home—it will be so much harder to do what I have to do.

Suddenly, he picks me up and turns around.

I cling to him. "Where are we going?"

"I'm not going to fuck you in this filthy bathroom."

As we leave, I blink around the room and, yeah, okay, I was seeing the room through *I'm-about-to-be-murdered* glasses before. Followed quickly by *fuck-me-now* glasses. It's disgusting. It needs a deep clean... followed by an exorcism and a speedy demolition.

Zane throws me back on the bed. The mattress springs protest and then erupt in a full-on riot as he falls over me. "It's bad enough I'm going to have to fuck you in this bed." He lifts my dress around my waist, his fingers hooking in the sides of my panties. "You should be in *our* bed. In *our* house."

I whimper at his words as much as the brush of his new facial hair over my hip, between my thighs.

He drags my panties down my legs and kisses his way back up, pressing my legs apart as he goes. "I should've had you like this every day, Mira. Do you hear me?"

He parts me with his fingers, and I don't hear anything except the whirr of blood in my ears, pulsing to the same beat I feel in my core.

Zane tastes me with tentative strokes at first that deepen with every shift of my hips, every groan I can't hold back.

When I fist his hair and haul him closer, he growls and tilts my hips to his mouth. He buries his face inside of me and I forgot anything could feel this good.

He's right. I need this every day.

How am I going to walk away?

"I need it," I pant, rolling myself against his mouth and his tongue. "Please."

All at once, he stops. Zane drops my hips and crawls over me. His lips are slick from me and his eyes are dark and blazing. "Say it again."

"Please?"

He shakes his head and curls his hand between my legs. "Say it again."

I frown before I realize what he's demanding. "I need it."

He rewards me with one finger, sliding it deep. He watches it disappear inside of me. "Again."

"I need it," I pant, arching to take another of his thick fingers. "I need *you.*"

Zane works his hand inside of me, curling and stroking until I'm fisting the scratchy comforter and panting his name. "You *need* me, Mira," he breathes against my neck. He kisses my stomach and my hip, his fingers never slowing. "You can't leave again. You have to stay. You need this."

If he's trying to change my mind, he's doing a world-class job. Consider me a convert.

Zane thrusts his fingers into me at the same time he seals his mouth over my clit, and I'm gone. Airborne. On my way to another dimension.

My body spasms and shakes, and he follows the rise and fall of my release, easing me down with gentle touches until I'm a puddle of relief on the bed.

"God, I missed the sounds you make when you come for me." Zane drags the straps of my dress down my arms and peels it off of me, throwing it to the floor. His pants are next and then he's stroking himself, studying every inch of me like I might disappear again.

And I will.

Soon.

But for now...

I wrap my hand around him, and Zane is more than willing to let me take control. He presses into my hand, his teeth biting into his lower lip. When I stroke the tip of him over myself, working him into the mess he left between my legs, his eyes drop closed.

"Fuck, Mira," he groans. "Like fucking silk."

In one move, he rips my hand away, pins our tangled fingers to the mattress, and sinks into me.

I whimper as he stretches me. When he's buried deep, he drops his forehead to mine. "Perfect."

I'm not sure if he means me or the way we fit together or the way this feels.

I agree, anyway.

"Yes." I lift my hips, rolling against him and taking him deeper. "Yes."

He retreats and then dips in and out of me in tiny increments that build a slow and steady fire in my core.

"Zane...!" I grab his ass and try to take him deeper.

"I want to touch you like this all night." He takes my nipple in his mouth, rolling his tongue over the pebbled tip. "I don't want it to end. We have so much lost time to make up for."

"We can't do it in one night."

We can't do it at all, actually. This is it. The end.

He teases me open once and again. He slides deeper with each thrust until he's finally filling me. Until I'm clawing at his back and catching my breath and—

"I'm coming!" I gasp.

I bite his shoulder to stifle my scream, but Zane presses me down to the mattress and watches me fall apart. The few seconds I can manage to crack my eyes open, he's studying me with a hungry expression.

He pulls out of me, still hard, and kisses down the center of my body. Then he grips my hips and drags me to the edge of the bed.

My hair fans out above my head, my limp arms stretched out to either side. I'm spent and Zane is sliding into me again.

"How many times can I make you come?" he asks, almost to himself. If there's a scientific study, I'd volunteer.

Heat is already building between my legs, and I toss my head to the side, weak and wanting. And I gasp.

"The door is still open!" I throw my arms over my chest like I might be able to retroactively keep anyone who might have walked by from seeing anything. "You never closed it after you—"

Zane scoops me into his arms, still inside of me, and carries me across the room.

The frame is cracked and splintered, but when Zane kicks the door closed, it latches somehow. He presses me against it and drives into me like we never stopped. Like this is the only thing we were made to do. The only thing we could ever need.

I kiss him, swirling our tongues together and telling him in the only way I know how that I want nothing more than to be here with him.

I want to stay, my kiss says. *I would give anything to keep you.*

My legs are wrapped around his waist and he finds my hands. Our fingers tangle together and he lifts them over my head, holding me between his hands and his cock. He drives into me until our lips break apart. It's all I can do to keep breathing and take him.

The door rattles in the frame and I'm sure everyone in the rooms beside, above, and below us can hear what we're doing, but I don't care. I'm too far gone.

"Mira," Zane pants, driving into me harder and faster. I feel his hips stutter and he's close, I'm close, *we're both so fucking close.*

My body quivers with the start of another orgasm that doesn't even feel possible when suddenly—

"More," Zane demands. He drops me to my feet and spins me around.

My hands slap against the wood door as he fills me from behind with a groan that I feel in every dark, shadowy corner of my heart.

If I loved him any less, I'd stay. I'd steal every last touch and kiss and orgasm he wanted to give me until my past caught up with us both and he had to pay the price.

But I don't. I can't.

I leverage myself against the door and arch my hips. He growls at the new angle, his fingers digging harder into my skin.

"Come with me," he demands.

I'm about to tell him it's impossible. I'm surprised I'm still standing.

Then his hand slides around my hip and he's circling my throbbing center and I toss my head back.

"How?" I ask in a breathless laugh as I clamp down around him again.

Zane curses under his breath, breaking the smooth rhythm his hips have been working into me. Then he seals our bodies together—his thighs flush with mine, his cock buried deep. I feel him jerk inside of me, and I grind against him, dragging out this moment as long as I possibly can.

"Holy shit, Mira. This is…"

His voice trails off, but I know. *I know.*

Zane comes inside of me for what feels like an eternity. Then he collapses against me, flattening me against the door until I can't breathe and I don't even want to.

Once we've caught our breath, he tucks my hair over my shoulder and kisses my neck, my shoulder. He slides out of me and carries me back to the bed.

We sleep. Or, I think we do. But when my eyes open again,

Zane is curled behind me, the hard length of him pressed to where I'm already wet.

He slides into me and we rock together until I'm burying my cries in the pillow and he's whispering in my ear, "You're safe with me, Mira. I'm going to take care of you. I'm never going to leave you. I'm never, ever going to leave."

"I know you won't," I whisper back.

But I will.

6

ZANE

I wake up to the shower running.

My body is heavy with sleep. Like I fused with the mattress while I was sleeping. It takes me a few seconds to remember where I am. To remember why my joints are stiff and there's a warm, heavy feeling low in my stomach.

I found her.

I smile and stretch an arm across the bed, but it's cold.

I jolt upright before I can piece it all together.

She's in the shower.

After last night, she probably does need to clean up.

I didn't plan to do any of that. My plan was to get into the room, grab her, and leave. I wanted to get her home as soon as possible.

Then she was there in front of me, and I couldn't think about anything else. Some ancient instinct rose up, and I needed her to be mine. I needed her to be mine again and again *and again.*

Even right now, I'm barely conscious and my cock is already rising to attention. I wasn't kidding about making up for lost time. We have weeks and weeks to catch up on.

I slide out of bed and pad to the bathroom door. I don't bother knocking, I just push it open.

A cloud of steam rolls through the door like smoke.

"Holy shit." I wave my hand in front of my face and water gathers on my skin. "Are you trying to boil yourself in there?"

The floor is damp and the steam is so thick I can't even see the mirror.

I rip back the curtain and…

It's empty.

She's gone.

I tear out of the bathroom and search the room again, as if she might have rolled between the mattress and the headboard like loose change.

I spin in a circle and *she's gone.*

Last night might as well have been a dream. I can still feel her on my cock. I can smell her in the dingy comforter. But she isn't here.

My phone rings. I dig it out of my pants on the floor. "Where are you?" I grit out.

But it isn't Mira on the other line.

"I guess you finally woke up," the P.I. says. "I've been calling you for hours."

I belatedly recognize the ringtone. I must have been tired if I didn't hear it for the last few hours. Weeks of no sleep and hours of fucking can really take it out of you.

Was that her plan? I think. *To exhaust me and run?*

"Where is she?"

"Your girl snuck out the bathroom window before the sun was even up. I followed her and she checked into a motel a couple towns over."

She left.

She's not just gone; she *chose* to leave.

I have to force myself to loosen my grip on my phone so I don't crush it in my hand. "You have eyes on her?"

"I'll send you the address and make sure she doesn't get away," he says. "I'd move quickly if I were you."

I pack up what little she left behind in the room in a mad dash and leave. The motel looks even worse in the daylight. The sun-washed green paint is the color of an old bruise and there's shattered glass glittering all over the cracked parking lot.

This is the kind of place I used to stumble out of in the middle of the day, sweating out the drugs and alcohol from the night before.

Mira absolutely doesn't belong here.

She can't want this over the life we could have together. Last night was enough to prove that. I know she wants to be with me. I felt it in every kiss, every curl of her body around mine. There's no way to fake this thing between us.

So how the fuck do I get her to stay?

I climb into my car, enter the address the P.I. sent into my GPS, and call Daniel as I screech out of the lot.

"Good news?" he asks in lieu of a greeting.

"I found her."

Daniel cheers and I hear muffled yelling. He's talking to Taylor in the background.

Good. I could use her input on this.

"Then," I add loudly, drawing their attention, "she ran off again."

Daniel cuts off his celebration. "What? What do you mean?"

"I mean, she waited until I was asleep and slipped through the bathroom window like a fucking ninja."

There's a shuffling sound and then Taylor's barking at me. "What were you doing sleeping in some cheap motel? You were supposed to grab her and bring her home!"

I don't answer, which must be answer enough.

"Men," Taylor spits in disgust. "You're all the fucking same. Sex is on the table and you let all of your well-laid plans— and the woman you love—go right out the window!"

"Why'd she escape through a window?" Danie's voice is faint in the background. "I thought she loved Zane."

"She does! But she's obviously running from something." Taylor clicks her tongue. "I should've figured it out sooner. Mira was always jumpy and she changed her locks more than any normal person should. Obviously, something wasn't right."

"Running from what? Is she in witness protection or something?" Daniel asks.

They start talking amongst themselves like I'm not even here, tossing around theories that are somehow even more wild than the truth.

"It's her story to tell," I finally cut in. "Mira will tell you when and if she wants to. But right now, all you need to know is that she thinks she's protecting all of us from her past. The only reason she wants to leave is because she thinks it'll put us in danger if she stays."

"Then tell her you don't care about being in danger!" Taylor snaps.

"I did."

"Tell her you'll protect her, then."

"I *did*."

There's another scuffle and then Daniel's voice comes through loud and clear. "Or, alternatively, you kidnap the woman you love and hold her against her will until she agrees to stay with you."

I snort. "She'll love that."

"It's not exactly romantic," Taylor muses, "but the plan has its merits. Mostly that I get my best friend back."

"I think it's a great plan," Daniel says. "Plus, you're doing it to keep her safe, which I think is *very* romantic. One day, she'll thank you."

I don't know if that's true.

I don't even think I care if it's not.

It would kill me if anything happened to Mira because *she* was trying to protect *me*. So I'm going to do whatever it takes to protect her.

Whether she likes it or not.

~

She is down the street grabbing food, the P.I. texts as I pull to a stop behind the dumpster behind the building. **No luggage with her, so I think she's coming back. Room 129.**

I could go chase her around town, but I think it's about time Mira came to me.

All it takes is the slide of my credit card along the inside of the door and the lock to her room pops.

The lights are off. The room smells like decades-old cigarette smoke and dust, but Mira wafts in the air. The floral scent of her hangs like a ghost in the doorway.

So I drop down into the rickety plastic chair in the corner, and I wait.

It can't be more than ten minutes later when I hear footsteps on the concrete outside. Then her keycard sliding in the door.

The second she pushes the door open, I grab her by the wrist and pull her into the room.

Her paper bag of food goes flying and she screams, but the sound chokes off when I pin her against the wall and she gets a good look at me.

Her green eyes go wide. She's teetering between shock and relief. "Zane."

"Considering what we talked about last night, you shouldn't be so surprised to see me."

She winces. "I'm sorry."

"See, I want to believe that, but it's hard because I believed you last night." I fight to keep my voice even. I don't want to yell and scare her, but frustration is simmering under my skin. "I believed you when you said you wanted to come home with me."

"I do." Her voice breaks. "I do want that, Zane. More than anything."

"Good. Then let's go."

I grab her arm and tug her towards the door, but she pulls back. "No. Wait."

"We played that game last night. I took things slow and then you waited until I fell asleep and crawled out the bathroom window like I was a terrible blind date you needed to escape from. I'm not letting you get away again."

She yanks hard, her thin wrist slipping out of my hold. I swear she's lost weight since I saw her last.

"What are you going to do, lock me up?" she spits. "Chain me to my bed? Might be a little traumatizing for Aiden to see me in handcuffs."

"It'll be even more traumatizing when you get yourself killed!" I roar, backing her into the wall.

I flatten my hand on the wall, flexing my fingers as I work out the urges I'm fighting to throw her over my shoulder and carry her away kicking and screaming.

Mira blows out a deep breath. "I can take care of myself."

My molars clench. I've heard that too many times. "How long do you think you can keep this up? Look at how easy it was for me to find you, Mira."

"My brother doesn't have the kind of resources you have." She lets out a bitter laugh. "*No one* has the kind of resources you have."

"Say that again," I demand. "Listen to yourself this time."

She frowns. "What?"

"No one has the kind of resources I have. You may be able to outrun your brother, but you can't outrun me. I won't let you."

Her eyes squeeze shut and she shakes her head. "You can't, Zane."

"I can." I grab her chin and force her face up to mine. I hold her there until her eyes open and she's looking at me. "I can and I will. I have more money than God already. Fuck hockey; I'll retire and spend my time dragging you home over and over again. As many times as it takes."

"I'm sorry I lied," she says softly. "I should have told you the truth last night. I just thought it would be easier if we got to… if we could say goodbye. I thought maybe you could let me go if we got one more night together."

I bark out a laugh. "Do you think one night with you is all I want? If that was true, I would've been done with you months ago."

"No. No, but—" She pinches her lower lip between her teeth. "You asked me to leave, Zane. At one point, you agreed with me. You thought it would be safest if I left."

"I was wrong!"

"You weren't!" she fires back. "You were thinking clearly and now, after last night, we're not. What about Aiden? Think about Aiden."

I *am* thinking about Aiden. I'm thinking about me and Aiden and Mira—the life we'll have together. For the first time in my fucking life, I'm thinking about weddings and happily-ever-afters.

"I love you." I drag my thumb down her jawline, over the thrumming of her pulse. Right now, it matches mine. "I love you, Mira."

She stiffens. "Don't."

I ignore her, massaging warmth into her cool skin. "I've never said that to a woman before."

She wraps her hands around my wrists, trying and failing to pull me away. "Don't waste it on me, then."

"You're not a waste, Mira. The time we've spent together, the time we're *going* to spend together... None of it has been a waste." I kiss her forehead and the end of her nose. I press my lips to hers, exhaling against her mouth when she won't kiss me back. "Our family is the only thing that matters. I fucked up when I told you to leave. I'm not going to make that mistake again. You belong with me and Aiden. You're going to live in my house and sleep in my bed. One day, you'll take my name."

A desperate sob escapes from her pinched lips. "Zane..."

"You're going to have my babies, Mira. *Our* babies. As many as you want." I can't help but grin. "They're going to look like you and me and we're going to love them and be together and—"

She's crying now and I brush my lips over the tears on her cheeks. I follow one to her jawline, her throat. "Tell me that's not what you want. Tell me you want me to let you go. Look me in my eyes and tell me you don't want to be with me, Mira."

She squares her shoulders and stares at me. "I don't want—"

But the words die in her throat.

Her chin wobbles.

She drops her forehead to my shoulder with a sob. "I don't want anything to happen to you or Aiden. I don't want to be the reason you get hurt."

"We're already hurting because of you. The only way you can stop it is by coming home."

Mira curls her hands around mine and holds the bundle of our fingers against her chest. She draws circles along my knuckles with her thumbs, thinking.

Finally, she looks up at me. "You have to know everything first."

"I already know everything I need to know."

She's mine. I'm hers. It's a tale as old as time and all that.

"I'm serious, Zane. I'm not going to let you risk Aiden when you don't even know the full story." She drops our hands and walks around me to the bed. She sits down on the end of it, her body curling in on itself. "I need to tell you what I've done."

I drag the plastic chair over and drop down, my knees enveloping both of hers. I grab her hand and press a kiss to her knuckles. "I'm listening."

7

MIRA

"I've never told anyone any of this before."

My hands are shaking, and I try to slide them under my legs to hide it. But Zane holds them tighter. "Just start at the beginning."

"For me, the beginning is when my mom left. I was little, so I don't remember a lot, but what I do remember... She loved to sing and dance. There was always music playing when she was around. She'd throw open the windows and turn on the radio and we'd dance."

I smile, my mind catching and stuttering on fleeting memories of holding her hands and being twirled around the living room. I'd get dizzy and fall over, giggling into the carpet. Then...

"She left me." I sigh. "I mean, I know she didn't leave *me*; she left my dad. But it felt like she left me."

"She should've taken you with her," Zane snarls. "A good mother would've done anything to protect you."

"I never understood that until I met Aiden. I know I'm not his mother, but I'd do anything for him. Including..." I swallow down the knot in my throat. "Including leave him, if I had to. Maybe my mom thought it would make things better. Maybe she thought my dad only yelled at her and, if she left, things would be okay."

Zane shakes his head. "She didn't think that."

I know he's right, but it's hard to think that both of my parents are monsters. I can't let myself go there.

"My dad was probably awful to her. He must have been. Because as soon as she was gone, he turned it all on me." I don't know when I started crying, but I swipe the tears from my cheeks. "He always told me how much I looked like her. I thought it was a good thing, but I was a walking, talking reminder of what he'd lost."

Of what he'd ruined, really.

Deep down, I've always thought my dad loved my mom, but he didn't know how to show it. He could barely even take care of himself. He scared her away and looking at me made him feel guilty.

"When I was thirteen, I cut my hair with kitchen scissors and dyed it pink. I was going through a phase." I tap my nose ring. "That's also about the time I let my friend talk me into piercing my nose in her bathroom. Don't recommend, by the way."

"There go my weekend plans," Zane says with a smirk. The smile doesn't reach his eyes, and I know it's just for me. He's trying to make this easier.

Just the fact that he's here makes it easier.

"My dad came home right after I'd rinsed the dye out, and I thought he'd be happy. Maybe he'd like me more if I didn't look so much like my mom, you know?" I blow out a shuddering breath. "The second he came inside, he could smell the bleach. He came looking for me in the bathroom and his face went redder than I'd ever seen it. I didn't know it at the time, but he'd just lost his job a few days earlier. Instead of going to work, he was drinking the day away at a bar. He was drunk and angry before he'd even walked through the door. He asked who I was trying to impress. He thought I must have a boyfriend. When I told him I didn't, he called me a liar and said I was a whore…"

Just like your fucking mother.

"I tried to get to my room, but he grabbed me by the hair and threw me against my brother's door. Dante usually tried to stay out of it, but that day he opened the door and looked down at me on the floor. I thought he was going to help me. I thought that, now that he was sixteen, he'd stand up for me, y'know? He was almost the same size as our dad by that point." I squeeze my eyes closed, and I can still see the way my brother's lip curled in disgust. The way he looked down at me like I was a pile of rotting garbage at his feet. "Dante spit at me and said they should shave my head to 'put me in my place.'"

A dangerous growl works out of Zane's chest, and I open my eyes. He's clenching his teeth hard enough that his jaw flexes. "Why wouldn't he protect you?"

"I've asked myself that question so many times." I stroke my thumb over his knuckles, comforting him while he's comforting me. "My dad never went after my brother. Maybe Dante wanted to keep it that way, so he joined his side. Or maybe whatever cruel streak there was in my dad was passed to Dante, too. Genetics, or something."

"You're not cruel." Zane lifts our intertwined hands to his mouth and kisses my fingers. "There's nothing cruel in your DNA, Mira."

The sound of my name—the name I chose myself—on his lips is like a balm over all the old wounds I'm reopening.

I blink away tears. "I like when you call me that."

He frowns. "What else would I call you? You told me that's your name. That's who you are to me."

My heart swells, and I don't know that I've ever been so broken and so hopeful at the same time in my life. My body doesn't know how to hold both things at once.

Which is why I cling onto Zane's hands even tighter.

So we can hold it together.

"Whether my brother was always cruel or our father made him that way, that day was the beginning of the worst years of my life."

"How could things have gotten any worse?" Zane growls. "The P.I. said you had a long history of broken bones and burns and bruises... ligature marks... Your father choked you, Mira."

I nod. "If I didn't stay out of sight when my dad was home, things would get ugly. Especially if he'd been drinking. He threw me against walls, knocked me out of chairs, pinned me to the floor by my neck. It was bad, but there was some relief: when he wasn't home, I was free... until Dante joined in." I chew on my lower lip, biting back a sob. "Big brothers are supposed to protect little sisters. I thought he was my friend.

Then, out of nowhere, Dante turned on me. One of them was always at home with me. If it wasn't my dad, it was Dante. If it wasn't Dante, it was my dad. It didn't matter what I wore or how quiet I was or whether I looked at them or kept my eyes on the floor—I was always doing something wrong."

You look nice, Dante would sneer if I ever dared put on a dress or fix my hair. *If you think you can convince the world you aren't trash, you're stupider than I thought.*

"Somehow, the mental exhaustion of it all was worse than broken bones. I preferred getting kicked around because at least my dad would get bored once I was on the ground. At least it would end. But they never, *ever* got tired of berating me.

"They broke me down until I didn't think I was worth anything. Even when I turned eighteen and could have left, I didn't think it was possible. How would *I* ever be able to escape *them*? They'd made me believe that I was worthless and hopeless. I didn't think I could do anything right. I thought I needed them." I shake my head. "Sometimes, I don't know who I hate more: the two of them, or myself for letting them get in my head. I hate who I used to be."

Zane quickly grabs my chin, forcing my eyes to his face. "The girl you used to be—Katerina—she survived. Don't forget that, Mira. Katerina did what she had to do to survive so that *you* could be here. She's a hero as far as I'm concerned."

I slide his hand to my cheek, nuzzling against his warm skin like it might be the last time. Because it might be.

"That's because you don't know the whole story," I sigh.

Zane nods gently, encouraging me to keep going.

It's the only reason I can swallow the lump in my throat and power on. Because more than anyone, Zane deserves to know this. He deserves to know everything about me. It's the only way I'll be able to trust whatever decision he makes next.

"The night everything happened—the night I killed him... It was my birthday. I doubt either of them even realized it," I say through a bitter chuckle. "They'd never celebrated my birthday before. But this was a big one. I was turning twenty-one, and more than I did at eighteen, I felt like an adult. I felt ready to head off on my own and start over. So, that was my plan."

I still remember exactly how it felt for the entire week before. The way I carefully and secretly packed a bag and hid it under my bed so they wouldn't find it. I practiced the speech in my bathroom mirror, whispering what I wanted to say to each of them more times than I could count.

I'm grateful to you, Daddy, for taking care of me and raising me, but it's time for me to take care of myself.

The lies were like slow-acting poison. The more I said them, the angrier I got. By the time my birthday rolled around, I was shaking with rage.

"Dante and my dad were in the living room watching football. Dante didn't live with us anymore, but he was there almost every night, anyway. They'd been drinking all day, and I might have been able to just slip out the back door without them noticing. But... I wanted them to know I was leaving. I wanted to see their faces." I shake my head. "I was so stupid."

Some nights, I dream that I'm walking through that living room. I can feel the threadbare carpet under my feet, barely covering the subfloor in some places. I can hear the low murmur of the television, my father's laugh at something my brother must have said. I can see their heads—one of them balding more than the other—peeking over the back of the twin recliners in front of the television. I walk and walk and walk, but I never make it to them.

I think it's my brain's way of protecting me. Of rewriting what happened that night.

Where would I be if I'd just left? Where would my father be?

"I had a whole speech planned," I continue, my voice as soft as a whisper, "but as soon as I saw them, I just blurted it out. *'I'm leaving.'* Just like that."

"Where are you going?" my father asked, bloodshot eyes sloshing over me. "I don't want you waking me up when you come back home."

As if he wouldn't be blacked out by then, anyway.

"You look like shit," Dante mumbled, not even bothering to look at me to confirm.

My father laughed. He laughed at my brother's cruelty the way he had a thousand times before, but I snapped. Everything I'd wanted to tell them for twenty-one years came pouring out of me.

"Then be grateful you won't have to look at me anymore," I spat. "I won't wake you when I come back because I'm never coming back. This house is hell on Earth and I hope you both burn here for eternity like the demonic assholes you are. I'm doing what Mama did years ago—what I should've done years ago. I'm leaving."

Zane whistles, and I blink out of the memory. My heart is racing, but I'm *here*. I'm not back in that house.

I'm with Zane.

I'm safe.

"I bet they took that really well," he says.

I don't want to go back into the memory. I've spent the last seven years repressing the hell out of it for a reason: it sucks.

But I trudge back into it, every word like walking through quicksand.

"It happened so fast. My dad was in his chair one second. The next, there was a crash and I was soaking wet. He was standing in front of me, and I couldn't figure out what happened. Until I heard Dante. *What the fuck did you just do?* It was the first time I'd ever heard Dante question our dad. It was also the first time I'd ever been stabbed." I wrap an arm around my stomach as a phantom pain ripples through me. "He shattered his beer bottle and stabbed me with it. He didn't even say anything. He just… stabbed me."

His face was cold. Flat.

"I dropped to my knees, and he looked down at me like I was a stranger. Whatever humanity I thought my dad might be clinging to, it was gone. He walked past me into the kitchen and Dante followed him. While blood was pooling in my hands, Dante followed our father."

"What are we going to tell people?" Dante screamed. *"She can't go to the fucking hospital again. She'll tell them what happened!"*

There was a pause—and then: "She can't tell them if she's dead."

"They were going to kill me," I explain. "I could hear them planning it in the kitchen. My dad had taken things too far and they knew I wouldn't lie for them. So I grabbed the beer bottle. It was my only weapon."

Zane smooths his hands up and down my arms. "You're shaking."

He's right. I'm trembling all over.

"You don't have to do this," he adds. "You don't need to—"

"I do." I pull his hands away, putting some space between us. "You need to know that I didn't flinch. As soon as my father walked in the room, I aimed for his face. His eyes. I was ready to gouge his eyes out, Zane. I was prepared to peel his skin from his skull if that's what it would take to kill him. But my aim was bad and I hit his neck. His carotid."

Some nightmares are just red. A sea of blood. That's what it felt like that night. Like I was drowning in blood. In the metallic smell of it and the slickness of it between my fingers.

"He dropped instantly. He didn't stand a chance," I whisper. "If I hadn't been wounded, I would've gone after Dante, too. But I was bleeding out and weak. When Dante stopped to help our dad, I knew I needed to leave. I was already in my car and pulling out of the drive when Dante came to the door. He told me he'd get revenge. And that's what he's been trying to do for the last seven years."

I feel lighter. Like I shucked off some weights I've been carrying for way too long.

But I'm still exhausted.

Getting all of this off of my chest has to be good, but there's going to be long-term damage. I'll never be back to "normal." I'll carry the scars of all of it with me for the rest of my life. I'll always remember what my family did to me, but I also have to remember what I'm capable of.

Zane sits back in his chair. "Is that all of it?"

I pinch my lower lip between my teeth. "Yeah. That's all of it."

Without another word, Zane stands up and walks to the door.

"Where are you going?" I breathe.

Slowly, he bends down and grabs my bag from the floor. Then he holds out a hand to me. "*We* are going home."

8

ZANE

"Are you sure about this, Zane?"

"Positive."

Still, Mira hesitates, her hand hovering over the doorknob.

"It's not one of those trick ones," I reassure her. "It won't shock you."

She spins around and then stumbles back, surprised by how close I'm standing. I haven't let her get more than a foot away from me since we left the motel. I'm not sure how I'll ever be able to leave her again.

"Aiden is in there," she states, as if it's news to me. "You're not just making this decision for yourself; it's for both of you. I don't know what my brother is going to do, and I don't want to put Aiden in danger. Maybe I should stay at another motel tonight while you take time to—"

I pin her against the closed door and silence her with a kiss. Her words shift to a helpless whimper against my lips. Then Mira is putty in my hands.

I could fuck her right here. On the doorstep, for whoever-the-fuck to see—I don't give a damn. It'd be so easy to peel off her—

It takes all of my self-control to pull away from her.

"I'm sure," I growl. "Now, let's go inside."

Reeves and Jemma had to drop off Aiden an hour ago, so I called Evan in to watch him. He meets us at the door with a nod for me and a warm smile for Mira.

"It's good to see you again, Mira." He points down the hall. "Aiden is in his room. I'll give you all a minute."

Evan slips into the hallway without another word, like the consummate professional he is.

"What if he hates me?" Mira grabs my wrist, squeezing until there are pins and needles in my fingertips.

"He doesn't."

"What if he's mad at me for leaving him?"

"He isn't."

"But what if he is?" she practically whimpers. "How am I supposed to explain all of this to him? He's too little to know why I had to leave, and I don't want to lie to him."

I spin Mira against my chest and cradle her face. "If he's mad at you, then we'll figure it out together. As a family. Everything will be fine."

She sighs and I feel a bit of tension drain out of her. "Are you going to kiss me again?"

I study her full lips for a beat too long. "Do I need to?"

"I wish you would," she whispers. "It would be a nice distraction."

I drift closer until we're a breath apart. "Later."

She shivers and *my God,* I don't know how I'm going to get anything else done for days. Weeks. There's too much of Mira that needs reclaiming.

But this comes first.

Mira squares her shoulders and walks to my four-year-old's room like she's facing a firing squad. Outside the door, she gestures for me to go first.

"Aiden?" I knock on his door. "Someone is here to see—"

Everything is lost in a high-pitched shriek.

A firing squad wasn't far off from the truth, because Aiden leaps off of his lofted bed and rockets towards Mira like a speeding bullet. Mira drops to her knees in the hallway and Aiden throws his arms around her neck and squeezes tight.

"You're back!" He draws back to look at her, the biggest smile I've ever seen stretched across his face. "I knowed you'd come back!"

I didn't have a single moment of doubt about whether I should bring Mira home or not, and now I know why.

They belong together.

Mira cries, kissing his cheeks and squeezing his hands. She inspects every inch of him like she's taking stock, making sure he has his fingers and toes and everything is in its proper place.

When she's finally done, Aiden collapses back into the hug. He presses his face to her neck and sighs. She smooths a hand through his blonde hair the way she has during so many bedtime books and bad dreams over the last few months.

Aiden pulls back again and holds her face in his small hands the same way I was only a few minutes ago. He squishes her cheeks until her lips are pouty like a fish and it makes him giggle.

Then he schools his expression into his best version of stern. "If you go again, I want to come. I don't want to be left here. I want us all to come. Me and Daddy and you."

Mira glances over at me, and I see the flash of panic in her eyes.

How do we tell him that Mira left for his safety?

How do we explain that Mira is being hunted by her own brother?

I kneel down on the floor and wrap my arms around both of them. "Mira isn't going anywhere, buddy. She isn't leaving again."

Aiden tries to stretch his arms to hold both of us the way I'm holding them. "We're gonna stay all together?"

"We're gonna stay all together," I assure him. "Forever."

"Was it a big, happy family reunion?" Evan asks when I step into the hallway.

He's posted against the opposite wall, a book open in his hands. He tucks it into his back pocket before I can see the cover.

"It's been two hours. You didn't need to stay."

He shrugs. "It's my job."

It really isn't. I keep Evan on retainer, but he wasn't even on duty today. He just came to sit with Aiden for an hour.

The only reason I knew he was out here at all is because I heard him sneeze after Aiden went down for a nap and Mira wanted to take a shower. I feel bad, but it's also more proof that he's the exact man I want to talk to.

"I actually wanted to run something by you," I say. "I'd like to expand your role to full-time security."

"For Aiden?"

I shake my head. "For Mira."

He frowns. "Does this have something to do with why she ran off?"

Like everyone else, Evan knows the barest details. If he agrees to the job, I'll tell him the rest. He needs to know everything if he's going to be able to protect her from Dante. For now…

"I can tell you there's a good reason I want her under close watch. Any time she's out of the house or I'm not here, I want you to be with her," I explain. "No one gets near her unless it's been pre-approved and cleared. Not servers at a restaurant, not anyone on my staff, not pedestrians bumping into her on the street. Not a single fucking person touches her without her permission."

"I have no problem there, but she's not going to like that," he warns. "If you can clear it with her, I want the job."

We shake on it. "Don't worry; she'll agree."

Whether she likes it or not.

9

ZANE

The shower is still running when I walk into the bedroom, steam billowing out of the crack in the door.

For a second, I have a flashback to this morning. Of walking into the dingy motel bathroom and finding the shower empty. I know Mira is in there, but I don't think that gnawing pang of anxiety that she isn't is going to go away anytime soon.

I push the door open.

Mira is little more than a fuzzy outline through the condensation on the glass, but she's *here*. That's more than enough.

I slip out of my clothes and ease open the glass shower door.

Mira is already looking at me. She keeps her eyes on me as she runs hands through her onyx hair. Water sluices down her shoulders and between her breasts. Her nipples are tight little knots.

"Miss me already?" she teases, her gaze dropping to my aching erection.

"I just needed to talk to you about some security updates." I step closer, a growl building in my chest when she meets me halfway, every inch of me pressed against her flat stomach. "This visit is purely business."

She swirls her finger over my chest, doodling in the mist gathering on my skin. "Should I be taking notes?"

I slide my hand between her thighs, gliding over her already-slick center. "Only if you're worried you'll forget something."

"I might," she gasps, "forget a thing or two."

"I can repeat myself." I spin her in my arms so I'm nestled in the swell of her ass. I dip a finger into her, teasing her open. "As many times as you need, Mira. Again and again and—"

She moans and her head falls back on my shoulder. Her eyes flutter closed as I touch her, and I could almost forget that I really did come here with another purpose in mind.

But I've always been good at multitasking.

"I have a new security system. It monitors the main door and the windows." I kiss her jaw and her throat, my other hand shifting higher to knead her full breast in my hand. "The code is 80085."

She laughs breathlessly. "*BOOBS*? Your code is 'boobs'?! Are you a middle school boy in math class?"

"No, I just wanted to hear you laugh. I'll give you the real code later, but you won't really need to know it."

"Why n—?" she starts to ask, but she loses her train of thought when I slide myself between her thighs from behind.

She arches against me, letting me work myself back and forth exactly where we both want me to be. She rocks against me, panting.

Suddenly, she plants her hands on the shower wall and looks back over her shoulder at me. Her green eyes are dark and that sinful bottom lip is pinched between her teeth.

"Fuck me, Zane."

She wiggles her hips and, just like that, there isn't a single other reason I came into this bathroom. There isn't a single other reason I exist on this planet, as far as this moment is concerned.

I band an arm around Mira's waist and pull her against me, sinking every inch of myself into her.

"Fuck," I growl, slapping my hand on the wall next to hers. I bite her earlobe and lick the water from her neck.

There isn't a single place where she isn't soft. A single place she doesn't fit me like a fucking dream.

Mira loops her arm back and around my neck. "This doesn't feel like business."

I drag out of her and drive back in, gritting my teeth against the urge to take us both there now. Because I could. *God, I really could.*

"You know what they say: if you enjoy what you do, you'll never work a day in your life." I tease in and out of her in small increments—an inch in and out, loving the way she clenches around me. The way she arches back looking for more. "And I fucking love what I do, Mira."

"Me?" she asks in a breathy laugh.

I hum my "yes" in her ear. "This. And taking care of you. Keeping you safe. It's all my job."

She stiffens, and I hate that she's still scared. That, even now, her past is hanging over us.

I slide out of her and spin her around. Before she can protest, I'm on my knees in front of her, her right leg tossed over my shoulder.

"That's why I asked Evan to watch you."

"Watch me?" she gasps as I drag my tongue over her. "*Now?*"

Even the suggestion sends a bolt of possession through me. I delve into her, claiming her inside and out until I don't think she'd care if Evan really *was* in the room watching. "No. This is all mine. Right now, you are all mine. But when I'm not here, I want someone to be with you."

Her fingers slip into my wet hair, dragging me closer. "Evan is already our bodyguard."

"Now, he's *your* guard." I kiss along her inner thigh until she whimpers, rolling her hips until my mouth is back where she wants it. "You'll be protected twenty-four-seven. Even when I'm not here."

She moans as I circle her clit, sucking and flicking until she's riding my mouth. "Yes, Zane. Holy shit. Yes."

I smile against her skin. "So, you agree?"

"Ye—" She falters. "Wait. No. No, I don't—Fuck. I can't think with your mouth on me."

I lower her leg to the floor and kiss my way up her body.

"I didn't mean you should *stop*," she whines, circling her arms around my neck. "But I don't need security. I can—"

"Take care of yourself," I finish. "Yeah, so I've heard. But I don't care. If you think you can take care of yourself, then—" Mira reaches for me, but I catch her wrist and pin it to her side. "—you'll have to *take care of yourself.*"

Her green eyes go wide as she catches my meaning. "You aren't serious. You won't touch me?"

"Oh, no—I'll touch you." I press her against the tile and find her entrance. She's so wet that I slide home in one thrust. Mira sighs. "But you won't come around my cock. I'll take you to the edge again and again and again—but you'll never, ever finish."

She tries to work herself against me, but I hold her hips against the tile. I pin her in place and only give her what I want to. An inch here, a slow stroke there. I circle my thumb over her center—but as soon as her breath catches and I feel her tightening around me, I pull away.

"Zane," she whimpers, "I need to come. Please."

"Then stop fighting me." I drag my tongue over her thundering pulse and follow the slope of her shoulder with my lips. "Tell me what I want to hear, Mira."

She huffs out a frustrated noise, and I tease into her again. She parts around me, whimpering as I slowly fill her…

Then I retreat.

"Let me come!" she cries, actually stamping her foot. "I need to—*Yes!* Okay? You can hire a bodyguard. I'll stop fighting you. Is that what you want to hear?"

I catch her full mouth in a kiss as I respond with a language we both understand. She gasps into my kiss as I drive into her, and I already feel her clenching around me.

"You're so close," I grit out. "I feel you."

Mira is too far gone for words. She moans and bucks against me until I press deep and she holds me there. Her fingers dig into my lower back as she takes me as far into herself as she can and falls apart.

I feel every ripple of her body, every pulse of her orgasm around me. She's falling and dragging me down with her, but I wait. I fight the bone-deep need to release until she's trembling and spent against the shower wall.

Only then do I slide out of her, gently lower her to her knees, and spill myself across her chest. She smooths her hands over her chest, spreading me across her skin.

This woman is perfect.

She's mine and I wasn't kidding before. My job now, more than playing hockey or becoming captain, is protecting her and Aiden.

My job is to keep them *safe*.

I fucking dare Carson or Dante or Peter Morris or anyone else to try taking them from me.

10

MIRA

"I know you're hired to watch me," I grunt, working through a few one-two combos on the punching bag, "but I don't think you have to *just* watch me. Read a book. Give the Stairmaster a spin."

Evan doesn't even act like he can hear me. His head swivels from where I'm dripping sweat in the corner, across the empty gym, and to the glass double doors that lead into the lobby. Just like the thousand other times he's done the same scan in the last half hour, there's no one else here.

Probably because Zane slid what I'm sure was an obscene amount of money to building management to keep the gym clear while I'm in here. Right now there's an *"Excuse our dust! Work in Progress"* sign hanging on the door. I'd bet dollars to donuts that that's Zane's doing.

"My glutes are fine," Evan drawls. "And I won't tell your boyfriend you were worried about that part of my anatomy. He'd probably fire me."

I roll my eyes. Evan and I both know that's a lie. The two of them can't be in a room together for more than ten minutes without someone asking for a workout regimen and bulking tips. They are in a muscle-ogling bromance.

"Firing you would mean leaving me exposed and vulnerable," I say in my best impression of Scarlett O'Hara. "Zane would never do that because I can't possibly be expected to take care of myself."

I sound bitter, but it's only because I am. I agreed to this arrangement under duress. Zane walked into my shower, set me on fire, and threatened to leave me like that. I felt like I was going to die if I didn't come.

Now, the only time I'm alone is when I go to the bathroom— even then, there's usually someone within a few feet of the door—and I'm feeling claustrophobic.

Is this what it's going to be like forever?

"It's only until the situation with your brother is settled," Evan says as if he's reading my mind. "Zane is right to be on high alert right now. Dante is a loose cannon."

I snort. "It's so weird to hear someone else talk about my brother. Most people don't even know I have a brother. Most people don't even know my real name."

"I won't tell anyone else, if that's what you're worried about."

I give him a tight smile. "I know you won't."

Zane explained why Evan needed to know the whole story, and for the first time in my life, the thought of someone knowing about my past didn't send a spike of panic through my chest. I didn't instinctively lunge for my suitcase and start planning my route out of the city.

Something like peace has taken root inside of me. The closest I can get to peace, anyway, while Dante is still lurking around the city like the Grim Reaper.

I just wish Zane could find the same kind of Zen.

"I think Zane should have full-time protection, too," I blurt. "Dante will go after him if he can't find me."

"Zane can take care of himself."

I strip off my gloves and turn to Evan. "How much did he pay you to say that? Because Zane may say he isn't worried about Dante, but I think he's lying."

I've woken up to an empty bed the last three mornings. Zane starts the night with me in bed, cuddling turning to kissing and kissing to fucking until my eyes roll back in my head and then flutter closed, in that order.

But when I wake up, he's gone.

It doesn't matter if it's sunrise or the middle of the night, Zane is gone. I have no idea when he's sleeping. Or *if* he even is.

Evan takes a quick scan of the gym again and then pushes off the wall, dropping his voice as he moves closer. "You need to give Zane some time. When you were gone, he was on edge. The man was killing himself trying to find you. All he wanted was to bring you home."

"And I'm here!" I throw my arms wide. "I'm home with him."

He arches a brow. "Do I really need to explain to you of all people that your past doesn't always pack away in a nice little box when you're done with it? Shit like that doesn't just go away, Mira. You're here, but now, Zane has to figure out how to *keep* you here."

"Then his job is done. Consider me a kept woman," I say. "I mean, I agreed to letting you follow me around like a stalker for the foreseeable future. That's about as 'kept' as I can be."

"You're going to have to give him some time," he replies. "You're also going to have to stop calling me a 'stalker.' I have baggage of my own, you know?"

I don't want to pry, but Evan must be able to read the frown on my face, because he continues with a sigh.

"A friend of mine had a stalker. An asshole ex-husband. It was a bad situation."

"Shit." My shoulders droop. "I'm sorry. I wouldn't have said that If I knew—"

He waves me off. "It's really fine. I know you didn't mean it like that. But that friend is why I got into security in the first place, and I take stalking seriously. More seriously than the fucking police do half the time, frankly."

I drop down onto the bench to shove my gear back into my duffel. Aiden and Zane will be back from school soon, and I want to be showered by the time they're back.

"Can I ask what happened to your friend? Are they okay?"

Evan smiles. "She's fine. Living in California now with her new husband and their Goldendoodle. I get Christmas cards —a saving-her-life perk, I guess."

"*You* saved her life?"

He shrugs humbly. "Kind of."

"Okay, well, that means you *definitely* saved her life. It's always the biggest heroes who act like they didn't do anything. Can I hear the story?"

Evan drags a hand across the back of his neck. "There isn't much to it. She grew up in an abusive home—kind of like you in that regard. Except, instead of getting out and finding someone nice like Zane, she found Tom."

I groan. "I hate him already."

"That's how I felt," he agrees. "I'd known Sariah since we were teenagers, and the moment I met Tom, I knew he was a piece of shit. But she swore she was happy and things were great. Then I saw her walking around town with a black eye. She finally told me the truth about Tom and I helped her move out of their apartment the next day. She lived with me for a few weeks."

I wag my brows in question and Evan shakes his head. "Nothing like that. We were always just friends. As soon as she could afford it, she got her own apartment. But Tom found her. Within a couple days of getting the keys, he was knocking on her door every night, all night."

"Did she call the police?" I ask.

"Would you have?" he retorts.

"That's—" I chew on my lower lip. "It's different. I'm wanted for questioning in a murder. I can't exactly trust the police."

"Yeah, well, neither could Sariah. She had some priors: minor stuff that stemmed from the rough childhood she had. Even though she was clean, she didn't trust the police. She called me, instead." Evan's eyes go glassy as he relives it all. "I slept over at her house the next night. The plan was for me to answer the door when he knocked and tell Tom to fucking beat it. Except, he didn't knock—he blew through the door with a shotgun."

I gasp. "Shit, Evan! What did you do?"

"I disarmed him," he says, the same way I'd say I shook someone's hand or waved hello. "I got the gun away, pinned him to the floor, and called the police."

"Did he go to prison?"

"Apparently, the only way he could go to prison for attempted murder is if I'd let him fire off a few more shots in the apartment first. I was too good at my job and all he got was breaking and entering." Evan snorts bitterly. "But he went away for six years before he got out for 'good behavior.' Whatever the fuck *that* means. It was enough time for Sariah to get out of town and start over, so that's all that matters to me."

I'm listening to Evan's story, but I'm also spiraling into a panic.

What kind of charges could they pin against Dante if he gets arrested? My brother hasn't touched me. Not since the night I fled that house. Maybe his calls to Hanna and Zane could be considered stalking? He broke down the door at my last apartment, but I doubt there's any footage to verify that.

If Zane and Evan catch him and he gets sent to prison, it probably won't be for long. He'll come back.

And I'll be right back where I started.

Running.

Hiding.

Afraid.

"Hey." Evan sits down on the bench next to me, his large hand heavy on my knee. "What's wrong?"

I blink up at him and realize I'm crying. "God, I'm sorry. This is embarrassing."

He hands me a tissue from his pocket. "Don't be embarrassed."

"I was just thinking... I don't want to get out of town and start over like Sariah did. I want to stay."

"You will. That's why I'm here."

I give him a sad smile. "Dante hasn't done anything like what Tom did to Sariah. In this story, *I'm* the murderer."

"No," Evan growls, shaking his head. "This is the kind of messed-up shit I'm talking about. The system never manages to help the people who need it most. You were abused your entire life, Mira. You finally get free and now, they want to lock *you* up? It's bullshit and I'm not going to let it happen. Zane isn't, either. I'm going to make sure Dante doesn't get close to you, and then I'm going to make sure you get the life you deserve."

I swipe the tears from my cheeks. "Thanks. But it's not my life I'm worried about. Zane is taking care of me, but I'm putting him and Aiden at risk, too."

"He knows that. He won't let anything happen to Aiden."

I know Zane will do everything in his power to protect Aiden. I know he doesn't want anything to happen to his son.

But the *what ifs* keep swirling in my head until I turn to Evan. "I need you to promise me something."

For the first time, the large man looks uncertain. "I don't know if I can do that."

"You can and you have to. I know you're being paid to watch me, but when I'm with Aiden, you need to swear to me that you'll protect him first. No matter what happens, Aiden has to come first."

Evan winces. "I made a deal with Zane. I signed a contract, Mira."

"Fuck the contract!" I snap. "We're talking about a four-year-old little boy we both love. You, me, and Zane would all throw ourselves under a bus to save him. You know that."

He nods. "Yeah, I know."

I hold out my hand for a shake. "So, promise me."

Evan stares at my hand. "This is pointless. Aiden is going to be fine."

"You don't know that. If Dante finds out where I am and who I'm with, he'll go after them to get me. Aiden is the easiest target." A knot forms in my throat, and I have to swallow around it. "My brother could use Aiden as bait to lure me out. Or as leverage to get me to go along with whatever he wants. You said yourself he's a loose cannon. We don't know what he's capable of."

"That is why Zane hired me to watch you and why Aiden is at a preschool with world-class security. You all are safe."

"But if we aren't—" I thrust my hand towards him again. "—I need you to swear that you'll save Aiden first. You know it's what Zane would want, even if he won't say it out loud."

Evan sags, and I know I've got him. Finally, he grabs my hand. "I'll protect both you and Aiden with my life."

I shake my head. "That's not what I said. I want to know that you'll choose him over me if it comes to it."

"It isn't going to come to that."

"But if it does," I grit out.

"But if it does," he sighs, "I'll choose Aiden over you."

Instantly, I can breathe a little deeper.

I can handle being followed around if it's what Zane needs to feel confident that I'm okay, but knowing that Evan will prioritize Aiden makes it even more bearable. There isn't much I can do to protect them.

But I can do this.

I squeeze Evan's gigantic hand with both of mine. "Thank you."

11

MIRA

"I want pizza!" Aiden plops down on the sofa next to me and rests his cheek on my shoulder. "And ice cream. And candy."

"Do you want to ride a unicorn and learn to fly, too?" Zane asks from the kitchen. "'Cause that's just as likely."

Aiden thinks about it for a second and then frowns up at me. "What does that mean?"

I bite back a smile. "I think that means it's not going to happen."

He sags lower on the couch. "No fair."

Funny, because I've had the same thought all afternoon. Since the moment Aiden came home from school with a finger painting he'd made of himself, me, and Zane.

None *of this is fair.*

I don't deserve a second of it.

The longer I'm here, the more danger the two people I love most in the world are in, and *they don't deserve that.*

Then Aiden dragged me to his room so we could play with his action figures and Zane caught me around the waist and pinned me to the wall in the hallway, kissing me until I was weak in the knees. Leaving them is impossible when they make staying feel so damn good.

I kiss the top of Aiden's head and he nuzzles closer.

Suddenly, there's a knock at the door.

Without thinking, I crush Aiden to my side. My heart is racing and my body is tense. "Are you expecting anyone?"

Zane saunters in with a smile that fades the second he sees me. "Fuck, Mira. I should've told you—Yes, I'm expecting some people. For both of us. It's a good thing."

I blow out a heavy breath, but the tension lingers.

"Ow," Aiden complains, shoving away from my ribs. "You squeezed me too much."

I kiss the top of his head again as Zane goes to answer the door. "Sorry, buddy. I didn't mean to."

Several voices I'd recognize anywhere float through to us.

"The fact my girl has been home for three days and I'm *just* now coming over is criminal," Taylor announces.

"Everyone should get out of the way," Daniel warns. "She will stomp on your toes with those heels. I'm immune—well, half-immune—but the rest of your little piggies are in danger."

Reeves laughs. "I think I can handle it. I used to skate with you, after all. You had two left feet on the ice even before you lost one of them."

There's a scuffling sound and I have to assume Daniel and Reeves are fighting, because it sounds like Jace is trying to break it up. But all the noise fades to the background when Taylor walks through the door.

She looks exactly the same. Which makes sense because it's only been two weeks.

But it feels like so much longer.

Taylor flicks her blonde hair over her shoulder and jabs a manicured finger at me. "I'm going to be so mad at you later. But first…"

She charges towards me, arms wide, and I meet her in the middle of the living room for a lung-crushing hug.

"Don't ever do that to me again!" she hisses into my hair. "I thought you were dead, girl. Or kidnapped. Or, worst of all, that you didn't care enough about me to tell me where you were going."

I laugh and only then realize how tight my throat is. And how wet my eyes are.

Taylor must hear it, too, because she jerks back with a gasp. "Are you crying?"

I try to quickly blink the tears away. "No!"

She passes her hand over my cheek and holds her wet fingertips in the air as proof. "You are! The emotional constipation has gotten a much-needed enema."

"Ew!" I laugh, pulling her in for another hug. "Don't make this moment gross."

Taylor hugs me so tightly my ribs ache. "Says the woman snotting on my favorite sweater."

"I'm not snotting," I mumble. But as I pull away from her, I wipe my nose with my sleeve. She might not be wrong.

While we had our moment, everyone else shuffled inside. They're loitering in the doorway, staring at me like I might clap my hands and disappear in a cloud of smoke.

I raise my hand in an awkward wave. "Hey, guys."

"*Hey, guys*?" Daniel mocks, shaking his head as he crosses the floor. "That's what you have to say to us after the hell you put us through? I was scared to death." He pulls me into a hug and his voice turns serious as he whispers in my ear, "It's good to see you, Mira."

The next five minutes is filled with the most hugging I've ever done in my life. My family wasn't big on displays of affection, to say the least. And despite all of my kickboxing experience, my arms are tired by the time I make it through the whole line.

Jemma hugs me the longest, swaying us back and forth like a pendulum while she hums happily in my ear. "I missed our play dates and your blunt honesty and Zane's good mood. He was miserable without you, honey. You can't ever leave again."

None of them know why I left, and I can tell they want to know all the dirty gossip. It's in the awkward way they sidestep that particularly large elephant, but also in the furtive glances they cast my way when they think I'm not looking. Like maybe an explanation will be tattooed on me somewhere.

Zane gets everyone a drink and they spread out around the living room, chatting and laughing. I follow him back into the kitchen, tugging on his shirt until he stops and turns to me.

"What is this about?" I ask softly. "Why didn't you tell me everyone was coming over tonight?"

He wraps his arm around my waist, holding me flush to him. "Because I wasn't sure you'd agree."

I narrow my eyes playfully. "That's not a good reason to go behind my back."

"It is when I think you really needed to see them." He curls a finger under my chin, lifting my face to his. "We've been hiding out the last few days, but your friends deserve to see you, Mira. They deserve to *know you*. In whatever ways you want them to."

My stomach swirls. I know what he means, but... "I don't know if I'm ready."

Zane bends and kisses me slowly, sending warmth swirling all the way to my fingers and toes. "Then just hang out, have a good time, and enjoy the pizza."

"We're having pizza?!" Aiden shrieks less than a foot away from us.

Zane and I both jump.

"Dang. You're a ninja, bud." Zane ruffles his hair just as there's another knock on the door. "And there's the pizza."

Aiden trails behind Zane to help pay the delivery driver and the next hour is madness. Taylor, Jemma, Rachelle, and I eat standing up at the island, watching with a mixture of amusement—and, in Taylor's case, unconcealed pining—as our respective men take turns wrestling Aiden and each other between bites of pizza.

"Why are men the way they are?" Jemma ponders as Reeves makes an impassioned argument for why Daniel can't use his prosthetic leg as a weapon.

"Someone call the ADA!" Daniel bellows. "This is discrimination!"

Taylor sighs. "Because we love them anyway. If we refused to put up with it, they'd get their act together and grow up."

Zane snags Aiden from the couch just before Aiden can dive-bomb him. They roll across the floor, Aiden giggling until he can barely breathe.

My heart swells. "Zane deserves this. After the last couple weeks, I'm glad to see him like this."

I realize what I said when the silence descends upon us. I tiptoed too close to the elephant no one wants to mention.

"Sorry," I mutter. "I made it awkward."

Taylor wraps an arm around my shoulders. "No, you didn't. I just didn't want to agree and make you feel like I'm piling on, but... yeah. The last two weeks have been hell for Zane. Daniel was seriously worried about him."

"Jace, too," Rachelle agrees with a wince. "Even Gallagher asked me what was wrong with Aiden. They were hurting without you, Mira."

My chin wobbles, and I bite down hard on the corner of my mouth to keep it together. "Things might not be much better for them now that I'm back."

Jemma opens her mouth to say something, but it's drowned out by a chant coming from the living room.

"Ice cream! Ice cream! Ice cream!" Daniel has Aiden on his shoulders and the men are marching towards the kitchen like marauding Vikings.

As Zane pulls a carton of ice cream from the freezer, I sneak up behind him. "Should I expect a unicorn within the hour?"

He shakes his head, but can't hide his smile. "Apparently. Right before the candy and flying lessons start."

Ice cream is doled out and, by the time people are scraping their bowls clean, Aiden is nodding off at the island.

"Time for someone to hit the hay." Zane scoops him up and uses Aiden's hand to give everyone a limp wave. "Tell everyone goodbye, buddy."

Aiden mumbles something, but his eyes are already slipping closed.

I watch the two of them disappear down the hall.

Then, like a switch has been flipped, the mood in the room plummets. It was all fun and laughing and chit-chat for two hours, but now, everyone is staring at their feet and drumming fingers on knees. Even Daniel can't manage to break the tension. Or, he doesn't want to.

My guess is the latter.

Finally, I clear my throat. "I know you're all here because of me, and I'm sorry."

"Sorry for what?" Taylor asks. "It's not like Zane put a gun to our heads. We wanted to come."

"We missed you," Jemma agrees.

The men all nod and give tight smiles.

"I know, but you all got a babysitter for this, right?" I look from Jemma to Rachelle. "Zane didn't tell me he was planning anything, and I feel bad that you all wasted a night coming to check on me. I'm fine."

Daniel slaps his knee. "You should apologize, dammit! What a miserable night I've spent hanging out with my best friends and eating junk food. It's been a nightmare."

I roll my eyes. "You know what I mean."

"I don't think we do." Jace shrugs. "We all *wanted* to come here tonight, Mira. Not just to see if you were alright—"

"Though we're glad you are!" Rachelle cuts in.

"—but to make sure we're alright, too," Jace carries on. "It sucked when you disappeared. It was scary."

"So, so scary." Rachelle squeezes Jace's hand and I can see tears in her eyes. "No one knew what happened, but with the way Zane was acting…"

"We knew it was bad," Reeves finishes when Rachelle gets choked up.

Daniel nods. "I've never seen him like that."

I shift my gaze to the floor and don't know how to lift it again. I was expecting everyone to be annoyed with me, at best. But this is all so much more complicated than I thought it would be. It's not like when I'd leave town before and get angry calls from a manager pissed I didn't show up for my shift.

These people… *care* about me.

I have no idea how to deal with that.

Jemma slides over, her hip bumping mine as she wraps an arm around my shoulders. A second later, Taylor is on the other side and Rachelle is kneeling in front of me.

"I'm sorry," I whisper through tears. "I thought I was doing what was best for everyone. I thought… It's complicated."

"Okay," Jemma nods. "It's complicated. But this isn't." She hugs me tight. "We're here for you."

"You can tell us anything," Rachelle agrees.

"I already know enough to blackmail you for eternity, and I haven't," Taylor adds. "That means you can trust me."

I laugh, but it's watery. Tears are pouring down my face, and the words come out with them.

I give the shortened version of what I told Zane the other day. They deserve to know what being friends with me entails. They deserve to know who I am and what I've done.

I tell them about my mom leaving, my dad's abuse, and my brother joining in. I say as little as I can about the night it all went sideways, but they don't flinch away from me or look horrified. I tell them I murdered my own father… and my friends just hold me tighter.

Wonders never cease.

"No wonder you're a stone-cold bitch! You had to be to survive." Taylor squeezes me tight. "I mean that in a good way, by the way."

Jemma nods. "We mean it in the *best* way. That's so much to carry on your own, Mira. I can't imagine."

I've spent years holding everyone at arm's length—rejecting them before they could reject me. The problem is, keeping everyone away meant I never gave anyone the chance to accept me, either.

I never gave anyone the chance to see all the broken, patched-together parts of me and love me, anyway.

Rachelle takes both of my hands and squeezes tight. "Thanks for telling us. Now, we can carry it with you."

12

ZANE

The door to Mira's apartment is shredded.

I feel like I've been here before—seen this before—but I can't think about that now. I need to find Mira.

"Mira!" I call her name, but my voice is hoarse. I can barely speak above a whisper.

The knife block on the counter is tipped sideways and knives are spilled across the floor. I bend down to grab one, but it slips out of my hand like a bar of soap. It skitters across the floor, leaving a trail of red across the carpet.

I look down at my hand and it's dripping with blood. But it isn't mine.

"Mira!"

The hallway to her room stretches and elongates. I keep walking, trying to dry my bloody hands on my clothes, but I can't get them clean. Everywhere I touch, there is more blood. It's still hot and the metallic tang burns my eyes.

I've been here before, *I remember suddenly.* This happened before and Mira wasn't here.

I start to turn back. I need to get out of here and find her.

All at once, the hallway slams down around me. My shoulders barely fit between the walls. I fumble with her bedroom doorknob, trying to open it before I'm crushed. My bloody hands slip over and over again before I can push it open.

I fall into her room, gasping... and land in a river of blood.

Sticky crimson soaks into the knees of my pants and splashes under my palms. I follow the path of the blood to Mira's bed in the corner, and a strangled scream tears out of my throat.

Mira is laying across her bed. Her arms are spread and her head is tipped over the end... revealing a deep gash across her throat from ear to ear.

No. No, no, no!

I pull her from the bed and cradle her in my lap. I try to hold her together, but her body is cold. The blood around me is congealing, turning rancid with every passing second.

Her flushed cheeks turn pale and then purple. Her skin shrivels and decays before my eyes, and all I can do is hold her and beg for it to stop.

No, no, no. Please no. Mira...

Warm hands hold my face, shaking me gently.

When I open my eyes, Mira is above me.

Mira—whole and perfect and breathing.

"Zane? Are you okay?" She runs her thumbs over my face. "I think you were having a nightmare."

Thank fuck it was just a dream.

But the weight of it is still on my chest. My heart is hammering and my palms are clammy like they're still covered in blood. In *Mira's* blood.

I curl a hand around her neck and pull her mouth to mine. She gasps in surprise, but quickly falls into the kiss. Our tongues tangle together and I savor every whisper of her breath across my face.

Alive. She's alive.

I flip us over, pinning Mira to the mattress beneath me. When I close my eyes, I see her as she was in my nightmare: pale and lifeless.

Then Mira drags her hand down my chest. I open them and she's looking up at me with a mix of desire and confusion. "Zane?"

Alive.

I've never needed to be inside of her more than at this moment. I want to feel exactly how alive she is. I want to feel her body responding to me. I want to feel her heart pounding and her heavy breathing on my neck. I want to taste every inch of her warm skin and claim it all as mine.

No one can hurt what is mine.

She fell asleep in my t-shirt, and I shove it up around her waist. She doesn't ask questions; she just lifts her hips so I can peel her panties down. I run a hand over her and she's already wet for me.

I kiss my way up her thigh, but Mira grabs my arm and tugs me over her. I arch a brow in question and she gives a quick little nod.

It's all we need to say before I press myself to her opening and slide into her warmth.

"Fuck," I groan, dropping my forehead to her shoulder.

Mira shudders and hooks her arms around my back. Her nails scrape over my shoulder blades. "I'm here, Zane. I'm right here."

Every night for days, I've woken up in a cold sweat. I'll check the bed and see Mira sleeping beside me, but I can't get back to sleep. I can't lie in the dark and do nothing.

So, I stand up; I pace the room; I check the security cameras.

I've gone through more late night cups of coffee this last week than is healthy or helpful, but how the fuck am I supposed to relax when someone wants to hurt this person I care about? How am I supposed to sit back and wait for some shadowy monster to show up and steal the one person that quiets all of the noise?

"Hey," Mira whispers. "Stay here with me."

I drive into her. "I'm here."

She shakes her head and taps my temple. "Stay *with* me."

I hold her gaze as I pump all of the panic and fear and anxiety into her. I watch her pupils dilate, watch as she drops her head back to the pillow and her lips part in a sigh.

We fall into a heady rhythm. My head is a fucking mess, but I can't think about anything else when I'm inside of her.

Mira pulses around me, whimpering that she's close. "Just like that," she moans, clawing at my lower back. "Please don't stop."

I slip farther over her with every thrust. She kisses my chest as I grip the top of the headboard and offer everything I have to hear her cry my name.

When she gasps against my skin, her pussy clenched tight around me, I finally let myself release.

I pour into her until we're both breathless and spent.

"Sorry," I pant when I'm done, rolling off of her and collapsing into the mattress. For the first time in days, I feel like I could sleep.

"It's not your fault," she says softly. "It's mine."

I was telling her sorry for waking her up in the middle of the night and fucking her. How is any of that her fault?

"What are you talking about?"

Mira pulls my shirt down to cover herself, but I can see her chin wobbling. "The nightmares and you not sleeping—I did this. I brought all of this shit into your life, and I'm so sorry, Zane."

"You have nothing to be sorry about."

I reach for her, but she slides away and scurries back against the headboard. "You told me to leave, and I-I didn't. I stayed around town. Part of me secretly hoped you'd come find me. But it was selfish. I should've left town right away and changed my name. Now, you and Aiden might be targets and you're so stressed you can't even sleep. I brought this into your life and—"

"I had a nightmare that you were dead," I blurt, if only to cut off the nonsense she's spewing. "I had a nightmare that I went to your apartment, but instead of finding it empty, you were dead. That is why I was upset. Because I thought I'd lost you."

I roll over to look at her and Mira is staring at me. Her eyes shimmer in the dark.

"You think you brought all of this bad stuff into my life, but… The only reason I've never felt like this before is because—" I consider each word carefully, measuring them out to be sure they're right. "—I didn't have anyone I cared about. It's because I've never felt for anyone what I feel about you."

I thought I loved Paige, but it was attraction mixed with getting high and the kind of delusion you need to feel like you're on top of the fucking world while your entire life is crumbling around you. Our relationship—with the massive exception of Aiden—was one long accident happening in slow motion.

But Mira is my choice. She's what I want.

"I love you."

"I wish you wouldn't." Mira reaches for my hand, squeezing my fingers on top of the comforter. "It would be so much easier if you didn't. It would be better if you cared less."

I tug her close and throw my arm around her waist. She tucks her face into my neck, still sniffling.

We fit together too well for this to be wrong.

"You've never said it back," I point out. She stiffens and I add quickly, "You don't need to. It's okay if you aren't sure. I'll wait."

We have all the time in the world.

"You broke up with me a couple weeks ago," she says softly.

"I told you it was a mistake."

"I know." She blows out a breath. "I know. But part of me is still waiting for the other shoe to drop. I'm waiting for you to change your mind now that you know everything. If I have to leave again, if you decide you don't want me, I d-don't know how I'll—*if* I'll survive it."

I can swear to her a thousand different times in a million different ways that I don't want her to leave, but I can't make her believe it.

What I can do is let her into every corner of my rotten heart so she can see the truth for herself.

"I have an idea." I sit up, leaning us both against the headboard. "Let's play a game."

13

MIRA

I don't mean to, but a surprised laugh bursts out of me. "Sorry, I didn't realize two in the morning was blocked off for *Chutes and Ladders.*"

Zane smirks, but it doesn't reach his eyes. There's still a shadow in them. The same one I saw when his eyes first opened.

I thought I'd lost you.

I can't shake the feeling that he'd be better off if I had died. That he and Aiden and all of our friends would all be safer.

"Not that kind of game." He twines his fingers through mine and lays our hands across his lap. "This thing between us is… intense. But it's still new. There's a lot we don't know about each other."

"You know more about me than anyone ever has," I admit.

Something sad flickers across his face, but he shrugs it off. "The game is One Truth Per Day."

I already don't like the sound of this. "Is that trademarked?"

"Considering I made it up thirty seconds ago, let's call it 'patent pending.' What do you say?"

I chew on my lower lip. "How long is this supposed to go on? I have more skeletons in my closet than most, but I don't have *that* many."

"It doesn't have to be deep, dark secrets. Just… truths. Things that are undeniably true about you or your life or your thoughts or the world in general. Whatever you want."

I quickly flick through the stack of most-recent truths in my brain.

My brother wants to kill me.

I'm putting everyone I love in danger.

If I was selfless, I'd leave and never look back.

I wince. "I don't know if I—"

"I'll start." Zane's calloused thumb smooths a circle over the back of my hand. "Today's truth is: I miss my family."

"Your parents?"

He nods. "And a younger brother. Caleb."

"You never talk about them."

"There isn't much to say." He sighs. "There isn't much to say that isn't fucking depressing, that is. I don't like to spend much time talking about all the ways I fucked up my rather charmed life."

I want to ask a million more questions, but I don't want to pry. His truth was that he misses them. He doesn't need to say more.

But he does.

"I hurt them," he admits. "When my addiction got bad, I stole from them and lied to them. I put them all through hell. They loved me and they never knew when they were going to get the call that I was in jail or the hospital or dead. It got to be too much for them, and they cut me off."

"But you're clean now."

"I got 'clean' a couple times before it stuck. They'd welcome me back with open arms and, by the end of the weekend, I'd slip cash out of my mom's purse and disappear for another six months."

I try to imagine that version of Zane—out of control and unreliable. But I can't picture it. He's so steady. So certain.

Zane Whitaker is the most stable thing I've ever had in my life. I can't imagine ever cutting him out of it.

"Part of my *get-your-fucking-life-together* process involved making amends. I wrote letters and apologized to them, but I never heard back." He lifts his shoulder in a shrug. "Maybe they got lost in the mail."

He tries to smile, but I can see how much it still hurts.

I curl against his side and rest my head on his chest. "They're missing out."

"I can understand why they did it. They had to protect themselves." He pauses. "Kind of like what I tried to do when I found out about you and your dad."

Toxic.

Abusive.

Is that what our relationship was like?

I lied to him, but it was because I wanted to keep him out of my mess.

Is that how he really feels?

"You're right," Zane continues, "that my life would be less complicated if you weren't in it. My life would be *completely* uncomplicated if I sat in a windowless room by myself for the rest of it. If I pushed away any person who ever tried to get close to me and spent every day alone, I'd never have another 'complication.'" He brings our hands to his mouth and presses a kiss to the back of my hand. "I also wouldn't have you."

A relieved sob bursts out of me, and I bury it against his ribs.

"My family pushed me away because of the choices *I* made—but you didn't do anything to end up in an abusive home and have to fight for your life. The choices you made, Mira, were to rise above all of that bullshit and, somehow, still be the best fucking person I've ever met. You're a miracle," he whispers against the crown of my head. "And I was an idiot for ever letting you go."

New truths pile up in my mind.

I love this man.

I never want to leave him.

Zane Whitaker is the love of my life and there's no coming back.

"Zane, I…" The confession sits on the tip of my tongue, but I don't want to hold him here if it isn't what he really wants. "My truth is that I'm positive I'm going to mess this up. Whatever this is—"

"A family. We're a family."

Tears stream down my cheeks and puddle on his bare chest. I wipe them away. "I've never had one of those."

"Yes, you have. With me and Aiden." Zane tugs on my arm until I'm sitting up. He curls a large hand around my jaw. "Aiden and I had no clue how to be a family until you came along. You were the glue that held us together before we even realized we needed it, Mira. We wouldn't have survived without you."

"You would have!" I cry out. "Look at your friends, Zane. As soon as you let them in and told them about Aiden, they jumped to help you. You've had a family for years; you just didn't realize it."

"Because I'd forgotten what it felt like to let someone get close. Until you."

First, he tore down my walls. Now, he's going straight for my mushy, exposed heart.

This isn't a fair fight.

I growl in frustration. "You keep saying that I did all of this, but I didn't. You're the one who saved me in that bathroom. You gave me a job and a place to stay. You're the one who introduced me to your friends and made me part of your life. I didn't *do* anything."

"You did." He takes my face in his hands. "Everything in my life was stable, which was nice for a while. Then Aiden showed up and gave me something to live for. Then you showed up and..." His blue eyes are searing as he studies my face. He traces over every line of me, a small smile pulling on his lips. "You gave me something to lose."

"Sleep?" I tease, my throat thick. "Your sanity?"

"Partnership. Excitement. Passion." He kisses each of my cheeks and my forehead as he checks off his list. Then he hovers over my mouth, his nose brushing against mine. "Love."

My heart aches and billows and expands in every direction at once. I've spent years telling myself I'd never get to have this. When Zane told me to leave, it confirmed all of my worst fears and theories about myself.

I don't know how to turn that part of me off.

I don't know how to be with him without hurting him.

"You don't need to say anything right now, Mira. The only thing I need you to do is stay." He kisses me and then makes his way along my jawline, his lips brushing against the shell of my ear. "Just stay and let me show you how good we can be."

14

MIRA

This can be good.

This *is* good.

Zane told me I can take all the time I need. He told me he'd be patient with me. He told me that he loved me, for crying out loud!

So why does it feel like I'm drowning?

I look over and Zane is still asleep. One arm is tossed over his head and his chest is golden and obnoxiously perfect in the sliver of light cutting through the blinds. He hasn't slept in this bed for an entire night since he brought me back from the motel.

At least one of us is doing better.

I clench my teeth and stare up at the ceiling. *I'm doing fine,* I insist silently to the whirring fan. *I'm doing great,* I inform the shadows.

The problem isn't Zane or whether or not I love him—because I do. I know I do.

The problem isn't even whether I want to be here or not. Because, again, *I do.*

The problem is that I went from being chronically single, bordering on full-time hermit, to *this*. To sleeping in a bed with a man who can make my toes curl just by looking at me. To taking care of *his* son, who is feeling more and more like *our* son with every passing hour.

I went from the relationship equivalent of a kiddy pool to fighting for my life in the open ocean that is Zane's unending patience with my bullshit. My "bullshit" being an unhinged brother with homicidal tendencies and a loose regard for the law.

"Mira?"

The little whisper no more than three inches from my ear almost stops my heart. I jolt like someone shocked me with defibrillator paddles and sit up to find Aiden standing next to my bed.

"Oh my God." I press a hand to my chest. "You really are like a ninja. Where did you come from?"

Aiden looks at me like I've lost it. "My room."

I chuckle. *Ask stupid questions...* "Do you need something, bud? It's early."

"I'm hungry," he whines. "I want pancakes. *Your* pancakes. The ones shaped like a mouse."

I saw the recipe in a kid's magazine in his therapist's waiting room and snapped a picture. As soon as I showed him, pancakes in any other shape were a disgrace. Mouse pancakes or bust.

It's been almost a month since I've made them. For some reason, I'm surprised he remembers.

I glance behind me and Zane is still asleep. I'm glad; he needs the rest.

I slide my legs to the side of the bed so Aiden and I can sneak downstairs, but then I stop. I remember Zane's wide eyes last night after I woke him up. He was shaking when he grabbed me and kissed me. He watched me like he thought I'd disappear.

If he finally sleeps through the night and then wakes up to an empty bed, he'll freak.

So I gently wake him.

Despite how much he's already slept through, his eyes pop right open. As soon as they settle on me, a lazy smile curls the corners of his mouth. "Good morning."

See? Toes = curled.

He fists his hand in the back of my shirt and tugs. "Maybe before Aiden wakes up, we can—"

"Too late," I squeak. I shift to the side so Zane can see Aiden.

He lets me go like I'm on fire and grins at his son. "Mornin', little man. What's going on?"

"Mira is gonna make pancakes! Mouse pancakes. With lots of syrup. And whipped cream. And chocolate chips. And—"

I whip around and tickle his side. Aiden squirms away, giggling. "You're going to get me in trouble with your dad."

Zane leans over and kisses the back of my shoulder. Awareness zips down my spine. "That all sounds good to me, actually."

Aiden grins. "We can do it?"

Zane gives him a thumbs up. "We can do it."

Aiden bounces around like a jackrabbit until Zane scoops him up and wears him like a scarf down to the kitchen. I help Aiden crack his first-ever eggs and Zane lets him pour an ungodly amount of chocolate chips into the pancake batter.

Half of the pancakes come out looking like birds that smashed into a window, but Aiden calls them all mice, anyway, and gives each one a whipped cream smile.

"Because we're all so happy," he explains, beaming down at his handiwork.

I bite back yet another completely inappropriate sob. It was so easy to enjoy time with Aiden and Zane before, because I knew it had an expiration date. I didn't need to sort through the sewage of my childhood trauma or overcome any demons because I was always, always going to leave. That was the plan.

Now, the plan is…

Well, we don't have a plan. Not explicitly. Not one that extends beyond stuffing ourselves with pancakes and spending at least an hour cleaning flour out from between the tiles on the floor.

It's hard to have a plan for the rest of your life.

The rest of my life. If I'm out here treading water, those words are a life preserver. They're a little break in the storm.

I want to do this for the rest of my life.

But I'm not sure I can.

After breakfast, Zane runs Aiden a bath. It always takes twenty minutes to convince him to get in the water, then an hour to convince him to get out. By the time Zane walks back to the kitchen, I can hear Aiden splashing and doing different voices for all of his plastic sharks.

"I don't think any of the syrup made it *into* his body. It's all on his face."

"That might be for the best. His sugar crash is going to be epic from the chocolate chips alone," I point out.

Zane leans against the counter next to me, arms crossed casually. He's wearing sweats and a plain tee and I'd slap him on any fitness magazine in existence. Actually, I'd rip him out of said magazine and tape him to my wall.

"I should've skipped the chocolate chips," he muses. "After pizza and ice cream and barely working out this last week, practice tomorrow is going to kick my ass."

"You're going back to practice?" I don't mean for my voice to sound so panicked. I'm *not* panicking.

I knew Zane would go back to work eventually. I just thought we'd have a little more time before real life came knocking.

He turns towards me, and I slap on a smile. "Good for you, I mean," I say hastily. "I'm glad you're getting back into the swing of things."

His brow arches. "'*The swing of things*'?"

"Yeah. Routine, sleeping, practice. It's good. Really good." I look down and realize I've been scrubbing the same sparklingly clean pan since Zane walked into the kitchen. "Great, even."

"Sure. I can tell by the way you keep saying it. It's very convincing." Zane gently pries the pan out of my hands and flicks the water off. I'm reluctant, but there's no way to resist when he pulls me against him. "One truth per day?"

"We already did one for today."

He wrinkles his nose. "The sun is up, so it's a new day. Do you have one?"

I chew on my bottom lip and try to pull something out of the tangled-up mess in my head. "I had fun this morning. This was nice."

Confusing and existential-crisis-inducing… but nice.

"I had fun, too."

"Is that your truth? Because you're kind of piggybacking off of me. It's a bit lazy."

His eyes narrow and he twists my shirt in his hands, arching me closer to him. "I am anything but lazy. You're gonna eat those words later tonight."

Goosebumps bloom down my arms. "Okay, then what's your truth?"

"I'm glad we're all home." Zane tucks my hair behind my ear. "Where we belong."

15

ZANE

"I hope that thing isn't glued to your hand." Coach Popov juts his chin towards my phone. "I need you ready to play this Friday, Whitaker."

I tuck my phone back under the bench where I stashed it before practice started. Every time there's been a break all day, I've made a beeline for it. Usually, I keep my phone in my locker, but "usually," my girlfriend isn't a flight risk with a psychopathic brother on her tail.

Considering the circumstances, it's a miracle I'm here at all.

I nod. "I'll be ready."

It's the closest we've gotten to talking about how I stormed out of the locker room before the last game. Coach could've torn up my contract if he wanted. I wouldn't have even blamed him. So, as much as I'd rather be at home, I'm grateful to still have a job.

As soon as Popov walks off, I lunge for my phone again. I

can't count how many times I've checked the security cameras or texted Evan.

Where is she?

What's she doing now?

What's her plan for today?

She's still in the condo, Evan texts for the fourth time in an hour. I don't need to read between the lines to catch his impatience, but I don't care, either. I'm paying him enough that I'd be justified in asking for second-by-second updates if I wanted them. Every fifteen minutes is nothing.

I'm about to ask him for another status report when someone slams into the boards in front of me and I jolt.

"When is your girlfriend gonna come back to root for us?" Davis asks. "I think she was my good luck charm."

"If she was anyone's good luck charm, she'd be mine," I warn.

Davis gives me a shit-eating grin. "Bring her around and we'll test that theory. See who she's more impressed by."

"Or I kick your ass into a hospital bed and you sit out another game," I snarl.

He's being a goofy idiot. *He's being Davis.* But my confession from the other night in bed is chafing a little, I guess.

I love her. I fucking love Mira. It's a first for me—the feeling and the confession alike. Possessiveness comes with the territory, it seems.

"Whoa," he laughs, raising his hands in surrender. "No jokes about Mira. Got it. I actually came over to see if you needed anything."

I frown at him, not sure what he means. Jace and Reeves and Daniel know what's going on with Mira and her brother, but it's not something we're publicizing. Davis is a friend, but he's a friend with a big mouth. He shouldn't know anything is going on until Mira is ready for the world to know.

As if reading my mind, he lowers his voice and leans in. "I don't know what the fuck is up with you, but it's clear things are... *tense* for you right now. If you all need a place to stay or to get away for a bit, my house is always open."

"Wow." I almost don't know what to say. "Thanks, man. That's—Thanks, but I don't want to put you out."

"You wouldn't put me out. Actually, I've been playing around with the idea of putting it on the market. I spend all of my time at my condo these days."

"At your fuck shack?"

"*Sex pad*," he corrects. "It's a luxury penthouse, not a wooden hut, thank you very much. But... yeah. I'm there most of the time and I hardly make it out to the house. Plus, everyone in that neighborhood is married with kids. I need to be around the young, vibrant people of the world."

It's not a terrible idea. Davis's neighborhood is nice. Safe, too. A gated community would ease some of my worries about all the people who walk past my building every day. Security is good, but we're in the thick of it. Mira barely even goes outside.

"I'd cut you a deal," he says. "Not that you need a deal. But if you were interested, we could make it happen."

"I'll have to think about it, but that sounds cool."

He arches a brow. "How cool? Cool enough that I shouldn't bother cleaning the place up for listing photos or…?"

I snort. "And here I thought *you* were doing *me* a favor. You just don't want to deal with listing it."

"Correct. Or going over offers or talking to strangers or reading through long, drawn-out contracts. Think it over," he says, already skating towards the other end of the ice where Cole is calling for him. "That fuckin' swingset you built last time is still there. You already acted like you owned the place. Might as well make it a reality."

Davis skates off before I can even pretend to be sorry. Aiden had a blast on that swing the week we stayed there. I don't regret it.

"Did I hear something about a swingset?" Jace asks. He and Reeves step over the bench on either side of me and drop down. "Rachelle has been hounding me about getting one for Gallagher."

Reeves shakes his head. "Don't give into the pressure. He's never going to use it. I built one for Jalen for Christmas and he doesn't touch it. The wasps love it, though. I had to get rid of three different nests underneath the slide over the summer."

"If I buy Davis's house, Gallagher can come over and share mine," I offer.

They both snap their attention to me. "You're moving?"

I shrug. "Davis just offered, but it's not a bad idea. Suburbia could be good to us. Maybe I could finally get some sleep."

There's only so many times I can wake up in the middle of the night and fuck Mira to calm myself down before I've got to get my shit together. And fucking her isn't a solution when I'm here and she's at home... without me... *vulnerable......*

Just like that, my heart rate is triple digits again.

"You installed that new security system," Jace points out. "And you have a bodyguard on her right now, right?"

I'm about to nod when Reeves adds, "Plus, Jemma is heading over there now."

"What?"

"Jemma is heading over there." He frowns. "At least, I think... Yeah, Wednesdays are her day. Tomorrow is Taylor's."

"Rachelle is taking Friday," Jace chimes in.

I shake my head. "What are you two talking about?"

"The schedule." Reeves circles a hand in the air like he's bored with trying to catch me up. "The women wanted to make sure Mira wasn't alone too much. Taylor's theory is that Mira is her own worst enemy and too much alone time will have her so deep in her head we'll never get her out."

"A distraction schedule." Jace shrugs. "At least, that's what Rachelle called it. For the foreseeable future, Mira will have two sets of eyes on her at all times."

Mira will probably hate that.

But I have to admit, it makes me feel better.

Mira said I'd already found a family with my friends, but this only proves that they are *her* family, too. They want to take care of her almost as much as I do.

Is this what it feels like to have a heart?

"Not all of us can afford to buy our position on the team." Carson's voice drifts across the ice towards me. It's like someone is running aluminum through a grater with how it sets my nerves on edge. "If anyone else bailed before a game, they'd be a free agent before puck drop."

A few of the rookies laugh, but most of them have the decency to glance nervously towards where I'm sitting. It's no secret who Carson is talking about.

"He isn't worth it," Jace warns under his breath.

"If I lost my focus every time I got some good pussy, I'd never show up to a game again," Carson chortles. "I guess I'm just used to it."

Last week, I probably would have flung myself over the boards and beat Carson into the ice. Not just for talking about me, but for bringing Mira into it.

Now... "I don't give a shit what he has to say."

Jace claps me on the back. "Good. You have enough to worry about. You won't become captain by killing Carson."

I don't give a shit about that anymore, either.

Becoming captain meant everything to me when I thought I had things at home handled. Now, all of my focus has to be on keeping my family safe. The only thing I want at the end of this season is for Aiden and Mira to be happy and healthy.

Anything else will be a bonus.

Coach blows a whistle for the five-minute warning. I stand up and start to stretch out.

"Oh!" Reeves snaps his fingers. "Jemma wanted me to ask about a sleepover for the boys tonight or tomorrow. Aiden was at our house so much there for a couple weeks that Jalen is missing him. He felt like he had a brother."

"Sorry again about—"

"I wasn't complaining," he clarifies. "We miss having Aiden around."

I give him a tight smile. "Maybe soon. For right now, I want to keep him home with me. Let him get used to our new schedule."

I also don't want yet another thing to worry about. Mira seems to think her brother will go after Aiden if he can't get to her. I don't want to believe it, but I'm also not willing to risk being caught off guard and something happening to Aiden.

Per usual, Jace seems to be able to read my mind. "Do you know any more about where Mira's brother might be?"

"I've kept the P.I. on retainer. He's working on hunting him down. In the meantime, I left an anonymous tip with the police about Dante. I don't want to lead them to Mira until she's ready, but if there's even half a chance that they'll be able to stop Dante before he can get to her, it's worth the chance."

"Do you think she'll ever be ready to talk to the police?" Reeves grimaces. "I mean, she killed her dad." I toss him a warning look and he flinches back. "None of us think she's guilty of anything, to be clear—but that doesn't mean shit to the law. She could go to prison."

"She isn't going to go to prison," I grit out. "She isn't going fucking anywhere."

Coach blows another whistle and we all hop over the boards to get back to practice. I'm already itching to text Evan again, but knowing Jemma is on her way to Mira is comforting.

Jace turns, skating backwards towards the center of the ice. "It sounds like you're doing everything you can for her. Now, I need you to get out on this ice and do something for yourself."

"Play hockey?" I guess.

"Sort of. I was thinking more along the lines of making Carson regret ever picking up a hockey stick."

I grin wickedly. "Ask and you shall receive, oh captain, my captain."

16

MIRA

"First, you hire a full-time bodyguard for me so I can't even use the restroom without it being logged somewhere—"

"Exaggeration," Zane declares from the other end of the phone line.

"—and now, you want me to gallivant around the city?" I groan. "I can't keep up."

That's true in more ways than one. Between Evan checking in on me approximately eighteen thousand times per day— *on Zane's orders,* Evan reminds me each and every time—and my friends not-so-casually "being in the neighborhood" on a daily basis, I'm exhausted. My social battery, already unnaturally low, is drained.

"I think it would be good for you."

I want to ask what he means by that, but a quick glance down at myself answers the question for me. I'm wearing Zane's boxers and doing a Sudoku puzzle on "Expert" level on my phone.

Maybe, just maybe, I need to get a life.

"One truth per day?" Zane suggests, charging ahead with his before I can respond. "I did not want to go back to practice and leave you alone all day, but being back with the team has been nice. I've always loved hockey and it feels good to do something I love."

"You do something you love almost every night," I childishly grumble.

I know Zane is still having nightmares, but when he finds me in the middle of the night and pulls me close, I don't mention it. We both need the comfort more than we're willing to admit.

Zane laughs. "And I'll do it again tonight—*after* you go out for lunch with your friends and enjoy yourself."

I sink down into the couch. "I don't even know what I'm going to wear."

Zane hums, thinking. "The green dress with the white flowers," he decides. "The one with the ties on the shoulders."

I can't bite back my smile. "You like that one?"

"Enough to rip it off you with my bare hands."

A shiver moves down my spine at the promise in his voice. Suddenly, I'm ready to get the hell out of Dodge.

If only so I can hurry right back.

$\sim$

"Zane said he called ahead to the restaurant so we'd have a private room." I study the cafe through the tinted window of Evan's car. What there is to study, anyway. The shop is narrow and wedged between two comically large buildings. "This place looks tiny. There's no way they have private rooms."

"No, probably not," Taylor agrees. "But Rachelle chose this place *because* it's tiny. If anyone we don't like comes in, we'll know it."

"And I can see the entire restaurant from here," Evan points out. "I won't move from this spot."

"But you're double parked."

He chuckles. "I dare a meter maid to try making me move."

I blow out a breath. This seemed like a bad idea back at the condo. But Zane wanted me to try and I wanted to pretend that I'm getting better. Now that I'm here, it feels like the world's *worst* idea. Being here—exposed and without Zane— is *"I know we're in a horror movie, but maybe we should split up"* kinds of stupid.

Dante hasn't made a peep since the day he broke down my apartment door and I fled down the fire escape. I could take that silence as a good sign. Maybe he doesn't know where I am or he's given up.

But I know what it really is: the calm before the storm.

He's lurking in the shadows somewhere, watching me. He's waited seven years—why not a few more weeks? All he has to do is wait for me to make myself vulnerable.

And here I am, playing Marco fucking Polo with a man who wants to kill me.

Taylor tugs on my arm. "Come on, Mimi. We're here, I'm starving, and Rachelle said this place has a caprese sandwich that is to die for."

My mouth falls open. "You did not just say that."

"Say wha— Oh my God!" She swats at me. "Don't be ridiculous. You are not going to die!"

"You don't know that."

"Yes, I do. Come on." She drags me across the backseat. "Wait for us here, Evan. We'll be back in an hour."

Evan gives her a salute. I glare at him for taking her side before Taylor slams the door closed.

The air is warm and a soft breeze toys with the hem of my dress. Even if this is a stupid idea, it feels nice. Then a sudden realization hits me: this is the first time I've been outside in a week.

I run through the last seven days in my head, and yeah, sure enough, the math is correct. I've taken the elevator down to the parking garage to load Aiden up for school, but we use the car drop-off line when we get there. I don't have to get out of the vehicle at all. Then it's back to the condo, where I workout on the first floor and spend the rest of the day inside Zane's unit. I haven't even been on the balcony because I was worried my brother might snipe me.

Last I knew, he only had a BB gun and a slingshot, but better safe than sorry.

A cloud floats out of the way and sunlight glows down on me. *Fresh air is magical.* I tip my head back and take a deep breath.

"Why do you look like one of those dogs who grew up in a lab and has never touched grass before?" Taylor asks.

Ouch. Accurate, but ouch..

I straighten my shoulders. "This may or may not be the first time I've been outside in a week."

She stares at me unblinkingly for a few seconds before she shakes her head. "I'm not going to get into the many benefits of Vitamin D for your skin and your brain, like how good it is for your bone health and the serotonin boost it gives you and—"

"Remember when you said you weren't going to get into it?"

"We're going to start going for walks." She says it like a threat.

Before I can argue, Jemma and Rachelle show up.

They smile and wave. We hug in front of the cafe, and I feel halfway normal for a second, even if I am still clocking all of the windows across the street that Dante could be watching me from.

Okay, maybe one-quarter normal.

But the second we walk into the cafe, the panic closes in.

This isn't a cafe; it's a shoebox. Outside, I had endless exit plans. I could pick a direction and run.

In here, I'm trapped.

If there is a back exit, I sure as hell can't see it. It's probably through the kitchen. A kitchen that anyone, including Dante, could sneak through and be on top of me before Evan could even get inside.

Rachelle tells the hostess we need a table for four and the hostess points to a booth in the back corner, but I'm hyperventilating. I can't breathe. It's like my lungs are encased in concrete.

"Mira?" Taylor lays her hand on my back, and I twist away from her. I hit the hostess stand with my hip and send a bowl of mints flying. The ceramic shatters on the floor and mints skitter across the floor. People nearby gasp and pick up their feet.

I don't even have the energy to be embarrassed.

I need to get out of here.

I whirl towards the front door, but a waitress is blocking my escape with a friendly smile and a broom. I have no idea how she got here so fast. "Watch your step, hon. I'll clean that up."

The socially competent part of my brain is screaming at me to *'Say something!'* But I just stare at the woman while I take wheezing breaths.

Her smile wobbles and her brows pinch together.

"Come on, Mimi." Taylor grabs my arm and pulls me out of the woman's way. "Let's sit down."

I let my best friend drag me through the restaurant, but when we get to the table where Rachelle and Jemma are waiting, I can't force myself to join them. There's an open spot on each side of the booth, but I don't know which way I should face. Do I want to face the door so I can see when Dante walks past on the sidewalk? Or should I face the kitchen so he can't attack me from behind?

It's inevitable that he's going to crash this party, so I should be prepared.

Taylor takes the seat facing the kitchen, which leaves me with no choice, but I still can't sit down.

"Mira?" Rachelle pats the bench next to her.

Sit down, I think. *Be normal.*

"Igottagol'llberightback." The words spill out of me in a garbled, breathless jumble as I spin towards the back of the cafe and dive into the closest bathroom. I'm not even sure if I'm in the women's or the men's, but I slam the bolt home and collapse against the door.

"You're fine," I whisper to myself. But it's hard to believe when my heart is doing its damnedest to fly out of my chest and splatter against the wall.

I squeeze my eyes closed and try to breathe.

I manage one shaky inhale when someone knocks on the door.

It's Dante.

He's here.

It's over.

"Mira?" Taylor knocks again. "Open the door."

I press a hand to my aching chest and blow out a breath. "Bathroom emergency."

"No, you're freaking out," she counters. "Let me in."

Taylor wants to help. Some part of me even wants her to help.

But another part of me doesn't want anyone to see me like this. Taylor has always called me the logical, level-headed friend. I'm the one who counts drinks and orders Ubers and never lets her run off with men she just met who claim they know Prince William personally. I may not have an online presence or a couch, but I'm good in a crisis.

Or so she thought.

Now, she knows the truth. What happens when she sees the mess I really am? What if she decides I'm not worth all the trouble?

She sighs. "Mira, let me—"

"No!" I drop my face in my hands. "I'm sorry. I just... Give me a second."

She doesn't say anything, so I assume she left. I wouldn't blame her. I just yelled at her through the door of a public restroom after embarrassing her in front of a cafe full of people.

There's a reason I've been a recluse for most of the last seven years: I'm a mess.

I'm trying to focus on my breathing, forcing air in and out of my tight lungs, when there's another knock on the door.

"Mira?" Taylor calls through the door again.

I squeeze my eyes closed. *I'm not ready.* "Just a few more minutes. I'll be out in—"

"It's Zane," she says.

I don't think. Don't hesitate. I whip around and yank the door open, ready to curl against his chest and let him carry me out of here like the giant baby I clearly am.

Except, it isn't Zane in front of me. It's Taylor.

"I see where I rank." She gives me a sad smile and holds out her phone. "I called him for you. He wants to talk."

I wince in apology and take her phone. Then I close and lock the bathroom door before I answer with a shaky voice. "Hello?"

"You've got a thing for public bathrooms," he murmurs.

His voice is warm and familiar and I let it wrap around me like a cozy blanket. Tears prick the corners of my eyes. "I can't do this."

"Yes, you can. You absolutely can. You're Mira fucking McNeil."

I snort. "It's funny because... I'm not."

"You are," he growls. "You're whoever you choose to be."

If that's true, right now, I'm choosing to be Katerina Costa. Right now, I'm every bit that scared little girl curled up in the corner, bleeding and crying.

I'm the person I swore to myself I'd never be again.

I close my eyes and cling to the phone like my life depends on it. "I'm scared, Zane."

"I know," he breathes. "You have no idea how much I wish I could—Fuck, if I could take all of this shit away from you, Mira, I would. I would. But, I can't."

"It's not yours to take away."

"But *you're* mine. Which is why I made damn sure that cafe was safe before you stepped foot inside. Evan is out front with a view of the entrance and the back exit is locked."

"You... you did?" I breathe. "It is?"

"I wasn't going to let you walk in there without being positive you were safe. I wouldn't ever put you at risk, Mira. Ever."

Tears pour down my cheeks, and I've lost track of how many times I've cried in the last couple weeks. Once the floodgates open, they are awfully hard to close. "I did this for seven years. I don't know why it's different now. I don't know why—"

Zane's words from the other night echo in my head.

You showed up and gave me something to lose.

The reason I ran from my brother for seven years without turning into a basket case is because, on some level, I didn't care if he found me. I had no friends, no family, nothing holding me in any one place. I was a ghost.

Now, I have all of that and more. I have a life to lose. A life I desperately want to keep.

And it's fucking terrifying.

The confession lodges in my throat. If Zane wanted me to give him one truth right now that's the only one that would rush out.

Thankfully, he doesn't ask.

"We can do this however you want," he says evenly. "If this is too much and you want Evan to drive you home, he will. But if you think you can handle it—"

"I can handle it," I choke out.

I *need* to be able to handle this. If I cower in the shadows, Dante wins.

"That's my girl." I can practically hear his smile through the phone. "Try to have fun. You deserve it."

17

MIRA

"We're really cranking it up to eleven." I barely resist chaining myself to the bumper of Evan's SUV as I watch hordes of people stream into the many, many exits of the outdoor mall in front of us. "Maybe we should quit while we're ahead. Lunch was a success."

"Success" might be a stretch, considering I spent ten minutes crying on the floor of what turned out to be the men's restroom. But, after that, I sat, I ate, I didn't hyperventilate.

So, yeah. *Success.*

"Nuh-uh." Taylor squeezes my cheek. "Say it with me: Vitamin D. This counts as our walk today."

"Bit public for a walk. Ever heard of a park?" I ask.

I'm not sure I'd trust any place with too many trees, though. I also don't want to be completely exposed.

Okay, maybe Zane should just rent out a gym with a walking track and I'll become a mole person who doesn't require sunlight.

"Have you ever heard of Lululemon?" Jemma bumps my hip. "I need new yoga pants. All of mine are worn out in the bum. It looks like I have a saggy diaper."

I doubt it. Jemma has never looked anything other than photo ready and she knows it. She's just being nice.

"While you shop for leggings, I need some of those juice glasses from Anthropologie." Rachelle is studying the mall map on her phone, creating a game plan. "Their website says they have some in stock. Who wants to come with me to scope things out? I want the bumblebee print, but I'll settle for cherries."

"No splitting up!" I yelp.

"But—" Rachelle holds out her phone to show me a picture of a drinking glass with little bumblebees pressed around the sides. "—I need a full set of these."

"No, we *need* to stick together. Right, Evan?" I snap my fingers for Evan to jump in and support me.

His silence is deafening.

I spin around to scowl at him and he shrugs. "You are my primary objective. I'm not being paid to watch anyone else."

So, if something goes sideways inside, Evan will protect me at the expense of my friends? "Then I'm not going."

"Vitamin D!" Taylor bellows.

At the same time, Rachelle loops her arm through mine and hands me her phone. "Look, Lululemon and Anthropologie are right across from each other. We don't even need to split up."

Jemma takes my other arm and the two of them together manage to propel me towards the building. "We stick together and we shop together. Then we eat giant pretzels together."

I can't imagine eating a thing. My stomach is in enough of a pretzel knot as it is.

"Whose arm do I get to hold?" Taylor complains from behind us. "You interested in being my escort, Mr. Bodyguard?"

"I should keep both hands free." Evan doesn't sound the least bit persuaded, even though Taylor brought out her sultry voice. He's in full business mode right now.

It makes me feel a little better about the hornet's nest we're walking into.

"Do I need to remind you that you have a boyfriend?" I call back.

Taylor laughs. "I wasn't asking for him to be *that* kind of an escort. Besides, my boyfriend made himself very memorable this morning. *Twice.*"

I wrinkle my nose. "Gross."

"It's about time Daniel found himself a good girl," Rachelle cheers. "He's too nice to be single."

Taylor leans between our heads, her voice low. "Between the four of us, I'm not a good girl and Daniel isn't all that nice, *if you know what I mean.*"

I stick out my tongue. "I repeat: gross."

Deep down—actually, not deep at all; it's pretty close to the surface—I'm happy for Taylor and Daniel. I want them both to be happy.

I just don't want to hear about it. Ever.

"Zane and Daniel are finally paired off. Now, it's time for Davis and Nathan." Jemma taps her chin. "Do either of you have any cute friends?"

"Half of my friends have already slept with Davis. The other half have slept with Nathan." Taylor shakes her head. "Those boys get around."

"And all of my friends are here," I admit sheepishly. "I'm pathetic."

"Or," Taylor offers, "spin team: you're selective and demand quality from your relationships. Hence, the top-tier selection of women you see before you."

"I second that," Rachelle pipes up.

Jemma lays her head on my shoulder as we walk. "Third. Nothing pathetic about us."

Jemma spoke too soon.

Thanks to the open air setup of the shopping plaza, I manage to make it through the doors and past the first few storefronts just fine. The wide walkways keep traffic flow light and there are narrow openings between buildings that work like little alleys to cut across to the other side of the circle or get back to the parking lot. I clock each and every potential exit as we walk, and I know Evan is three steps behind me doing the same thing.

Then someone screams.

I jolt so hard my knees almost buckle before I realize the woman at the sunglasses hut isn't screaming; she's laughing at something the man at the perfume cart said.

Jemma and Rachelle are a few paces ahead, so they don't notice. But Taylor grabs my elbow. "All good there, Mimi? You've got your newborn baby deer face on again."

"Fine," I squeak out. "Just jumpy."

Which is true.

I'm also jumpy when one of the teenagers next to us drops their phone on the concrete.

I'm jumpy when a bird caws in the ornamental trees separating the sidewalk into right and left.

And I'm jumpy when anyone decides to dare exit through a door I happen to be walking past.

By the time we make it to the other side of the plaza where the shops we want are, I'm not sure my nerves can handle the long walk back. I'm like one of those fainting goats: one more scare and I'm going to go stiff-legged and hit the ground.

"Pathetic" might have been an understatement.

"Leggings or glasses first?" Jemma asks, holding out her two hands like she's Morpheus in *The Matrix*.

I want to ask for a third pill—one that poofs me back to the condo and dresses me in Zane's boxers.

Rachelle chews on the corner of her lip. "The bumblebee glasses are really hard to find…"

"Weirdly specific juice glasses, it is," Taylor decides, leading the charge and dragging me along with her.

I cast a quick look over my shoulder and Evan gives me a wave as he follows us through the door.

He's watching over us. We're fine.

Until we walk inside and into the middle of what has to be a mosh pit.

People are jammed in shoulder to shoulder. There's a line from the registers at the back of the store all the way to the front doors. And people are still shopping, cutting back and forth through the line and winding around intricate displays.

"Oh, no!" Rachelle groans. "It's the house and home sale."

"What's the house and home sale?" I ask as a woman reaches past my face without so much as a glance in my direction to grab a set of dish towels with dogs printed on them. "Is it a cult?"

"No, but it means my juice glasses are probably gone."

Taylor whispers in my ear, "Definitely a cult."

I manage a laugh, but then a new wave of people pushes through the doors and we're washed into the crowd. I can see Jemma above the crowd because she is a walking, talking goddess amongst us mortals, but Rachelle and Taylor are nowhere to be seen.

"Hey! That's my teapot." A woman lunges around me to snatch a floral teapot from the shelf behind me. She only avoids elbowing me in the ribs because I dodge out of the way.

"This has got to be against fire code," I mutter.

There's a loud whistle, and I spin around to see Evan waving an arm over his head. He has eyes on me, and he points towards the back of the store.

The last thing I want is to go deeper into this chaos, but there's no way to tell him that without crowd surfing over the heads of people willing to maim for home goods. So I duck my chin and head towards the back corner.

But with every step, the hairs on the back of my neck stand up. I feel like someone is watching me.

It's absurd, because I'm surrounded by people on every side. Of course someone is watching me. Evan, for one. My friends are in the crowd somewhere, too. They could be watching me.

But the sensation trickling down my spine is specific and unrelenting.

I scan the faces around me, but I don't recognize anyone. They also don't seem to be paying any attention to me. What am I compared to overpriced vases and golden snail bookends?

But I glance over my shoulder, anyway.

And immediately face forward again.

My heart is pounding and I don't even know what I saw. Not really. It was just a flash of someone behind me. A figure that ducked behind a shelf of coffee mugs before I could see any identifying features.

If it was Dante, I'd know...

Unless he's working with someone else. Unless he, God forbid, has a girlfriend. Maybe he's told her lies about me and she wants to help him.

I just need to get to the back corner of the store. Evan will meet me there and I can tell him what's going on.

But I can't stop myself from looking back again.

As soon as I turn around, the same person in a dark jacket squats down behind a rack of floral bath towels.

"Shit," I hiss.

An older woman scowls at me and turns in the opposite direction, a squirrel-shaped vase clutched to her chest. I ignore her. It's easy because all I can hear is my blood thrumming through my veins and the distant *Psycho*-style music screeching ominously in the back of my head.

Dante is here.

He found me.

I look around, but I can't see Evan, so I have no idea if he can see me.

Will Dante make this fast and stab me in the middle of this crowd? Or will he manage to drag me away from my friends and my bodyguard so he can take his time with this revenge? Will I disappear without a trace?

I start shoving people out of the way, ignoring their protests and grumblings. I can see the "Fitting Room" sign hanging from the ceiling, but a wall of women sifting through bed linens are in the way. I divert through a room full of drawer knobs and puzzles. *What is this place?*

Just as I duck around the knobs and cut back over towards the fitting rooms, a dark-clad figure blocks the doorway in front of me.

This is the end.

A scream lodges in my throat and I stumble back into a small pyramid of puzzles just as I realize my stalker isn't Dante.

The puzzles crash to the floor, but the store is so loud that almost no one notices. I barely even notice.

I'm too busy staring at the woman in front of me.

"Hanna?" I breathe.

I used to dread every time she made an appearance. This time, I'm almost relieved.

"Mira," she sneers. "I thought that was you. It wasn't hard to pick you out. I just looked for the person barreling through the crowd like she thought she was better than everyone else."

My brain is having a hard time keeping up with the situation. *Are we in danger or not?*

It's hard to tell, but the deep scowl lines around Zane's ex-assistant's mouth can't be a good sign.

"Listen, I don't know what this is about, but I don't want—"

"Don't act like you're innocent," she fumes, stalking towards me. "You know exactly what you did. I worked with Zane for *years* before you showed up."

"Would you like a medal?" I drawl.

Her eyes blaze. "No, I want my job!"

She lunges towards me, and I just barely manage to hop over the mess of puzzle boxes at my feet and get out of her reach. "What the hell is wrong with you? I'm not the one who got you fired."

Even if Evan is close by, he's probably on the other side of the wall. He might have lost me in the crowd and not know where I am. It's not ideal, but at least Dante isn't here. I can manage Hanna on my own just fine.

"It's not a coincidence that you show up and I'm out of a job. You were threatened by me," she spits. "You turned Zane against me because you were jealous."

"Zane and I almost never talked about you." I have to bite back a laugh. "Why would I talk about you? I barely even know you."

"But I know Zane." Hanna's face is as red as her hair. Her eyes are tiny pinpricks locked on mine as she reaches into the nearest bin and pulls out a hefty glass doorknob.

Okay, red alert. Crazy woman with a makeshift weapon.

"I've been there for him for *years*," she hisses through clenched teeth, as if she hadn't made that point abundantly clear already. "I was waiting for him to realize how perfect we'd be together. I was loyal to him."

"Is that why you didn't tell him his son was in the hospital?" I roll my eyes. "*I* didn't get you fired. You got yourself fired by being a selfish bitch."

Hanna's mouth opens like she's going to scream. If she does, I don't hear it. I'm too focused on the doorknob she's swinging at my head.

Years of kickboxing takes hold of the situation before I can even think.

I swat Hanna's doorknob-wielding arm out of the way with my left and uppercut with my right.

It's a solid hit.

Almost in slow motion, Hanna's teeth clack together. Her head snaps back and she sprawls backward, taking another pyramid of puzzles and two bins of doorknobs down with her.

It's a big enough crash that people take notice.

A woman with an armful of tapered candles bends down next to Hanna to check on her—ignoring me shaking out my fist less than a foot away.

"She hit me," Hanna howls, pointing a trembling finger at me as blood dribbles down her chin. "She attacked me."

"I defended myself!"

"I saw the whole thing. It was self-defense." Taylor plants herself next to me and circles an arm in the air. "We need security over here!"

"Oh, I don't know if—"

Before I can even get the words out, a severe-looking woman with an earpiece walks over with a security guard already in tow. "I want both of you out of here. Now."

"Bullshit!" Taylor argues. "My best friend was attacked in your store. She's the victim!"

"She hit me first!" Hanna cries, holding her jaw with both hands.

Taylor looms over her. "Open your mouth and *I'll* hit you again."

Hanna shrinks back and the woman with the candles wanders off to stand with the growing crowd of onlookers.

I grab Taylor's shoulders and pull her back. "Down, girl."

"Was it really self-defense?" she asks under her breath. "Did she swing at you? Are you okay?"

"She tried." I study my right hand. My knuckles are turning purple. "That's the first time I've ever punched anyone. Turns out jawbones are hard."

It also turns out…

I know how to fight.

Which means I have options. I can run, but I can also plant my feet and defend myself. I can fight back.

Something like pride swells in my chest.

The security guard adjusts his belt and then waves for me to follow him. "Our policy is to remove anyone who is being violent. You both need to go before I call the police."

When I don't move, he starts trying to usher me towards the door, even though Hanna is still lying on the floor whimpering for all to hear.

Suddenly, a shadow falls over us. The security guard's eyes flare wide, and I don't need to look behind me to know Evan has entered the fray.

"And you need to keep your hands off of my client if you'd like to keep them attached to your wrists," Evan growls.

The manager frowns. "'Client'?"

Her eyes dart from me to Evan and back again. I can see the questions mounting. *Who is this woman? Why is she so important?*

Evan takes the manager aside and explains the situation to her—who I am, who he works for. Within minutes, the guard is asking for security footage and Hanna is being escorted out of the store.

"Finally," Taylor groans. "That bitch needed to be put in her place months ago. Better late than never, I guess." She turns to me, running her hands down my arms. "Are you okay?"

"Yeah." I grin. "I'm great."

18

ZANE

I've barely stepped out of the locker room when the P.I. pops up in front of me.

"Fuck." I glance around, but I'm alone. The rest of the team is still making their way off of the ice. "Again, phone calls are great. Preferred, actually."

His face is flat as he hands me a slip of paper. "I got a new number. Another job went sideways, and I lost my phone. And my contacts."

I wince. "That can't be good for business."

"It's good for my survival, so I'll take the loss."

I slip the paper into the side pocket of my duffel. "Is that all or do you have information for me?"

"Nothing yet." The pinch between his brows is the most emotion I've seen from him since we met. "The guy is nowhere. I'm starting to wonder if he hasn't skipped town."

I've floated that same idea to Mira more than once over the last few weeks. Some days have been so fucking pleasant it's hard to remember someone out there wants to snatch it all away.

Mira hasn't forgotten. Not for a second.

Knocking Hanna's lights out at the mall was a surprisingly big confidence boost and inspired her to get back to kickboxing a couple days per week, but I can see it in her eyes every time I look at her that she still thinks Dante is prowling.

"Keep looking," I order. "He's out there."

"And if he isn't?"

"Then I waste a shit ton of money and you get paid to do nothing," I fire back. "And I have more than enough money. Do you?"

"Fair enough." He waves his new phone in the air. "Text my new number when you get a chance. If I ever find this ghost, I want to be able to give you a call."

I text the number on my way down the hall and pocket my phone.

The hallways are buzzing with staff working the game tonight. A woman I recognize from before the game waves at me from behind a merch table. I signed a poster for her son on my way to the locker rooms. I normally keep to myself before a game to make sure I'm in the right headspace. It's headphones on, the rest of the world tuned out. But I knew we were going to win—which we did—and then I'd get to go straight home to Mira. I couldn't have been in a better headspace.

It was the same last week, even though it was an away game. We beat the Firebirds 3-1, mostly thanks to Cole being a beast in the net and Jace and I operating on some superhuman wavelength.

He knew where I was going to be all night. Carson might as well have taken a seat in the upper deck for all the good he did out there. Then, as soon as we shook hands and did our good sportsmanship routine, I hauled ass out of L.A. so I could crash into bed next to Mira six hours later.

"I could've handled one night alone," she scolded as she curled herself possessively around me in the pre-dawn hours.

"I know you could've." I kissed her forehead and held her right back. "But I couldn't."

Next week, we're playing in Denver. I can't drive thirteen hours, so I'll have to get my own flight out instead of flying home with the team the next morning. But I'll make it happen.

Things are good with the team again, and so long as I give it my all during the games, Coach doesn't give a shit where I sleep. When I sprinted for the exits after the game tonight, he just tossed me a two-finger wave.

For the first time in a long time, it feels like I can get the Angels to the Stanley Cup and make sure I'm there for my family.

I can still see fans funneling through the main doors and heading for the front exits, so I keep walking towards the side door. Security will move the barriers to let me out of the parking lot and I'll be home in twenty minutes. If Aiden isn't asleep, I can help put him to bed. We've been reading a series of graphic novels about a little girl who lives with trolls. I may be twenty-five years outside the recommended age range, but I want to know what happens next as bad as he does.

I'm digging for my keys and mentally mapping out the fastest way to get home, so I don't see the figure stepping out of the shadows until he's on top of me.

"Holy f—" I throw up an arm and pin the man against the wall by his chest before I can even clock who it is.

The man nervously laughs and raises his hands in surrender. "I didn't mean to surprise you."

I scan his face—middle-aged, graying hair, looks nothing like Mira.

Not Dante.

I ease back, still not lowering my arm. "And I didn't mean to shove you against a wall. It's a reflex."

"I know. I saw the game." He hitches a thumb towards the rink. "I've seen a lot of your games now. Those reflexes are why I'm here."

I narrow my eyes. "You want an autograph or something?"

"More like a signature." He gives me a slimy smile. "I'm a scout."

I drop my arm. "Oh. Yeah, no thanks. Have a nice night."

I take a step towards the door, but the man shifts in front of me. "I came all this way to talk to you." The look on my face must be lethal because he raises his hands again. "I know you're busy, but I'd love to tickle your ear for a few minutes."

"And I'd love if you didn't ask to tickle my anything," I growl. "I'm not interested."

But the guy doesn't take a hint. He follows me down the hall to the doors. "You're talented, but I think we both wonder if you're living up to your potential here."

I don't want this guy following me to my car, so I stop and face him. He has to stumble backward to avoid slamming into my chest. "And where do you think I could live up to my potential?"

He smirks. "Does that mean you're intrigued? I promise you we can pay you more than you're making."

Fat chance. My contract broke records when I signed it a few years ago.

And even if he could double my pay, it wouldn't be worth it.

Aiden loves his school. He has friends. *I* have friends. I just got Mira back and we've found a rhythm. I wouldn't fuck it up for all the money in the world.

I pretend to consider it and shake my head. "Nah. I'm good."

His face falls. I'm sure it isn't often he waves money under someone's nose and they don't even take a sniff. "You haven't even asked who I work for. You'd be starting for one of the best teams in—"

"I'm good," I repeat, waving a hand over my shoulder as I turn away. "Don't follow me. Pinning you the first time was a reflex. Next time, it'll be on purpose."

∾

Mira rolls over as I close the bedroom door. "You're late."

"Only by thirty minutes." After the scout slowed me down, there was an accident on the highway. Traffic was backed up for miles. I was on the verge of driving down the ditch when cars finally started moving again. "How are you already asleep?"

"I guess I'm tired." She lifts a shoulder in a shrug. There's a thin, lacy strap peeking out of the blankets, so I know all hope isn't lost. "Aiden fell asleep before the game was even over. You played great."

I kick off my shoes and slide in next to her. "You're right; I did play great. It's almost like I deserve a reward or something."

She arches a brow. "They named you a star of the game. Isn't that enough?"

"Did they? Must've slipped my mind." My fingers find silk between the sheets and I grab a fistful, tugging her across the mattress towards me. "I need a proper celebration."

Her body bends to mine. She hooks her hands behind my neck and her knee over my hip. "What does a proper celebration entail?"

"Me. You." I kiss her jaw and the soft spot beneath her ear. She exhales softly and just like that, my cock could hammer nails. I should be exhausted after the game, but I couldn't go to sleep now even if I wanted to. "Lots of orgasms."

She hums in thought even as she rolls her hips against me, drawing a deep growl from my chest. "I suppose. But only because you earned it."

I roll her so she's straddling me, her pale pink lingerie finally visible. I bunch the material around her hips and rock between her legs. "One truth?"

She sinks her teeth into her lower lip. "You first."

I'm barraged with too many possibilities to count.

I love you.

I want this forever.

Nothing could ever make me give this up.

But Mira is still holding back. As nice as the last few weeks have been, she is still halfway turned towards the door. I don't want to freak her out.

"You're beautiful," I settle for instead. "Your turn."

She grins like a cat and slides down my body, stopping when her perfect mouth is a breath away from the erection tenting my boxers. "You deserve a reward."

19

MIRA

This can't be happening.

I look from Zane to Aiden's therapist like one of them is going to rip open their shirts and reveal they're wearing a wire. The other will probably start pointing out hidden cameras.

"Really?" Zane asks, looking from the therapist to me with the exact same expression.

He can't believe it, either.

Dr. Turner chuckles. "You two look shocked. Is anything going on with Aiden at home that I should know about?"

"No, he's been great," Zane says.

"Perfect," I echo. "Absolutely perfect."

Everything has been perfect. For weeks.

Which is why I have every last one of my guards up.

In my experience, times like this are usually when life decides to remind me of the pecking order. Just when I think things are hunky dory, I find myself under a piano on the pavement.

"Well, great." Dr. Turner clicks her pen closed and leans back in her chair. "I concur. And that's my official, professional opinion."

A wide smile spreads across Zane's face, but he still circles a finger in the air. "You're gonna have to hit me with that all good news again, Doc, or I'm gonna swear I made this up."

"Aiden is doing exceptionally well," she repeats slowly. "He's improved leaps and bounds from where he started, especially where it concerns processing negative emotions. Even during the little hiccup last month, Aiden continued talking to me. He could express himself. And that's because you've created a home where he feels safe."

Zane lets out a choked kind of laugh and I reach over and grab his knee. He instantly folds his fingers around mine, taking my hand instead. "I know he's doing well. I can see it. I guess I just expected to be the only one."

"Then I'm happy to prove you wrong," Dr. Turner says. "Anyone who spends any time with Aiden must be able to see how happy he is in your home. You're doing a great job with him, Zane." She shifts her focus to me. "Aiden speaks highly of you, too, Mira."

My heart squeezes.

I was Aiden's "hiccup" last month. The reason his progress dipped at all is because I left him. I have no idea how to make sense of the joy and the fear mingling inside of me at that realization. Do I get credit for helping to solve a problem I created?

Nothing about Zane seems conflicted. He is beaming as he thanks Dr. Turner and then leads me out of her office with a hand on my lower back.

"Well?" I breathe as we walk down the hallway towards the waiting room. I have half a mind to glance up at the ceiling. *Any baby grands suspended up there by thin, fraying ropes?*

"Well." Zane turns to me. "What are you thinking?"

I'm not sure if he's asking me for my one truth of the day or not, but I give it to him anyway. "I'm thinking I'm glad I didn't mess Aiden up."

"You?" he snorts. "You made everything better. I'm glad *I* didn't mess him up. Part of me expected her to look me in my face and tell me I was a fuck-up."

I grab his arm and pull him to a stop. "You don't think that, do you? That you're a fuck-up? Because you're not. You're amazing with Aiden."

"I think Aiden is amazing, and I happen to be around." He shrugs. "I feel like I've barely done anything. He's just... He's the best."

Emotion presses at the backs of my eyes. "He really is. But so are you. Dr. Turner said so."

"All I heard is that Aiden struggled when you weren't around." Zane curls a hand around my jaw and strokes his thumb over my cheek. "So did I. And it was my fault. I sent you away."

"You did what you needed to do for Aiden. Because you're a good dad. I don't blame you for that."

As the words come out of my mouth, I realize exactly how true they are. I always understood why Zane asked me to leave, but some part of me still hung onto it as a reason not to get too comfortable here.

He could change his mind about you. Don't let yourself count on this.

But it's too late. I'm comfortable. Stay-here-forever, never-want-to-leave kind of comfortable.

Before I can say any of that, a little head pokes around the end of the hallway. "Daddy!"

Aiden comes tearing down the hall and Evan appears behind him. "Sorry. He heard your voices. I couldn't keep him contained."

We all know Evan could keep him contained if he wanted to, but people have a way of giving Aiden exactly what he wants. It's hard not to—he deserves the world.

"What are we doing now?" Aiden bounces and Zane scoops him up, cuddling him tight.

"I think you're heading home with Evan and Mira. I have to go back to work, bud."

Aiden throws his arms around Zane's neck. "I want to come with you!"

"You'd get bored. And Mira would have to sit in the stands with you. You'd have more fun at home."

Aiden frowns. "No, I wouldn't! Please, Daddy!"

Zane looks to me, a question in his eyes, and I shrug. "I don't mind watching you play. It could be fun."

"I'll tag along," Evan offers. "In case he changes his mind and wants to come home. Plus, I wouldn't mind catching the Angels in practice."

"You all might be bored out of your mind, but..." Zane shifts Aiden up onto his shoulders. "Let's go."

~

I don't know how anyone could be bored watching this.

Zane looks amazing out there, and not just because he's tall and broad and he keeps grinning up at where we're sitting in the stands. He's in complete control of every part of his body. I'd look like a newborn giraffe on ice, but Zane is running drills like he could do them in his sleep.

He skates through the obstacles like they aren't even there and fires off a vicious shot. Cole has blocked everything that's come at him for the last half-hour, except for Zane's shots.

Yet again, the puck rips the back of the net.

"Come on!" Cole complains. "You're making us look bad out here, man."

I would have to disagree. Zane looks very, very good.

"Yay, Daddy!" Aiden jumps up and down on the bleachers. Zane tosses him a thumbs up, and Aiden grins.

I love them.

The thought has found its way to the forefront of my mind more and more often lately. It's turning into a second heartbeat. Something vital to my day-to-day life.

I love them.

Zane has been so sure for weeks now that this thing with us is going to go the distance, but I'm not at all used to getting what I want. It's taken every second of the last few weeks— every kiss, every tear, every drop of sweat shed during kickboxing—for me to even begin to believe that I might get my happy ending.

I love them more than anything.

And I need to tell Zane.

After a few more drills, the men shove the obstacles to the side of the rink and start goofing off. Half of the team is in the weight room, so the ice is relatively clear when Zane calls up to us. "Want to come down, A?"

I've never seen Aiden move so fast in my life. He bounds down the bleachers and Jace is at the boards waiting for him. He lifts Aiden onto the ice and then holds his shoulders as he skates him over to Zane.

There's a smaller rink on the back of the building where kids can take ice skating lessons, and someone comes from that direction with a pair of rentable skates for Aiden.

As soon as Aiden is skated-up and on his feet, the professional hockey players turn into children. I can see exactly what they must have been like at eight and ten and twelve, playing hockey and learning to love the game. They all take turns helping Aiden with his skating and shooting the puck.

A few of Aiden's shots go wide, and I can tell he's getting upset. His little shoulders slouch and he hangs his head.

Zane skates over and kneels in front of him. He pushes the stick back in Aiden's hand and walks him through a few practice swings before it's time for Aiden to try again.

"You got this, Aiden!" I cheer from the stands.

My voice echoes more than I thought it would and my face burns. But Aiden stands a little taller, so I don't care. I'll be that hockey mom if I have to.

Aiden lines up the puck and gives it his best swing.

It almost looks like a slow motion replay. The puck bumps and skitters over the ice so slowly, I'm not sure it's going to make it. But when it gets close, Cole makes a big show of diving for it a full foot ahead of where it is. The puck comes to a slow stop in the middle of the net... and the rink goes wild.

Evan and I clap and cheer as the men on the rink take turns skating Aiden around on their shoulders, hooting and hollering.

"I did it!" Aiden shouts when he gets close enough for me to hear. "I scored!"

Nathan is taking his lap with Aiden when the doors at the far end of the rink open. I can see the rest of the team waiting just outside in the hall, but it's Coach Popov who blasts through the doors.

"Whitaker!" he roars. He's so mad that he almost forgets he isn't wearing skates and steps onto the ice. He grabs the boards for balance and hooks a finger at Zane. "We need to talk. Now!"

A hush falls over the rink. When Zane makes it to his coach, everyone in the room can hear every word.

"When were you going to tell me the good news?" he growls with vicious sarcasm. "When was I going to get let in on the secret, eh?"

I swear I see a piano-shaped shadow around me.

Zane shakes his head. "I don't have a secret."

Coach Popov snorts. "No, I guess it isn't a secret anymore. Maybe congratulations are in order. Have you already signed the contract?"

"What are you talking about?" Zane leans in, probably in an effort to get his coach to lower his voice.

"I'm talking about you abandoning this team and moving halfway across the goddamn country," his coach barks. "I'm talking about you talking to the scout from Detroit!"

20

ZANE

"I didn't talk to any fucking—"

The denial is halfway out of my mouth before I remember the guy from the other night.

Coach shakes his head. "I thought we were past this shit, Whitaker. I shouldn't be blindsided by something like this."

"I didn't talk to any scout," I snarl. "I'm not trying to leave the team."

The "team" in question is standing in a loose circle around mine and Coach's little show. I can only imagine what they're thinking right now.

I can only imagine what Mira is thinking. Of course, today of all days, she's sitting in the stands.

Coach Popov's neck is red and veiny. He waves a warning finger at me. "I shouldn't need to remind you that I have the footage. I saw you talking to him."

I look Coach directly in his eyes. "I talked to the scout, but I—"

"You have some fucking nerve," he growls. "After everything this team has done for you."

"—I didn't *ask* to talk to him," I continue. "He showed up on his own."

Someone behind Coach laughs, but I can't tell who it is. Instead, I glance over my shoulder to where Mira was sitting. She's moved down the stands and is hovering right behind the bench, watching every second.

Coach jabs me in the chest again, forcing my attention back to him. "Scouts don't fly halfway across the country to talk to players who aren't interested. They wouldn't be here unless someone thought you were looking to switch teams."

"I'm not looking to trade! Why would I want to—" The doors open and I see Carson slip into the hallway.

And suddenly, it all makes sense.

It takes every ounce of self-control I have to stay standing here and not hunt the motherfucker down and beat him with my skates. "Someone set me up. They want it to look like I'm not committed to this team."

It's the only explanation. No one else would waste their time trying to recruit me. Not unless they'd gotten direct word that I was looking to trade.

It would make sense why the scout looked so shocked I wasn't interested.

Coach is staring at me like he's trying to burrow straight through my skull. Finally, he sighs. "I don't know if I can trust you."

His words hurt worse than he probably knows.

But Jace skates over, skidding to a stop next to me. "Coach, why would Z want to leave? Things are going well for him. He just got his kid in preschool."

"That's hard to do!" Reeves chimes in. "There are long waiting lists."

Jace nods. "He's settled here. Why would he be looking to leave?"

"I'm *not* looking to leave," I repeat loudly enough for everyone to hear. "It's a misunderstanding. That scout caught me after the game and wanted to chat, but I told him I wasn't interested."

"Who wouldn't be interested?" Lars, our backup goalie, shrugs. "Sorry, man, but… Changing teams comes with a pay raise. It would be weirder if you *weren't* interested."

There's a murmur of agreement before Davis slaps his stick against the ice. "This is bullshit. Don't pretend you all didn't read the articles talking about how much our boy was paid to come to the Angels. Who do you think is going to top that pay?"

I don't love flaunting all of the zeroes that come along with my contract, but it's a fair point. It would be a tough number for most teams to beat.

"Maybe it's not about the money," one of the rookies tosses out. "It's because you don't want Carson to be your captain."

Even when Carson isn't here, his puppets talk for him.

My molars grind together at the thought. "You're right; I don't want Carson to be captain. But I wouldn't throw away what I've built here in a tantrum. If Carson beats me out for captain, then I'll deal with it. I'm not going anywhere."

I don't know what I expect, but a nod of agreement would be nice. Maybe some thumbs up, something that lets me know my team is behind me.

But there's nothing.

No one says a word.

They don't believe me.

I don't owe anyone an explanation about my life, but I can't be at odds with the team. I probably lost out on being captain when I bailed right before a game to go track down Mira, but this goes deeper than that. If my teammates aren't behind me, I could get fucking wrecked on the ice. It's dangerous for me and bad for them.

"I'm not going anywhere!" I repeat, spinning in a slow circle. "And it has nothing at all to do with any of you."

"You sure know how to flatter me," Davis drawls.

"I love this team," I say to him and everyone else. "I have no intention of leaving. But the real reason I'm staying is because I love my kid."

On cue, Aiden peeks his head out from behind Nathan. He shakily makes his way over to me, catching himself on the legs of my teammates until his little arms are wrapped around my thigh.

I pat his head. "I love my son and he's happy here. I wouldn't take him away from his friends and his school if I didn't absolutely have to. But also, I—" The words catch in my throat, and I have to clear it. "I'm staying because I love a woman."

Mira is already walking around the stands to get closer, probably to grab Aiden from me, but she freezes between sections 108 and 109. I can see the whites of her eyes from here.

Davis whoops and Jace and Reeves clap their sticks against the ice until half the team has joined them.

Once they quiet down, I keep my eyes pinned on Mira's. "I've built a life here for myself in the last few months. There are too many things in this city that I don't want to give up, and no amount of money could pull me away."

Mira swipes at her cheeks, and Jace grabs Aiden like he knows before I do that I'm going to go to her. I skate over to Mira and she meets me at the boards.

"You're making a scene," she whispers through a laugh.

"Coach started it." I lean towards her, voice soft. "Do you believe me?"

She nods without hesitation. "Of course I do. Even before you confessed your undying love for me in way too public of a setting." She blushes. "I trust you, Zane."

Warmth spreads through my chest. "I should've told you about the scout, but it wasn't important. I didn't even catch which team he was from. I told him I wasn't interested right away."

"It's okay. It doesn't matter to me. Even if you did want to leave, I'd go with you." Mira leans close, her warm vanilla shampoo wrapping around us both. "Because I think—I'm pretty sure I—" She blows out a frustrated breath. "One truth?"

I throw an arm back to the teammates thronged behind me. "I think I'm good for today."

"I know. It's my turn." She gives me a nervous smile. "My truth is... I can see it: the future you want, the life you outlined for us. At first, I wasn't sure, but lately, I can see it. And I want it."

I'm not breathing. "Yeah?"

"Yeah." She nods. "We're a forever kind of family, Zane. I'd follow you anywhere. I love you."

Before I can stop myself, I grab Mira by the waist and haul her over the boards and onto the ice. She yelps in surprise, but the sound is lost when I kiss her.

We meld together. She's standing on her tiptoes on top of my skates, and I have every single one of her soft curves pinned against my body. In my mind, we're the only people in existence.

"There are children present!" Daniel calls, splintering the moment.

I glance over and he's leaning against the doorway, watching the spectacle with Aiden at his side.

"And me," Davis adds. "I don't want to see this, either."

Nathan snorts. "Right? I've never felt more single in my life."

Slowly, everyone devolves into either making fun of me for being a lovesick puppy or sullenly heading for the locker rooms.

I know some of the team still don't believe me, but there's nothing I can do about that right now aside from show up every day and be consistent.

Reeves skates over. "I don't want to be crude, but have you changed your mind about that sleepover? Aiden just asked if he could play with Jalen. I could take Aiden right now and keep him for tonight if you—"

"Do it."

My hand tightens on Mira's waist. If I could get everyone out of this arena, I'd throw her down and take her right here.

"Yeah, I thought so." Reeves bites back a laugh. "I'll bring him home tomorrow morning. Late." He looks from me to Mira, who is still gazing up at my face. "Maybe after lunch. I'll text you."

Mira drops her forehead to my chest. "Everyone knows what we're about to do."

"That explains the jealous looks I'm getting."

She pokes me in the rib. "Best behavior, Whitaker. Your coach is coming."

I keep my arm around Mira, but then to face Coach. He looks stern, but his face is back to its normal shade. He sighs. "I should've checked with you before assuming the worst."

I bite back several smartass comments. "I appreciate that."

"But if you really were set up, then you need to fix it," Popov warns. "I've had enough of petty jealousy causing drama on my team."

Carson. He's had enough of Carson.

But I bite that back, too.

I nod. "I'll take care of it, Coach."

As soon as he's gone, Mira fists my jersey. "When are you planning to take care of it? Now or…?"

"Later," I growl, pulling her close. "Definitely later. Right now, I have plans."

21

MIRA

"Table, couch, or bed?" Zane asks as soon as we're through the front door. There's an urgency in his voice that tells me he wants to get this over with as fast as I do.

"Thai food in bed would be a bad idea," I decide. Then again, after the torturous car ride, first to the Thai place, and then to the condo, where Zane's hand kept sliding higher and higher under the hem of my dress, caressing my thigh... I can't imagine sitting an entire table length away from him. "I vote the living room."

Sitting on the couch might be detrimental to the eating portion of the night, but I don't actually care. Then again, couch shenanigans might still involve eating. Just of a very different variety.

He dumps our takeout containers on the coffee table and dishes out spring rolls and pad thai like we're being timed.

I touch his knee with my fingertips, afraid I won't be able to stop if there's any more contact between us. "We don't have to do this."

"Your stomach growled," he grits out.

It really did. Audibly. For a second, we both thought something might be wrong with his car before we realized the growl was coming from the passenger seat.

I was nervous about Aiden's therapy appointment, so I barely ate breakfast. Then I assumed I'd be going back to the condo afterwards, but we went to the arena instead. It's been a solid eight hours since I've eaten anything more than a protein bar.

I shrug. "Stomachs growl. It's what they do."

Steam is rising off of the noodles in a slow swirl, and my mouth is watering. The problem is, another, more insistent part of me has been soaking wet since Zane dragged me onto the ice and kissed me silly.

He slides my plate closer to me. "Eat."

"I imagined this differently." I snap my wooden chopsticks in half and stab them into the noodles. I know I'm pouting, but I don't care what my stomach says; I'm hungry for Zane, not Thai food. "When I told a man I loved him for the first time, he was supposed to be so overcome with emotion that he ravished me on the spot."

"It was a pretty public spot."

"Fine," I concede. "A closet, then. Lots of equipment closets in the arena, I'm sure."

"Lots of cameras, too."

He sounds so rational. So level-headed. It's maddening when I've spent the last hour with my heartbeat firmly between my thighs.

I turn to him with a scowl. "How are you so calm?"

Zane slowly lowers his chopsticks and turns to me. He's all sculpted golden stubble and dreamy blue eyes. I can't look at him without imagining the scrape of that stubble between my legs. Those eyes hovering over me, black with want as he—

"It's thrilling to score a goal in hockey. The feeling of slapping the puck and watching it sail into the net... It's unreal."

I blink at him, dazed at the subject change. "Is that supposed to be an innuendo?"

The corner of his mouth twitches into an almost-smile. "*But, if I try to score every time I get the puck, I'll miss most of my shots. Sometimes, the conditions aren't right.*"

"Are you—" I make a show of looking over my shoulders before I face him again. "Are you talking to me right now?"

The conditions could not be more right. If he'd touch me where I want him to touch me, he'd know that already.

Zane leans over and the world narrows. He's an inch from me, his breath warm against my lips, his thumb brushing back and forth over my jawline. My breath catches and I'm prepared to sacrifice our dinner by swiping it all to the floor so he can throw me on the coffee table instead.

"Right now, the conditions aren't right," he says in a low rumble. "You're hungry, and you're no good to me if you starve to death."

What about if I spontaneously combust from sexual frustration?

I swallow hard. "I won't starve in the next hour."

"That's the problem." He tips my chin up and drags his eyes over my face, down the line of my neck. He bites his lower lip, and I've never seen anything more sensual in my entire life. "The plans I have can't be contained in one hour. I need you strong if you're going to make it through the night."

My brain short-circuits. I feel his words fizzing in my chest and tingling in the tips of my toes. I've forgotten how to speak, how to eat. Which might be why Zane grabs a bite of food and holds it to my lips.

I accept it, never letting my eyes shift from his. Watching me slurp noodles can't be cute, but he looks utterly captivated.

Finally, he blinks and hands me my chopsticks. "Eat."

I don't taste a single bite of the food I shovel into my mouth. We eat in silence. Mostly because, if either of us says anything, the fraying restraints keeping us apart will snap and I'll be in Zane's lap before he can say "pad woon sen."

Zane is still eating when I slide my takeout container across the coffee table, but before I can even lean back, Zane scoops me up and places me on his lap. My knees are on either side of him. His hands drag down my waist, trying to bring me closer, but I resist.

"Thai breath," I protest. "I was going to brush my—"

He catches my lips in a kiss, easing his tongue into my mouth as I soften into him. I sink onto his lap and go dizzy with the evidence of how much Zane wants this pressing against my panties.

"I don't care," he pants, breaking away long enough to slide the straps of my dress off of my shoulders.

The material bunches around my waist and Zane groans when he sees I'm not wearing a bra. He takes one nipple into his mouth and then the other, lavishing attention with his tongue and rough strokes of his thumbs along my ribs and the undersides of my breasts.

He works down my body, sliding the dress lower and lower until I have to lift my hips so he can slide it down my thighs. I get momentarily tangled in the material, but Zane doesn't hesitate. He lifts me up and sits me down on the edge of the coffee table. One by one, he frees my legs and tosses the dress to the side. Then he drops to his knees between my spread thighs.

"This is mine." He drags a knuckle over the seam of my lace thong. "You want to be mine."

It's not a question—more of a reverent observation. But I nod anyway. "Forever."

His eyes flare as he shoves the lace aside and parts me with a claiming lick.

I whimper and slide my hands into his hair. He takes his time adoring every wanting, hidden part of me, but there's nothing gentle about it. Zane drags me relentlessly to the edge with lips and teeth and, *fuck*, his tongue and fingers, too.

He thrusts into me, fucking me with his tongue while his thumb draws dizzying circles over my clit.

He was right: I would have passed out. Even with food in my belly, I still barely have the energy to work my fingers through his hair and hold on for dear life as he drives me to an orgasm that steals my breath and leaves me limp on the coffee table.

"Holy shit," I breathe, throwing an arm out to the side and accidentally tipping over the leftover pad thai.

Zane doesn't seem to notice. He's kissing his way over my hip and my stomach. He slides me off of the coffee table and back into his lap on the floor. While I'm still floating in post-orgasmic bliss, Zane unzips his pants and pushes into me.

I cry out as I sink down onto him. "Wait! I wanted to—"

I don't know how to finish the sentence. Because I want it *all*.

I want to watch Zane fall apart in my mouth.

I want to peel him out of his clothes and taste his salty skin.

Most of all, I want this to last and last and never, ever end.

"We will." He grabs my waist and pulls me against him, burying himself in me until there's no more space. Until we're sealed together and I can feel the last ebbs of my orgasm fluttering around him. "We're going to do all of it, Mira. But I need you now."

I nod because I lose the ability to speak when Zane lifts me up and then fills me in another slow thrust.

He scrapes his gaze over my flushed neck and pinched nipples. Then his eyes settle on where we're connected, where he's disappearing into me again and again.

With one tug, he shreds my thong off of me and tosses the ruined scraps over his shoulder.

I'm completely naked on top of him, fully at his mercy—and there isn't a single part of me that's scared.

I want him in every way it's possible to want another person, and I don't know another way to convey that except to bring his lips to mine.

Zane kisses me and fucks me until we're breathing too hard, until our focus shifts to where we're coming together and falling apart.

"Fuck," he growls, digging his fingers into my waist. "You feel amazing. You're amazing."

I curl my hands in the hair at the nape of his neck and rock against him. I meet each of his movements with my own until I feel his hips stutter. Zane's face creases and his mouth drops open. I feel him twitch deep inside of me, and knowing that I can bring him to this takes me right down with him.

I clench around him, and he holds me tighter, deeper, as we pulse together until I collapse against his heaving chest and his arms fall loosely around my back.

We lie there together for a long time, breathing and coming back down to Earth.

Then we slide apart and shift into normalcy. Zane takes off his shirt and pulls it over my naked body. He cleans up the spilled noodles while I package up the leftovers and stash them in the fridge.

When I come back from the bathroom after finally dealing with my Thai breath, Zane is leaning against the counter with a glass of water. He hands it to me and I take a long drink.

He fists the loose material on either side of my waist and tugs me against him. The air shifts and, just like that, I'm a bow strung tight again. "Pick your poison: table, couch, or bed?"

"What's wrong with the counter?" I pat the countertop familiarly. "This quartz has seen some things."

Those "things" being my bare ass and what was, up until that point, the best sex I'd ever had in my entire life.

Zane smiles. "I fucked you here because I knew that, if I took you to bed, I'd never let you leave. I was trying to convince myself that this was temporary. I was an idiot."

"You had a lot going on at the time. We both did."

We still do, I think. But I don't want to bring Dante into this moment. Not yet.

Zane goes still, and I'm worried it's too late.

"I didn't think I wanted this, Mira." He indicates the air between us. "I never wanted kids with Paige. I was messed up when we were together, but I knew enough to know that we couldn't take care of a child. And I thought I just didn't want them. But then there was Aiden. And now..." He hooks his hands around my lower back, bending me against them. "I just didn't want to raise them with *her*."

My heart is in my throat. I can barely talk around it. "Are we having the kid talk right now?"

I *just* managed to tell Zane I love him for the first time. I meant it, but I don't know if I'm ready to plan out our entire future. Especially when a not-insignificant part of me is waiting for the other Dante-sized shoe to drop.

"No. *I'm* having the kid talk," he says, clarifying absolutely nothing. He brushes a thumb over the confused crease between my brows. "I didn't want to freak you out before—but if you're really in this, I want you to know exactly where I'm at."

I swallow down the joke that's sitting on the tip of my

tongue, waiting to diffuse the tension and gets us back to fucking as soon as possible, and nod instead.

"I want absolutely everything with you, Mira." He exhales. "*Everything*. I want your body and your heart and a lifetime together. I want you to be there for Aiden and to carry my babies. I want kids that are half you and half me and all wild. I want a forever family that no one can take away from me."

I'm hanging on his every word, with him... right up until the end.

I drop my eyes, watching as I run my fingers along the hem of his shirt, back and forth. "I can't promise that. I want to, but... With Dante out there and everything with my dad, I don't know if I can—"

"I've been talking with Hollis about everything." Zane grabs my chin and brings my eyes to his. "He thinks there's a way you can get out from under the accusations."

Hollis? His agent? I remember Zane saying something about him once being an attorney, but there's no way Hollis has handled a case like mine before.

"They aren't accusations. I killed my dad." My voice hitches. "I did it. I'm guilty."

Zane holds my face, brushing tears away from my cheeks that I didn't even know were there. "We don't need to figure everything out tonight, but I want you to know that you have options. I want you to know that, when you're ready, I'll be here to help you every step of the way."

I want that. God, do I want that.

But what if Hollis can't help me? What if I go to the police and they slap cuffs on me and lock me away?

I could lose Zane and Aiden and the beautiful future he's painting for us.

I bite my lip. "I just think—"

"Take your time." Zane kisses me slowly like he's trying to prove we have all the time in the world. "Think it over. When you finally tell me what you want, I want you to be sure. Because I am, Mira." He drops his forehead to mine. "I'm so sure. I know exactly what I want."

My head is swirling with a thousand different things I want to say, but I hold it all in. "Okay. I'll think it over."

"Good. Now, I ask again—" He tugs me against him, his eyes dark, and his voice a devastating rumble. "—table, couch, or bed?"

I don't even need to think about it. "Bed. Pronto."

Zane picks me up and throws me over his shoulder. He carries me, laughing, all the way to his room where he dumps me on the bed. I'm giggling until he takes off his pants, and then my mouth goes dry.

And for a few hours, I forget about the future. I forget about my past and the ways it's tied around my ankle like a cement block. I forget about the world beyond the edges of this bed. Beyond the places Zane touches and tastes and fucks me.

When it's late—so late I'm starting to get hungry again, but there's no way in the world I'd ever leave this bed—Zane folds our hands together over my head and presses into me.

I'm wet and ready. He slides home like he belongs there, like we should always be like this.

"Fuck, I still want you," Zane groans, driving deep. "I'm inside you and I *still* fucking want you."

"Zane…" I can barely breathe. I'm exhausted and full and it still isn't enough.

When is it going to be enough?

The steady drive of his body into mine pushes us both into what has to be the last orgasm of the night, because I don't think the human body can take much more than this.

I clench around him and Zane stutters, groaning into my skin and kissing my chest. "I want you, Mira."

"I want you, too." I squeeze his fingers and he brings our hands to his chest, holding them between our bodies. I kiss his knuckles and promise him the most I can right now. "I'll always want you."

22

ZANE

The score is tied.

The Firebirds have only had seven shots on goal, but four of them have gone in. It's been all I can do to keep us level. But it won't matter if Cole doesn't get his ass in gear.

"What the fuck is going on?" I skid to a stop in front of the goal.

"Talk to the D," Cole spits, flinging an arm towards Davis and whichever of the rookies is subbing in for Nathan on the first line. I think it's Grant, but I don't turn around to check. "They're letting everything through."

"They're not the reason you're letting two-thirds of the shots in," I bark. "I'm about to ask Lars to take over."

Cole's eyes narrow. "I can handle my shit just fine, Whitaker. Worry about your position; I'll worry about mine."

"Subs are called by Coach," someone behind me says. "Not you."

I turn around and it is Grant. He's watching me carefully.

He's one of Carson's goons, and I know that by the time we hit the showers, there will be whispers that I'm power-hungry.

"You're right. Because if it was up to me, you'd be parked on the fucking bench!" I can practically feel the cameras around the rink zooming in. The commentators are probably living for this drama. "Cole wouldn't have shots to fend off if you were doing your goddamn job."

Grant starts to mutter something under his breath, but I'm not in the mood to brawl with my own teammate. I skate past him and get into position.

"You good?" Jace asks.

I should ask him the same thing. Gallagher is home sick and Rachelle called to say she was coming down with the same thing as we were boarding our flight. I know he's been distracted, and it shows. He should be the one kicking Cole's ass into gear, but instead, he left it up to me.

I shrug him off, grinding my molars together to work out some of the frustration simmering under my skin.

It's wild to think I came into this game feeling great. Even the promise of a postgame red eye flight back to Phoenix couldn't dampen my spirits.

If anything, knowing I'd be back home before the sun came up tomorrow made me feel even better.

Mira is committed to our family.

I left Phoenix knowing that she'll still be there when I get back. I also left with a quickie in the shower that Mira promised was just a sample of what I'd get when I came home to her.

The fact that I have the image of her full lips wrapped around my cock playing on a loop in my thoughts, and yet I'm still the only person on this ice with my head in the game, is insane.

The puck drops and Jace slices it to Reeves. The defenders have been on my ass all night, so I've had to fight for even the slimmest of openings.

Reeves charges forward, and I cut towards the net to find a through line, but he loses the puck to the Firebirds' right wing. I curse under my breath and follow the puck, only to see Grant steal it back.

Maybe the rookie isn't useless after all.

As soon as the thought crosses my mind, I watch Grant turn to me, and I swear I hear ominous background music. Like I'm being circled by sharks in *Jaws.*

Reeves is wide open and off to Grant's left. He's the move. Grant should pass to him.

But the puck is already moving towards me.

I have to look down-ice to complete the pass, and I curse before I even touch the puck. Because I know this isn't going to end well.

Grant knew it, too.

The second the puck is in my possession, a wall of muscle slams into me from my blind spot. Both Firebirds defensemen drive me into the plexiglass, and I fucking crumple.

As I crunch against the boards, the only thing I can think is what Aiden must be thinking. I know he and Mira are watching the game at home.

Is he scared?

As soon as the defensemen give me the space, I stand up, though pain is scorching through every inch of me. But fuck the pain—I don't want Aiden to see me lying on the ice. I don't want him to worry for even a second that something bad might happen to me.

The world isn't on its usual axis and my legs are wobbly, but I'm fine.

My ears are ringing and there's no other feeling quite like having your lungs crushed like Whoopee Cushions, but... *I'm fine.*

Grant, however, is dead.

Before I can do what I should have done earlier and elbow Grant in the jaw, Reeves is in front of me. "Sit down, man. You got wrecked."

I brush him off. "I'm fine."

"No, you just got checked by two of the biggest defensemen in the league. Sit. The fuck. Down." Reeves waves an arm over his head and the medical team is already skating towards us.

"It was a fucking suicide pass," I grit out. "He knew I was going to get rocked. *Grant knew.*"

I may have a concussion, but I also know it wasn't all Grant's idea. Carson put him up to it.

Carson is also the reason half the guys on the squad think I'm planning to cut and run to another team.

I'm fine to walk, but I sling my arms over the shoulders of the med team, anyway. They're trying to do their jobs, and I'm not going to make it harder for them.

I drop onto the bench and lights flash in my eyes, checking my pupil dilation. They're asking me questions, but I barely register my own answers. Carson is buzzing around, watching the action like his career depends on it.

Probably because it does.

"Is he good to go?" Coach asks.

Before the med team can answer, Carson growls, "He needs a sub. I'll go in."

At the start of this game, I would've held my tongue. Now, I'm just pissed off enough to be a little stupid.

"This is the only way you can get any ice time. Is someone gonna hobble me in the parking lot at the next game?"

"I didn't do a fucking thing. I was on the bench while you handed the game away," he spits.

Cindy zips the first-aid bag and gives me an apologetic smile. "He should sit the rest of the game out. I don't see signs of a concussion, but just to be safe."

"Deluth." Coach tips his head towards the ice. "You're in."

Carson might as well shoot off party poppers as he skates onto the ice. He looks every bit as proud of himself as I know he is.

Reeves adjusts his helmet. "I should let that asshole get checked and see how he takes it. Fifty bucks says he cries."

"Don't." As much as I want to see Carson get exactly what he has coming for him, I won't do it at the expense of the team. "Carson and Grant work well together, but don't expect Grant to watch your back. Get the puck to Carson when you can. He's an asshole, but he's a good shot."

Reeves gives me a two-finger salute and I slump on the bench.

Coach is standing next to me, arms crossed, eyes on the ice. "You're a bigger man than I am, Whitaker."

"You'd let Carson get checked?"

I don't actually believe it. No one is more even-keeled than Coach. He keeps his mouth shut and his head down. It's hard to get embroiled in drama when you mind your own fucking business.

He shrugs noncommittally. "I wouldn't stop it if someone else wanted to make it happen, I'll tell you that. Not if someone had given me as much trouble as Carson has given you."

"Is that why you weren't captain of your team? Too set on revenge?"

Coach bites back the start of a smile. "I wasn't captain, but I learned something important: you don't need a 'C' sewn into your jersey to be a leader."

23

MIRA

"I'm going to be honest: I don't fully know why I'm here." Taylor adjusts her smartwatch on her wrist and tightens her ponytail. "Am I acting in a bodyguard capacity or is this more for moral support?"

"*Evan* is the bodyguard." I hitch a thumb to where Evan's hulking shadow can be seen through the frosted glass. "*You're* here because you came to pick me up for pre-kickboxing coffee even after I told you I had other plans."

Truth be told, I knew Taylor didn't hear me tell her I had other plans. She was prattling on the phone about picking me up and grabbing lattes, and I realized all at once that I didn't want to go see Hollis by myself. So I let her organize picking me up at the condo, knowing full well oat milk lattes were not in our future.

Sue me.

We are at an attorney's office, after all.

I told Zane I wasn't ready to make any decisions about how to handle the PR nightmare that is my bloody past, but he told me I should at least go and figure out my options. I agreed, but only because he was supposed to come with me. But that was before he got checked in the game last night, and I begged him not to rush home on the first flight to Phoenix.

Head injuries + overnight flights = bad news, I texted. **I'd rather have you alive tomorrow than dead tonight.**

After a lot of back and forth, he finally agreed to sleep in Jace's hotel room—on the condition Jace would wake him up every few hours—and fly home with the team today.

Which means I had a vacancy in the "moral support" department.

Taylor swirls the collection of fountain pens in the cup Hollis has on the corner of his desk. "So, what does this guy think he can do for you? My dad has good lawyers, you know. If you want help, I can get it for you."

"I don't even know if I want help. I'm just here to talk. Or, listen, I guess." I sigh. "I want to hear what he thinks."

Taylor hums, unconvinced. "This guy is a sports agent, right?"

"And a former attorney." Hollis pushes through his office door with a smile. "I don't practice much anymore. This consultation is a favor for my favorite client."

I jump to my feet, but Taylor just juts her hip out defiantly. "How do we know we can trust you? This is a big secret my bestie is carting around. You could destroy her if you wanted to."

"Taylor!" I hiss.

"What?" she shrugs. "I'm looking out for you. I don't know this guy. Neither do you. If you'd asked me for help, I could've given you the number of an attorney I trust."

I never quite know what to expect from Taylor, but her getting territorial over where I go for legal help wasn't on my bingo card.

Hollis doesn't flinch. "At this exact moment, I have no less than fourteen pieces of information with the power to blow up headlines the world over. But it's my job to make sure that *doesn't* happen. If confidential information leaks out of this office, I'm out of a job. It's something I work hard to avoid."

Taylor narrows her eyes for a second and then nods once. "Okay, Mimi. You can trust him."

"Yeah, I know." I brush her aside and shake Hollis's hand. "I'm sorry. She's just here because—actually, I don't know why she's here."

"Then maybe she'd be more comfortable waiting in the lobby." It's a suggestion, but it's really not a suggestion at the same time.

Taylor looks at me, silently confirming that's fine before she slips into the hallway with Evan.

"Sorry," Hollis says, softening immediately. "I prefer one-on-one consultations. I like to control the ears in any room. If there's a leak, I want to know who is responsible. Because I know it won't be me."

"That makes sense." I fold my hands between my thighs. "I don't really know where to start."

"How about the beginning? I've gotten your story secondhand, but I'd like to hear it from the source to keep things clean."

"Okay."

I don't know why I'm shaking. You'd think by this point I'd be used to telling my horror story to people. I went from not telling anyone for the first twenty-six years of my life to telling a new person every couple of days. It should be easier by now.

Spoiler: it isn't.

I offer Hollis the same shortened version of events I gave our friends the night they came to Zane's condo, but it's still a very fresh Band-Aid I'm ripping off here.

When tears pool in my eyes, Hollis slides a box of tissues my way, and then waves for me to continue.

At the end, he doesn't offer apologies or condolences. He just leans forward and steeples his hands in front of him. "You have two options, as I see them. You can either pretend Katerina Costa ceased to exist the day your dad died and hope you never get caught. Or you can turn yourself in."

His options are a one-two punch to the chest. It takes me a few seconds to remember how to breathe. "Those aren't—I thought you were supposed to give me options. *New* options."

Zane made it sound like there might be a way out of this mess for me. The dark, cynical parts of me didn't believe him. But the soft, mushy parts of me that melt against him in the night and pinch his ass while he makes our morning coffee grabbed onto that little bit of hope.

Now, it's being yanked away.

"Sorry; let me explain." Hollis plucks a pen out of the cup on his desk and sweeps a clean piece of paper in front of him. He draws two circles on the page. "You have two options. No matter what happens from this point forward, you either tell people you killed your father or you don't. Those are the big picture options, but—" He draws lines coming out from each circle in every direction like rays of sunlight. "—each option comes with an array of smaller options."

I frown down at his drawing. Maybe Taylor had a point. This guy might be a quack. "Okay, so I confess that I killed my dad and they, what, let me pick my jumpsuit color?"

"It's about the tone." He points a finger at me. "For instance, you could have folded your hands demurely in your lap and requested that I explain what those options would look like. Instead, you scowled and hit me with sarcasm."

I wince. "Sorry."

"Don't apologize." He waves me off, completely unbothered. "The only thing that matters to me is making sure I get the best possible outcome for you. So, in the case of confessing that you killed your father, you have the option of showing deep remorse for your actions, but explaining that you had to do it to save your life. Or you tremble and shake and look as scared now as the day it all happened, which would garner you some sympathy, especially with the battered women crowd."

I can't hide my grimace. "So we're manipulating people?"

"No, you're selling them your version of the truth," he corrects. "If you hit people with nothing but the facts, they'll assume the worst. If you want the truth to go down easy, you have to flavor it with some emotion. You have to give them a hero *and* a villain—someone to root for."

I look at the pen-drawn rays coming off of the sun and wonder how many of those options end with me in a jumpsuit I may or may not get to choose the color of. "You think I could be someone to root for?"

Hollis smirks. "By the time I'm done with you, they won't have a choice."

∼

Zane calls me thirty seconds after I walk out of my meeting with Hollis. "How did it go?"

I'm not sure who has been sending Zane second-by-second updates, Evan or Hollis, but I don't even care. My head is spinning and Taylor abandoned me to caffeinate. I need someone to talk to.

"Well, he laid out my options."

"Was he an asshole about it?" Zane asks. "I should've been there with you. Hollis can be like that, but he knows what he's doing. I told him not to overwhelm you at the first meeting."

"He didn't. Well, he did. But it isn't his fault; I think I'm just easily overwhelmed right now." I blow out a breath. "He thinks I need more evidence of my abuse."

"What the fuck does that mean?" Zane snaps. "You have evidence. The P.I. found all of those hospital records. What does he want, video footage and a play-by-play commentary?"

I shudder at the thought. "He said the hospital records are a good start, but it might not be enough to prove that my life was in danger, which is what we need to do to prove that I was acting in self-defense."

"Okay, okay…" Zane's voice trails off. "What about character witnesses? That kind of thing matters in a trial. There are so many people who would get on the stand for you. We'll prove that you aren't violent or a threat. I'll get up there and tell everyone that I've seen how scared you are of your brother and—"

"No!" I say it loudly enough that Evan catches my eye in the rearview mirror. I give him an apologetic smile and lower my voice. "I appreciate that, Zane. Obviously. The fact that you'd do that for me—"

"I'd do anything for you," he growls.

My chest tightens. *That's the problem.*

"If I decide to do this, there's a chance it doesn't go well, and I don't want to take anyone else down with me."

"I'm not going to let anything happen to you."

"But you might have to," I argue. "Because you have Aiden to think about. If they charge me with murder and find out you knew about it, you could be charged with aiding and abetting. Hollis said as much."

Zane is so quiet I think the call might have dropped. When he does speak, his voice is soft. "That isn't going to happen, Mira."

I wish I had the luxury of being that optimistic.

"But if it does, I need you to be prepared to tell the police you didn't know a thing about it. You need to tell them that…

that you had no idea who I was—no idea what I'd done." I hate that my voice wavers, because I mean every single word. "I don't want Aiden to lose both of us."

"It's not going to happen."

"But if it—"

"But if it does," he cuts in with a weary sigh, "I'll do what's best for Aiden. I swear."

The weight on my chest eases a bit. I feel like I can breathe. "Thank you."

"When are you coming home? I want to see you."

"Are you at the apartment already?" I check the time on the dash. "Did your flight get in early?"

"Jace and I flew in a few hours ahead of the team. Like I said, I wanted to see you."

There's a promise in his voice that zips straight to the core of me. I have half a mind to tell Evan to turn the car around and take me home.

I groan. "I want to, but I thought you wouldn't be back until this afternoon. Taylor and I signed up for a kickboxing class in fifteen minutes."

"Go ahead. Take the class. But when it's over… come straight home to me."

The woman behind the front desk gives me a tight smile when I walk in. I guess she isn't used to members having their bodyguard sweep the gym for threats before they can enter.

To be fair, I'm still not used to it, either.

I can't help but feel like walking around with Evan puts a bigger target on my back than if I pulled the incognito celebrity move and wore a baseball cap and sunglasses everywhere I go.

I scan the front lobby and the juice bar at the back, but I don't see Taylor yet, so I head to the locker rooms.

As much as I want to get out of here and get home to Zane, I also need to burn off some of the anxious energy buzzing through me.

I don't know why the meeting with Hollis has me so on edge. He told me I shouldn't even consider turning myself in until things with Dante are resolved.

"The way you describe him, I don't think your brother will be on your side," Hollis said. "So, it'd be best to wait until that situation is handled before you start a new one, if you know what I mean."

Maybe that's my problem: I didn't know what he meant. I still don't.

How do I *handle* things with Dante? What will it look like when that situation is *resolved*?

Is it when I sit down with him over coffees and we work out all of our issues?

Or maybe when he's dead?

One of those things is never going to happen, and the other is something I'd like to avoid at all costs. One body buried in my figurative backyard is more than enough.

I punch in the code to the locker room and try to shake off my bad juju at the door. Aside from being with Zane and Aiden, kickboxing is one of the only things that can turn my brain off. I can come here and pretend I'm just like the stay-at-home moms here for the free daycare or the influencers taking mirror selfies. I can be normal. I don't want to ruin it by bringing my emotional carry-on with me.

The locker room is humid and smells like the complimentary seabreeze shampoo they keep in the showers, but I don't hear any movement. The tile walls echo every tiny sound, so it's easy to know if you're alone. Yet another reason I like being here.

I pull out my phone and text Taylor. *You're going to be late.*

One minute away, she responds immediately.

Yeah, right. She'd text that whether she was actually one minute away or still standing in line at the coffee shop.

I'm going to tell Jordan where you've been. She'll be so disappointed.

The three dots appear and then: *Snitches get stitches, Mimi.*

Jordan is the only trainer at the gym that Taylor hasn't been able to woo into post-class protein shakes at the bar. Taylor has a weird obsession with proving that she's every trainer's favorite client. Something about paying for their time bothers her, but that's for Taylor and her therapist to work through. The fact remains that Jordan is intense about punctuality and thinks caffeine is an addictive drug. Taylor is definitely *not* her favorite client.

I drop my phone in my bag and dig around for the key to my locker. After around the twelfth time I showed up to class without my gloves, Taylor rented us both permanent lockers. I resisted the handout, but I have to admit it's been nice.

I'm debating splashing some water on myself before I head out so Taylor will think I've been here long enough to work up a sweat when I pull my locker open and freeze.

I blink, trying to decide if I'm seeing what I'm actually seeing.

Red. Everywhere.

It's coating the walls of my locker, dripping from my gloves.

Blood.

No.

I shake my head, trying to logic this away. *It can't be blood. Why would there be blood in my locker?*

I lean in and I can smell it—not the metallic tang of blood, but something… fruity.

I swipe a trembling finger across the sludge at the front of the locker. It's thick and cold and—I bring it to my nose— strawberry-flavored.

Someone put jelly in my locker?

"What the fuck?" I mutter, carefully pulling my gloves out. They're absolutely slathered in jelly. This wasn't an accidental jar explosion. Someone meticulously painted strawberry jelly onto every inch of my gloves.

I carry them over to the sink and do my best to wipe the jelly away with a towel before I start rinsing it down the drain.

The whole time, my heart is thundering in my chest.

It's just jelly.

My hands are shaking.

It's just jelly.

I'm trying to talk myself back from the ledge my brain is galloping towards when the locker room door beeps and then careens open.

"I still have three minutes before I'm late!" Taylor screeches. "I can make it!"

Screw the napkins and the gym's pipes—I blast the water and start scraping the jelly down the drain as fast as I can.

"I might pee my pants during class because I absolutely chugged my iced latte on the way here, but I made it!" Taylor skids to a stop in front of her locker... which is right next to mine.

My locker is like a red, gaping mouth next to Taylor, but she's so busy peeling off layers that she doesn't notice.

I whirl around and slam my locker closed just as her head pops through the neckhole of a spandex tank top. She looks me over carefully. "You look pale."

"No, I don't."

"Yes," she insists, crossing her arms, "you do. And sweaty. I think I know why."

How can she know? I'm not even sure I know.

Maybe this was a random prank... that looks like blood... that someone pulled only on me. It's probably a social media trend to recreate crime scenes out of condiments.

But how did they know my locker code? *How did he find me?*

Taylor nods. "Oh, yeah. I see the truth written all over your face. It's the guilt. It's eating you alive."

"What?" The word squeaks out of my dry throat.

"You feel guilty for betraying your best friend." Taylor slings an arm over my shoulders. "But it's okay. You can make it up to me. I'll let you tell Jordan that I was stopping to get the latte for you, which is why I was almost late."

The sigh of relief I release is audible. It transitions to a choked laugh. "Okay. Yeah. Sure."

She doesn't know.

No one needs to know.

I don't know for sure what even happened. This is probably nothing.

Taylor turns around and frowns. "Why are your gloves in the sink? And sopping wet?"

I scramble for an excuse, something that means my life isn't falling apart and my brother isn't breathing down my neck. Anything that means Taylor won't think twice about what's happening here. Because she'll tell Evan, who will tell Zane, who will throw the life he has earned and worked hard for overboard at the slimmest chance to save mine.

Despite what Zane promised, I know he'll sacrifice everything to keep me safe.

I can't let anyone go down with me.

"There was a spider," I blurt. "A big one. I drowned it."

Taylor looks from me to the gloves and back again slowly. Finally, she wrinkles her nose. "You should've killed it with fire. That's the only way to deal with spiders."

24

ZANE

It is absolute carnage. Everywhere I look, sheer carnage.

Kids are skidding across the ice on everything *except* their skates—knees, butts, the occasional face. People should sign waivers before they step out here. This rink is an insurance nightmare.

"I'm doing it!" Aiden calls, clumsily stomping in his skates across the ice. "I'm skating!"

That's a generous way of putting it, for sure. But he isn't face-planting on the ice like the girl in the sparkly unicorn helmet behind him, or clinging to the boards and screaming for help like the twins in matching velour jumpsuits, so I give it to him.

"You're doing amazing, bud!"

The dad of the twins tosses a longing look towards Aiden before he goes back to convincing his little gremlins to let go of the wall.

Aiden grins. "Can Mira see me? Is she watching?"

I can tell he wants to look into the stands to check, but he learned very quickly that, where his head goes, the rest of his body follows. If he turns his head, he'll end up on his ass.

I look for him. Mira is sitting in the middle of the stands, a white bobble hat pulled down over her ears, her dark hair in long braids. She smiles when she catches me looking, and the gooey warmth that fills my chest is lowkey embarrassing.

"Yeah, she can see you. She says you're doing great, too."

Aiden lowers his head and tries to skate faster. I can tell it's taking every bit of his concentration because his tongue is sticking out the side of his mouth and his face is all squished up.

It's not too far from the way Mira looked when she first got on the ice. To be fair, she warned me in the car ride over that she wasn't going to be any good on ice skates, but she does everything else so gracefully that I didn't believe her.

I should have.

It was like trying to teach a millipede to skate. There were limbs flailing everywhere. I was so busy trying to keep her from cracking her skull open on the ice that I couldn't even help Aiden.

"If you don't put me out of my misery and let me take these skates off," she gasped, almost eating shit when a ten-year-old skater whizzed past her and upset her very delicate equilibrium, "the universe is going to put me out of my misery for you. I'm going to die out here."

I helped her to the edge of the rink and she's been safely in the stands ever since.

Aiden has been a lot easier to train.

After a half-hour of slow laps around the ice while holding my hands, he's able to skate mostly unassisted now. On his third lap without any help at all, he waves me away. "I can do it by myself."

"Are you sure? I can follow along behind you if—"

"I'll do it by myself," he insists.

I skate away, hands raised. "I'm sure you can. I'll go talk to Mira while you take a solo lap."

I skate for the exit and Mira walks down the bleachers to meet me on the bottom row. "He looks good out there. A little more practice and he'll be a pro."

"He's already talking about being on a hockey team. He wants to be a forward. Naturally."

"Like father, like son," she agrees. "Do they have teams for four-year-olds?"

"There's actually a peewee league that runs through the Angels. Some of the trainers and rookies help coach. I might sign him up." I shrug. "Maybe I could even coach."

Mira smiles. "Aiden would *love* that. And it would give me a good excuse to paint my face and make glitter signs."

I can see it perfectly: Aiden tumbling out of the car with all of his gear, Mira decked out in team colors. She and Taylor would make a perfectly obnoxious cheering section. And even though PDA is very much not her jam, Mira would kiss me over the boards before every game.

I tug on the end of her braid. "You'll be our good luck charm."

She winces. "I'm not so sure about that."

My hackles rise. Something has been off with her since she got back from kickboxing this afternoon, but I don't know what. Admittedly, there wasn't a lot of time to figure it out.

She got home an hour later than planned, saying something about a "situation" she had to handle at the gym. Before I could ask about it or make good on my promise to clean her up in my shower, Aiden blew in with Evan thirty seconds later. He was talking a mile a minute about how he desperately needed to learn to skate so he could keep up with Jalen, who just started lessons all of one week ago. Ten minutes later, we were headed out the door for the rink.

"I never got to ask about what happened at the gym." Our legs brush as I turn to her. "About why you were late."

Mira goes rigid. Her green eyes flare wide. "What? When? Nothing."

I arch a brow. "You want to try that again? Maybe your second take will be more convincing."

Her braids bounce against her shoulders as she shakes her head. "Really, it was nothing. Nothing happened. I just—" She looks at me, and goddammit, there's *something* there. Something she isn't telling me. She blinks away before I can figure it out. "I stayed late to work out some frustration. I think talking to Hollis freaked me out a bit. That's all."

"I should've been there," I grit out.

She was worried about a possible head injury and begged me to stay, but I could've paid a flight attendant to check on me through the flight. I should've flown home to be with her, regardless of what she wanted.

"No, you shouldn't have. You probably shouldn't even be

here." She sweeps her fingers over the side of my head. "You need to rest. How do you feel?"

I snag her wrist. "I'm fine. You're the one I'm worried about."

"You don't need to worry about me anymore." She gives me a smile that doesn't quite reach her eyes. "I've sworn off ice skating. It's only solid, unfrozen ground for me from here on out."

"I'm serious, Mira. You don't have to do anything you aren't ready to do. We can go to Hollis and handle this whenever you think the time is right."

"Or whenever Dante shows up," she mutters. "Whichever comes first."

She doesn't mention her brother directly very often. It feels a bit like Voldemort or Beetlejuice. If we say his name, we might summon him.

Mira's cheeks flush despite the chill of the arena. She tips her chin towards the ice. "Aiden looks steady out there. Way better than kids out there twice his age. He really must take after you."

I want to push, to promise Mira that Dante isn't going to get anywhere close to her. But I decide to let it go.

For now.

Aiden finishes his first lap and waves up at me as he starts in on the second. "God help our future kids," I mutter.

She snaps narrowed eyes to me. "What is *that* supposed to mean?"

"You know what I mean. Half of their DNA is going to be yours and balance is not a guarantee."

"This is not a good way to convince me to have your babies, Zane Whitaker!" She swats at me between every other word.

I can perfectly imagine Mira pregnant with my babies. *Our family.* That gooey warmth is back and filling up my chest. "You know it's true."

"Yeah, but only I can say it," she argues. "You're supposed to lie and tell me I looked like a swan out there."

"You did," I agree. Then I add, "A dying swan. With one wing. And no feet."

She puts those flailing limbs to good use, but I fend her off, eventually capturing her gloved hands and cradling them against my chest. "If I tell you you looked graceful, will you be convinced?"

"Convinced of what?" Her eyes rove across my face, and I can tell when she finds the answer to her question. Her smile slips. "I thought you wanted me to take my time to think about it."

"I do, but that doesn't mean I won't try to persuade you in the meantime."

Her full mouth tilts into a smirk. "Telling me I looked graceful is a start."

"Mira, you looked extraordinarily graceful out there." I dip my chin, holding her gaze. "Especially when you tripped over your own skates and almost crushed that little girl and her mom."

She shoves away from me, laughing despite herself. "You're terrible at this."

"I guess so. I've never been good with words. I prefer to use my mouth for other things."

She casts a sidelong glance my way, but it's not until her teeth sink into her lower lip that I know I've got her. "Like what?"

"I'll show you tonight." I lean in, my lips brushing against her cheek. "I'll convince you again and again... *and again...*"

25

ZANE

While Mira is putting Aiden to bed, I get a text from the P.I.

Word is the brother is back in town. I don't have eyes on him yet, but tell your girl to watch her back.

Fuck.

It was stupid to hope that Dante would move on. He's been after Mira for seven years; what's a few more months of waiting compared to that?

But, stupid as it seems, I'd let myself start hoping. Every day with Mira and our little family makes me believe that life really might work out for us. I pulled myself out of hell when I got sober four years ago. This life with her could be my reward.

But life likes to remind me that nothing is ever that easy.

I text Evan. ***P.I. says Dante might be back in town. Have you seen anything?***

Nothing, he texts back. *But I've been on high alert. Mira was on edge all day.*

I'm not sure if it's a good or bad thing that I'm not the only one who noticed. I was ready to write it off, but if Evan is noticing it, too…

"I don't know how kids are able to fight bedtime." Mira rubs her eyes. "Thirty minutes in that dark room with a sound machine going, and I'm a goner."

I drop my phone face down on the counter. "Maybe we should get one for our room. We can fall asleep to ocean waves every night."

I could use all the help I can get. I'm still waking up most nights in a panic to make sure Mira is still next to me.

"Or we skip the sound machine and move to a deserted island. We'll open our windows and fall asleep to the *real* ocean lapping against the shore." She wraps her arms around me and rests her cheek on my chest.

The team still hasn't completely forgiven me for the rumor I didn't even start that I'm looking to be traded. They'd never speak to me again if I up and abandoned them for some island in the middle of nowhere. No matter how nice it sounds.

"You thinking about making a getaway?"

I mean it to be a joke, but Mira's breath catches. She goes stiff in my arms and all of my internal alarms go off.

I grab her shoulders and hold her away from me. "Are you?"

"N-no. No!" She shakes her head. "I'm not. It was just a joke."

I want to tell her what the P.I. said about Dante and ask if she's seen anything. I want to show her Evan's text message for proof I'm not crazy. Other people can see something is wrong with her, too.

But she feels like a wild animal sometimes. If I get too close or push too hard, she'll get spooked. I could lose her.

I grip her chin and tilt her face to mine. "Tell me your one truth."

Her lips part and then close. She frowns, and *fuck*, I want to wipe it away.

"Come on, Mira." I brush the pad of my thumb over her full bottom lip. "I can't quiet all of the noise in your pretty head if you don't let me in."

"It's pretty loud in there," she whispers.

"Is that doubt I'm sensing?" I arch a brow. "If you don't think I can handle it, I can't wait to prove you wrong."

"I know you can. But I don't know i-if I can. Handle it, I mean." She squeezes her eyes closed for a second. When they open again, they're glassy. "What if I let you carry some of it, Zane? What happens when I get used to having you here and then… and then…"

"And then *nothing*." I pull her close, cupping a hand around the back of her head. "We're going to be there for each other and carry each other's shit and nothing is going to change that."

Her chest shudders on an inhale. "My one truth is that I'm terrified that something will. I'm terrified I'm going to lose you."

"Is this still about the meeting with Hollis? You aren't going to prison, Mira. You didn't do anything wrong."

"I know a lot of people who would disagree with you," she mutters.

"They'll have to go through me if they want to arrest you."

She jerks back. "*No.* That's exactly what I'm afraid of. We're both going to get all tangled up in this and you aren't going to be able to rip free. You're going to go down with me, and I don't want—"

"Too fucking bad!" I don't mean to, but I press her back against the wall. I loom over her until I'm staring down into her wide, green eyes. I know I'm probably scaring her, but the feeling is mutual. I capture her mouth with mine and kiss her until we're panting. I drop my forehead to hers. "We're tangled up already, Mira. It's too late to avoid it."

"It's not. We can—"

"I love you," I bite out. "I love *you*. All of you. Your heart and your stubborn head and your baggage. I love who you were and who you are and who you will be."

I wrap my arm around her waist and bend her against me. We're close, but it's not enough. I've never had this kind of urge to be inside someone before.

She whimpers. "Zane…"

"You've been through so much, and you could have let it make you cold and bitter and angry. But you spent your time making sure your best friend didn't get murdered by her Tinder dates." She lets out a watery laugh, and I trace the line of her smile with my lips. "And fake dating a stranger so he could keep custody of his son. You take care of everyone else. It's way past time that someone took care of you."

I slide my hands under the hem of her dress and work slow circles over her hip bones. She rocks against me gently, driving me fucking mad with every brush of our bodies.

"I didn't want it to be like this. I was supposed to leave. None of this was supposed to land in your lap." Tears roll down her cheeks. "I wish…"

Her voice trails off, and I kiss her, drawing the words out. "Tell me."

"I wish we'd met in a different life. One without all of this mess."

"It wouldn't matter. There's no version of me that doesn't love every version of you. In every alternate universe, you and I are just as tangled up."

She opens her mouth like she's going to argue—I'm more than used to it by now. But I don't want to argue.

I kiss her back into the wall and lift her legs around my hips. Her lips are salty from tears, but with every twist of our tongues together, she softens. I press myself between her legs and she moans. Her hand twists in my hair, dragging me closer.

"You want this," I growl.

It isn't a question, but she nods.

"You want me."

She answers by slipping her hand between us and undoing my pants. When her fingers curl around me, I can't fucking breathe. It's like I'm in a vacuum. It isn't until I slide her panties to the side and press into her that I can finally inhale again.

Mira gasps, and I tug on her lower lip with my teeth. I fill her with a slow, relentless thrust and watch as she takes me.

"Say it," I snarl. "Tell me what you want, Mira."

"You can feel what I want."

She's talking about how wet she is, and she's not wrong. I rub my thumb over her clit, spreading her wetness over where we're connected.

"Say it anyway."

Her eyes roll back. She throws out an arm for something to hold onto, grabbing onto the handle of the refrigerator until her knuckles are white. "Y-you."

I drag out of her and drive in again. She gasps in my ear, her body quivering around me. "I want you. So much. All the time."

"I was supposed to take you to bed and do this right," I remark with a grimace.

"No!" She fists her hand in my shirt, her other arm still tossed over her head. "Don't stop. Please."

I couldn't stop now even if I wanted to.

I pin her hips to the door of the pantry and fill her again and again. "I'm supposed to be convincing you."

Mira wraps her hand around my neck and rolls against me. She chases her own pleasure until she's bouncing against me, crying out with every shift of our bodies together. I'm barely clinging on.

Before I lose it, I press into her, driving her back against the wall and holding.

"Please," she whimpers, trying to wriggle free. "Zane, I'm convinced."

I press an open-mouthed kiss to her lips and her neck. "Don't say it because you want me to fuck you. Don't say it if it isn't true."

She scrapes her fingers down my back. "I'm not. It's always been true. There's no one else I'd want a family with."

Talking about kids should not make me this wild, but possession curls low in my gut. The urge I have to be inside of Mira grows into something instinctual. Something raw and feral.

I touch her jaw and force her heavy eyes to mine. "Say it."

Her lips are swollen as she says, "Of course I want your babies, Zane. I love you."

I'm not sure how we got there, but we're on the floor. I drag her dress down her shoulders and bunch the material around her waist so I can wrap my mouth around her nipple.

She groans, her back arching off the floor, and I press my hands to her spine. I haul her against me and hold her in my lap as I fuck her.

She looks in my eyes and her expression is tinged with heat. She's as lost to the feeling as I am. When she shoves against my chest and forces me back, I let her. Her hands smooth over my chest and lower. She reaches for me like she keeps expecting me to disappear. I grip her waist and we grind together until I feel her clench around me. Until she goes limp against my chest, and I have to hold her steady and fill her from underneath.

"I love you," she pants against my neck. "Holy shit, Zane... I love you."

Mira presses her hand to my cheek as I cry out and spill into her. I come hard, kissing her fingers and her palm on every ragged exhale.

I slowly work my way down her arm and across her collarbone. When I reach her lips, they're salty again.

I pull back to see she's crying.

"Are you okay?" I brush her tears away. "What's wrong?"

She shakes her head. "Nothing. It's... it's nothing."

"Mira—"

"No matter what happens," she says, laying her head on my chest, "I'm just glad I'm here with you. In this reality."

26

MIRA

"God, I love a boozy brunch!" Taylor declares, raising her wine for the third toast in the last half hour.

I tap my glass to hers. "It's four in the afternoon."

"Yeah, well, some of us don't have to wake up at the ass crack of dawn to get kids off to school. I slept in today. For me, this is brunch."

To be fair, this is brunch for me, too. I dropped Aiden off at preschool, went to the gym for a kickboxing class, and then had to distract Evan with some fake threat in the parking lot so I could ask the front desk about security footage in the locker rooms.

The woman looked at me like I was soliciting her for pictures of her feet. "It's illegal to have cameras in the locker rooms for... *obvious* reasons."

I tried to convey to her that I wasn't trying to get naked footage of my fellow gym-goers and was, instead, trying to see who vandalized my locker, but first impressions are hard to undo. She thought I was a creep and had no intention of being part of whatever weird fetish she thought I had.

"Me, too!" Jemma chimes in. "I mean, I still had to wake up at the ass crack of dawn to get a kid to school, but I went to bed at eight last night. I slept for, like, nine hours. Going to bed early is as close to sleeping in as I get these days."

Rachelle shakes her head. "I have no idea how you can sleep when Reeves isn't home. When Jace is gone for games, I sleep like shit. I tossed and turned for a couple hours last night before I got up and deep-cleaned the fridge." She shivers. "Some of the leftovers in there were older than Gallagher."

I didn't sleep well, either.

I haven't in days.

Evan stayed in the spare room last night at Zane's request, and I didn't even attempt to argue. Having someone close by helped me get at least a couple hours of sleep in the big, empty bed. Then I woke up early this morning and found a black jewelry box sitting just outside my door.

Panic sliced through me for half a second before I saw Evan's large note on the floor next to it. *Zane asked me to leave this for you.*

My hand shifts to the necklace sitting just above my collarbone the way it has repeatedly all day. I run my thumb over the little charms and smile.

"What's that?" Taylor swats my hand out of the way and lets out a tipsy scream. "Oh my God!"

The patrons of Café Bisou glare at our table over their patisseries, and I slap a hand over Taylor's mouth. "Can we not make a scene?"

She mumbles something about Zane and jewelry before she rips my hand away and keeps going at full volume. "—never thought I'd see the day that my bestie would be in a real relationship." She waves Jemma and Rachelle closer. "Look at this! Hockey sticks with their initials."

My friends lean in, fawning over the delicate charms. On the back of each hockey stick is a "Z" and an "A." For my boys.

"That is the sweetest thing I've ever seen. Can Zane give Reeves gift-giving tips? To him, that 'Dick in a Box' song is not a joke." Jemma's smile wavers somewhere between a laugh and a grimace. "He would absolutely give me his dick in a box."

I decide not to tell them that the necklace also came with a note in Zane's handwriting. I have it folded inside of my purse right now. I reread it in the parking lot like a smiling idiot before coming inside.

I plan to get you a much more expensive piece of jewelry the second I'm positive you'll accept it. Until then, I'll claim you like this.

I'd say I'm hearing wedding bells, but it's more likely they're blaring alarms. I still haven't told anyone about the Smuckers murder scene I found in my locker, though Zane came incredibly close to fucking it out of me the other night.

I want to imagine wearing a white dress and getting married to Zane. I want to picture Aiden as a little ringbearer and me pleading my undying love for Zane in front of all of our family and friends.

But with everything else going on right now, dreams of a wedding quickly morph to include buckets of pig's blood and fiery death.

Not exactly the genre of daydream I'm going for.

"Shit!" Rachelle jumps up, almost knocking over our teensy cafe-style table and earning even more glares from the people around us. "We gotta go, girls. The open house starts in half an hour."

Taylor offers to pay the tab. "It's the least I can do since you all are about to spend your night looking at preschool art."

"I'm actually kind of excited," I admit. "A couple months ago, Aiden was drawing pictures of me as a head with arms and legs growing out of it, but now, he does bodies with necks and everything."

"Wow. *Necks*," Taylor drawls. "I see we're setting the bar high."

I'm not just excited to see a picture of me with a neck; I'm also excited because the team's plane arrived a couple hours ago and the men are meeting us at the school.

As soon as we pull up, my head is on a swivel, searching the crowd for Zane.

Rachelle elbows Jemma as we walk through the doors of the school. "Zane knew what he was doing with that necklace. He is *sooo* getting lucky tonight."

"Again," Jemma pants, "someone tell Reeves. I'd be hunting for him like that if he left me cute gifts, too."

Rachelle spots Gallagher standing in front of a full-sized self-portrait that looks mostly like a chalk outline of a dead body, and she splits off. Then Jalen stands on a table in the back corner of the gym and waves his arms over his head, calling for Jemma.

"There's my hooligan." She squeezes my arm as she leaves. "Catch up later?"

I nod and navigate through endless tables of soap boats and lemon batteries and dioramas that explain the water cycle until I see a shock of blonde hair sitting on top of a set of broad shoulders.

As soon as Aiden sees me, he starts smacking Zane's forehead. "She's over there! I see her!"

Zane winces and nods. By the time I make it to them, he's sliding Aiden off of his shoulders.

"We couldn't find you and we got desperate. I almost lost an eye." Zane pulls me in for a quick kiss. Our lips press and hold for slightly longer than necessary. When he pulls back, Zane's gaze shifts to my necklace. "You like it?"

My hand flies to the hockey sticks for what has to be the hundredth time today. "I love it. More than anything. Thank you."

"I meant what I said in that note." He leans in, his voice low enough that I feel the rumble of it in my toes. "Give me the sign and I'll get you something even better."

I try to match his smile, but it's bittersweet. From where I'm standing, that kind of happily-ever-after moment is a long, long way off.

Before Zane can notice my half-assed smile, a woman with a red braid and a prairie-style dress pops her head in. "Hi there! I'm Mrs. Wilson, Aiden's teacher."

Aiden darts between me and Zane to wrap his arms around Mrs. Wilson's legs.

"You just saw her an hour ago, bud." Zane tries to pry Aiden back, but he holds tight.

Mrs. Wilson laughs and squeezes him back. "It's okay. This is the best part of the job. Preschoolers always let you know exactly how they feel about you."

I don't look to confirm, but I swear I feel Zane's eyes slip to me.

I'll have to tell him about the locker eventually. But not until I'm sure it was Dante who did it. There's no sense freaking everyone out if it was some random, senseless prank, after all.

I'm halfway lost in my head, trying to decide what kind of search I'd need to do to find out if teenagers are pranking people with strawberry jelly, when Aiden's voice cuts through my thoughts.

"This is my dad." He loops one arm around Zane's leg and then loops the other around mine, tugging on my knee. "And this is my mom."

The record that is my life scratches.

I stand perfectly still, afraid that any tiny movement might shatter this obvious daydream I've stumbled into.

"It's so nice to meet Aiden's parents." Mrs. Wilson shakes Zane's hand and then holds her hand out to mine, oblivious to the riot of thoughts bouncing around my head. I don't move until Zane nudges me gently in the side. I finally take her hand and she grins. "Aiden talks about you both all the time."

I should be listening. Mrs. Wilson is telling us how great Aiden is doing in class and how many friends he has. She's rattling off a list of accolades and praise that I would be absolutely giddy to hear if I wasn't deep in an existential spiral.

Zane answers for both of us, saying all of the right things, I'm sure. Even though, again, I'm existentially spiraling.

Mrs. Wilson points Aiden towards Gallagher's self-portrait and the two of them head over to admire his classmate's work.

As soon as Zane and I are alone, he turns me towards him. "You're freaking out."

"Nope. I'm fine."

"You're not." He massages warmth into my arms. "But you should be. Aiden loves you."

"But I'm not his mom," I blurt.

It hurts to say it. To admit the undeniable truth out loud.

"As much as I want to be, I'm not. And I'm not sure I should let him call me... *that*. What would Paige think?"

"I have no idea what Paige would think. Because she's dead." I gasp and Zane just shrugs. "She isn't here. But *you* are. I don't intend to erase Paige or lie to Aiden about anything, but I've told you from the beginning that you're good for Aiden. He loves you."

"I love him, too. Of course I do. But—"

"You can stop there. That's all that matters. *You love him.* As far as I'm concerned, he's as much yours as he is mine." Zane pulls me against his side, and I can see the whole gym. All the families that look as normal here as we do. "We all belong to each other now, Mira. And nothing is going to change that."

Zane's words stick with me the rest of the night. While I admire Aiden's family portrait and we walk around, hand-in-hand, to look at all of the science projects.

On the ride home when Aiden recaps every single moment from the entire event, even the ones we were there for, while Zane squeezes my thigh across the console.

Especially when I poke my head in Aiden's door as Zane is putting him to bed.

They're huddled under the blankets with a book between them. The reading lamp in the corner casts them in a soft, yellow glow.

"Goodnight, buddy."

Aiden smiles so hard his eyes go squinty. "Goodnight. I love you!"

Emotion clogs my throat and it takes two tries before I can squeeze the words out. "I love you, too."

I slip across the hall to my bedroom and, alone in the quiet, give myself permission to imagine this forever.

I may not know what a normal family looks like, but surely I can figure it out. Hell, maybe we already have. Maybe this is it!

We all belong to each other now. Nothing is going to change that.

Can that be true?

I lean against the door under the weight of a future I want, but don't know if I can have, until I *need* to do something.

I kick my sandals into the closet and straighten the books on my nightstand. Then I drag my gym bag off of the end of the bed and move to hang it on the hook behind the door, but a slip of paper falls out.

It floats to the floor like a falling leaf, swaying back and forth before it comes to rest on the carpet.

It might as well be a grenade.

Without even looking, I know this is the other shoe I've been waiting for.

I don't even want to touch it, but I force myself across the floor and pick it up with trembling fingers. Somehow, after all these years, I recognize his handwriting.

I remember strawberries were always your favorite. Sorry I missed you. Catch you next time, little sister.

Before the words can even sink into my panicked brain, I sprint into the bathroom and flush Dante's note down the toilet.

It was him. He's here.

My heart is racing and I'm trembling, but when I hear Zane come into the bedroom, it's still his words that echo in my head.

This family is mine.

And nothing is going to take that away.

27

ZANE

Owen takes one look at Daniel from across Cam's Cafe and his top lip curls.

"I told you I shouldn't have come," Daniel hisses.

"Don't be scared," I reassure him, nudging him into the restaurant. "He's old. You can take him."

Honestly, I'm not sure that's true. Owen's knees are made of fucking crabmeat, but he has a pull-up bar hanging from his bedroom door and does twenty reps before he even takes his morning piss. That, plus his surly attitude, might give him the advantage.

"Obviously, I could take him," Daniel snaps. "It's offensive that was even in doubt. But I shouldn't be here. I thought this was just dinner. I didn't know it was a meeting. These should be closed."

"It *is* just dinner. Relax." I clap Daniel on the back and weave my way through the cafe.

Owen watches us approach with narrowed eyes. When we're still far enough away that he shouldn't be talking to us yet, he slams his coffee down. "So scared you brought backup, Whitaker?"

The people at the tables close by eye us warily, especially when Daniel erupts in nervous laughter.

"I'm just here for the chicken fried steak." He holds his menu like a shield and slides into the booth. "Good to see you again, Owen."

"Wish I could say the same, lad." Owen arches a bushy brow at me. "How many times have you rescheduled on me?"

Five... maybe six? Owen and I were never out of touch, exactly, but we haven't sat down for our regular chat in a long time.

"I had a lot going on." I grab the carafe in the center of the table and pour myself some coffee. "How have you been?"

Owen ignores my question. "The times you have a lot going on are when we need these meetings the most."

What I mean to say is: *You're right, Owen. I've missed our meetings, too. I'm sorry.* Instead, it comes out as, "If you were really worried about me, you would've broken my door down by now."

"Is that what you want?" he growls. "I thought we were past that, but I can root through your drawers if that's what you want. Give me a spare key and I'll drop in unannounced. Maybe I'll get another peek of your bonnie lass in the bare scud."

"If you're talking about seeing my girlfriend naked, you'll be the one who needs a bodyguard," I growl.

Daniel whistles loudly and opens his menu. "Wow, what a menu. So many options. What are you both getting?"

"Naked or not, I'd like to see your girlfriend," Owen says, tossing an annoyed scowl at Daniel. "Since the lass showed up, you've disappeared. It makes me wonder…"

"I disappeared because *she* disappeared. Because I was so busy trying to get her home, I didn't have time to think about a drink or fall off any fucking trolleys."

Owen knows Mira was gone. He knows I was torn up about it. I expect this to be the end of his interrogation.

I should know better.

"And now, she's back and you have nothing *but* fookin' time," he says. "So, have you?"

Daniel is reading the menu under his breath, his finger sliding across each menu item like he's a first grader learning to read. I'm not sure why I thought he would be a good buffer for this conversation.

"Have I what?" I grit out.

Owen extends his thumb and pinky and tosses back a signed drink. "Have you found yourself some time to get sauced?"

"Fuck you."

"You sound mighty defensive for someone *on* the trolley."

First, my teammates don't trust me. Now, Owen.

I slide out of the booth and stand up. "It's been nice to catch up with you, too, O. I've been through a lot lately, but it's good to know you have unwavering faith in me."

Owen shakes his head, unfazed. "I stopped putting my faith in addicts a long time ago. I dinnae even have faith in myself. It's why *I'm* still in the program."

"So am I."

"Oh? When was your last meeting?" he fires back.

"Did you know they have steak and eggs?" Daniel asks no one in particular. "And dumplings! Man, this place has everything."

I roll my eyes and focus back on Owen. "It's been a while. Like I said, I've been busy."

"Okay, then you'll go this week."

"I'm fucking sober, goddammit!" The couple in the booth next to us glance over, and I give them a scowl. If they want to run off and tell some tabloid that Zane Whitaker is talking about sobriety in a shitty cafe downtown, they can go for it. I don't fucking care because—"I'm clean. I'm good. I'm... I'm better than ever, actually."

Owen's face softens. He's an asshole, but he just has a tougher brand of love than most people are used to. I think the weeks apart lowered my immunity.

"That'll be great for people in the program to hear. That there's life on the other side." He grabs his jacket and slides out of the booth. "Call me when you're taking your sobriety seriously again. In the meantime, I'd love to have the bairn over to my place again soon. It's been a wee bit since I've seen him, seeing as you've been so *busy*."

Daniel doesn't say anything until Owen is out of the restaurant and halfway down the block. He leans across the table. "I hate you for bringing me here."

"You could've vouched for me. Told him I'm not drinking."

"I also could have put my balls on the table and handed him a mallet!" He shivers. "That man is scary. But... he's not wrong."

"Not wrong about what? I *am* sober. I wasn't—"

Daniel waves me off. "I know that. I'm talking about a meeting. You used to go all the time."

Yeah, back when I spent countless hours alone with nothing but the devil on my shoulder for company. Some nights, the thought of going to a meeting first thing the next morning was the only thing that kept me from slipping down to the liquor store on the corner or hunting down the number of my old dealer.

"It's been a long time since I needed that."

"So go to a meeting before you need it." He shrugs. "You've finally got your wily ducks in a row. Now, you need to keep them that way."

"What are you talking about?"

"I'm talking about your *bonnie lass*," he says in the world's worst Scottish accent. He leans in close. "Did Owen really see Mira naked?"

"Close enough," I growl. The day Owen burst into the house, Mira was practically comatose in bed. The only reason Owen didn't see her naked is because I threw a blanket over her. He was tearing through the house, and she was terrified.

I'd like to avoid that ever happening again.

"A meeting would keep him off my back," I admit. "It'll also keep him out of my house. The last thing I need is him destroying the place again."

"You should spend more time with him. If he could see you with Mira, he'd be less worried."

"Maybe. But they didn't get off to the best start."

Only because I didn't tell Owen about Mira until she was living in my house. He had every right to be on edge. If Mira was any other woman in the world, moving her in that fast would've been a disaster.

But she *isn't* any other woman in the world.

She's *my* woman.

Daniel lets off another low whistle. "God, you really do have it bad."

I turn to him and only then realize I'm smiling like an idiot. I quickly flip it upside down and scowl at him. "You have no room to say shit. Let any loud-mouthed blondes boss you around lately?"

Daniel puffs up, straightening his navy bomber jacket. "Yes, actually. She picked out this outfit for me."

I give him a look that lets him know I absolutely rest my case.

"But we aren't living together," he argues. "I like Taylor. She's fun. But if she up and left me tomorrow, I'd drink about it— maybe watch one sad movie about it—and then I'd move on."

"Bull-fucking-shit!" I scoff, earning me another glare from the older couple across the aisle. "You'd be a wreck."

"The same way you were?" He smirks, trying to corner me, but it won't work.

Because I'm not afraid of the truth.

"Yeah, the same way I was. Because you know you love her."

He huffs. "I never would have thought that, out of the two of us, *you* would turn into the sappier one."

"I'm not being sappy; I'm being realistic. Mira is the one."

"So when are you going to make it official?" He holds up his left hand and wags his ring finger.

"Soon."

At that, Daniel about falls out of the booth. "You're kidding. *I* was kidding. You're serious? Are you kidding?"

"Yes? Or... I don't know how to answer that, but I'm serious. It's going to be soon."

"Well, son of a bitch." He raises his coffee mug in a toast. "Nathan will be disappointed, but everyone else will be happy for you."

"Why does Nathan care?"

"He had a little crush when he first met her and has been secretly hoping things between you two weren't that serious." Daniel lifts one shoulder in a casual shrug, like he isn't telling me information that might get our good friend Nathan killed. "But Nathan has a crush on everyone."

I grind my molars together. "Yeah. I guess he does."

Daniel eyes my face and smirks. "You better lock her down real soon before someone else tries. Otherwise, you might lose your girl *and* be sent away for murder." Suddenly, Daniel grabs his knife and fork like he's a hungry cartoon character. "Our food is coming."

The waitress is making her way towards us, and I check the time on the red neon clock above the counter. It's later than I thought.

Just as the waitress stops next to our table, I hold out a hand. "Actually, can we get these in a to-go box? We need to get going."

"Of course," she says cheerfully, spinning away as Daniel's face falls in horror.

"No!" he cries out. "Why?"

"You can eat in the car."

"But why?" he bemoans, sinking down in the booth. "I'm starving."

"Because we're going shopping."

28

MIRA

A loud pop goes off in my ear, and I almost hit the deck.

"Another balloon down!" Davis cheers, tossing back another tequila shot to go with it.

At this rate, this drinking game is going to kill him.

And the popping balloons are going to kill me.

I've been on edge for days—longer, actually, but the last few days have been especially bad. That's what getting a threatening note from your murderous brother will do: fry your nerves and fuck with your head.

I should probably be huddled in a dark closet, taking long, measured breaths until this whole thing is over. Instead, I'm at a five-year-old's birthday party, standing in front of a balloon arch that is swiftly losing its battle with the sun and picking at the same plate of food I've been holding for the last hour.

I haven't been eating much at all lately.

Or sleeping.

Or talking to Zane.

It's hard when, every time I look at him, all I can see is Dante's creepy note. And all I can hear is a little voice in my head calling me a *dirty rotten liar who lies.*

"Friends don't keep secrets from friends!" Rachelle shouts over what I believe is a Kidz Bop cover of Nicki Minaj. I think she might be talking to me and my guilty conscience, but she's over by the juice table shaking Jemma by the shoulders. "Don't be a gatekeeper."

Jemma laughs and shakes her off. "I'm not gatekeeping! I really don't remember where I got the balloon arch for Jalen's party. I'll look back through my email when I'm home."

Another balloon pops and I yelp, spilling half of my plate on the patio.

"Shot!" Davis shouts.

Rachelle just groans. "That stupid thing is going to be gone before we even do cake."

Jace shifts behind his wife, squeezing her shoulders. "Look at Gallagher. Does it look like he cares?"

Aiden and Jalen double-bounce Gallagher so hard that he smashes against the mesh wall face first. His cheeks are squished into a deformed grin before he can right himself and go straight back to bouncing, laughing the entire time.

The kids have been in the bouncy castle since the moment Rachelle opened the sliding glass door and released them into the backyard. We're going to have to drag them out of it when the party is over. They might not even come out for cake.

"No," Rachelle sighs. "He doesn't. But *I* care. I paid a stupid amount of money for that dumb arch."

"Wait? How much did you pay?" Jace turns to face her just as a pair of muscular arms slip around my waist.

I spasm like I'm being electrocuted and drop the other half of my plate.

"Oh. Shit." Zane laughs, kicking the food into the grass where Davis's dog has been lying in patient, dedicated wait. "Didn't mean to scare you."

I force a smile on my face. "It's okay. I just didn't think anyone was behind me."

"Makes sense. You're being a bit of a wallflower." He kisses my cheek, his stubble scraping over my neck. "A beautiful wallflower. One I've been thinking about... plucking? That sounds weird. Sniffing? No, worse."

I don't have to fake a laugh now.

"I've been thinking about doing whatever sounds sexiest the second we get back home and Aiden has his sugar crash," he hums against my skin. "How about that?"

Before I can respond, another godforsaken fucking balloon pops, and I yet again.

Davis calls for another shot and then frowns down at his dog. "Who in the hell gave Anita little smokies?"

"Who's Anita?" Jace asks.

Davis points at the French bulldog on the ground. "Anita Bone, M.D. I introduced you after I adopted her last month."

"That still doesn't explain why Dr. Bone is at my son's birthday party. I tripped on a hole she dug in the grass."

Davis is denying any and all wrongdoing on behalf of his dog while Jace shows Davis the swelling around his partially rolled ankle, and I'm enjoying the show. But Zane turns me to face him.

"Something is wrong," he accuses.

"I know." I hitch a thumb over my shoulder. "Anita didn't dig that hole. It was Aiden. He used a plastic spoon."

He shakes his head. "Not with them. With *you*."

Instantly, the noise of the party dies down. The world fades away. It has a tendency to do that when Zane is looking at me like this.

I want to deny it, but I know it won't do any good.

"Something has been wrong for a few days," he continues. "You think you're hiding it well, but you aren't."

"I don't even think that. It's why I've been avoiding you. Because I knew you'd get it out of me." I blow out a breath. "But it's not you, Zane. It's not about you or Aiden or… *us*."

I should tell him. I should've told him the second the note fell out of my duffel bag.

No, I should've told him when I opened my locker and found the psychopath's version of an edible arrangement.

Zane sweeps my hair behind my ear. "I'm not going to force you to talk today. There's enough security around this party that I know for a fact you're safe. But eventually…"

"You won't have to force me. I'll tell you myself." I lean

against him, my chin raised so I can look into his eyes. "Just… not today."

I don't want to pop our happy little bubble until I have to.

I know I've never been cared for by anyone the way Zane cares for me. It's not like there's been a lot of competition, not even from my own parents. Still, it's special.

Few people get to be loved by someone like Zane Whitaker. I don't intend to take it for granted.

"Promise me that, if what you're hiding is dangerous, you'll tell someone." He cradles my face gently. "It doesn't even have to be me. Just… tell someone."

I curl my fingers over his. "I promise."

Later, when Zane is busy making sure the boys don't accidentally beat each other with sticks instead of the piñata, I keep my promise.

Evan is leaning against the back gate. "Enjoying the party?"

"Oh yeah. Juice boxes and PG-rated covers of songs I used to get hammered to. What's not to love?" I lean against the fence next to him. "Are you having fun?"

He lifts a shoulder, his eyes shifting from the driveway to the street beyond. "I don't think I'm being paid to have fun."

"Right." I dig the toe of my shoe into the dirt, trying to decide the best way to bring this up. After almost no consideration, because I'm too much of a coward and might chicken out if I think about it too hard, I decide to jump straight into it. "I need you to look into something for me."

"Professionally?"

"Yes. I need you to check with the staff at the gym. See if they have any security cameras set up."

"They do," he says, turning to fully face me. "I know they do. Why do you need to see them?"

Whatever I ask, he could report back to Zane. I know that's true. Some part of me is even glad that it's true. Zane and I can both trust Evan, which is why he's good at his job.

But it also means I have to be careful.

"I want to know if Dante has been by," I say plainly.

Still, his shoulders tense. "Is that why you've been skipping kickboxing the last few days? Have you seen him? Do you know where he—"

"I don't know anything."

"I've been keeping a close eye on things at the gym, but I'll check again," Evan says. "I can ask them for footage and take a closer look, if you're worried."

Zane gets a blindfolded Aiden aimed in the direction of the piñata and then turns around, looking for me. Our eyes meet across the lawn, and my insides light up like a switchboard.

"Thanks. It's just a precaution." I manage my first real smile in days. "I'm sure everything will work out just fine."

29

_____

ZANE

"This is an open meeting, but you really don't have to come if you don't want to." I squeeze Mira's hand as we walk down the stairs. "Evan is just outside. He can take you back to the condo. I'll go by myself."

"Zane." Mira pulls me to a stop. She's a step ahead of me, our eyes almost on the same level. "I want to come with you. Please don't be nervous."

"I'm not nervous." She arches a brow, and I drop my head to her shoulder. "Fuck. Fine. I haven't been this nervous for a meeting since my first one. I've only ever gone to these by myself."

"Well, I'm happy to be your first." She gives me a teasing smile. "But if you don't want me here, then I can leave. It's up to—"

I yank her forward, catching her with a kiss.

She hums contentedly against my mouth and my hand slides

over the curve of her waist, across her hip. I pull her against me, pressing her where I want her until—

"You're at the wrong building," someone croaks from way too close.

I snatch Mira around the waist and haul her down to my step before I realize we've been caught by a woman half my height and three times my age.

The old woman takes a shaking step down the stairs to get past us. "Sex Addicts Anonymous is at the Greek Orthodox church down the block." With that, the woman leaves, her witchy cackle floating back to us as she wobbles away.

Once she's down the stairs, Mira laughs against my neck. "How does she know where sex addicts meet?"

"Don't ask questions you don't want the answer to."

I grab her hand and lead her into the dingy church basement full of addicts.

Folding chairs have been set up in a circle. As opposed to most meetings I attend first thing in the morning before practice, almost every seat is full. Mira and I have to squeeze between a middle-aged couple in matching striped shirts and a young guy FaceTiming with a woman who looks old enough to be his mom.

"Do you want any coffee?" I point to the refreshments table. "It's actually pretty good. Caffeine is the only drug we're allowed, so we know how to do it right."

"That's okay. Now that we're here, *I'm* nervous," she admits. "I don't know what this will be like."

Before I can prep her, the secretary for this meeting stands up and opens up the proceedings. They pass the donation plate to collect enough money to pay for the cookies and coffee—I toss in everything in my wallet. Then the first speaker reads from the Big Book.

When he's done, he lowers the book and raises a hand. "Hi, my name is Dan. I'm an alcoholic and I just had my second sober birthday last week."

People clap, including Mira.

He tells his story of addiction and betrayal and then opens the floor to the rest of us.

The couple next to us share the woman's addiction and the way it affected her husband. The guy next to me holds up his phone so his mom can tell the room—with her spotty internet connection—how proud she is of her son for coming clean to her and being sober for the last twelve days. When I glance over, Mira is dabbing at her eyes.

Halfway through the meeting, I stand up.

I don't have time to think about it before all eyes are on me. "Hey. My name is Zane. I'm an addict, and I've been clean for four—well, free from drugs for over four years." I scratch the back of my head, trying to ignore the shame swirling in my gut. Then I feel Mira's knee brush against the back of my calf and it dissipates. "I haven't had a drink for three months, and I plan to keep it that way. But we all know how that goes."

Self-deprecating laughter ripples through the room, and I already feel more at home. Like it or not, these are my people. Their scars match mine.

"Yeah, so, I haven't told my story in a while. I did a lot at the beginning because it's all I could think about. How it all started and how I never wanted to go back there. Then, over time, it all got kind of hazy. I felt... different. Better. I sat

back and let other people talk. Then I stopped coming, and...
Anyway, I'm back and I thought I'd share."

There's another soft round of applause before I begin.

"For me, it started with a girl and party drugs. My ex had
been in and out of the program a few different times before
she met me, though I didn't know that at the time. I thought
we were just having some fun, but pretty soon, our 'fun'
turned into week-long benders, which turned into a high I
rarely came down from. I was using as often as I could, as
much as I could handle. More than once, I couldn't handle it.
I almost OD'd three different times."

Mira lets out a soft gasp. Then her leg is a steady presence
against mine. Like she needs the contact as much as I do.

"Eventually, there was an accident," I breathe. "I was fine, but
my best friend... He lost his leg. I made choices that didn't
ruin my life; they ruined someone else's. That's when it all
clicked for me. I cleaned myself up and spent the next few
years staying sober, but always feeling like I was one slip up
away from being the person I used to be. Then—Then I met
my son."

I spare the group the made-for-TV drama of Paige keeping
Aiden a secret until after she died. The group is, by
definition, anonymous, but I don't want the gritty details of
Aiden's life leaking out without his consent.

"I met my son and things fell into place. I wanted to be sober
for him. And then I met the woman I love, and I wanted to be
sober for her, too." Mira's leg gives a reassuring little nudge
against my calf. "When I was in my darkest place, I didn't
think it was possible to feel like this. I was convinced that I
wasn't made for something as soft as love. But now, I know
that it's that soft kind of love that makes you strong. I've

never felt steadier. I'm not just living for myself anymore; I'm living for them. I want to be the best version of myself so I can get even sort of close to being worthy of the people I have in my life."

When I sit down, Mira is wiping her eyes. She twines her fingers through mine and doesn't let go the rest of the meeting.

When it wraps up, we walk back up the stairs hand-in-hand. We're heading to Evan's SUV parked down the block when Mira suddenly tugs me into an alley.

I'm about to tease her and say we might need to hit up that meeting at the Orthodox church, after all, but then I see her face. The yellow security light behind the church brushes her in harsh shadow. Her brows are pinched together and her tongue wets her lower lip.

Her hands fist in the front of my shirt, and I don't say anything, giving her a second to think.

Finally, she blows out a breath. "Losing my mom broke my dad. He always had a drinking problem, but when she left… he had nowhere to hide. Whatever front he'd been putting on for people of a happy wife and a happy home were gone, and he was exposed. It's when things got really bad for us."

Her voice breaks, and I wrap my arms low around her waist, holding her close.

"I can see now, looking back, how scared Dante must have been, too. Our dad never hurt him, but first, it was my mom. When she left, it was me. Somewhere in his head, my brother must have thought that he'd be next. Maybe that's why he—" She shakes her head. "Maybe if our father had gotten sober—gotten help—Dante wouldn't have turned into the monster he became. Maybe we could have been something like a happy family, if there is such a thing."

I curl my palm around her cheek, stroking away a single tear. "There *is* such a thing."

I know because we have it.

Right now.

Right here.

Mira gives me a sad smile. "Thinking that we might have been able to figure our shit out and love each other helps me sometimes. Because thinking that my family falling to pieces was inevitable is… It's too fucking bleak. I don't want to live in a world where there was only one ending for us. I want possibilities."

I want to give her those possibilities. As many as she wants.

"But when I sat there and watched my dad fall apart after my mom left—when I watched my brother fall in line with what my dad wanted him to be because he was terrified of the alternative—I swore to myself that I wouldn't depend on anyone else to survive. Because being dependent turned my dad and my brother into monsters, and I didn't want the same thing to happen to me."

"It couldn't," I whisper, kissing her wet cheek. "You're too good, Mira. It never would have happened to you."

"I wanted to take care of myself because then I'd be my own responsibility. I wouldn't get hurt by another person or be the person doing the hurting. It was easier to be alone, until…" She looks up at me from under wet lashes. "Until it wasn't. Until you."

I meet her eyes and say nothing. It's not my turn to speak. It's hers.

"It's so fucking scary to love you this much. But I think..." She swipes her sleeve across her nose. "I finally realize that it's not that I can't depend on people—it's that I have to depend on the *right* people. And you're the right kind of person, Zane. The best kind of person."

She draws in one more shuddering breath, glances away, glances back at me.

"Which is why I need to tell you something."

Her voice trails away as her eyes do. She's looking down at the pavement, and I can feel her shaking.

"Mira..."

"I should have told you right away, but I didn't want to hurt you. Or scare you. Or myself, honestly." She shakes her head. "I didn't want to tell you because I didn't want to make it real."

My heart is in my stomach. I grip her chin, forcing her eyes to mine. "Tell me. Now."

"Dante," she whispers. "He found me. At the gym. There was a note in my—"

I drop her face and grab my phone. I dial the P.I.'s number by memory. It goes to voicemail, and I'm not supposed to leave a message, but fuck him. "He's on fucking top of her. You should have known. Find him. Now."

When I hang up, Mira grabs the phone out of my hand and wraps her fingers around mine. Now, it's my hand that is shaking.

"I told Evan. I should have told you, but I told Evan at the party. He's looking into the security footage at the gym. Please d-don't be mad." Her chin wobbles.

"I'm furious, Mira. Fucking furious." I cradle her face in my hands, holding her like she's fragile. Because she is. "Not *at* you, though. At *him*. At myself. He got close to you, and I wasn't there. He was so close and—"

"I'm fine." Her hands wrap around mine. Her fingers are cold. "I'm okay."

The bone-deep need to be inside of her burns through me, and I know I won't be able to relax until I can feel her. Until I can prove to myself that she's here and alive.

So I haul her against me, our lips crashing together in the dark alley.

When I pull away, it's only because I need to get her home. Because I haven't even started with her yet. "He isn't going to hurt you. I won't let him."

She stretches onto her toes for one last kiss. "I know."

30

MIRA

I hear the key in the door first.

It's way too early for Zane to be home. I know because, this morning, he dragged me out of bed and into the shower with him.

"I want a few more minutes with you," he said, kissing my neck as he shifted me into the warm shower spray. "We have media today, and I'll be gone until dark. I need more."

Last night should have been more than enough. But it wasn't. For either of us.

So now, I'm on the couch, a pleasant kind of ache between my legs, staring at the front door with wide eyes.

It goes quiet for so long I almost convince myself it was a distracted neighbor trying the wrong door. Or maybe I was hearing things.

Then three loud knocks resound through the condo.

I fly off the couch and fumble for my phone. Like every horror movie ever, it's upside down and I have to turn it around. Then my fingerprint doesn't unlock the phone once, twice, again, again.

"Shit!" I whisper, finally unlocking the phone right as Evan's name flashes on the screen. I swipe up instantly. "Hello?"

"Daniel is heading up to the condo," he explains. "I just saw him park in the garage."

Panic gives way to annoyance, and I stomp over to the door and fling it open. "You scared the shit out of me!"

Daniel winces, his spare key still in his hand. "You know, I realized after I put the key in that maybe now isn't the best time to let myself into Zane's place. Even if I've had this spare key for years and I knew him way before you did."

"Remember this argument when I decide to let myself into Taylor's apartment with my spare key," I threaten, stepping aside to wave him in. "I'll wait until the two of you go on a date and then show up around midnight with a Jason mask and a bloody ax... y'know, since I've known her longer than you."

Daniel eases by, hands raised in surrender. "Touché."

I close and lock the door, checking the bolt twice before I can walk away. "What are you doing here?"

"Allegedly, I'm here to grab Zane's backup car key because—" Daniel utilizes finger quotes. "—*he locked his in his car.* But, astute as I am, I know he actually sent me here to watch you."

I frown. "But Evan is here to watch me."

"No, Evan is here to make sure no creeps make it into the building."

"He's not doing a very good job," I tease. "*You* made it into the building."

Daniel just rolls his eyes and reaches for the remote, flicking the television on. "You should be so lucky to have my company. I'm a delight."

Daniel is, admittedly, kind of a delight.

Especially since, thirty seconds before he gave me a mild heart attack, I was lying on the couch wondering what I was going to do with my day. Aiden is in school and I would usually go to the gym or maybe out for coffee with Taylor, but telling Zane about the note that may or may not be from Dante really did make the whole situation more real to me.

My brother might be out there. Waiting. Watching. So, it's easier to stay inside. Where I'm safe...

And unbelievably bored.

Daniel flings a couch cushion at my face that I only barely manage to bat out of the air.

"Hey!"

"You were looking dangerously serious." He goes back to flipping through the available streaming options. "I think that's what I'm here to put a stop to."

"How do you plan to do that?"

He shrugs. "You're young and in love. Isn't that enough of a reason to smile?"

"It's actually kind of the problem," I blurt before I can stop myself.

There's a reason this arrangement with Zane was supposed to be emotion-free. There's also a good reason I tried to leave and never look back. Everyone would be safer if I wasn't in love with Zane.

Daniel threatens me with another pillow. "Are you going to elaborate or do I need to use this?"

"Neither. I had an emotional purge last night, and my tank is empty. If you want to stay here, you need to be a distraction."

He gestures to himself flopped on the couch, his prosthetic stretched across the coffee table. "I'm here. I think that's enough, don't you?"

"Definitely not. I can watch TV by myself." I snatch the remote out of his hand and turn the television off. Then I start to clap to a slow beat. "Dance, monkey, dance."

"No wonder you and Taylor are friends," he grumbles. "You're both borderline abusive."

I sit up. "There we go! That's something! Tell me about you and Taylor. What's going on there?"

I know far more than I need to about the frequency (and duration) of their overnight visits, but I'd like to hear things from Daniel's, hopefully PG-rated, perspective.

"There's nothing to tell. We're dating. It's good."

I glare at him long enough that he finally peeks at me out of the corner of his eye. "Taylor is my best friend in the world. Up until a couple months ago, she was my *only* friend," I explain. "Which means you better say something a whole lot better than that if you want to be with her."

He scowls. "You know how I feel about her."

"I do. Which is why I need you to be man enough to admit it."

He barks out a laugh. "Is that what a man is made of these days?"

"If you mean 'emotional intelligence' and 'vulnerable honesty,'" I say, "then yes."

Daniel slouches deeper in the couch, trying to ignore the holes I'm boring into the side of his head. But finally, he throws up his hands. "I'm super into Taylor, okay? Is that what you want to hear?"

"Yes, it is. Thanks for sharing."

But now that Daniel has started, he can't stop. "When I'm not with her, I think about being with her. She's the only person I want to talk to. I smile whenever she texts me, and the other day, she fell asleep on the phone and I stayed on the line and listened to her breathing." He spins towards me, shaking my arm for dramatic effect. "I listened to her *breathe*, Mira! That's crazy!"

"Sort of. But it's also sweet. It's also not surprising. You were following Taylor around like a little puppy a month ago with no shame whatsoever. It makes me wonder why you're all clammed up about it now."

He snaps his fingers and points at me. "Exactly. I was trailing after her like a lovesick puppy an entire month ago! And here I am, four weeks later, *still* trailing after her."

It takes me a few seconds to understand what he's saying. When I do, I grab the pillow he tossed at me and fling it back at him.

"Ow!" he complains, hugging the pillow with both arms like the pathetic manchild he is. "What was that for?"

"For not just calling me and asking if Taylor is as into you as you are her! I'm her best friend, Daniel. You don't think I might have been able to help you out?"

He frowns for a second. Then realization dawns and Daniel sits straight up on the couch, shifting his prosthetic onto the cushion so he can face me. "Mira, is Taylor into me?"

"No. Not at all," I drone.

His smile slips, and I hit him with the second pillow I locked and loaded without him noticing.

"Obviously, she is!" I yell while he glares at me for sucker punching him. I don't even care; he deserved it. "Yes, Taylor is super into you. You can tell by the fact that you are the only person she's dating, she's sleeping over at your apartment, and you're the only man I've heard her talk about for months."

I don't want to fully sell out my best friend to her current love interest, but if I was a recluse when it came to dating, then Taylor was a door-to-door saleswoman. She went from one guy to the next with no hesitation.

Until Daniel.

"Really?" In a second, Daniel is back to the lovesick puppy I recognize from a few weeks ago. "I've never felt like this about anyone. Even before my accident." He pats his leg. "Being part cyborg isn't exactly a turn-on for most."

"Use it as a litmus test. If a woman is an asshole about it, she isn't worth dating."

We slip into a long silence. Daniel doesn't seem to mind; he's just grinning stupidly to himself.

But my mind wanders back to the AA meeting. To Zane talking about the accident that changed everything for him.

"I actually don't know much about what happened." I tip my head towards his leg. "Zane doesn't like to talk about it."

Before I can even get the question out, Daniel zips his lips closed. "You need to talk to your boyfriend about that."

My stomach flips nervously. "Why? You were there, too."

"Yeah, but my experience is a hell of a lot different than his, I'm sure. Given the fact I was drunk and then woke up days later in the hospital."

I've just been assuming it was a bad car accident. Is there more to it I don't know about? Did Zane crash on purpose? Did he—

Daniel reaches over and pats my knee. "Zane doesn't open up to pretty much anyone, so I don't want to steal his chance to tell you the story himself. That's all it is. Don't freak out."

I want to argue because I'm nosy, but Daniel is trying to be a good friend. So I decide to let him.

We end up turning the TV back on to watch way too many episodes of *House Hunters International*. With only our commentary to go off of, you'd think every couple on the show were bloody dictators who wanted five beds, four baths, and a tiled mud room with good drainage where they could string their victims from the walls.

When it's time for Daniel to go, he is halfway to the door when he turns around and pulls me into a tight hug.

"What is this for?" I ask, my words muffled against his shoulder.

"I've always wanted a sister, and you're gonna be the closest thing I'll ever have." Daniel pulls back, another sappy smile on his face. "And that's fine by me."

I turn into one of those chocolate lava cakes: stone-cold on the outside, but an ooey-gooey pile of mush on the inside. "Thank you."

"You're welcome." He claps me on the shoulder. "Now, I need to go track down the woman I'd love to make my girlfriend. Catch you on the flip, Mirabel."

Daniel leaves, and I realize he did a better job of distracting me than I thought he would. I haven't thought about Dante all day, and by the time I meet Evan in the parking garage to get Aiden from school, I am in a certifiably good mood.

I walk around to the driver's door and knock on the glass. Evan rolls down the window, one eyebrow arched.

"Mind if I drive?" I ask. "I kind of miss it."

He studies me for a couple seconds before he hands the keys through the window. "Sure, why the heck not?"

The answer to that question is that his SUV might as well be a cruise ship and I haven't driven so much as a shopping cart in weeks, but it still feels good to get behind the wheel.

"You're a natural," Evan lies, gripping the door handle with white knuckles.

When his phone rings, he has to force himself to let go to answer it.

"Hello, this is Evan." He nods and hums along with whatever the other person is saying. Then, suddenly, he goes rigid. "When was the last time?"

I try to stay focused on the road, but it's hard when the hair on the back of my neck is standing tall.

I know what this call is about before he even hangs up.

"Dante?" I ask in a whisper, afraid to say it too loud and ruin this surprisingly good day.

"That was the security guard at the gym. They watched the footage and... It was him, Mira. Dante was at the gym. He left the note in your locker. He..." He looses a weary breath and tosses his phone in the cupholder. "He found you."

I open my mouth to say something. I'm not sure if I need to comfort Evan or myself, but there's no time.

There's only a blur of motion.

A screech of tires.

His door caves in. The giant SUV twists and turns like we're in a garbage disposal.

Then everything goes black.

31

ZANE

"You didn't actually need your spare keys, did you?" Daniel asks. "Because I did not grab them."

I shift my phone between my chin and my shoulder so I can keep signing the unreal stack of team posters in front of me. There's some kind of fundraiser for the children's hospital coming up. The first thousand people to donate twenty dollars get an autographed poster, I guess. I don't know the details; I just know I'm supposed to put my name on all of them, and this beats doing more press.

"I did not need my keys."

"Ha!" Daniel crows. "I knew it. I told Mira that."

"You were supposed to be discreet."

I could tell Mira was more freaked out about a possible Dante appearance than she wanted to admit, and I didn't want her to be alone all day. Since all the girls were busy, I sent in my fourth choice: Daniel.

"Then you should've said that when you sent me over there instead of making up some stupid excuse. But it's fine. I handled things like a pro."

"What the hell does *that* mean?" I slide a finished stack of posters to the end of the table and reach for another one. Jace and Davis were in here signing with me, but they left to check out the catering spread the owners called in. I'm holding off on eating in hopes I can wrap up here and be home in time for dinner.

"It means that I distracted your girl until it was time for her to do school pickup while simultaneously finding out top-secret info about mine."

"About Taylor?"

"What other girl would I be talking about?" he snaps. "Yes, Taylor. I now know that she is super into me."

I pause, waiting for Daniel to say something groundbreaking, but apparently, that is it. "Right. Everyone knows that. What else?"

"Well, I didn't know it! But now, I do, and I am going to go seal the deal."

I'm reluctant to ask what deal he's planning to seal and what part of his anatomy he intends to seal it with, but I'm saved the trouble when my phone rings.

"Other line," I tell him, trying to remember where I recognize the number on my screen from, but it hovers somewhere in the back of my mind, just out of reach. "I'll call you back."

I answer and a soft, musical female voice greets me. "Mr. Whitaker, it's Aiden's teacher, Mrs. Wilson."

"He's not in trouble, is he?" I'm teasing, but Mrs. Wilson doesn't laugh.

"I'm calling because it's getting late and no one has come to pick up Aiden."

My brain buffers. It takes way too long for me to respond.

"No, my—His mom should have come to get him by now." Mira should have been there thirty minutes ago. Daniel just said that she left to do school pickup.

"The parking lot is empty and Aiden is the last student here," she explains. "Is there anyone else who can come pick him up?"

My mind is spinning off in a thousand different directions, but I need to focus. One problem at a time.

"Yes," I tell her, the plan forming as the words are coming out of my mouth. "My best friend will be there. Daniel Patterson is his name."

"Is he on the approved list of family and friends who can pick up?"

"He's the first name on the list. Don't release him to anyone else except for Daniel Patterson," I reiterate, already feeling something ominous stirring in my gut. "He'll be there soon."

I hang up with Mrs. Wilson and call Daniel back.

"You said Mira left to get Aiden, right?" I bark the second the line connects.

"Yeah. Right after I did. Actually, I was across the street grabbing an iced latte for my lady—you should never show up empty-handed—and I saw her and Evan pull out of the garage."

Shit.

"I need you to pick up Aiden."

Daniel hesitates. "From school? Why? Mira went to get him. Can you hear—"

"Can you get him or not?" I snarl. My fingers are itching to punch in Mira's number. To hear her voice. To feel her body against mine. I need to get off this phone now. "Can you do it, yes or no?"

"Yes! Yes, obviously. But what the fuck is—"

"I'll fill you in later."

I hang up and dial Mira's number. Before the first ring, I'm already on my feet and heading towards the locker room.

Something is wrong.

Something is so fucking wrong.

The phone rings and rings and Mira never answers. I don't even wait for her voicemail before I hang up and call Evan instead.

Evan has never not answered my calls. First thing in the morning, middle of the night, hell or high water—he always answers.

Until today.

Someone says something to me as I pass, but I don't hear them; I'm too busy scrubbing through the cameras at the house. I see Mira and Daniel watching TV for a long time before they get up and… there she goes. She grabs her phone and her purse and walks calmly through the front door. She wasn't running or panicked.

She left… and now, she's gone.

I open my locker and am reaching for my duffel when a hand clamps on my shoulder.

Instinctively, I throw my elbow back to shake them off.

Nathan jumps back, hands raised. "Shit, man. I've been saying your name. Someone is here to see you."

"Who?"

He shrugs. "I have no idea. Coach told me to come get you. They're in the media room waiting for you."

I shove past Nathan, ignoring his grumbling complaints, and sprint down the hall to the media room.

I have no idea what to expect when I open the door—maybe Dante, maybe Mira and Evan here to surprise me with the worst prank in the world—but a police officer never crossed my mind.

The officer has his thumbs hitched in his pockets, a gun gleaming on his hip. Coach is standing off to the side, arms crossed, mouth tense.

I've seen this movie.

I know what it means when an officer comes knocking on your door.

She can't be gone.

I storm into the room, all racing heart and pumping adrenaline. "What in the hell happened?"

"Easy, Whitaker." Coach presses a hand to my chest, and I swipe his arm away. He holds flat hands in front of me, steadying me like I'm a raging bronco. "Listen."

I don't want to listen.

She is fine.

She has to be.

Mira has to be okay.

The officer tips his head to Coach in thanks and turns back to me. "You're Zane Whitaker?"

"Yes," I bark. "Who the fuck else would I—" I swallow down the frustration and nod. "I'm Zane Whitaker. What's going on?"

"Mr. Whitaker," The officer speaks slowly, like he's getting paid by the second, and I want to shake the rest of the words out of him as much as I want him to never finish his sentence.

But he does. He gives me a tense grimace and says, "I'm sorry, but there's been an accident."

32

ZANE

I screech to the hospital, narrowly avoiding three different accidents myself. I'm only as careful as I have to be to make sure I get there in one piece.

She needs me.

Mira is alive. I know that much. Because the second he told me she was in an accident, I grabbed the cop by the front of his shirt and demanded he tell me every fucking detail.

"You can't do a damn thing from jail," Coach hissed, dragging me away from the officer. "Calm down, son."

But there is no such thing as "calm" when Mira is hurt. When I'm still ten minutes away and she needs me.

Mira is alive, I remind myself, blowing out a deep breath.

I also learned why Evan didn't answer his phone, either. He and Mira were both in the car and they both had to be rushed to the hospital from the scene. I didn't ask about the asshole who hit them because I could really care less, but apparently, the cops are still looking for them.

"He got away?" I growled.

I don't know how someone can send Mira and Evan to the hospital, yet come out okay enough to flee the scene, but I made a silent vow to hunt them down and ensure the motherfucker gets exactly what is coming to him.

At the hospital, I slam to a stop halfway up some curb and don't bother fixing it. I'm not even sure I close my car door behind me. The only thing I can think about is getting inside.

Finding Mira.

Touching Mira.

My phone buzzes and I read it as I'm running.

DANIEL: *I have Aiden. I'm taking him to Reeves's house. Jemma is there and said she'd watch him.*

Aiden is safe.

Mira is alive.

I repeat those facts to myself again and again as I keep sprinting down one hall after the next.

My phone buzzes again, but it isn't Daniel—it's the security system at home.

Front Door Alarm Activated.

I can only watch the recorded footage for the front door camera, not the live feed. From the glances I steal down at the footage as I take an elevator up to the fourth floor, everything looks fine. But the rest of my life is melting down around me—why not my security system, too?

I try to see the live footage again, but the app freezes and then crashes.

"Fuck!" I roar, squeezing my phone hard enough it should shatter before I decide it might be useful over the next few hours and pocket it instead.

I barely know where I am, and the letters *PACU* printed on the wall in thick, black font aren't helpful.

Turns out, screaming obscenities at the top of your lungs is helpful. No less than three nurses pop out of rooms and head my way. One of them is saying something into a walkie, and I'm sure security will be here within the minute.

"Mira McNeil," I growl to anyone who will listen. "I'm looking for Mira McNeil. She was in an accident. A car accident." Saying the words out loud makes me feel nauseous. When I first got to the hospital to see Daniel, I was still coming down from all the shit I took the night before. I barely remember it.

But I'm painfully sober now.

"This is the Post-Anesthesia Care Unit," one nurse says.

I stare at her blankly, waiting for her to say something useful.

"I don't need to know where *I* am," I snap. "I'm looking for my—" *Wife* sits on the tip of my tongue, but I bite it back. "Girlfriend. I'm looking for my girlfriend."

The woman shakes her head. "The PACU is for post-surgery. If she was just in an accident, she might still be in the OR. You'll have to check with the front desk."

"You shouldn't even be here," an older woman interjects. "You don't have a visitor's badge. Who let you in?"

The stairwell at the end of the hall opens and a security guard strolls in. I don't have time to wait for this to go down. I turn back the way I came, heading down to the first floor.

Another alert from the security system buzzes in my pocket, but I can't think about that now. Not when I have no idea where Mira even is.

The elevator doors open on the main floor and Jace and Owen are standing there like they're waiting for me.

"Well?" Jace asks.

I throw up my hands. "I have no fucking idea. I can't find her. Or Evan."

"Hospitals and their fookin' useless policies," Owen mumbles as he stomps towards the front desk.

I move to follow him, but Jace grabs my shoulder. "Have you heard anything at all? Coach mentioned something, but no one knows what's going on."

"There was an accident. Mira and Evan were brought here." The weight of everything I don't know sits heavy on my chest. It's hard to breathe. "That's it. That's all I have."

"They're going to be fine." Jace has no way of knowing that, but *fucking hell,* I want to believe him. "It's going to be fine. Daniel dropped Aiden off with Reeves and Jemma, and then he'll be here. We're all going to be here."

It's nice of him, but it doesn't help right now. There's only one person I want to see.

"She's his lassie!" Owen barks at the stiff-backed elderly woman manning the front desk. "Who else would you tell about her condition?"

The woman presses her thin lips into a firm line. "I can only talk to her family."

"She doesn't have any family." I hurry over and place my palms on her desk. "Her parents are gone, no siblings. I'm all she has. Please."

The woman stares at me for a heavy second... then she checks her computer and writes something down on a slip of paper. She doesn't look up as she passes it to me. "I can't give you any information since you are not family. It goes against hospital policy."

On the piece of paper is a room number.

I'm so grateful I could kiss this woman, but there isn't time. I hustle down the hallway, tossing a hurried thanks over my shoulder.

Mira is alive.

She'll be okay.

She has to be okay.

～

Mira is not okay.

If she was okay, she wouldn't be lying unconscious in a hospital bed.

If she was okay, I wouldn't be on the phone with Rachelle's sister, who happens to be a nurse, going over the blurry photos I sent her of Mira's medical chart.

I pace up and down the narrow space at the foot of Mira's bed, my phone glued to my ear. "The nurses won't tell me shit and I haven't even seen a doctor yet."

"That's a good thing," Rachelle's sister says. I think her name is Kate or Katie or Kathleen. She said it, but I wasn't listening. "If the doctor isn't around, it means there are more serious patients to attend to. And based on her chart, it looks like she's just there for observation."

I glance back at the bed and it physically hurts. Seeing her in the bed, her cheek sliced open, her hands limp at her sides... it aches. "I'm observing her and she's fucking unconscious. Shouldn't someone be doing something about that?"

"I'm sure the first thing they did when she arrived was check her for signs of a traumatic brain injury. That's why she's still there for observation. They'll want to wait until she wakes up to make sure nothing is seriously wrong."

Someone plowed into Mira and got away, while she's unconscious in the hospital. The fuck isn't "seriously wrong" about that?

Katie, or whatever her name is, assures me she doesn't see anything alarming in Mira's chart. I try to let her confidence reassure me, but it doesn't do shit.

I move a chair to the edge of the bed and take Mira's hand in mine. Her fingers are cold, and I curl my hands around them, blowing warm air over her skin again and again.

"You're going to be fine," I whisper. "You just have to wake up."

After a few minutes, her eyelids twitch and my heart jolts. I lean forward, studying her face. "Mira?"

Nothing. No movement. Just the soft, steady sound of her breathing.

I drop back into the uncomfortable chair next to her bed just as the door flies open.

"Evan is awake." Daniel waves me towards the door, his every movement frantic. "You go talk to him. I'll stay here with Mira. Go, go."

Evan is just down the hall. I jog to his room.

There's a pretty, dark-haired nurse taking his blood pressure. The cuff is wrapped around the arm not covered in scrapes and purpling bruises. Even with all that, Evan doesn't look like he's in pain.

"You look healthy to me," she's telling him. "Most people I see in an accident like that are more banged up from the airbags, but you're so big…" Maybe I'm imagining things, but it looks like the nurse's hands linger around his arm as she removes the blood pressure cuff.

He gives her a warm smile. "I count myself lucky."

The nurse notices me and steps back guiltily from Evan's bed. "Looks like you have a visitor. I'll leave you two alone."

If Evan is sad to see his pretty nurse go, he doesn't show it. The only thing on his face is guilt. Before I can say anything, he dips his head.

"Fuck, I'm so sorry, Zane. I shouldn't have let her drive."

"The police said the accident wasn't her fault."

"It wasn't," he agrees. "The light was green and Mira was doing fine, but I would've been more alert if I was driving. Maybe I would have seen the car coming. I could have gotten us out of the way."

"No offense, Evan, but I saw a picture of the car." The mangled metal took me right back to that night four years ago. To the blood on my leather interior. The smell of oil and gas in the air. "It hit on the passenger side. If you'd been driving, it would have been Mira sitting in the passenger seat."

I don't need to explicitly say that I'm glad it was him and not Mira. I'm glad he's okay, too, but if I had to choose...

Evan thinks that over and blows out a heavy breath. "You're right. It could have been so much worse."

"Did you see who it was?" I ask. "The other driver?"

He shakes his head. "I didn't see a fucking thing. We were driving and then—lights out. I was telling Mira—" Evan's eyes go wide. "Shit, I was telling Mira about Dante. It was *Dante*."

I stiffen. "In the other car?"

"No. Or, maybe. I don't know." He waves his hands like he's scattering a swarm of gnats around his head. "But it was Dante at the gym. I'd just gotten the call from the security guy at the gym that Dante was on camera. He was *inside* the gym. *Inside* the women's locker room."

I knew that was the most likely possibility, but I still didn't want to believe it. I wanted to cling to what little hope there was that Dante would move on and leave Mira alone.

Before I can come up with anything more profound to say, my phone buzzes. It's the damn security system again. **Front Door Alarm Activated.**

I'm about to swipe away the notification for the third time when I realize...

"What is it?" Evan asks, on high alert even from his hospital bed.

Maybe none of this is an accident.

"Nothing. Rest up," I tell him, hurrying out of his room.

Owen catches me just outside the door. "Whoa there. Moving quick for someone with no place to go. Your lady is still asleep."

"The alarm at the house keeps going off. Mira's brother is in town and I have to—" I look from my phone to Mira's hospital room down the hall. I can't be in two places at once, but fuck, do I want to be.

"You want it checked out?" Owen asks. Before I can nod, he grabs his keys from his pocket. "I'll go take a look."

"Owen, no. It should be me."

If only so I can be the one to wring Dante's neck and end this for Mira. I want it to be me.

"Don't argue with me, son. You should be in there with your heart." He jabs a finger at Mira's room. His scowl doesn't match his uncharacteristically soft words. "You need to be the face she sees when she wakes up."

I want to argue, but I can't. I know he's right. Already, I'm inching towards Mira's door, drawn towards her.

"If you notice anything weird at all, call the police," I tell him. "Don't go in there alone, O. It isn't worth it."

Owen looks me over slowly from head to toe. His lip curls as he ambles past me and remarks with his trademark brand of withering, scornful love, "Oh, fuck off, Zane. Don't tell me what to do."

33

MIRA

There's pain.

Or maybe there isn't.

I'm not sure which option is worse. I'm not sure of anything, really.

My eyelids are cemented closed and I'm stiff all over. My back, my hips, my—*fuck*, my neck. I try to tilt my head and pain ricochets down my spine and makes my back and hips hurt all over again.

"Mira?"

Everything aches, but the sound of his voice cuts through the pain.

A warm hand squeezes my fingers, and I realize someone is holding my hand. Not someone—*Zane*.

I struggle to lift my eyelids, cracking them open just enough to singe my eyes with daylight and wince.

"Shit. Sorry."

Zane's hand is gone. A second later, the bright light shining through my eyelids dims. I tentatively crack my eyes open again.

It's dark, but then his face is there. There are shadows under his eyes and he looks pale, but he's the best thing I've seen in... well, I don't know how long. But it doesn't matter.

"Wherever I am, it can't be all bad," I rasp. "You're here."

He smiles and brings my hand to his lips. He kisses each of my knuckles like they're precious to him. "You're in the hospital."

Suddenly, I hear it. The beeping of the monitor behind me. The murky glug of my IV.

The crunch of the metal as the SUV spun across the intersection...

"The accident!" I gasp, sending another sharp pain down my spine. "I'm so sorry, Zane. I asked Evan to let me drive. Don't be upset with him. It was my fault."

"Don't apologize."

"But—"

"Don't," he repeats, squeezing my fingers, "apologize. I just spent the last four hours praying to every higher power I could think of, waiting for you to wake up. If you think the first thing I want to do now that your eyes are open is get mad at you, then you must have hit your head very hard."

Tears fill my eyes, and Zane gingerly leans over me to kiss them away.

This is what it means to be cared for. To be cherished.

I'm not sure I'll ever get used to it. Part of me hopes I don't.

"Is Evan okay?"

"He's fine. Sleeping it off down the hall."

Thank God for that.

A doctor comes in and looks me over, but he doesn't find anything of note.

"The scrape on your cheek will heal up in a week or so, and the aches and pains should go away," he says. "Unless anything changes over night, I'll let you go home in the morning."

"Thank you, Doctor." Zane shakes the man's hand, but his voice is cold.

"Is he the person who crashed into me?" I ask as soon as the doctor is gone. "You looked like you wanted to deck him."

Zane settles on the very edge of the chair next to me, like he can't get close enough. "I wanted to deck everyone who works in this hospital. They wouldn't tell me anything."

"Why not?"

"Because we aren't family." His fingers shift over mine, lingering on my ring finger. "It was the same way when Daniel was in the hospital. I had to get everything secondhand through his parents, but it took them an entire day to get here. For twenty-four hours, I was in the goddamn dark."

"I'm sorry." He scowls at me for apologizing again, but I wave him off. "I just mean I'm sorry that I didn't think about the fact that you've done this before. With Daniel."

I can only imagine what kind of memories this is dredging up for him.

"Well, you should've thought about it. Then you could've made sure some idiot who wasn't paying attention couldn't crash into you, since you obviously have control over things like that. This really is all your fault, Mira."

I shove his shoulder, ignoring the jolt of pain that shoots up mine when I laugh. "You know what I mean."

"I do, but *you* don't seem to understand *me*." Zane slips gracefully into the bed with me. "I want you to stop apologizing. You didn't do anything wrong. It's not like you spent hours getting wasted and then offered to drive. You didn't choose this."

The casual self-deprecation is almost worse than if he was emotional.

"You were a different man, Zane. You weren't thinking clearly." I lean against his chest. "I didn't know you back then, but I know for a fact that you wouldn't do anything that might hurt the people around you."

"Not anymore. Not after what happened to Daniel." He strokes my side through the scratchy hospital gown. "I hate that that's what it took for me to get my shit together. Daniel had to lose his leg—and it had to be my fault—before I could see how bad things had gotten." He huffs out a bitter laugh. "Some days, the guilt of seeing Daniel was the only thing that kept me sober. How fucked up is that?"

"I don't think it matters *why* you stayed sober. I doubt Daniel would even be upset. Actually, he'd probably love knowing he was the reason you stayed clean."

"Probably." Zane smirks, but just as quickly his smile falls and he grips my face. "But I don't want anything like that to happen to you. I don't need the guilt to keep me going—I need *you* to keep me going."

"I'm not going anywhere." Even as the words leave my lips, my eyes are blinking closed. I'm exhausted.

Zane's mouth whispers over mine, feather soft. "Promise me. Promise me you'll stay with me, Mira."

I know I shouldn't make promises I might not be able to keep, but I've never wanted to keep a promise more than this one.

I can't even tell if I'm dreaming anymore, but I don't care. I sink deeper into the curve of his chest and his arm around me.

"I promise."

"Good." His breath is hot against my neck, his whispered words sending goosebumps across my chest. "How am I ever going to let you out of my sight after this?"

My thoughts swirl away. I can feel myself slipping into sleep no matter how much I want to stay right here—with Zane, in his sights, next to him forever.

As if he can read my mind, his arm tightens around me. Before I give myself over to sleep, he whispers behind my ear, "You're everything, Mira. My whole world."

34

ZANE

"You're absolutely sure about this?" Hollis looks at me over the stack of freshly-signed papers. He holds them like he's ready to tear them in half at the tiniest sign of indecision from me.

But I've been absolutely sure since the moment I scheduled this meeting.

"Would you stop asking me that?"

"Never," he laughs, sliding everything into a folder labeled **Whitaker, Z.** "Do you know how often I deal with people who are pissed off because Daddy signed his estate over to his side piece and cut his children out of it?"

"How often?"

He considers it for a second. "Twice. But that was two times too many. I have to make sure you are of sound mind so that I can look your descendants in their faces and tell them it was your decision, not mine. I need my conscience to be clear."

"Consider it clear then. First, because I'm of sound mind. Second, because Mira is *not* my side piece." I narrow my eyes in warning. "And third, because I didn't cut Aiden out of anything. Everything we've done here is standard stuff."

Hollis arches a brown in disbelief. "Nothing about you and Mira is 'standard.'"

He has no idea how right he is.

Though I'm sure Hollis is referring more to the fact that I made sure Mira will become Aiden's legal guardian if anything ever happens to me. And that she'll have access to all of my accounts, including the money set aside for Aiden in his guardianship trust.

"Are you expecting some great tragedy to befall you or something?" he asks. "Do I need to be worried?"

"I'm not expecting anything. Then again," I add, "maybe we should all be expecting something."

It's been a week since Mira's accident, but all I've been able to think about is the fact that I didn't have access to any information about the most important woman in my life because we weren't "family." As if the government gets to tell me who my fucking family is.

What would've happened if something had happened to me? Where would Aiden have gone? Would Mira have been taken care of?

Mira was released from the hospital the next day, Owen assured me everything was as it was supposed to be at the house and with the security system, and life has been quiet and peaceful for the last week.

But I couldn't relax until I knew I'd done everything I could to take care of Aiden and Mira.

For the first time in seven days, I can take a deep breath.

Hollis smiles and crosses his arms. "I'm not going to tell a client of mine to be *less* prepared, but I have to ask again..." He leans across the desk, his eyes boring into mine. "Are you sure about this woman?"

I lean forward, matching his intensity with my own. "I've never been more sure of anything in my entire life."

It's later than normal when I get out of Aiden's room. He talked me into reading two extra chapters of his book, but we both dozed off during the second one.

I stumble out of his room towards the living room, rubbing my eyes. But Mira isn't on the couch where I left her.

Or in the kitchen.

And I smile—because I know exactly where she is.

I smell the lavender bubble bath before I even open our bedroom door. In the ensuite, candles flicker and I can hear the gentle lapping of water.

I cross the room and lean against the doorway. Her eyes are closed, her head resting on the lip of the tub. The water is up to her chest, but I can still see the soft swells of her beneath the surface. My cock twitches.

"It's not safe to bathe alone," I warn.

She smiles, still not opening her eyes. "What a shame. It's my new favorite thing."

She's taken a bath every day since the accident. The doctor told her it would help with the muscle aches, but it's not doing a damn thing for me. I've been purposefully gentle with her since we left the hospital—a task that has become almost impossible when I have to see her naked in my bathtub day after fucking day.

"Do you want some company?" I ask.

Her eyes snap open. The way she tugs at her lower lip with her teeth makes me wonder if I'm not the only one who has been undergoing a kind of torture. This is the longest we've gone without touching since I tracked her down to that dingy motel.

It's been too long.

"You're a little overdressed," she remarks.

I respond with the dramatic unbuttoning of my pants, and her laugh does as much for me as the sight of her. Knowing she's here and happy... I can't think of anything I want more than that.

She watches with hungry eyes as I peel my shirt off and toss my clothes in a pile. She sits up to make space for me, her breasts rising out of the water like she's fucking Aphrodite. Water streams over her shoulders and down her chest. By the time I sink below the surface, I'm rock hard.

Mira notices.

She swirls her finger over the surface of the water. "Did you want a bath, too?"

"No." I catch her hand and pull her gently towards me, helping her straddle me. "I want you."

Mira plants her palms on my chest, and everything about her is soft. Her hips, her touch, her smile. Her hair is twisted into a knot on top of her head. Dark strands slip free, sticking to her neck.

"You're perfect."

"Tell that to all my bruises," she mumbles.

With a frown, I lift her arm to look. A deep purple bruise rises out of the bubbles and stains her ribs. I gingerly press my lips to it, tracing the edges with my mouth and my breath.

She tips her head back in a sigh. "How are you making a bruise feel sexy?"

"Because it's proof you're still here with me." I work my way around her ribs, swirling her nipple in my mouth and nipping across her collarbones. "Do you have any idea what went through my head when the police showed up to tell me about your accident?"

She curls her fingers through my hair, pulling me closer. "I'm so sorry."

I press my tongue to her pulse point, feeling it jump when my hand slides between her legs. The water is warm, but I can still feel how hot she is. "What have I said about apologizing?"

"I'm sorr—I mean…" Her lips part on a sigh, but she's smiling. "I don't know what else to say."

"How about: *Please, Zane, have mercy. Fuck me.*" I wrap my hand around myself and slide through her folds, back and forth and back and forth. I tease her with my dick, driving us both nearly to the edge faster than should be possible. But it really has been a long time.

Mira rocks against me. "Please, Zane. Have—"

That's all she gets out before I slide into her.

Inch by inch, Mira sinks onto me, sealing our bodies together until I'm drowning in her.

I'm shaking with the need to pin her against me and fill her hard and fast, but I move slowly, gently.

"The second I felt you like this, I knew there'd never be anyone else. I knew no one would fit me the way you do."

It's not just the sex, even though the sex is genuinely unbelievable. It's the way we fit in everything. The way her body settles against mine when we're sleeping. The way we move around the kitchen on sleepy mornings.

"If I'd known it was a test, I would've tried harder." She grips my shoulders and rides me slowly, setting the pace.

I spread my hands across her hips. She gives into my touch, arching against me and mewling. I flick the pebbled point of her nipple with my tongue.

"You're so goddam edible. There's nowhere I don't want to taste."

"Then do it." She moves faster. The water laps against the edges of the tub, threatening to spill over, not that I give a shit. The entire place could be underwater, and I'm not sure I'd notice.

"Oh, I will," I tease, kissing the slope of her throat as I pulse into her, meeting her rocking thrusts. "But first, I want to feel you come."

'

She gnaws at her lower lip. "Oh, yeah? Then what?"

We die, I think. That's what it feels like now—dying in some glorious final bang, pun fully intended. I'm not sure how anyone survives the heat building between our bodies.

"Then I carry you to our bed," I pant, "and lick you until you come again."

She cries out, her body beginning to pulse around me. "And then?"

The fact she wants more is why we're perfect. We can't get enough. We never will, either of us.

Black creeps into the edge of my vision. I'm half out of my body already, absolutely lost in her. But I manage a breathy laugh. "Then I press you back against a wall, wrap your legs around me, and fuck you. The way we did the first time. The way we did when I found you in that motel."

Mira wraps a hand around my neck and bends backward. "Sounds like you have it all planned out."

I close my eyes, a stupid smile I can't hide spreading across my face. "You have no fucking idea, Mira. I've had more than enough time to think about it. I know exactly what I want to do with you."

"Tell me every last detail," she breathes.

"I will." I slip my hand from her hip and press my thumb to the point directly between her legs. "But not until you come."

On the next roll of her hips, her breath catches.

And she dissolves like sugar in the water.

Mira melts against me, her face buried in my neck as her chest heaves and her thighs tremble. I wrap my arms around her, pinning her close, and drive into her. Again and again until I'm groaning into her skin.

"Perfect." I lick the water from her shoulder and she rises up to look at me. Her eyes are bright, like she's glowing. "Fucking perfect."

"I didn't realize poetry was on the schedule. You're a natural talent." She smiles and smooths her fingers across my chest. She has to know what she's doing to me. When her lips tilt in a half-smile, I'm positive she does. "Okay, I came. Now, it's your turn. What are you going to do with me?"

The words slip out without any hesitation, as easy as breathing. "I'm going to marry you."

35

MIRA

Zane is still inside of me. The last pangs of my orgasm are lightly pulsing around him. Goosebumps spread across my skin as the bath water cools and evaporates. His thumbs stroke half-moons over my ribs and his skin is blazing hot.

But I'm numb to everything except the panic.

"What did you just say?"

Zane gives me an easy smile like he isn't turning my world upside down. "Marry me, Mira."

My heart stops and then... then, I almost laugh. Because I must have misunderstood.

"You want to get married someday, I know." I press my palm to his chest and his heart is beating oddly fast, even considering we just had sex.

"Not 'someday.' *Now*. Right now." He leans forward until his breath whispers over my cheek. "Marry me, Mira."

"Oh." I shrink back like he's a live wire. Actually, a live wire in the bathtub might be less shocking than the words coming out of his mouth. "That's a question. You're asking me to marry you."

"A couple times now. If you don't answer soon, I might start to worry."

The answer swells inside of me, stealing my breath. *Yes. Over and over again, yes.*

But I swallow it down. "You don't have to do this, Zane. You don't—I see what's happening here, but I'm okay. I'm alive and the doctors all fully expect me to live. One hundred percent chance of survival."

"I'm aware." His brows pull together. "If there was a chance you'd die, we'd be having a much different conversation, believe me."

"I just mean, we have time. So much time."

Zane studies me for a moment. Then he shakes his head and starts to climb out of the tub. "Maybe this will make more sense with clothes on."

Water shimmers across his tan skin. Muscles shift and pull as he pads naked across the tile floor, and my mouth goes dry. I want him again.

I want him forever.

The thirsty little voice in my head is begging me to accept and fuck him until we're both too old and gray to care about such things, if that's even possible. I can't imagine ever not needing him the way I do now. I *love* him.

Which is exactly why I bind and gag that little voice and try to let cooler, less horny heads prevail.

I look away, staring at my shivering legs beneath the cooling water. "I know the accident was scary, but I'm not going anywhere. You don't have to rush into anything you aren't ready for."

"You think I'm not ready?" He has his boxers back on, so it's a little safer for me to take a peek over at him. But he's still too gorgeous for words. I'd have to be the dumbest woman alive to refuse him.

I lift my shoulder in a shrug.

Before I can lower it, Zane is at the edge of the tub, plunging his hands into the water to wrap around me.

"What are you doing?" I try to fight, but I'm wet and slippery, and he's, well, *him*. He lifts me like I weigh nothing and plants my feet on the cushy bath mat.

Without a word, he dries me with a towel, making sure to be gentle with the bruises on my side and my hip where I smashed against the center console as the SUV spun through the intersection.

"I can dry myself," I mumble, but the words come out so softly I'm not sure he can even hear me.

I'm glad.

I don't want him to stop.

Zane dries every inch of my skin with the same meticulous attention to detail and tenderness he used to set me on fire just a few minutes ago. He does everything in his life with a singular, driven focus.

Which is why I don't want him to jump into marriage with me on a whim. I don't ever want to be something Zane Whitaker might regret.

When he's done drying me off, he tosses the towel away like we're beyond clothes and scoops me back into his arms.

"Are you mad?" I ask, trying to understand the slant to his brows and the flex of his jaw. "I really do love you, but—*What are you doing?*"

Zane places me on the bed and then crawls over me. His broad body stretches above me, and we should be talking this out.

Then again, he is strong and warm, and maybe we can afford another round before we make any big decisions.

The dirty voice in my head wins out. I press my palms to his bare chest and drag them lower, smoothing over his still-damp skin.

I hear his bedside drawer open and close. "I'm showing you how ready I am."

I look between our bodies at the bulge in his boxers and bite my lower lip. "I can see that."

But before my hands can make their way there, Zane pulls away. I sit up, instinctively following him. I'm about to protest—maybe even beg for him to come back if things get desperate enough—when he slides off the end of the bed and holds out a black velvet box.

I stare at it.

And stare.

And stare some more.

All I seem to be capable of is staring and blinking and breathing.

"You don't think I'm ready," he says, flicking the box open. I catch a glimpse of something large and shimmery inside, but I can't focus on it. I can't look away from the slow smile spreading across Zane's face. "But I already have the ring I'm going to put on your finger."

"When?" I croak.

He knows exactly what I'm asking. "Two weeks ago. I bought it a few days before Gallagher's birthday party."

"Before the birthday party. Before… *before* the accident."

The timeline shuffles. Pieces click into place. A picture is forming in my mind and my throat is tight.

Zane must be able to read my face, because he sets the ring box on the bed and grabs my hands. "I was going to wait until after things with your brother were figured out, but I don't want to wait anymore."

"Because of the accident."

"The accident woke me up to what it would feel like to lose you," he agrees. "Yeah."

I'm already shaking my head. "I don't want you to marry me because you got scared. I'm not going anywhere."

He pulls me to the edge of the bed. "I know you aren't."

"Then we don't have to do this, Zane. We can wait for a better time. When we're both thinking clearly."

"I'm thinking clearly."

That makes one of us. It's hard to think at all when that spiced wintergreen smell I love so much is wafting off of his skin. When he's holding my hands and looking at me with those piercing blue eyes.

"You were in the hospital, Mira, and that was—" He closes his eyes, wincing against the memory. "—fucking awful. But the worst thing was that I couldn't get to you. I was running around that hospital, desperate to find you, and no one would tell me where you were. Loving you wasn't a good enough reason, apparently."

My chin wobbles. I lean my forehead against his shoulder. "I'm sorry."

"Don't be sorry. Don't apologize." He lifts me off of his shoulder and holds my face. "Just marry me."

I open my mouth to respond, but Zane is there. His lips catch mine. Our tongues tangle together like he's trying to find the words I'm afraid to speak. Like he's trying to coax the answer out of me.

I fall against him with a moan. If he wants to convince me like this, I think I might just let him.

Finally, he breaks away with a growl, his hands dragging possessively down my arms. "Tell me you can't live without me."

"You *know* I can't live without you." I kiss his jaw. His throat. I free one hand and tug trembling fingers through his damp hair. "I don't *want* to live without you, Zane. Ever."

It's easy to say because it's the truth. There isn't a single part of me that doesn't love him.

Zane pauses for a second. Then his leash on his control snaps. He crawls over me again, pushing me back on the mattress. His mouth blazes across my body, kissing and licking and stroking until I'm squirming under him. Until my hips are moving at a rhythm all their own, trying to close the distance between us.

"I told you I had our future all mapped out." He looks up the length of my body, catching my eyes. His are dark. He wraps his hands around my inner thighs, parting my legs to make room for him. "I told you I'd lick you until you come."

I swallow. "I remember."

"So you'd better give me a good reason why we shouldn't get married before you come... or I'm going to put that ring on your finger and make you my wife when you're too worn out to fight back."

"I'm not going to be able to think. I can't—" Just his breath against my center steals mine away. I try to squirm, but he holds me steady. Zane stares up at me like a man starved, and I'm already quivering. "I won't be able to come up with anything."

He smiles. "That's the plan."

Zane sets to work all at once. There is no build up, no slow easing in. He sets his lips to me and feasts.

I cry out, my body shifting up the bed for some space, but Zane follows me. He pins his arm over my hips to hold me down and works his tongue over every nerve ending I have.

"I-I can't," I gasp, curling my fingers in his hair. "Zane, I need—"

"You better start talking." He slides a finger into me, twisting and curling. "You're already so wet."

The hunger in his eyes and the filthy words coming from his lips don't help. He flicks his tongue over my clit, and I have to lie back and toss my arm over my eyes to even attempt to clear my thoughts.

"It's not safe," I pant. "I p-put you and Aiden in danger just by being here."

He gives me a slow kiss and pulses a second finger into me. "I tried to live without you once. It was hell, Mira. For me *and* for Aiden. I refuse to do it again."

My hips roll against his fingers without my permission, and I force myself to lie still. "We've only known each other a few months. It's too soon."

"Says who?" He works his tongue and his fingers in a maddening rhythm that has my body clenching for more. "I would've asked you sooner, if everything else wasn't going on."

My thoughts are trapped behind a haze of heat and pleasure, but I snatch at his words. "There! We can't because—" My mouth opens in a silent moan as Zane curls his fingers against me, stroking a spot that sends fire up my spine. "—because Dante is still around! We're still in danger. We don't know what's going to happen!"

"Even more reason to make sure I'm protecting you in every way I know how. With my money and my body." He licks me between words. "With my heart and my name. It's all yours, Mira. Every bit of it."

I struggle for some excuse, some reason why I shouldn't let myself have every damn thing I want, but it's impossible to think now.

Zane works another finger into me and I'm full and rolling against his mouth and his hand and every piece of himself he'll give me.

Because I want it all.

My orgasm tears through me hot and fast. I cry out, clamping down around his fingers and shuddering with every brush of his tongue against me.

He kisses me gently, coaxing me back down to earth. Then he crawls over my body. "Marry me, Mira."

I hook my arms around his back and haul him closer, but Zane resists. He snags my wrists and pins them to the bed. He reaches for something and I don't realize what it is until he's holding my ring finger, a cool bit of metal poised above the tip.

"Marry me," he growls. "Live with me and be with me. Raise Aiden with me. Make a family and a home with me because there's no one else I'd rather do it with." He looks down at me, his expression softening. "Marry me, Mira."

Tears are already pouring down my cheeks. Whatever strength I had to resist before is gone. I nod. "Okay. Yes. Yes."

Zane slides the ring on my finger and then turns my hand over in his palm. He studies our hands and smiles.

And I need him now.

I grab his face and pull him to me. I kiss him hard, stopping only to catch my breath when he slides into me to the hilt.

"I want this," I breathe against his mouth. "I want you, Zane. So much. Forever."

Now that I've said yes, it's unthinkable that I ever could have said anything else.

What was I made for, if not to be with this man? If not to love him and be loved by him?

"You're mine." Zane grits his teeth. "You've been mine since the day we met. Since the moment I saw you. *Mine.*"

He's shaking, trying to hold back, trying to wait for me. But I want to see him clearly. I want to watch the strongest man I've ever met fall to pieces because he loves me.

I press my left hand to his chest, just over his heart. "I'm yours, Zane. Take me."

His hips stutter and he growls dirty, beautiful things against my neck, my breasts, my mouth as he spills into me.

A few minutes later, when he's lying next to me and drawing idle circles across my stomach, I ask, "So when's the wedding?"

"I'd say right now, but that seems too soon. Especially since I still have plans for you."

"Again?!" I feel like jello, but Zane wags his brows at me.

Somehow, heat is already building between my legs. *Oh, alright. If I must.*

"So, since tonight is booked, I'm thinking a week from today."

I laugh, but Zane doesn't.

"You're kidding."

Again, silence. He just watches me.

"You are kidding, aren't you?" I ask.

Slowly, he crawls over me, his skin scraping against mine.

"Zane...?"

He grins over the length of my body, and I forget what we were even talking about for hours and hours.

36

ZANE

"I thought you were kidding, Zane!" Mira is standing at the kitchen counter with my laptop open in front of her and her phone wedged between her cheek and her shoulder. She's frantically scribbling things down on a yellow legal pad, but all I can really focus on is the red jersey that falls around the tops of her thighs.

I step behind her and kiss the slope of her neck. "You look good in my name."

"We'll see how good I look when I age three decades in one week!" She swats me away from her neck and goes back to list-making. "We can't get married in a week. Who gets married in a week?!"

"Probably the same people who move in together after a day," Daniel chimes in from the living room.

Mira spins around, her pen pointed at him like a weapon. "Who invited you?"

"You did!"

She frowns. "Oh, right. Then... make yourself useful! Find a florist or... or a place for the ceremony!" Mira gasps and spins towards me. "Where are we going to get married, Zane? Everything is going to be booked up, and we can't do it in a public park or Dante could ruin it. We'd have a Red Wedding on our hands."

"I'll handle music," Daniel suggests. "My cousin plays the cello. She's only fourteen, but she's first chair in her school orchestra. Then again, there is no second chair, but..."

Mira whirls towards him with her pen, but I grab her shoulders and spin her into me, if only to save my best friend from another amputation. "We'll get married at our house."

She looks doubtfully around the condo. I know exactly what she's thinking. It's big, but not *that* big.

"Not here. Our new house."

"What new house?" She must find the answer written on my face because her eyes go wide. She hangs up with whoever she's been on hold with for the last twenty minutes and gapes at me. "You bought a *house*? Without telling me?!"

Daniel oohs from the living room like I'm a kid who just got called to the principal's office, but I ignore him and focus on Mira. "Davis has been wanting to sell his house, and I told him to hold off for a couple weeks so I could think."

"His sex pad?" Her top lip curls. "I do not want to live in—"

"Not his apartment in the city; his *house*. The one we stayed in." The place where we spent a perfect week cooking and playing and going for walks. It was one of the better weeks of my life. Now, it can last forever. "I texted him last night after you went to sleep and told him we wanted it."

"You bought a house without telling me?" she snaps again, turning her pen on me. "We have been engaged less than twenty-four hours, and you've already made a giant decision without consulting me?"

"Do you want me to call and tell him we don't want it?"

"No, obviously not," she snaps. The messy knot of hair on her head wobbles and a few new pieces fall around her face. "That house was perfect, and I want us both to be buried there. I'm thrilled."

I press my thumb to the edge of her downturned mouth. "You should let your face know."

She tries to hold onto her frown, but it wavers when our eyes meet. She wraps her arms around my middle, her chin resting on my chest. "I'm annoyed that I'm trying to plan a wedding in a week and flailing, but you're somehow making the exact right decisions. How do you always know what to do? Tell me your secrets."

I swear I hear Daniel snort from the living room, but it's going to take a lot more than that to break me out of the bubble we're in. I grab Mira's hand and pull her away from the kitchen counter and into the hallway.

The second we're out of sight of the living room, I press her against the wall. "Do you want to hear my one truth for today?"

She shakes her head. "No, because you're going to say something sweet about how much you love me—"

"—endlessly—

"—or how you'll like any decision I make for the wedding—"

"You're agreeing to marry me. Your decision-making skills are obviously impeccable."

She thumps lightly at my chest. "But what I *need* to hear is how in the hell I'm going to pull off a full wedding ceremony in seven days, Zane. Can't we just elope? There's got to be a non-Elvis-themed chapel somewhere nearby. Or, what the hell? Elvis it is! Let's get married and have the King of Rock and Roll seal our eternal vows himself."

"As good as I'd look in a tuxedo t-shirt, I want to do this right, Mira." I tuck a strand of hair behind her ear. "We're doing it fast because I can't wait 'til the end of the season. I want to wear an actual tux and I want you to wear a white dress. I want to kiss you in front of Aiden and all of our family and friends so that they know who we are to one another. So that everyone knows how serious I am about making you mine for the rest of our lives."

Her cheeks flush even as she scowls. "Dammit. I knew you were going to say something sweet."

I lean forward, my hand gripping her hip. "I also want to carry you down the aisle and over the threshold so I can rip that white dress off of you and fuck my wife in every room of our new house." We've shifted closer with every word. I can feel Mira's exhale against my lips when I smile. "Or was that too sweet for you?"

She blinks up at me, slightly dazed. "My one truth is that I don't think I care what our ceremony looks like as long as I get the reception you just promised me."

I hook a hand behind her thigh and bring her leg over my hip. I'd be happy to give her a taste of what she has to look forward to right here and now—

Until there's a knock on the door.

"I'll get it!" Daniel calls.

Mira drops her leg and pulls away from me. "Who is that?"

Before I can answer, the door flies open and the condo is filled with voices.

"Daniel told me Zane bought a ring two weeks ago, and I've been *dying*!" Taylor shrieks. "I'm no good with secrets."

Neither is my best man, apparently.

"Tay!" Daniel hisses. "I was sworn to secrecy. You weren't supposed to know."

"No one told me," Jemma says, "but Reeves and I are happy for you both, anyway. Aren't we?"

Aside from our friends, only Hollis knows about the proposal. I need to tell Coach—*invite Coach*, actually. And most of the team, Carson and his goons excluded. Then I'll have to tell the team's PR people so they can draft a statement before the press gets wind of the wedding and rumors start to build.

Mira might be right. A week could be a tight turnaround.

"I don't even see them," Reeves mutters. "Are they here?"

"Yeah, probably feeling each other up somewhere," Daniel sighs. "They've been nauseating to be around all morning."

For the first time all morning, Mira smiles. She buries her laugh against my chest. "What are they all doing here?"

"I called in the cavalry." I tip her chin up and kiss her, long and slow. "I'm going to give you the wedding of your dreams, Mira McNeil."

37

ZANE

Davis tugs on the lapels of his suit as the tailor measures his inseam. "You're really taking this whole 'hooking up with the nanny' thing to the next level, Z."

I shoot him a lethal look in the three-paned mirror and he holds up his hands. "No nanny jokes. Roger that."

"You've gotta be careful what you say around this one, Davy." Jace wraps his arm around my shoulders. "He's newly coupled and feeling territorial."

"Mira and I are not *new*. We've been together for…" I've known Mira for almost five months, but we weren't *together* that whole time. There was some fake dating and then some back-and-forth. She was also gone for an entire month, which I probably shouldn't count.

Jace saves me the trouble of doing the math. "Newly committed, I mean. Something happens when you make a woman your wife."

Reeves whistles. "It really does. Jemma and I paid for this all-inclusive honeymoon package, but I don't think we left the room once. I'd say it was a waste of money, but we put that room to good use."

"Mira and I aren't doing a honeymoon. Not right now."

It was an easy decision to make. Neither of us wanted to leave town without Aiden, not while Dante is still lurking in the shadows. And there are just too many unknowns with traveling. I promised her we'd postpone and I'll take her on the best first anniversary trip anyone has ever had.

"No honeymoon?" Daniel exhales. "What's the point of getting married if you don't get to lounge on a tropical beach somewhere afterwards?"

"I guess I'll just have to settle for a lifetime of happiness with the woman I love," I drawl.

Davis gives that idea two thumbs down, and I'm beginning to severely question why he's in my wedding party.

"Don't worry," Jace assures me. "Rachelle and I would love to have Aiden over for a few days after the wedding while you and Mira *test out* your new relationship."

"Yeah, test it out in every room of *my* old house." Davis holds out his fist for a bump that I do not reciprocate. "You're welcome, by the way."

"I'm paying you over market value, so *you're* welcome," I fire back.

The tailor finishes with Davis and moves on to Daniel. Every one of us has a tux for all of the media and events that come along with the team, but I really am trying to do this right. The bridesmaids are going to be in matching dresses. The groomsmen are going to wear matching suits. It's going to be as legit as a backyard wedding can be.

About the time the tailor is finishing with the groomsmen, Evan pops his head through the front door.

"Are you ready for him?" Evan asks. "We explored every inch of the toy store down the block, but we can find something else to do if we need to."

"We're ready for him," I say. Aiden squeezes around Evan's leg and sprints towards me. I kneel down, catching and swinging him into my arms. "Did you have fun?"

"There's a 'mote-control dinosaur that has a swinging tail," he announces. "It was green and Evan said it costed one dollar."

Evan shakes his head. "One *hundred* dollars."

Aiden ignores him, grabbing onto the collar of my shirt. "Can I have it? Please?"

I screw up my face, thinking it over. "Hmmm… How about if you hold still while you get measured for your tux, then we'll go back and buy it when we're done?"

One hundred bucks is steep for a bribe, but I'm trying to make this move as smooth as possible for Mira. Keeping Aiden happy is part of that.

"Yes!" he shrieks, squirming out of my arms to run towards the tailor and then standing straight and still as a statue on the dais. The faster he gets measured, the faster he gets his dinosaur.

Smart kid.

∾

His resolve doesn't last long. Fifteen minutes into the process of trying on suits, I'm glad I have some collateral.

"This shirt is itchy," Aiden moans, squishing up his neck.

The tailor pulls a paper tag out of the collar. "It's just the tag, buddy."

Aiden shakes his head. "It's itchy everywhere. My tummy. And my elbows. Even my butt."

"The shirt isn't touching your butt, bud."

He looks at me like I can't possibly know anything about the pain he's going through. "I don't want to wear this."

"You're saying what we're all thinking, little man." Davis raises a fist in solidarity from where he and the rest of my groomsmen are loafing on the couch. If Mira could see them, lounging and not doing anything remotely productive, she'd kick all of their asses straight out the door.

I put myself between Aiden and the bad influence of my teammates. "We'll be done soon and we can go get your toy dinosaur."

"Then I never have to wear it again?" he asks hopefully.

"Well, you have to wear it at the wedding. But only for a couple hours. Just until the wedding is over."

"But you and Mira are already married," he pouts.

"We're together, but we aren't married yet. That's what the wedding is for."

Aiden spins around so fast that his shaggy blonde hair whips across his forehead. I mentally add *haircut* to my growing to-do list. "But you live together! Jalen's parents live together and sleep in the same bed and they're married. What does a wedding do?"

"That's true," Reeves chimes in. "Good point, Aiden. Do explain to all of us how that works, Zane."

I flip him off behind my back so Aiden can't see.

"Mira and I love each other very much, so we want to show everyone how much we love each other."

Aiden's blue eyes narrow as he thinks very hard about something. "Does marrying mean you have babies?"

"Oh, shit," Davis hisses through a laugh. "The baby talk. Little man does not waste time."

Reeves leans forward to whisper, "This is probably Jalen's fault. We had a version of the talk with him last week. He's been telling all of his friends."

"Open and honest communication. That's what kids need," Daniel adds. "I vote we tell him."

I wave them all off. "Marrying does not mean we'll have babies. If you're worried about that, don't be. It's just a party."

He lifts his chin and looks directly in my eyes. "I'm not worried. I want you to have babies. Lots of them."

My groomsmen erupt in more childish laughter, and Mira's elopement idea is sounding better and better by the second.

"Oh, yeah?"

"Yeah." He nods. "I want a little brother."

I can't help but smile. At the thought of Aiden in the backyard, a little toddler trailing after him, yes—but also at the thought of Mira in her frilly sundresses, her hand on her growing bump. Of Mira pregnant with *my* baby.

"It might be a sister."

"Both!" Aiden adds excitedly. He grabs my sleeve and tugs. "Can we have both?"

"It's not completely up to me, buddy. We'll have to talk it over with Mira."

"But we have more rooms at the new house," he argues. "You and Mira share one and I can share, so then we can have…" He twists his face into deep concentration. "Five babies!"

"That is one pragmatic kid," Daniel muses.

"I'd love it if we had five babies." I kneel down. "So how about you and I both talk to Mira and try to convince her that you need five brothers and sisters?"

"I won't even get the dinosaur for one dollar. We can save the money. For the babies."

I pull him in for a hug and kiss the top of his head. "You're the best big brother already."

38

MIRA

"Are the flowers here yet?"

Taylor doesn't even look up as she nods. "Yes."

"And the cake?"

"Chilling in the downstairs fridge as we speak."

I worry the lace of my dress between my fingers. At this rate, all the beading on the front of my gown is going to be gone by the time the ceremony starts. "Oh, crap. The catering! I didn't order—"

"Tablecloths," Taylor drawls. "You thought of that last night, texted me in a panic, and I bought some at Home Goods on my way over this morning. There are only four tables, so I won't even ask for reimbursement. I am nothing if not generous."

I sigh, but it does nothing to loosen the knot of anxiety in my chest. Even with all of the help I've had at my disposal, it's been there all week.

"Girl, breathe." Taylor inhales slowly and exhales, but I can't even pretend to follow her. It's hard when I'm too busy hyperventilating.

Me being on the verge of a mental breakdown is why Jemma and Rachelle decided to be anywhere other than this room, I'm sure. That... and I asked them to double-check that all of the bulbs in the string lights are working.

The realization hits me all at once.

"Oh, God, I'm a bridezilla! I need to go grab Jemma and Rachelle. They should be in here, not working in the backyard."

Taylor blocks my path to the door and shakes my shoulders. "Don't make me slap you, Mira. It will smear your makeup."

"And it would hurt."

"And it would hurt," she agrees. "Though that's not my main objection. Also, it's your wedding day and the only thing I should be doing is pinching you because you feel like you're in a dream! That's the kind of blood, sweat, and tears I've put into calling up every favor I've been saving with businesses all over the city to make this wedding happen on time."

"God, you're right." I go to clap my hands over my face, but I stop when I remember the painstaking work the makeup artist put into my eyeshadow. So I end up staring at my palms. "Everyone has put so much work into this, and I'm so stressed I haven't even thanked you all."

Taylor wrenches my hands away. "No, you're so stressed that you haven't even enjoyed it! You've gotta stop and smell the flowers, Mimi."

She leads me towards the tall, gold-framed standing mirror in the corner of the guest room we've commandeered as the Bridal Suite.

Zane and a horde of hockey players moved most of our stuff from the condo to the new house a couple days ago. Most of the boxes are unpacked, but this room was left intentionally bare. Today, when I arrived, there was a velvet sofa, the gilded mirror, and the softest robe I've ever felt in my life. *From Z* was the only thing written on the note left behind.

Zane stayed over at Daniel's last night. It's only been eighteen hours since I last saw him, but it's almost embarrassing how much I miss him.

Taylor jerks me to a stop in front of the mirror and stands over my shoulder. "Look at yourself."

For the first time all day, I do just that.

There wasn't time for a custom wedding dress, but I found the perfect off-the-rack gown at the first boutique we went to. Zane loves my sundresses so much that I went for something without a lot of structure. Sheer tulle straps flow into a lace bodice with floral appliques that trail down the flowing skirt. Even if I'd had a full year to search for a dress, I still think this is the one I would have chosen.

The makeup artist took my half-sarcastic direction of "totally natural, but ethereal and flawless and angelic" very seriously. My skin is glowing. And for the first time in a week, my hair is in thick waves over my shoulders instead of a tangled knot on top of my head.

I smile. "I look—"

"Absolutely fuckable," Taylor finishes. "Too hot to handle."

"Taylor!"

She shrugs shamelessly. "I call 'em like I see 'em, darling, and Zane is going to lose his mind when he sees you."

At that moment, someone knocks on the door. Taylor throws herself in front of me like a shield. "I don't care how convincing you think you are, lover boy, you can't see her until the wedding!"

"What? Zane has been trying to see me?" I instinctively start to look for my phone before I remember Taylor stripped it off of me first thing this morning. The same way Daniel, apparently, stole Zane's phone.

The door cracks open and Daniel's face appears. "It's just me and—" His eyes go wide at the sight of Taylor in her bridesmaid dress. Taylor chose the strapless version of the silk rose dresses I selected and Daniel seems to approve wholeheartedly. "You are a goddess, Tay. Absolutely gorgeous."

"You're supposed to compliment the *bride*, idiot." Taylor rolls her eyes, but her cheeks are a brighter pink than they were a second ago.

Daniel pivots to smile at me. "You are radiant, Mira. Can we come in?"

"'We'?"

He throws the door wide to reveal that my hallway is absolutely stuffed to the brim with a thousand pounds' worth of hockey players.

"We aren't supposed to see her!" Davis covers his own eyes and throws a hand over Reeves's while he's at it.

Jace just stretches onto his toes to give me a wave over their heads. I laugh and wave back.

"Jace, avert your gaze!" Davis barks.

"I'm not the one marrying her, dumbass. Plus, Daniel already saw her."

Daniel puffs up his chest. "As is my right as the best man."

They jostle back and forth, all of them trying to squeeze into the narrow hallway.

"You swear there isn't a groom hiding between all that muscle?" Taylor peers into the group with narrowed eyes. "If Zane sneaks his way into the bridal suite, my best friend is going to have a eunuch for a husband."

"We solemnly swear." Daniel raises his hand in a scout's honor salute, Reeves crosses his heart, and Davis kisses two fingers and blows it towards the sky.

Jace just shakes his head at the men with their eyes closed and pushes past them into the room. "We're alone. And we wanted to talk to you."

I must be trained to expect bad news because my stomach flips. "Is everything okay?"

"Absolutely not," Davis announces, still shielding his eyes with one hand and using his other to clumsily bat at Jace and Daniel. "We came in here to do something sweet, but these asshats are just pissing all over tradition. I said, Avert your eyes, gentlemen!"

Jace throws up his hands in exasperation and turns his back on me as Daniel winks and does the same. So now, I'm staring at four broad, tuxedo-clad backs.

Davis sighs in relief. "There. *Now*, everything is fine."

"Superstitious moron," Jace mutters under his breath. "Well, I *was* going to say that you look lovely, Mira, but apparently, that's against the rules."

Reeves raises a hand. "I'll say it! You look lovely, Mira. Zane is going to lose his mind."

"That's what I said!" Taylor gasps. "Absolutely fucka—"

I'm glad no one is looking because I slam an elbow into Taylor's side and shove her back towards the couch. Her opinion does not need to be repeated to the groomsmen, thank you very much.

"Anyway," Jace carries on, "we just wanted to come as a group and tell you how happy we are that this day is finally happening."

"'Finally'? We got engaged a week ago," I remind him.

"Yeah, but Zane has been a grouchy sad sack for years," Davis offers. "The man was miserable and didn't even know it until you came along."

I want to argue. I almost convinced myself this morning that marrying Zane is too selfish. I'm clearly bringing chaos into his life.

But if his best friends don't see it that way, maybe I'm not ruining Zane's life after all.

Daniel sighs. "What this graceless oaf is trying to say is that Zane has never been happier than he is with you. We're thrilled to be here to support you both."

The lack of sleep and excitement are clearly getting to me

because I have to blink away tears that threaten to ruin my mascara. "Thanks, guys."

"Also," Reeves adds, "Zane is our boy, but we'll absolutely kick his ass if he fucks things up with you."

"Amen to that!" Taylor calls from the couch.

I laugh. "Thanks for that, too, I guess."

"Okay, that was sweet, but you all need to go." Taylor jumps up and ushers the men out the door. "We have bridal duties to attend to. No more men allowed."

As soon as the men are back in the hallway—and Daniel cracks the door open one last time to blow a kiss to Taylor—she slams the door shut and leans against it. "I'm gonna be honest, they kind of stole my thunder."

"Were you also planning to tell me that Zane has never been happier?"

"Please." She rolls her eyes. "Zane is fine, but you know you are my number one—then, now, and always. The only person whose happiness I care about in this relationship is yours. Which is why—" She looks uncharacteristically serious as she takes my hands. "—I'm also so happy that this day is finally happening."

"Again, just to reiterate, we've only been engaged for one week."

"But I've been watching you put yourself last for years." Taylor gives me a sad smile. "Up until a few months ago, you never showed any interest in dating."

"That never stopped you from trying to set me up on terrible dates."

"I would've respected your pledge to singlehood *if* I hadn't been able to see how lonely you really were."

Tears prick the back of my eyes again. I chew on the corner of my mouth to keep my chin from wobbling.

"I know I'm the here-for-a-good-time-not-a-long-time friend in this relationship. I take my duties to keep the mood light and never take things too seriously *very* seriously." She folds my hands against her heart. "But I want to tell you that you're my best friend in the world, Mimi. Even when I knew you were keeping secrets from me. Even when you were scared of your own shadow and refused to buy new furniture."

I laugh, a tear finally slipping free.

"Even when you'd run off and bail on me for months at a time." She gives me a quick, stern look that softens just as fast. "You've always been the best, most loyal person I know. I'm so glad you overcame the bullshit your family put you through so you can finally get the happily-ever-after you deserve."

Before she can even finish, I throw my arms around her neck and squeeze.

"God, you are a real softy now," she teases, squeezing me back.

She isn't wrong. But I'm not sure I mind.

"You're my best friend," I whisper. "I love you."

"I know." She draws back and swipes her fingers under my eyes, cleaning up my mascara. "Now, pull yourself together, woman. We've got a shotgun wedding to get to."

39

MIRA

"Why is everyone crying?"

Aiden is holding my hand as we walk across the flower-strewn patio towards the makeshift aisle that cuts across the lawn, casting horrified looks in every direction.

We have a small gathering of people. Zane's teammates and their wives are in the first few rows of chairs. Owen, Evan, and a woman who looks suspiciously like a nurse I recognize from the hospital are in the back and the only people I can see from this vantage point, but every single one of them is crying. Owen keeps squinting up at the cloud-covered sun as if it's simply the light bothering his eyes instead of the ooey-gooey emotions he claims not to have.

I squeeze Aiden's hand. "I think it's because they're so happy for us."

Aiden frowns like he doesn't buy it, and I can't even blame him. One day, he'll look back at pictures of him in a tiny tuxedo, leading me down the aisle to his dad, and he'll understand why no one can keep their shit together.

Actually, the thought of him as a teenager, reminiscing about the day we legally became a family, has me teetering on the edge of losing *my* shit, too.

I hear Taylor's warning in the back of my mind. *If you ruin your makeup before you get down the aisle, I will not forever hold my peace. I'll object to your wedding, Mira McNeil, I swear to God. Do you hear me?!*

But the second the orchestral music swells and Aiden and I pause at the top of the aisle, my makeup doesn't stand a chance.

Zane is waiting for us, looking sharp in a navy tux and a wide smile. His eyes flick from me to Aiden and back like he can't believe we're his, and I've never loved him more.

I know there are other people here, but I don't see them. I can't focus on anything except the little boy holding my hand and the man just in front of us, who has always held us both.

When we make it to the top of the aisle, Zane kneels in front of Aiden and offers him knuckles. "You nailed it, kid. I couldn't have walked her down the aisle better myself."

Aiden fist bumps his dad and then throws his arms around his neck. It's already an adorable moment, but when he reaches grasping little fingers towards me, my heart melts. I kneel down next to them, not caring at all if I get grass stains on my dress, and hug my boys.

"You're crying, too?" Aiden shakes his head, and I can't help but laugh.

"Happy tears, A. I'm crying very happy tears."

And I continue crying happy tears while Aiden climbs up next to Reeves and Jalen in the front row and Daniel welcomes everyone to "the wedding of the decade that we've only known about for three days."

He reads from some printed-out wedding ceremony guide he must have found online, but I don't hear a word. Zane runs his thumbs over my knuckles, back and forth, and traces his eyes over every detail of my face. It's impossible to think about anything when he's looking at me like this.

Suddenly, Zane opens his mouth, and it takes me far too many seconds to realize that it's time for vows.

Panic claws up my throat because I didn't prepare anything. At some point in the chaos of this last week, we decided to do our own vows.

"I don't want someone else's words in my mouth while I'm making my vows to you," he said, and it sounded so damn good when he said it that it was all I could do to contain my drool and nod.

The problem is, I don't have a single clue what I'm going to say. I never stopped long enough to plan something.

Zane steps close and drops his voice so only I can hear him. "I think this moment should just be for the two of us, don't you think?"

My chest unclenches. *Talking to Zane*—I can handle that. "Just me and you."

He wraps his arm around my waist and presses his lips to my cheek before they settle next to my ear. His voice is deep and steady.

"For a long time, I didn't think I was capable of taking care of another person. I could barely take care of myself. How could I be any good for anyone else? Then I met you." He kisses my cheekbone. "You made me feel good enough, Mira. You made me feel worthy. You taught me how to take care of my son and, every second we spent together, I realized more and more how much I wanted to take care of you, too. I just —" He laughs softly against my skin. "I love you, Mira. More than I thought I was capable of. It would be my honor to spend my life taking care of our family and putting you both first."

I'm not sure I've stopped crying since Aiden walked me down the aisle, but it's a bona fide literal and emotional downpour now. Zane pulls back and, seeing how much I'm crying, immediately closes the gap again. He holds my face in his hands and brushes my tears away.

"I don't know what to say," I blubber, falling against his shoulder. I'm probably leaving makeup smears on the fabric, but I can't bring myself to care. "I-I love you so much, Zane. I didn't think I would have any of this. Love. Happiness. *You*. But—" I gesture to him with both hands. "You're here and I never want to be without you. I promise I'll love you and Aiden as long as I live. With everything I have."

I can't imagine my blubbery, on-the-fly vows are anything to write home about, but I look up to see that Zane is tearing up, too. His eyes are dark and glassy as he jerks me against him.

I fall into the kiss without any fight. I sink against his mouth, bend to his touch. When he tips me back and nips at my lower lip, I'm not sure why he isn't taking this all the way to the ground to see this show all the way through to its inevitable conclusion.

When Zane sets me upright and pulls away, I'm dazed.

Then Daniel clears his throat, and I remember where exactly we are. "I swear I'm getting to that part of the ceremony next. If you all can just hang with me for another thirty seconds, this will be over."

A laugh moves through the crowd and my cheeks heat. It only gets worse when I meet the intensity in Zane's eyes.

For a second there, he was just as lost as I was.

"By the power vested in me by the great state of Arizona and the kind people over at BECOMEAMINISTERRE-ALQUICK.COM, I now pronounce you husband and wife. Zane," Daniel says warmly, stepping back, "*now*, you may kiss your bride."

I expect Zane to grab me the way he did a second ago, but he reaches for my hand with practiced calm. Gently, he pulls me against him and cradles my cheek.

His lips settle over mine, patient and hungry and promising something much deeper the second we're alone.

When he pulls away far too soon, the smile on his face is the most tender thing I've ever seen. His eyes sweep over me as he whispers, almost to himself, "My bride."

40

MIRA

"Are you absolutely, positively, one hundred percent sure you all want to leave?" I spin in a circle as our friends clean up the reception before my very eyes.

Not even half an hour ago, Zane and I were having our first dance under the glow of the string lights above us. White flower petals covered the dance floor and Zane twirled and dipped me so smoothly I almost felt graceful. Halfway through it, Aiden escaped Daniel's hold and ran across the dance floor. He threw his arms around our legs and Zane scooped him up so we could all dance together.

Nothing in my life has ever felt more right.

Now, Taylor, Jemma, and Rachelle are blowing out candles and clearing dishes. The hockey players are mostly eating leftover canapes and hiding wine bottles inside their jackets, but still, they're making quick work of everything, each in their own way.

"It's barely even eight o'clock." The sun is setting behind the distant mountains, painting the sky in jewel tones.

"It's past my bedtime." Rachelle gives a fake yawn and points towards where Aiden and Gallagher are drooping in their chairs. "It's past theirs, too."

"Yeah, we laughed, we cried, we danced, we drank." Taylor shrugs like there's nothing left on the list of possible wedding verbs. "Now, it's time for us to go."

I spent a week straight planning this day and now, it's over. We're married.

We're married.

I want to hit pause and savor the day a little longer. I want to spend a few more minutes with the people we love.

Then Zane wraps his arms around me from behind. He hasn't had a drop to drink, but there's something intoxicating in the air. He feels heavy on my shoulders, his body loose and relaxed and at ease in a way I haven't seen in way too long. "I hope you're not tired. I have plans for you, Mrs. Whitaker."

I barely resist letting out a wolf whistle, reversing course, and pushing everyone towards the doors. *Okay, party is over.*

My heartbeat kicks up, and I wonder when this will go away. When will I get used to the magnetism that is Zane Whitaker?

All at once, something occurs to me and I gasp. "I'm Mira Whitaker now."

I've been so busy the last week that I didn't have time to come to terms with everything that would change when I became Zane's wife. My name being one. I roll the idea around in my mind and smile.

Mira Whitaker.

I feel Zane's matching smile against my neck. "Say that again when we're alone. I like it."

Twenty minutes later, once the perishables are packaged in the refrigerator and anything that might blow away in the night is strapped down, folded, or stashed in the back of Daniel's truck, Aiden grabs me and Zane by the hands.

"I know you just had your marry, but Jalen wants me to stay at his house tonight." He delivers the news with a somber face, like he's telling us something we don't know. "I'm gonna do that."

Zane and I both bite back a laugh. "We'll miss you every second, son," Zane says in all seriousness. "But we understand."

I kiss the top of his head and remind him to grab the overnight bag I packed for him twelve hours ago from the closet. Jemma and Reeves wave as they follow the boys into the house.

Next, it's Taylor's turn to grab my shoulders and look deeply in my eyes. "I know you just had your marry, but it's time for me to leave so you can get railed by your husband."

"Taylor!"

She laughs and ducks away when I try to swat at her. "I'm sorry—the deep and meaningful bullshit was for before the ceremony. Now, I've had a little too much wine and your husband is looking at you like he wants to eat you."

I follow the flick of her eyebrows and, well, she's definitely not wrong.

Zane is talking to Jace, but his eyes keep slipping to me. His jaw is set in the soft glow of the lights and he ditched his jacket somewhere an hour ago to roll his sleeves around his forearms. He looks even more unbelievable than usual.

Mine. He's mine.

The reality that this man belongs to me snaps into place all at once. Something feral claws at my chest and I barely resist the primal urge to walk across the lawn and pin him to the ground.

"Wow. Yeah. That's my cue." Taylor backs away. "I'll see you whenever you're done…" She flits a finger from me to Zane and back again. "*Later.* I'll see you later. Probably in a few weeks."

I'd be annoyed with her if she wasn't spot on. Once I fall into Zane, I don't think I'll want to come up for air for a good, long while.

Taylor whispers something to Rachelle and, after a quick look at me, Rachelle crosses the yard and pulls Jace away by the elbow.

"I was in the middle of—" He starts to argue, but Rachelle tosses a pointed look at me and Zane, and Jace blanches. "Congrats again, you two! Bye!"

They walk around the side of the house, and Zane and I are finally alone.

"Our friends aren't much for subtlety." His voice is a deep rumble that sucks out all the oxygen in my lungs. He's stalking towards me with purpose, and I should be scared. A man like *him* looking at *me* like *that* should register some instinctual alarm bells, but all I feel is heady anticipation curling low in my belly.

Mine.

I'm Mira Whitaker, and he's *mine.*

"To be fair, neither are we. I think we made them uncomfortable."

"Good." He doesn't slow or stop as he wraps his arms around my waist and walks me back until I'm pressed against the brick wall of the house. *Our* house.

He plants his palms on either side of my head, caging me in with his body. The heat rolling off of him is insulating against the evening chill. "I've wanted to get you to myself all fucking day. Even before I saw you in this dress."

His fingers smooth over the delicate tulle straps, and I'm painfully aware of how easily he could shred this dress off of me… and how much I wish he would.

"You're the one who wanted a formal wedding. I would've gotten married in front of Fake Elvis—twenty minutes in and out—but you wanted our friends and family there."

"Maybe I wanted to draw it out. Maybe I'm into edging." He nuzzles his stubbled cheek against mine. My body vibrates where he touches me. I can't take it, but I also need more. "Waiting almost drove me crazy. You've been driving me to distraction for hours. It's a miracle I got through my vows without dropping to my knees and tasting you."

Speaking of miracles, it's a miracle I'm still human-shaped instead of a melted puddle of desire on the ground.

I press my hand to Zane's chest just to make sure he's real and this isn't all a dream. His heart thuds against my palm a bit too fast. "We're married now, you know."

His eyes flutter closed like I just said something sinfully dirty. "Believe me, I'm aware."

"If I remember right, your plan was to marry me and then carry me over a threshold before you rip this dress off of me with—"

I yelp as Zane scoops me into his arms and carries me towards the patio doors.

I think he's going to turn down the hall towards our room, but he turns for the kitchen instead. He sets me on the spacious counter littered with party leftovers, and I don't even have time to complain about the bite of the cold marble through my dress before Zane slips the straps down my shoulders and has me bare from the waist up.

"I thought you were going to rip it off with your teeth."

"It's pretty and you look good in it. I don't want to ruin it." He scrapes his teeth over my shoulder instead, kissing his way over my collarbone while he curls both hands around my chest. He lifts my breast to his mouth, moving over me with gentle nips until his control slips and his teeth sink into me.

"You bit me!" I yelp.

"I already told you," he growls against the sting, kissing away the tenderness. "You look edible."

The bite already feels good. I want him to do it again. But I lift my chin. "Well, I'm not. If you keep that up, *I'll* be ruined."

When he looks up at me, his eyes are dark and his smile is vicious. "You're not so fragile, Mira. You can take it."

Before I can find the words, Zane pushes me back onto the counter. The marble is frigid on my skin, but my body flames where Zane touches me. He lifts my hips and slides my dress down, discarding it somewhere on the floor. Calloused fingers scrape over my legs, hesitating over the garter belt around my thigh and the lace arching over my hips.

"Just for me," he breathes against the inside of my leg. Goosebumps explode in his wake. Every part of me is alive and responsive.

I should be doing something in return—touching him, making him feel as worked up as I am—but I lie back and let Zane explore. He kisses my knees, my thighs, the crease of my hips, then strokes his thumb over the triangle of lace at my center.

And just like that, I pretty much cease breathing.

I grab at his shirt and try to pull him higher, but he shrugs my hands away and takes his time, as if we have an endless amount of it. As if there is no limit to how long we can taste and touch and tease.

Come to think of it, he might be right.

He parts me with his hands, planting stubbly kisses along the hem of my panties. He must be able to see how wet I am, smell it, taste it. I'm throbbing and it's a miracle I haven't finished from the anticipation alone.

"I chose these because they were supposed to drive you crazy," I complain, squirming to get his mouth where I want it. "You were supposed to go wild and rip them off of me."

I feel him smile. Feel a wide-mouthed kiss pressed to my very center over the fabric. "As a kid, if I liked the wrapping, I would peel the tape from my presents and fold the paper neatly for later. I liked taking my time."

"You were one of those kids?" I groan. "You *definitely* like edging, then."

"You're the prettiest present I've ever seen, Mira Whitaker. I don't want to rush it." His hands span across my thighs, his thumbs stroking devastating vibrations on either side of my pulsing pussy.

"Zane…"

He takes mercy on me and slides the lace to one side. His warm breath washes over my wetness before his thumb settles there, stroking.

He's barely touched me, but I'm deranged. I'm trembling with how much I need him.

I throw my arms out to my sides. Cups tip over and my fist lands in something solid, but Zane's lips are on me now and nothing else matters.

"There," I moan, hooking a leg over his shoulder. I slide my hand through his hair, holding him where I want him, arching my hips against his mouth. "Oh, God, right there."

He hums against me, working his tongue faster, tasting me like his grip on control is slipping as fast as mine.

My hand closes in his hair, pulling tight—too tight. He growls and tosses my hand to the side. It lands in something solid again, but my body is on fire. I feel like I'm coming out of my own skin. I stroke my hands over my chest to keep myself together, massaging to the pace of Zane's mouth.

"Touch yourself. Don't stop," he orders, but I already am. I couldn't stop even if I wanted to.

Some primal snarl rips out of Zane's chest and he lifts my

thighs, holding me open so he can bury his tongue inside of me.

And I collapse like a dying star.

Bright white burns behind my eyes as my body pulses again and again. Zane keeps going, following my cues. As I'm coming down, he coaxes me back to reality with soft kisses.

When the last of it ebbs away, I slump to the counter, breathless.

Zane starts making his way over me again. He drags his tongue over my stomach and around my breast. I open my eyes and see a clump of white in his hair.

"What is—" I work my hand through it, rubbing the cream between my fingers. "Is that *frosting*?"

He lifts his face and his tongue is out, a dollop of frosting on the tip. He swallows, his throat bobbing beautifully. "I think we ruined our wedding cake."

I look over and see what my hand kept hitting. The bottom tier of our chai cake with vanilla cream cheese frosting is perfect—except for a deep gash in the side closest to us. It looks like a bear mauled it. There are actual claw marks.

Whoops.

Zane follows the trail of frosting I unknowingly left across my stomach and over my breasts. He straddles me on the counter, eating and tasting until I'm pulsing again.

"I want some."

He swirls his finger in the mess at the hollow of my throat and holds out some frosting, but I shake my head.

I reach for the cake, swipe my hand through the frosting, and then dip between our bodies. Zane frowns until my hand slides into his pants. Until I stroke frosting over him from base to tip.

We clumsily switch positions, and he hisses when his back hits the cold marble.

"You're not so fragile," I tease, arching a brow. "You can take it."

He grins and dips a frosting-covered thumb between my lips. "My cruel wife."

His pants are covered in frosting and spilled champagne, so they stick to his skin when I peel them over his hips. Zane kicks them off the rest of the way while I fumble with the buttons of his shirt.

He took his time with me, but I don't have nearly the self-control my husband does. The second Zane is bare beneath me, I plant my hands on his thighs and take him in my mouth.

"Fuck." He loops my hair around his fist, holding lightly as I move over him.

I swirl my tongue over the frosting at his tip, and Zane breathes my name. He thrusts into my mouth like he can't help himself, his lips moving around broken phrases and words I can't hear. When I slide deeper, pressing my nose to his stomach and swallowing around him, he roars.

Sugar and Zane explode on my tongue.

When he's finished, he grabs my arm and pulls me over him. The marble is warm under us now, and he settles me against his chest.

"Have I told you how incredible you look?"

A weak laugh bubbles out of me. "You're remembering me from an hour ago. It's too late for compliments now. I'm wrecked."

He drags his finger through the sticky mess of my chest, slowly circling my nipple until the skin pebbles for him. "Wrong. I don't think you've ever looked better."

That doesn't stop him from peeling me off of the ruined island and carrying me straight to the shower. Steam billows and swirls as we soap each other up. I work shampoo into the frosted mess of his hair and he drags his hands over my skin, making me feel dirty in a way soap could never touch.

We dry each other off, unwilling to stop pawing at each other for even a second.

Our bedroom is a maze of half-unpacked boxes, but the bed is made.

"Did you do that?" I ask, pointing to the tucked corners and mound of pillows.

"I unpacked the most important things first."

I start to reach for a box labeled *Clothes*, but Zane catches me around the waist and pulls me onto the bed. "Like I said, I only unpacked the important things."

"Clothes are pretty important."

He rolls me against him, fitting his body behind me like we were made for this. "Not right now they're not."

It's easy, the way he slides into me. I've been wet and ready for hours—days, really—and Zane sinks into me with one thrust. He presses a hand flat to my stomach, holding me against him as he drags out and fills me again. The friction is excruciatingly good. I reach back to touch his neck, his hair, whatever I can reach, because I need to hold onto something or I swear I'll float away.

"Do you think this will go away?" I breathe. "The way I need you? The way you need me?"

Zane laces his fingers through mine and brings our hands to his lips. He kisses each of my knuckles. "It might change. When we've been married for ten years, twenty, fifty—"

"You'll be so old by then," I tease, gasping when he shifts a little faster inside of me like he's trying to prove exactly how young he still is.

"—so maybe it will look different, but it will never go away, Mira." His hand strokes over my stomach, dipping between my legs to circle my clit. "You're wrapped up in my DNA. Needing you is part of who I am now."

When he groans against my neck that he's going to come, I slide away from him and lie flat. If Zane is confused, he pieces things together fast. He kneels over me, stroking himself as his neck tenses and his arms flex. The low lamplight paints him in pale golds and soft shadows. Zane gives himself fully to everything he does, including pleasure. It's mesmerizing to watch. I touch myself while I stare up at him, falling at the exact moment he spills onto my chest.

He dries on me and my fucking God, it's insane how much I love being marked by him, inside and out.

His cum on my skin.

His ring on my finger.

His love and his heat and his last name surging through my veins.

Zane lies down next to me, and we might fall asleep. I'm not totally sure. My eyelids are heavy, and he's warm and solid at my side. I do know we lie there for a long time before he gets up to snag tissues from the nightstand.

He cleans me up with a lazy smile. "We just showered and you're already dirty again."

"I don't care. I wanted you everywhere. Inside and out." I reach out and stroke my fingers down his stomach. His muscles twitch and flex. "I wanted you to mark me, Zane."

His smile slips and his eyes darken. His voice goes rough. "Fuck, Mira. You can't say shit like that to me."

"Why not?"

He falls over me, catching himself with his hands on either side of my head. "Because I'm already getting hard again and I want to fuck a baby into you."

Zane told me to take my time. He told me to think about whether I wanted kids or not, but in the end, there wasn't much to think about.

"You can." I bite my lip. "Right now, if you want."

"You're on birth control."

"I was. I—" The words catch in my throat. I'm going to sound insane. Hell, I might be, but the truth tumbles out of me, anyway, for better or worse. "I stopped three days ago. I thought it could be like a wedding gift. That maybe you'd… that maybe you'd want to…" My cheeks warm, and I shake my head. "It's crazy; I know it is. That's why I didn't let you finish inside. I didn't want to force you. But when I thought about this night, I didn't want there to be anything between us or our future. We don't have to, but if you want—"

Zane steals the words from my lips. He kisses me hard, picking me up off the mattress so we're chest-to-chest. So I can feel how fast his heart is racing.

When we break apart, he's panting. "I *want*. All I fucking do now is *want*, Mira." Our foreheads press together. "Ever since I met you, I want it all."

I wrap my hand around him and he takes my hips. We fall together like a sigh, sinking back together in a kind of frenzied haze I've never felt before. I ride him in long, slow strokes, rising and falling down every inch of him.

"I already want to come," he grits out. He sounds half-amazed.

"Do it." The way he's filling me has me teetering on the brink.

But Zane shakes his head and pushes me back onto the mattress. "I want this to last. I don't want to stop."

He slides into me and it's too good. I cry out. "We'll die."

I believe it. Death by excessive orgasms. We've got to be setting records here.

"Then we'll die together." He slides his hands into my hair and kisses my neck, licking my pulse as he fucks me faster and faster.

I hook my legs around his thighs and pull him closer. I claw at his chest and cry his name and lose myself to whatever this madness between us is.

I'd say it's love, but if that's true, we must be the first two people who have ever felt it.

Because no one has ever fit together the way we do.

"I'm going to put my baby in you," he groans, pumping faster. "You're mine, Mira. All mine."

I arch off the bed, so close to the edge my vision is going black. "I'm yours."

A deep hum rumbles through his chest. "Say it again."

"I'm yours, Zane." I tug my hands through his hair and give myself over to everything he has to give. "I'm all yours."

He grips the top of the headboard and spills into me in long, powerful strokes. My orgasm stretches and carries until I think I really might die.

Hearts shouldn't beat this fast. Bodies shouldn't burn this hot.

Then Zane collapses on top of me, and everything is just as it should be again.

"That was more official than any ceremony." He sinks into the mattress next to me and flattens his hand on my quivering stomach. His lips brush against my jaw as he whispers, "*Now*, you're officially Mira Whitaker."

41

MIRA

"Oh, no."

Zane's voice drifts into the bedroom where I've been dutifully putting clothes on hangers for an eternity. If it takes ten thousand hours to become an expert at something, then I'm definitely a leading expert in the field of clothes hanging.

My knees pop as I stand up straight for the first time in way too long and head off to find my husband.

The thought still brings a smile to my face. *My husband.*

Zane Whitaker is my husband.

"Hello?" I pad barefoot down the hallway, poking my head into rooms to look for him as I go.

Compared to the madness of planning a wedding in one week, unpacking has been leisurely. A relaxing stroll in the park compared to the Ironman Triathlon.

But the office is still a catastrophe. I actually pull the door closed so I don't have to think about the computer cords and filing cabinets that will need to be organized at some fuzzy, distant point in the future that will never come if I have anything to say about it.

Aiden's room is entirely unpacked, though. All of his superhero action figures have made themselves at home on the top row of his bookshelves, and he has a giant bean bag chair that he's sneakily slept in three times this week. Between his "cool" room—his words, not mine—and the swingset Zane set up in the backyard months ago, Aiden is little more than a blur in passing, usually running from one to the other.

I was worried how he'd adjust to Zane and me getting married and the move happening at the same time, but he acts like nothing has changed at all.

In some ways, it hasn't.

Zane and I still find each other under the blankets most mornings before we stumble to the kitchen for coffee. Then it's a mad dash of showers and breakfast and shuttling everyone off to practice and school, which takes longer now that we're in the thick of suburbia.

We still cook together. Aiden chops fruits and vegetables with his plastic knife while Zane and I bicker over the difference between a "simmer" and a "rolling boil."

In the evenings, we read picture books and take turns making Aiden giggle until he's too sleepy to keep his eyes open. Zane and I pretend we're going to start a new show or maybe call some friends, invite people to sit under the lights of the patio, and chat, but we don't make it past wondering who we should invite before we're stumbling towards our bedroom.

In other ways, it's completely different.

Unlike before, where I could hear a countdown clock ticking down the seconds, Zane and Aiden are mine. *Forever.*

I'm not sure that's something I'll ever get used to. I kind of hope I don't.

"That's just great," Zane groans again.

I throw up my hands. "This is the worst game of Marco Polo ever. Where are you?"

"Sunroom."

I wrinkle my nose. "We have a sunroom?"

"That's the problem!" I follow the sound of Zane's voice through the living room to a set of French doors. There's been a curtain over the glass since we moved in, but it's pulled back now, revealing a—

"Sunroom!" I spin in a circle, gaping at the sunlight streaming through the windows onto warm-flecked tiles. "I thought those doors went to the garage or something. How did I not know this was here?"

Probably because I've been too busy scaling Mount Neverending Clothes. I haven't done much exploring. Plus, by the looks of it, this little room wouldn't be visible from the front of the house. And the wooden trellis along the patio blocks the view of this room from the backyard.

"The doors have been locked since we moved in. I just found the key."

Zane is wearing his work clothes—a pair of old jeans with a fraying hem and a dark t-shirt—and he still looks like he's ready for the fine people at *GQ* to show up any second for a photoshoot. He's sitting on a pristine-looking wicker couch, a frown tugging on the corners of his mouth.

It's the same frown he wore the three different times the people from the security system company came out to problem solve why our system keeps failing to arm.

"Someone looks glum." I walk over to him, stopping between his spread legs. "Is it the security system again?"

"No. It's that I just found a new room in the house."

I look around and wait for him to elaborate, but he doesn't. "You're going to have to explain this to me real slow because I'm not following. This room is incredible. I might live out here."

I can already picture fairy lights hanging around the edge of the room, candles glowing on the table in the center. I could curl up on the couch with a book.

"It is incredible. We'll get a lot of use out of it," he admits. "The trouble is, we're going to be late."

I look at my bare wrist even though I've never worn a watch a day in my life. "No, we have hours until we need to leave for the volunteering event. Aiden is still at school."

This volunteering opportunity is the first team/family event that Zane has invited me to as a newly-minted member of his actual family. I've met everyone on the team before, but I still want to make a good first impression as Zane's wife, even if we aren't technically announcing that to the press just yet. Being late is not an option.

"Hours?" His hands slide up my thighs, curling around my ass under my sundress. "Oh, then everything is fine."

I let out a breathless laugh. "The stress of the last week is catching up to you. You're not making any sense."

"Then let me make myself clear." Suddenly, he pulls me onto his lap. My knees settle on either side of his hips. "As you know, I've been on a tireless crusade to fuck you in every room of our new house. After finally catching you in the laundry room last night—"

"*Attacking* me in the laundry room last night." I kiss his cheek and reposition, noticing the hard bulge between his legs for the first time. "I was trying to put a load in the washer and you threw me on top of the dryer like an animal."

"—I thought I'd christened every room, but now, here's a whole new room that I haven't touched you in."

Understanding dawns, and I start to scrabble away from him. "Zane, we can't. Aiden gets out of school in an hour and I have unpacking to do!"

He loops a strong arm around my waist, jerking me back against him. Already, the friction is devastating. "Some things are more important than unpacking, Mira. We have to make this house a home somehow."

"With our *things!*" I laugh, trying and failing to fight off his grabby hands. "We make it a home by *getting rid of the cardboard boxes.*"

He nuzzles his stubbly face into my neck while his hands slide higher and higher under my dress. "Agree to disagree. How about we do it my way first… and then one more time, just to be safe. *Then* we can do it your way."

There's no point arguing. Mostly because I don't want to.

I sink against him and we christen the wicker couch.

And the tile floor.

And one window that now needs a good cleaning before anyone comes over and sees my handprints on the glass.

Zane kisses me on the cheek, agreeing to disagree yet again. "I like the handprints. They make the place look lived in. It adds character."

Against all odds, we make it to the volunteering event with plenty of time to spare.

On the way over, Zane told me that the team does these community events every few months—fundraisers for cancer research, donating books to underfunded public schools—but this event is a first.

A fact that seems to be upsetting Taylor more than anyone.

"Usually, I just take some shots of the guys huddling up with underprivileged kids or holding onto a big check, but what am I supposed to do with this?" She flings her arms at the rundown brick building with **Domestic Violence Shelter** painted on the side.

I actually teared up when Zane told me we'd be organizing donations for the shelter. Places like this fed and clothed me more nights than I can count, especially right after I ran away. Being here is a reminder of where I started and how far I've come.

"These people have powerful stories, Tay. The team is doing great work here."

"I know that, but I can't ask these people to sign waivers to be used for promotional material. Some of them are literally running for their lives," she hisses softly. "Plus, as nice as this is, it's a bummer. It doesn't roll off the tongue the way 'we're helping to cure cancer' does."

I snatch her phone out of her hand. "Stop thinking like Social Media Coordinator Barbie and just be here as Daniel's girlfriend. I don't think he invited you here to document anything."

She chews on her lip. "Yeah, but my dad will be pissed if I don't. As much as he wants to pretend these events are just to give back to the community, everything is about PR. Fans eat this shit up. Then they buy merch and season passes and flood his pockets with cash. It's the way of the world."

I want to disagree, but she isn't wrong. Even though this is supposed to be a family-only event, I notice a journalist making the rounds, asking questions. It's why Zane is keeping his distance from me: people know we're dating, but we don't want to hard launch our marriage outside of a domestic violence shelter. It's called "reading the room."

A woman who works for the shelter finds Taylor and me with our hands empty and quickly puts us to work sorting clothes so they can be washed by a line of industrial washing machines.

An hour ago, I would've said I never wanted to see another pile of clothes in my life, but I don't mind this. It feels good to help people the way I wish I'd been helped.

"This whole thing is boring, right?" A petulant groan cuts through our work and Carson Deluth flops on the pile I'm folding, chin resting on his fists. "I don't know who came up with this charity, but playing hockey with kids is way more fun."

Carson has been flashing smiles at me for the last hour. I know he's only doing it to get under Zane's skin, but I'm not in the mood to be a victim of his small dick energy. I hoped I'd make it through the entire event without actually having to talk to him. Seems my luck has run out.

Thankfully, where luck ends, Taylor Hall begins.

"Yes, because we shouldn't do anything for others unless it's fun," she sneers. "If I remember right, you weren't at the last hockey clinic, Carson. But I remember seeing pictures online from your ski trip. That looked *fun*."

God, I love her.

I bite back a smile and drop my head, pretending to be very focused on whether the hot pink shirt in my hands should go in the darks or the colors pile.

His eyes narrow, but his oily smile stays firmly in place. "There weren't enough volunteer slots for everyone on the team. I guess that's the benefit of this one: everyone can help *and* bring a puck bunny plus-one."

Taylor grins, but only I can see the fangs beneath the smile. "Weird, because I didn't see that you had a plus-one. Is she here or…?" Taylor makes a big show of looking around the warehouse before she gives him a pitying frown. "Don't worry, I'm sure you'll find someone desperate enough to ride your schlong for the next volunteer event."

Carson's smile finally slips, but as he opens his mouth to speak, a deep voice cuts in, sending a shiver straight to the core of me.

Zane keeps his eyes on me as he growls at Carson. "The rookies are unloading more boxes from the truck if you need something to do. Talking to my—to *the* women doesn't count."

Everyone from the wedding has been sworn to secrecy about our marriage until the news is officially announced. Apparently, that vow of silence extends to Carson Deluth.

"And what have you been doing?" Carson drawls.

Zane points to a pyramid of boxes twelve feet tall, and Carson's mouth twists in a frown. As he turns away, I hear him mumble, "Maybe these people should get a job and buy their own clothes. It's what the rest of us do."

Taylor hitches a thumb in the direction of the door he disappeared through. "That one doesn't have a charitable bone in his body. Just pure asshole, through and through." She gathers up a load of colors and waddles off to find an open washer.

Zane is still staring at me, his fists tight at his side. "What did he say to you?"

"Nothing. Really. Just being his usual charming self." Zane doesn't even crack a smile. I reach over the clothes between us and grab his hand. "Really, it's fine. He's an asshole and I can take care of myself."

Something flares in Zane's eyes, and I realize what I said. And how many times I've said it before.

Before I can say anything else, Coach Popov claps a hand on Zane's shoulder as he passes by. "This was a good idea, Whitaker."

Zane shrugs, looking unusually sheepish. "Thanks."

"What was a good idea?"

Coach Popov gestures around. "This."

I look back and forward between the two men, trying to put the pieces together. "This charity? Like, the domestic violence shelter?"

"Yep. Whitaker thought we should stretch our charity muscles and do something with some real-world impact. I think it's going well." Coach turns, taking in the hockey players and staff unloading boxes and washing clothes. "We might make this an annual thing."

Coach wanders off to help the people organizing crisis kits. I'm glad, because my eyes seem to be leaking.

"You didn't tell me this was your idea," I snap at Zane.

"You didn't ask."

"I didn't know I needed to ask." I shove his shoulder gently, but he catches my wrist and presses my hand to his heart. "I figured someone on staff chose the charities."

"Usually, they do. But I wanted to do something special." His blue eyes find mine. "I wanted to do something to honor you."

For years, I didn't think anyone could love me. My family didn't. Couldn't. Why would anyone else?

Then I met Taylor and thought, maybe, if I kept my past to myself, people could come to care about me. So long as it was easy, and I didn't make them work too hard for it.

But the fact that Zane Whitaker, my husband, not only loves me as I am now—healing and more or less whole—but also wants to honor the scared, hopeless, broken woman I was seven years ago?

I don't know what to do with that.

I open my mouth to try to say *something*, but I'm a blubbering mess.

Zane walks around the pile and pulls me to his chest. "I didn't plan to make you cry."

"I'm just so happy." I stretch onto my toes and give him a watery kiss. "I love you so much. And I'm so happy to be your wife."

42

ZANE

I didn't expect the wedding to change much in my life, but somehow, everything feels different.

Mira and I still live together, but we're in a house that we own.

We already had Aiden to take care of, but now, we're trying for more kids and talking about baby names while we lie in bed.

At the risk of sounding like some happy schmuck in a movie montage, my world is so much bigger now. There are so many possibilities—and Mira is in every single one of them.

It's a good fucking life.

"How's marriage treating you?"

I spin around, ready to tell Davis or one of my other idiot groomsmen that the news is still on the down low.

But instead, standing behind me is the very last person I want to see.

Carson fucking Deluth is wearing a smirk he has no right to. He leans in, speaking in a harsh whisper. "Sorry, was that supposed to be secret? You and Mira were just so cute at the charity event. She was *so happy* to be your wife. I thought it was public knowledge."

I run my tongue over my teeth. "It's rude to eavesdrop."

"It's also rude to cheat on your brand new wife."

I slam my locker closed and turn to face him fully, arms crossed. "What?"

"That's good." He circles a finger at my face. "That's a very believable frown. If you do this with Mira, she just might believe you haven't been fucking another woman for the last six months."

I can't help it, I laugh. "I think you've Googled my name one too many times, man. You're deep in the trashiest tabloids if you believe that."

"I don't need to believe it; I just need enough other people to. And since your past is checkered at best and I have a firsthand witness willing to go on the record—" He lifts his shoulders in a shrug. "Well, I like my chances. Let's put it that way."

Adrenaline is thrumming through my veins, but my body is oddly still. My heart rate is steady. My head is clear.

"Why?" I grit out.

"Because I deserve to be captain," he spits. "You've fooled a lot of people, but I know better. So does your assistant. Or your ex-assistant, I suppose. It was actually her idea to start the cheating scandal. Apparently, she wants to destroy your wife as much as I want to destroy you. We have that in common."

There are still people in the showers, but otherwise, Carson and I are alone. It's dangerous. I could kill him and no one would see a thing.

And fuck, do I want to kill him.

"Mira won't believe you or Hanna."

"Maybe. Maybe not." He seems relaxed for someone carrying out blackmail. "If you drop out of the race for captain, you won't have to put that theory to the test."

Again, I laugh. But it comes out sharp and bitter. "This is really about being captain?"

He ignores me, lifting his chin in challenge. "Between the cheating scandal and making the announcement that you're now a married man, reporters are going to be crawling all over you. It'll be bad press for the team. Coach would never let you become captain after that."

Carson is threatening my future career, but all I can hear is that he's sending the media my way. *Mira's way.*

I've finally carved out some peace and quiet for her, and he wants to shatter it with cameras and publicity. If Dante doesn't know where our new house is yet, he will once my face and a million ridiculous, scandalous headlines are plastered all over the internet.

He'll find her. He'll come for her.

I hear Mira's voice from the other night in my head. *I can take care of myself.*

I know she can. I also know she didn't mean it the way it sounded—she didn't mean that she doesn't want me to take care of her—but the words still stuck.

How many years are we going to have to be together before she realizes that *I* will take care of her? That she doesn't have to do it alone anymore?

I'm not sure, but that thought is the reason I don't waste time saying another word to Carson Deluth...

I just launch myself at him.

Carson yells as I slam into his chest, but the sound dies when the air rushes out of his lungs when I take him to the floor. My vision is red. I'm operating on some deep, animal level as I rear back and drive my fist into his stupid fucking face.

Again and again.

Carson gets a few shots in, mostly to my ribs and my chest. I grunt, but I don't slow down.

Not until hands grab me from behind.

"Whoa, Zane!" Jace is shouting in my ear, utilizing every decibel of his captain's voice. "Back off. Enough. Stop!"

Davis and Nathan are picking Carson up off the floor, but I'm still lunging for him. I can't stop. Not when he's threatening my family.

Not when he's coming after what is mine.

Jace spins around to face me and plants both hands on my chest. "Zane, look at—*Look at me!*"

Finally, I tear my eyes from Carson's bloody nose and his split lip. Jace's face is red, but his eyes are pleading.

"Stop," he growls. "Don't do this."

"He threatened Mira!" I spit loud enough that my voice echoes off the stone walls. "He came for my family because he wants to be the fucking captain. How—" I lean around Jace, talking only to Carson now. "How do you not realize I'm out of the running for captain? I have been since I walked out of this locker room before we played the Firebirds. If you haven't put that together, maybe you're too stupid to be captain."

A few whispers echo through the locker room. It's the first time I've said out loud what everyone has been thinking.

I'm not going to be captain.

But I don't care.

"I don't regret leaving, by the way. I don't regret it because, as much as I love this team, I'll do anything to protect my family. From the media, from people who want to hurt them, or from fuckheads like you—"

I lunge again, but Jace pins me against the locker. "Zane, seriously. Enough."

I fight him for a second before I sag back, hands raised. "I'm done. I'm done. He isn't worth it."

Jace doesn't buy it, though, and I don't blame him. He keeps his hands on my chest as the rest of the team starts to file in like a bunch of rubberneckers here to see an accident.

But I don't care about any of them. I jab a finger at Carson as he swipes his wrist over his bloody lip. "You're a piece of shit, Deluth. You're shady and you don't give a fuck about anyone but yourself. I can put up with your bullshit—until you start fucking with my family. Don't ever," I spit, leaning over Jace's shoulder to get as close to Carson's face as I can, "threaten my family again, or I'll end you."

"That's enough." Coach is standing in his doorway, leaning against the frame. I'm not sure when he got here, but he looks as tired of this shit as I am. "Show's over. Clear out and go home."

Carson's face flames red. He dips his head as he passes the office door. "Sorry, Coach."

Maybe I'm still high on adrenaline, but I swear Coach's eyes narrow.

I may not be in the running for captain—but after this little stunt, Carson might not be, either.

43

MIRA

The last few weeks have been a dream, but Dante was always lingering on the periphery. Whether I wanted to acknowledge it or not, he was a shadow in the picture, a dark cloud over the party.

Now, standing in a sea of screaming people, he's the entire picture. I can't look anywhere without thinking about him sitting out there somewhere.

Watching me.

Waiting.

"Do you see him?" Taylor asks.

I stop my scan of the stands and whirl towards her. "What? Who?"

There's no way I said what I was thinking out loud, but maybe I'm not playing off my paranoia as well as I think I am. Maybe it's obvious I'm one loud noise away from dropping to the deck and rocking in the fetal position.

This is the first time I've been in a public space since before the car accident. I haven't even been going to kickboxing, not that I had a lot of time for working out classes with wedding planning and unpacking going on. But still, I should've thought this through. I shouldn't have let Aiden guilt me into coming with his puppy dog eyes and his pouty lower lip.

"Who do you think? Your hubby," she whispers low enough so no one else can hear. She points to the ice, where Zane is waving.

The girls in front of us think he's waving at them and scream, but I lift Aiden over their heads and point out Zane.

"Daddy!" He throws both arms over his head, waving them so wildly that it actually sparks an impromptu wave from the crowd.

The entire arena moves as one and we stand up and hurl our arms in the air three times before it finally dies out.

"I did that!" Aiden beams, trying to sit down, but bouncing in his seat from pure excitement. "Everyone did what I was doing!"

As if Aiden needs even more reason to crawl out of his skin, Taylor hands him a family-sized box of candy that she nabbed from the owner's box behind us.

The box we were supposed to sit in until Aiden complained that he couldn't see anything from there and we were too far away.

The box where Evan is stationed, currently watching me like a hawk... if a hawk's goal was to protect me from harm, not eat me.

A buzzer sounds and the players skate out onto the ice. Taylor shakes her head. "Wow. Zane is starting."

"Why do you sound surprised?"

"Why do you not?" She arches a brow. "I figured Popov would bench him after what happened in the locker room the other day."

"What happened?"

"Oh… did he not tell you?" Taylor winces. "Maybe I shouldn't, either. I don't want to cause trouble in paradise."

I grab her arm, digging my nails in deep. "You love causing trouble. Now, open that big mouth of yours, Taylor, or I'll dive in and drag the truth out of you."

"Why am I both terrified and turned-on right now?" She pries her arm out of my grip. "Daniel came home from work the other day and said Carson and Zane got into it in the locker room. Something about Carson threatening you to get Zane to back out of being captain." She shrugs, like I'm not hanging onto every single detail. "I don't know, but it sounded intense. And kind of hot. People would pay good money online for any cell phone footage, but Daniel swears there isn't any."

"Carson threatened me?" I shake my head. Surely Zane would've told me about that.

Unless he's trying to protect me.

I saw his face the other night when I told him I could take care of myself. Zane wants to take care of me, but keeping me in the dark isn't the way. If he didn't tell me about Carson's threat, what else has he been keeping from me?

"Classic Carson stuff." Taylor dismisses the whole thing with a wave of her hand. "He's an asshole and I'm glad someone finally broke his nose."

"Zane broke his nose?!"

She shrugs. "That's what Daniel said, but he can be dramatic sometimes."

Zane broke someone's nose at work and didn't say a word. I had no idea. *What other signs have I missed?*

I thought Dante might have slunk back to whatever hole he crawled out of after he was caught on camera at the gym, but the truth might be that I'm not on the receiving end of information anymore and I'm too cushy in my brand new life to realize I'm in danger.

I glance at the young girls in front of us and the family off to our right. I look for a familiar head of dark hair or a red laser sniper dot aimed right at my chest.

When the puck drops and the crowd roars, I jolt and instinctively reach for Aiden's shoulder.

"Ow," he complains, frowning down at the gummy candies he dropped on the ground.

"Sorry, A," I mumble.

The players on the ice are little more than streaks in my vision. My chest is tight, so heavy I can't lift it to inhale fully. I'm surviving on tiny sips of air.

I just need to make it through the first period and then we can go back to the box. Or I'll pretend to be sick and we can leave.

Another roar moves through the crowd, and I shrink in my seat like a turtle hiding in its shell.

I try to keep my eyes on Zane—nothing can go too horribly wrong when he's here—but I have a hard time tracking him in the sea of red. So I shift my gaze to the back of the heads in front of us, but I keep imagining one of them turning around.

My brother's face grinning at me.

I spin around, looking for the nearest exit in case of an emergency and the realization that there are *so many* people sitting behind me—people I don't know; people I can't see—makes my chest clench even tighter.

The crowd roars again and I yelp. Actually yelp.

"That's your man!" Taylor grabs my arm and waves it in the air, and I think I'm going to be sick.

As she drops my arm and it slaps against my side, someone touches my shoulder.

I whip around so fast, my purse smacks the girl in front of us in the back of the head. She complains and Taylor apologizes, but I'm looking up at Evan. And for the first time in I-don't-even-know-how-many minutes, I take a breath.

"Are you okay?" he asks, voice low. The people behind him are leaning around him, whining about their view being compromised by a walking, talking giant. "You look nervous."

I can't even answer. All I can do is pinch my lips together and shake my head.

"Come on."

Evan helps me out of my chair and whispers something to Taylor. She gathers up Aiden and his candy and follows after us.

My heart races as we mount the stairs, as people in the stands turn to look at us, confused. Maybe they recognize me from the paparazzi pictures. Or they might just be annoyed at the people blocking their view during the game.

Either way, I don't relax until we're in the box and the door is closed.

"Shit, Mimi." Taylor rubs my arm. "You should've told me you weren't doing well. We could've come up here."

"I thought I—" I blow out a harsh breath, ignoring the tremble in my voice. "I thought I could take care of it on my own. I guess I was wrong."

While we wait for the players to file out of the locker room, Evan doesn't leave my side. He's my shadow, and I want to hug him. I want to give him a raise. I want to send him on an all-expenses-paid trip to Aruba... except then he'd leave my side, so I scrap that idea and decide to talk to Zane about giving him a raise.

"Aiden is with Jemma in the box," he reminds me softly. "They aren't supposed to leave until I go back to escort them."

"Thank you, Evan. Really. For everything. I was losing it back there and—"

"It's my job." His voice is curt, but he presses a friendly hand to the back of my shoulder, steadying me.

The players start filing out and the panicked part of my brain is convinced Zane won't be with them. Every situation has only one outcome and it's the worst-case scenario.

While I was freaking out, Dante got into the locker room and is holding Zane—

Then Zane turns the corner with damp hair and a wide grin, and I want to collapse. From relief and exhaustion. It's tiring being this doom-and-gloom about everything.

When he snags me off the wall and loops his arm around my shoulders, I sink against his side.

"You left your seat."

I feel him looking at me, but I can't bring myself to look at him. As soon as I do, he'll see exactly how messed up I am.

"We wanted to go to the box instead."

"Before the game, Aiden couldn't stop talking about how excited he was to be in the crowd." Zane shakes hands as we pass people, but his arm never leaves my shoulders.

"It was crowded."

"As most crowds are," Zane agrees. "You agreed to sit with him down there. What changed?"

"Nothing. I'm—"

Suddenly, his lips are against the shell of my ear. "Don't lie to me, Mira."

"*Lies.* Let's talk about lies," I snort. "Have there been any fistfights you'd like to tell me about?"

We're at the end of the hall now, well beyond the people waiting in the tunnel, and Zane grabs my arm. He turns me into him gently. "You're mad at me?"

It would be easy to funnel everything I'm feeling into a

simple emotion like anger, but it's way more mixed up than that. I press my fists into my eyes. "No, I'm not. I'm sorry."

"Don't be sorry. Tell me what's going on."

I drop my hands and finally meet his eyes. "I think I need to go to therapy."

He searches my face, and just like I suspected, every thought in my head is laid bare in front of him.

"This is about Dante," he guesses.

"I thought I could handle the crowd because the last couple weeks have been fine, but I...I couldn't."

My hands are shaking.

I'm a married woman now. I have a house and a little boy who is as good as my son as far as I'm concerned—but some part of me will always be that terrified little girl hiding in her closet. I'll always be shaking and trembling, looking over my shoulder to make sure no one is there waiting to hurt me.

I clench my teeth to keep my chin from wobbling. "I got cocky. I've been locked away with you and Aiden for the last couple weeks, and I thought—I thought I could—"

"Take care of yourself?" Zane offers.

I could grind my molars to dust right now and it wouldn't matter. My chin wobbles.

Before I can say anything, Zane pulls me against his chest. "You don't *have* to take care of yourself, Mira. That's why I'm here. It's why I hired Evan. It's why Taylor was sitting next to you and Owen was in the row behind."

"He was?"

Zane nods, kissing my temple. "I would never leave you there alone."

"I felt like I was going to die," I breathe. "I felt like I was falling apart. Aiden was next to me, and I could barely focus. I felt like I was putting him in danger, and I hated it."

"Then what I'm doing isn't enough."

I jerk back. "No. No, that isn't—"

He shushes me gently. "I'm tough, but even I can't protect you from what's inside your own head, Mira. If you think therapy will help, then I'll get you the best fucking therapist this side of the equator."

The storm in my chest eases and I press my cheek to the space just above his heart. "Thank you."

"Thank *you*," he echoes back, "for wanting to be the best version of yourself. Not just for you, but for our family, too. We need that. All of us do."

44

MIRA

Daniel frowns as he flips through the wedding pictures.

"What's wrong now?" I ask with a frown of my own.

He plops the album in the middle of our cafe table and grabs his coffee. "Nothing. I just still think a scrapbook would have been a better idea. We could have put little descriptions with the pictures. *'Here's everything you've missed since you abandoned your son.'*"

I roll my eyes. "The goal here is to build a bridge between Zane and his parents. I don't think accusing them of abandonment sends the right message."

"Suit yourself. The pictures are fine, but they lack the judgment I think his parents have earned."

Daniel was fully supportive of sending a letter to Zane's parents when he thought I was going to drag them for not supporting Zane in his sobriety or being around to meet their new grandson and daughter-in-law. I may or may not have kept the ruse going just long enough to get their address from him before I confessed the truth.

Now, he's my reluctant chaperone for this errand while Evan watches us from some parking space nearby.

"The way Zane explains it, the situation was complicated. He hurt them over and over again. They thought cutting him off was the best thing for him."

"Yeah, to help him get sober," Daniel argues. "I don't know if you've looked around recently, but Zane is sober! He's doing amazing."

"Which these pictures will prove!" I fan the photos out in front of us. "Now, stop being a butthead and help me pick an appropriate first kiss photo."

"Impossible. You two were tongue-fucking before God and your gathered guests."

"Taylor is rubbing off on you," I accuse. "And that is *not* a compliment."

"All I'm saying is, skip the first kiss photo unless you want Zane's parents to think he's taken up a side gig in public softcore porn."

I roll my eyes again, but Daniel has a point. I might hide the first kiss photos in my bedside drawer and only pull them out once every blue moon. Maybe on nights Zane is traveling for work and I'm alone… and lonely.

My cheeks flush as I slide the photos into my purse. "Fine. No first kiss photos. Now, we need to go through all of these pictures and get rid of every picture with a champagne bottle or someone holding champagne. Or something that looks like champagne. Or pictures where someone looks like they could possibly be drunk."

Daniel sets the entire stack aside. "You better start looking at stock photos online and get really good at Photoshop, because all of these pictures are out."

Getting rid of any picture with alcohol in it actually does get rid of most of the reception photos, but I end up with a healthy stack of ceremony photos inside a manila envelope, on which I write Zane's parent's address in my best handwriting.

"Here you go." I hold the envelope out to Daniel.

He stares at it like it's a dead frog. "What am I doing with that?"

I point to the USPS collection box at the end of the street.

He immediately starts shaking his head. "When I signed up to come with you today, the job was described to me as 'intimidating muscle with a side of eating pastries.' This is a job for an errand boy."

"Yeah, well my actual muscle—" I point to Evan's hulking frame in the car three spaces away. "—told me I can't leave this seat unless it's to get in his car, so you have to do it for me."

Grimacing, Daniel snatches the envelope out of my hand and mumbles something about how marriage is going to my head, but all I feel is a spark in my chest.

This is what it feels like to have friends.

People I can count on. People who will stick around even when I'm being my most annoying self.

I sip on my chai latte and watch Daniel walk down the street to the post box.

The coffee shop is tucked on the side of a narrow strip of businesses. We're out of view of the main road and the only people pulling into the lot are here for the coffee shop or an elderly woman coming for a glass bead workshop at the art studio next door.

So, when a dark car with deeply-tinted windows circles the lot once and then again, passing by the only empty spaces and making their way closer to me, I notice.

Evan does, too.

Through the windshield, I see him sit up. He reaches for the volume knob in the car. He checks his mirrors.

I know he's seeing the same thing I am. I can tell he's worried.

It's better *and* worse that way. This is the one situation where I'd rather be crazy than right.

The car rounds the corner, moving closer to the building, and my heart is a wild thing in my chest. Nervous energy zips through my body. Every part of me wants to duck and run for the hills.

It's just a car, I tell myself. *Other humans exist in the world. They're not all out to get you.*

The car rolls to a slow stop along the curb. In my peripherals, I see Evan's door open. But he's too far away. He can't see what I'm seeing.

The flick of dark hair.

A flash of white teeth.

The interior of the car is dark—so dark I can barely see through to the driver's side—but that doesn't change the fact that I know exactly who I'm looking at.

For years, I've been running from him, but now, all I can do is sit here. Wait.

Tremble.

"Who was that?" Evan asks.

The car slithers away along the curb, and I'm afraid to move in case he circles back.

Evan pulls out his phone and points it at the car. It takes me a second to realize he's taking a picture of the license plate.

Suddenly, the car stops, and I wait for the flash of the reverse lights. *He's going to come back and finish me off.*

But it's Daniel who moves.

It happens fast. Daniel turns his head, smiles at the person inside the car. He takes one step and then another.

Desperation overrides my panic, and I croak out. "Dante."

Evan tenses. "What?"

"I-it's Dante. It's—" I regain control of my body all at once and jump up, my chair tipping over behind me. The table rattles and my chai latte goes flying. "Daniel!"

Daniel turns towards the sound of his name just as Evan grabs my arm, blocking my view.

I don't know what he's doing; all I know is he's in my way. I try to shake him off, squirming to get past him. "Daniel," I gasp. "You need to help Daniel!"

Evan starts to move me towards the coffee shop door. "You're my priority. I need to get you somewhere safe."

"Daniel!" I scream again.

It doesn't matter. The car is already screeching away. I fight and claw against Evan's hold, but he doesn't budge. In the end, that doesn't matter, either.

Daniel appears over Evan's shoulder. "What the fuck was that about?"

Relief overwhelms me. Tears prick my eyes and I shove past Evan and wrap my arms around Daniel. "Are you okay?"

Dante was so close. He could have—

I can't let my mind go there. Can't think about how helpless I was to do anything at all.

"Are *you* okay?" he asks. "Why were you screaming?"

"That car—" I point at the empty space where Dante was idling a second ago. The car is gone. I don't even know which direction he went. "That car stopped and you—"

"I gave him directions," Daniel finishes. "He was lost."

Maybe I am crazy.

I shake my head. "No. I *saw* him. He smiled at me."

"What did he look like?" Evan is sending off texts rapid-fire. I don't know who he's texting until my phone rings.

It's Zane. I know it before I even check.

I bring the phone to my ear, not able to manage more than a whisper. "Hello?"

"Where are you?" Zane growls. I hear movement on his side of the line. I'm sure he's leaving work right now, already heading to where I am. "Are you safe?"

Yes.

No.

Define "safe."

"It was Dante." I'm trying to convince myself as well as him. Maybe I'm making it up. Maybe I've lost my mind. "I saw him, Zane."

Daniel curses. "Your brother? Are you sure?"

Before I can answer, Evan turns to Daniel. "What did he say to you?"

"He asked for directions. He asked where— *Fuck.*" Daniel bites his lip and turns to me, an apology in his eyes. "He asked for directions to Paradise Valley."

"Mira?" Zane snarls. "Are. You. Safe?"

"No." I blink and a tear rolls down my cheek. "He found me."

45

ZANE

My phone buzzes on the nightstand, pulling me from the liminal land of half-sleep I've been wandering through all night. I don't know what time it is, but it's definitely too fucking early for my alarm. The sun isn't even up.

The buzzing stops, and my eyes slip gratefully closed. Mira's body is warm against my side, and I want to stay here as long as I can. The panic I felt when Evan texted me yesterday isn't something I ever want to experience again.

As she laid awake last night, crying and pouring out all of the messy thoughts in her head, I wasn't sure if I was holding her for her or for me. Probably both.

It didn't help as much as I would've liked.

My phone vibrates again. And again. By the time I slip away from her and grab it, my notifications are like a firehose.

I hiss against the bright screen as a text from Daniel appears, almost blinding me. *Is the marriage embargo lifted?* He follows up with a link to a news article.

BABY ZADDY: PHOENIX ANGELS' ZANE WHITAKER TAKES A BRIDE.

And another.

FROM HOCKEY HUNK TO HOCKEY HUSBAND: CAN ZANE WHITAKER STAY TRUE?

No one keeps their private life private quite like star of the Phoenix Angels, Zane Whitaker. One Twitter account with an associated true-crime style podcast exists purely to track down Zane Whitaker's conquests because the man himself refuses to kiss and tell. A few months ago, in a bombshell reveal, the world found out that Zaddy Zane became a real-life Daddy... **FOUR YEARS AGO!** *Given how tightly his lips are sealed, is it any wonder he skipped straight over announcing his engagement and had a secret wedding? Well, fear not—we have all the details of his special day and the woman he has pledged his heart to.*

The article is replete with anonymous quotes from women I've supposedly slept with in the last four years. One of them claims I flew her from Europe on my private jet for a single hookup. As if I'd ever be that desperate.

The rabbit hole of gossip featuring me is endless. For every trashy article, there are three dozen more, as well as a dozen email requests from journalists looking for an interview.

There's exactly one email I actually open. *Releasing the wedding announcement might be too little too late, but give me the go and I'll post it. - Hollis*

I should've known punching Carson in the face wasn't going to change his mind. He's like poison ivy—if I don't rip him out by the root, he'll just keep coming back.

I glance over my shoulder and, miraculously, Mira is still asleep. Her cheek is pillowed on her arm and she's breathing, deep and even.

I held her last night and promised I'd protect her. I swore I wouldn't let Dante hurt her, and I meant it. I won't. Not physically.

But there are other ways to hurt someone. Even I can't protect her from all of them.

I slip out of bed and down the hall. Sleep isn't happening, that's for damn sure.

I'm making the world's strongest pot of coffee when Evan texts. *I'm outside. Thought you might need backup this morning.*

I unarm the security system and crack the front door. Thirty seconds later, Evan is shuffling into the kitchen, hands in his pockets.

"The road outside was clear," he says by way of hello. "No photogs or journalists yet."

It won't be long, though. Barely two weeks of wedded bliss, and now, we're going to have nosy assholes banging on our front gate from sunup to sundown.

"I didn't ask you to report this morning."

He shrugs. "It felt important. Especially after yesterday."

Evan and Daniel were practically carrying Mira inside when they got back to the house. She kept telling me she was fine, but her face was pale and she was shaking. It took most of the night for the tremors in her hands to go away.

"Did you see him?"

Evan shakes his head. "No. The windows were tinted. Daniel couldn't identify him, either, but Mira was positive it was Dante."

I wish even a small part of me doubted her. I want to think this is all a misunderstanding and Dante isn't really hunting her down—but I've clawed my way out of enough trenches to know hoping for the best doesn't get you very far.

"Does your P.I. know anything?"

I clench my teeth. "With how much I'm paying him, he should. He can't pin Dante down. The fucker is like a ghost."

"I was hoping maybe I could corroborate my information with what the P.I. had just to make sure it's legit, but—"

"What information?"

Evan slides his phone across the island to me. "I didn't recognize the car from yesterday, but I took a picture of the plates. It's the same license plate number that was on the car outside of the gym. And the car that crashed into us."

If I had been doubting Mira, there wouldn't be any room for it now.

"So it was him."

Evan nods. "Unless she has more than one assassin coming after her."

"He's not an *assassin*," I snarl. The word is far too official for whatever revenge fantasy Dante is indulging. "He isn't going to touch her."

We look at each other in silent understanding. No one is going to touch my wife. Not now, not ever.

"I'm going to do everything I can to protect her, but..." Evan sighs and leans across the island. "Listen, I don't want to overstep, but I think Mira should see somebody. A professional. I've been in this situation before. I've known people who have had to live scared for years on end... It can really fuck with your head."

The thought that I can't be everything Mira needs bristles, but Evan is right. "She wants to see a therapist. I think it's a good idea, but..."

"Who can you trust?" he finishes for me. It's half-question, half-sad inevitability.

I drag a hand over the back of my neck. "Right now? No one."

Evan leaves to post up outside, and I don't tell him not to. It'll be nice to have another layer of protection between the outside world and my family.

As soon as Mira is awake, I tell her about the information leak.

"We knew this was coming, I guess." There are dark circles under her eyes, and I wish I could whisk her away from all of this.

Maybe a honeymoon wasn't such a bad idea, after all. At least we'd be out of the city.

"As soon as Carson made that threat, I should've told Hollis to release the announcement," I admit. "I naively hoped Carson would keep his fucking mouth shut. Or that he would finally piss someone off enough to get himself killed."

She turns and reaches for my face. Her hand is cold when she cups my cheek. "Hope isn't naive, Zane. It's all we have."

That's not quite true. When I'm holding her, I have everything.

Those words are on the tip of my tongue when the doorbell rings.

Mira stiffens, but I press a kiss to the center of her palm. "It's probably Evan."

"Evan is here?"

"He was worried about you. It's just a precaution."

I can see through the glass around the door that it's Evan on the porch, but his face is obscured by a massive bouquet of red and white flowers.

"What in the hell are these?" I open the door wide and usher him inside.

Mira gasps. "Pretty."

"*Heavy*," Evan corrects. He places the vase awkwardly on the entryway table.

"Are they for the wedding?" Mira asks. "Who are they from?"

Evan wipes his damp hands on his jeans. "I didn't ask. A delivery driver dropped them at the end of the driveway. I don't know if there's an envelope or not."

"It's probably from a news outlet," I grumble. "They're always pulling shit like this, trying to sweeten me up for an interview."

"Next time, ask for donuts. Preferably cream-fi—" Mira's voice drops off at the same time a small card falls to the floor.

Her face is pale, her mouth open in a wordless cry for help.

"Mira?"

She doesn't answer. She's shaking, tears gathering on her eyelashes.

I snatch the card off the floor and read the scratchy handwriting inside.

Congrats on the wedding, little sister. Sorry I missed it. I'll be there for the next big thing, I promise. —Dante

46

MIRA

I run my finger along the bottom edge of the passenger window. I wonder how much force it would take to shatter it.

More strength than I have, I think. Especially with how many weeks it's been since I've so much as looked at my kickboxing gloves, let alone put them on.

"Nice day out," Evan says next to me, scrambling for anything to talk about other than the obvious. "Sunny."

"Is this glass bulletproof?" I ask.

He sighs. "So much for my attempt at distraction."

I arch a brow. "Talking about the weather was your go-to distraction technique?"

"My job title is 'bodyguard.' Idle chit-chat isn't in the job description."

"So, let's skip the chit-chat then. Tell me—" I rap my knuckles on the window. "—are these bulletproof?"

He hesitates for a beat too long before he relents. "Yes, but you're supposed to be thinking about something else. 'Healthy diversions,' right? That's what the therapist said."

"The therapist is a hack. What kind of professional tells someone who is being hunted for sport to destress with 'long walks?'" I snort. "I'll be sure to savor my trips from the bedroom to the kitchen, since I can't leave the freaking house!"

It's not like I even want to. As soon as the bouquet from my brother arrived, our sanctuary in Paradise Valley went on lockdown like Fort Knox.

Sitting in this bulletproof Popemobile is the closest I've come to fresh air in a week. Even my therapist's office has an underground parking garage so I can go straight from the lot to an elevator that takes me to her floor. I'm growing pale like a mole person.

"Your case is... unique. Helping you would be a steep learning curve for any therapist."

I know he's right. In all honesty, I liked Dr. Navarro. She's smart and empathetic. She listened to my story of patricide and woe without any outward judgment. Plus, the breathing exercises she recommended helped me navigate my way out of a panic attack this morning when I woke up and Zane wasn't in bed next to me.

"Yeah, well," I grumble, "if I launch myself through the car door when Aiden's teacher opens it, don't mind me. It's just the imprisoned person's response to finally experiencing fresh air."

We're a few minutes later than normal to get Aiden since we

came from the therapist's office, but there's still a healthy line of cars in the pickup lane.

Zane and Evan both thought I could tag along for this errand without anything too traumatic happening. Though, last time I came to pickup, one of the "Bouncy Hair Moms," as Jemma likes to call them, invited me to a "Wine & Whine Night" at her house. Apparently, the idea is to get drunk and complain about our children and spouses. I politely declined, because my frontal lobe is still intact.

Now, I'm desperate enough for social interaction that I might take her up on it.

But as we pull through the roundabout, I forget all about the Bouncy Hair Moms. Aiden is nowhere in sight. I see Jalen standing with a few other boys in a group by the doors, but Aiden's blonde head isn't there.

"Where is he?"

Evan doesn't answer. His brows are pinched as he flashes our family's badge through the window to the teacher on duty. She holds up a finger before she disappears into the building.

"Is this normal?" I ask. Evan's jaw flexes in a way that tells me it's not. "He must be waiting inside."

"That isn't what I asked."

Then I see Aiden through the glass, smiling and chatting to the teacher, and the tension in my chest evaporates. I blow out a ragged breath that would disappoint Dr. Navarro, but I don't care.

Aiden is okay. That's all that matters.

The teacher opens the car door and helps Aiden into the

backseat. "Sorry about that. It's school protocol to keep a student inside after an unsuccessful pickup attempt."

I smile and start to wave her off, ready to forgive anything, since I'm beyond relieved and this is the first conversation that I'm not paying for in a week.

Then I hear her.

Actually hear her.

"'Unsuccessful pickup attempt'? What does that mean?"

"His uncle." She smiles, her head tipping to the side like a dog hearing a high-pitched noise. "He said he'd call you and clear it all up. He wasn't on the list."

I inhale, count to four.

Exhale, count to seven.

But I think I'm counting too fast. And I'm not actually sure I'm breathing.

"Aiden doesn't have an uncle," I rasp.

"But he had your same beautiful dark hair. He must be related to you." The woman smiles, but there's an edge of confusion now. "Uncle Dante...?"

The principal's office is dark. She pulled the blinds once we were inside so no one from the pickup line could look in and see us. The last thing I need is the moms chatting about our drama at their next Whine Night.

Aiden is playing on a school tablet in the corner while Evan talks with the security team, reviewing footage.

Everyone else has a job. But I'm just numb.

Until I hear Zane's voice in the hallway.

"Where is my family?" His voice is a deep rumble. I expect the ground to open up and swallow us all.

"Mr. Whitaker." The receptionist sounds terrified. I don't blame her. "Your wife is—"

"Here." I don't remember standing up and moving across the room, but I'm in the doorway now. My legs shake, and I have to lean against the frame to stay standing.

Zane is almost glowing. I swear there's a dark aura around him. Some avenging angel here to save the day.

But his fury softens when he sees me. "Mira."

He crosses the room and folds me in his arms. I have no idea how many people are watching us, but I'm too far gone to care.

"I'm sorry," I gasp against his chest. "I'm so—This is my fault. I'm sorry."

It hits me all at once. How close Dante got. How any number of tiny things could have gone differently so my brother could have left with Aiden. With my son.

My stomach twists and my chest aches. It feels like I'm being wrung through a pasta maker.

Zane's chest hitches to say something, but Aiden's giggle interrupts him.

He still hasn't seen his dad yet. Aiden is sitting in the corner of the office with headphones on. He has no clue how much danger he was in. He has no idea that he has become the center of my world—and how, because of that, he's never been in more danger.

I hope he never has to find out.

Zane takes my hand and leads me back into the receptionist's office. He tosses a half-formed question her way and she points us to a dark room on the other side of the office. *"Counseling Space"* is on a plaque next to the door.

Zane doesn't bother turning on the light as he closes the door behind us and pulls me against his chest. His hand cradles the back of my head. His lips are soft against my ear.

"None of this is your fault, Mira. None of it."

I want to believe him so badly, but I shake my head. "Dante wants to hurt me. He went after Aiden because I love him. He did this because I've been hiding from him."

Zane pulls back, his strong hands bracketing my cheeks. His eyes are as bright as the sky outside. I want to lie down and get lost in them.

"Dante did this because he's fucked in the head," Zane spits in disgust. "Nothing he has done or will do is any reflection on you, Mira. Do you hear me?" I try to look down at the greige carpet, but Zane grips my chin and forces me to look at him. "Do you *hear* me?"

"I hear you." My voice wavers. His face blurs as tears fill my eyes. "… but I don't believe you."

His jaw ticks, and I don't realize we're moving until my back is against the wall. He pins me in place and looks at me like he's afraid I'll disappear.

"I love you," he growls. "Do you believe that?"

There's not a single doubt in my mind. "Yes."

"I will do anything—fucking *anything*—to keep you safe. Do you believe that?"

Again: "Yes."

"I would never put Aiden at risk. Do you believe that?"

"Of course I do." I hold his hand. "We'd both do anything to protect him."

Including leave. Those words hang unspoken. If Zane registers they're there, he blows right on past them, smoothing my hair away from my face.

"Then believe me when I tell you I don't blame you for a thing, Mira. Believe me when I tell you that none of this is your fault, and believe me when I say I'm not going to stop until you're finally free from your past."

I fist my hand in his shirt. Dr. Navarro should hear about the effect being close to Zane has on me. Forget mindful breathing. Just touching him—feeling his heartbeat under my palm—settles something wild inside of me.

"I don't want you to sacrifice anything for me, Zane. Especially n-not—" I hiccup and swallow down a cry. "Especially not your son."

He kisses my cheeks to take my tears away. "Nothing is going to happen to Aiden. I'm going to keep him safe, just like I'm going to keep you safe." He grabs my hand, turning it over to run his thumb along the diamond on my finger. "You belong to me now, Mira. You have my ring and my last name and my protection. I will never let anyone hurt you." He kisses my knuckle and looks up at me. "Do you believe that? Do you believe in me?"

I nod. It's easy this time. "More than I've ever believed in anything."

47

ZANE

When I went to get dressed twenty minutes ago, Daniel and Taylor were hunched over the island, scrolling through an endless list of takeout options for dinner.

As I make my way back to the kitchen, not much has changed.

"Pizza," Daniel argues. "Children love pizza."

"Which explains why *you* love it so much." Taylor hip-checks him out of the way and snatches the phone. "If I have to watch *Teenage Mutant Ninja Turtles* tonight, I'm doing it with egg rolls. End of story."

I round the corner into the kitchen, adjusting my cufflinks. "You two really don't have to do this. If you want to go to the ceremony—"

"As a member of the team staff, I had to vote on who got which award and, spoiler alert: none of them were for me." Daniel arches a brow that is enough of an explanation. In case it isn't, he adds, "Plus, everyone is still pissy about us not making the playoffs. It's a negative energy."

"Says the man who didn't have to sit and watch tape from that game for the last two days," I grumble.

We lost to the St. Louis Mules even though their star player spent half the game in the penalty box for absolutely wrecking Davis and Carson. Simply put, they outplayed us. Jace tried to give a speech after the game to inspire some hope for next season, but the guys didn't want to hear it.

I couldn't even blame them. My head was already at home with Mira and Aiden.

"You could go just to get dressed up and for the free drinks," I suggest.

But Taylor waves both arms in front of her like she's warding off a demon. "Absolutely not. We went to a fundraiser on my dad's behalf last night. I spent eight hours in stilettos with rich men twice my age who wanted to talk to my cleavage way more than they wanted to talk to me."

"And I couldn't even punch them in their dentures for ogling my lady," Daniel grits out.

"It was a nightmare," she concludes. "Tonight, I want to wear sweats and eat garbage."

"Fine," I relent. "But if you change your mind, I can ask Evan to come sit with Aiden just as easily."

He's been spending most of his nights the last couple weeks patrolling the perimeter of the property, anyway. I try to make sure to account for the extra hours in his paycheck, but he doesn't even tell me he's out there half the time. As far as I'm concerned, he's priceless.

Daniel gasps in outrage. "No one can replace Uncle Daniel! Not Evan, not anyone. How dare you even suggest it?"

Taylor rolls her eyes. "What he's trying to say is that we would love nothing more than some extra time with our favorite nephew."

"Our *only* nephew," Daniel points out. "But even if we had a dozen, Aiden would still take the cake. I'm happy to be his bodyguard for the night."

Suddenly, a blonde mop of hair pops up between their legs. "I don't need a bodyguard. I already have one at school."

"Yeah, but can your bodyguard at school do this?" Daniel picks Aiden up and tosses him over his shoulder like a sack of potatoes. He flips him around until Aiden has done a full three-sixty and is back on his feet.

"No!" Aiden giggles. "We're in school. It's not allowed. Hank just stares at me all day."

It's been weeks since Dante tried to pick Aiden up from school, and we've been in a stasis. Nothing has changed, for better or for worse. On one hand, it's nice. On the other, I get the feeling Dante is planning something.

That's why I hired Hank.

He meets Aiden at school every morning, watches him all day, and then hands control to Evan at pickup. It's just another layer of security. Another bit of insurance. One less thing for me to worry about.

Still, my list of worries could fill phone books.

I hate that I might be handing some of that anxiety to Aiden, too. Last night at bedtime, he asked me why he needed a bodyguard at all.

"Is there a bad guy after me?" he asked, eyes wide with fear.

I told him the truth. As much as I could, anyway. Even though it broke my heart.

"I'm doing everything I can to protect you," I assured him. "It's why I hired Hank. He is there to make sure no one gets close enough to hurt you. You'll be safe."

"So... someone wants to hurt me?"

"No. Of course not. But..." How do you tell a five-year-old that someone might want to rip his family apart? How do I explain that he's nothing more than a pawn in Dante's game?

How do I explain that I'll fucking kill Dante if he touches my son?

"Is it Mommy?" he asked softly.

It's like I could see his innocence shattering in front of my eyes, and I was the one holding the hammer.

I wrapped my arm around him. "I'm going to protect you and your mom, no matter what. You are both going to be safe, okay? That's what's important."

Aiden let it go and he didn't have any more questions for me this morning, but I still wonder what he makes of all of this. Will his life be an endless maze of guards and security systems and locked doors? Or will Dante be gone before any of this shit can traumatize my kid?

Those thoughts are swirling around my head when Aiden gasps, pulling my focus.

He's staring down the hall, his mouth split in a wide-open grin. "Princess."

I follow his gaze and the noise in my head goes fuzzy.

Before I know what I'm doing, I'm moving down the hall, only one thought in my head.

Mine.

"You're a fucking goddess," I breathe.

Mira waves me off, but her dark waves slip over her shoulder and her red-painted lips tilt into a smile. They match the burgundy of her dress.

The material traces a low line across her chest—a line I plan to follow with my tongue later. And I have devious plans for her thigh-high slit.

"You look good yourself." Her green eyes slide down my suit and back up, her cheeks turning pink. "Ready to come home with a neck full of medals?"

I loop my arm around her waist, pulling her close because I can't help myself. "There are no medals."

"Trophies, then."

"No trophies, either." I lean in, my lips moving against the shell of her ear. "Except for you."

She pulls back just far enough to bat her long lashes at me. "Being called a trophy wife is not the compliment you think it is."

"That's only because you have no idea how well I treat my trophies."

She smiles—her full, vibrant smile that knocks me back a half-step—and I start to consider if maybe we should skip the team's awards ceremony and stay here.

Then Daniel clears his throat behind me. "Just thought I'd

remind you two that we're still back here. You know, in case you'd forgotten."

I turn back to Mira. "I don't think they're gonna let us sneak back to the bedroom, so I guess we should go."

She holds out a dainty hand, her wedding ring gleaming in the hallway light. "Lead the way, Mr. Whitaker."

48

MIRA

"Oh my God!" Jemma's voice is slushy as she grabs my arm, shaking me even though she's talking to the entire group. "We're just down the street from that bar."

She blinks at us all, waiting for someone to say something.

Finally, Reeves steps in. "My darling, we're downtown. There are a hundred different bars. We're actually in one right now."

"We're in a steakhouse that has a bar," she argues. "That's different. But you know the one I'm talking about. The one with the—" She wiggles her arms in the air like seaweed and then flashes her hands like a strobe light.

Miraculously, Rachelle snaps her fingers. "The cocktail lounge that has bubble machines in the floor!"

"Yes!" Jemma hugs Rachelle. "I knew someone would get it. You're so smart." She kisses Rachelle sloppily on the cheek and twists back to me. "Do you know the place, Mira? Have you been there? Do you want to go?"

She's firing so many questions at me, I can't keep up. "Oh, uh—"

"We've been to that cocktail lounge before." Zane's hand tightens on my waist. "We had a great time. They have nice bathrooms, too. Spacious."

Jemma is too busy making afterparty plans that she is definitely going to be too drunk to attend to find Zane's comment weird.

"Do you *want* everyone here to know we had sex in a public bathroom?" I hiss under my breath.

No one is paying any attention to us, though. Jemma isn't the only one who made good use of the open bar. The rookies are playing a very obvious game of beer pong in the back corner, despite the wall of muscle they've employed to try to hide it from the coaches. And everyone else is gathered around tables, sharing highlights and horror stories from the season.

Zane and I are the only ones left on this far edge of the room. The low lights have us almost hidden in shadow.

I feel the exhale of his laugh against my ear. "No, but I'm down for round two if you are."

Heat curls low in my belly, and I have to lean into Zane's side to stay standing. "But we'll miss the ceremony."

"It's already over. Jace retired. That was the big news of the night."

Everyone knew this would be Jace's final season, but there still wasn't a dry eye in the house when he stood up in front of the team and thanked them for all the good years. Davis was an inconsolable mess and muttered something about boycotting Jace's media announcement next week.

As soon as Jace finished his speech, he huddled up with Coach Popov in a corner and hasn't left since. I keep wondering what they're talking about, but Zane is convinced it isn't important.

"We should at least stay until Coach Popov dismisses us."

"We aren't kids in school," he teases. "I had no idea my wife was such a rule follower."

"And I had no idea you were in such a hurry to leave your own award ceremony!"

"I'm in a hurry to get out of here so I can get into you." He dips his chin and takes my earlobe between his teeth. As if we aren't standing in the middle of his work function!

My body flames and I slap my hand on his thigh, digging my nails in as a warning. I'm not sure if the warning is for him or myself.

"It feels like I'm starting to convince you." His tongue flicks out to drag across my neck. "Come on, Mira. Leave with me. Let me take you out of here and fu—"

Shrill feedback from the mic blasts through the speakers and everyone winces.

"Sorry." Coach Popov taps the microphone a few times like that might help. "I'm more comfortable barking orders from the sidelines than using a microphone."

Everyone laughs while I give Zane a smug *I told you so* look. He just shifts behind me and loops an arm around my chest, pinning me against his body.

"The night may be young for you all, but it's late for me, so it's time to wrap this up so I can get home." Coach Popov pauses for another laugh. "I was going to make this announcement myself, but it feels right to let your former captain announce his successor."

Zane's arm tightens around me as Jace joins Coach on stage and grabs the microphone. I wrap my hand around Zane's, squeezing his fingers.

"I swear I'll make this quick. You all have heard enough from me tonight."

"And for the rest of our lives!" Davis jeers loudly.

Jace ignores him, continuing on. "I love this team. It's been my home for the last six years, and I couldn't walk away without making sure I left it in good hands. Which is why I'm thrilled Coach is letting me announce the next captain of the Phoenix Angels."

Carson sits up from where he's been holding court in the corner. His eyes flick over to us, but I look away quickly.

Zane said he could stay on the team if Carson became captain, but I can't imagine how. I've been mentally preparing myself for a big move if, for some reason, Carson's name comes out of Jace's mouth. I don't want to leave the family we've found here, but I'll do it for Zane.

"First," Jace adds, "I just want to give a quick thank you to the coaching staff for putting so much thought into this decision. It wasn't an easy choice, but you listened to the team and took everyone's opinions into account. We all appreciate that."

Zane lets go of me just long enough to join the smattering of applause.

"Without further ado, I'm thrilled to announce that your next captain will be... Zane Whitaker." Jace gestures towards Zane and I with a flourish, but...

Zane doesn't move.

Applause erupts around us, but Zane keeps holding onto me.

I try to wriggle away so I can clap or hug him or *something*, but his arm stays tight around my chest.

"Zane," I hiss, looking over my shoulder, "did you hear that? You're the captain."

I finally get a good look at his face, and he's...

Smiling. A wide, ear-to-ear, stupid happy grin. He's looking around at his teammates, taking it all in.

It's been a crazy few months where almost nothing has gone right—but this? This is perfect.

"You deserve this," I tell him, kissing the inside of his wrist. "You deserve it all."

Zane finally whirls me around and hugs me.

Davis starts a slow clap that evolves into a sloppy rendition of *"He's a Jolly Good Fellow,"* and Zane reluctantly lets go of me. He gives me a quick kiss on the cheek before he's roped into hugs and handshakes and claps on the back.

Coach Popov shakes Zane's hand and leads him off to talk shop, I'm sure. I'm beyond happy for him, but I also want this moment to be about him. Zane has been working for this for years, and I don't want to get in the way.

I make my way through the crowd towards the bar. I have a feeling Zane isn't going to want to rush off after that announcement. He'll want to stay and bask in the glory a little while longer, as he should. So I order an iced tea. It's been my drink of choice all night. Zane told me I could drink, but I told him I'd rather stay sober with him.

The bartender has to go into the kitchen to get my tea, and as soon as she's gone, a hand snakes around my wrist.

For a split second, I think it's Zane.

I turn around with a smile...

Until I see who is actually standing behind me.

Then, before I can rip my hand away from him, Carson Deluth is pulling me through a side door and into a dark hallway.

49

MIRA

The music in the main dining room has gotten louder. Even with the door shut, it pulses through the walls.

No one would even hear me scream.

That doesn't stop me from trying.

"Let go of me!" I try to twist away from Carson, but his grip is crushing. My bones grind together, and a whimper forces its way out of my mouth.

"You've been in the spotlight all night," he slurs. "Don't get shy now."

He twists my arm between us, never loosening his hold, and pins me against the wall. His breath is toxic. Every exhale stings my nose and makes my eyes water.

"You're drunk, Carson. Don't do this."

I'm not sure what his plan is, but it can't be good. Not if he's bringing me out here. Not when his eyes are bloodshot and there's a level of crazy in them I've never seen before.

He towers over me, all six-plus feet of him looming overhead and blocking out the light. "I didn't do anything. *You.* You are the one who fucked all of this up."

"Me? What did I do?" My heart is racing, but I try to stay calm. I focus on breathing in and out the way Dr. Navarro taught me. I place myself *here and now* instead of in my childhood home, curled against the floorboards.

I'm not that little girl anymore.

"You turned that piece of shit addict into someone people want to root for," he sneers.

I stretch onto my toes, getting as close to eye level with him as I can. "Zane has *always* been someone to root for. Long before I showed up."

He barks out a cruel laugh. "How much is he paying you to say that? Is this marriage between you two even real?" He's still pinning my wrist against my chest, but with his other hand, he curls a finger over my bare shoulder. "What are your rates? I might want to pay to play."

I wrench against his hold again, but he shoves me even tighter against the wall. My chest is tight, and I can barely breathe, but I drum up enough air to spit, "I'm not a prostitute; I'm his wife."

A lazy smile curls the edges of his mouth. "Maybe that is true, but I don't give a fuck. Because he will never be my captain."

Carson lunges for me like he's going to bite me, and he might as well. His lips smash against mine so hard I taste blood.

I kick and scream—and then Carson is gone.

It takes me a second to understand why. To realize that there is another hulking shape in the hallway with us, and he's yanking Carson back by the scruff of his neck.

"Get off me," Carson grumbles, stumbling.

But before he can catch his balance, Zane rears back and punches him in the jaw.

I swear it happens in slow motion. Carson's head snaps to the side, spit flies, and his eyes roll back in his head. He's unconscious before he hits the ground.

Then Zane is in front of me.

"Tell me where he hurt you. What did he do?" He ghosts his hands over me like he'll be able to feel where I'm hurting. "Are you okay?"

"I'm okay. I'm okay." Adrenaline is thrumming through me so hard I'm starting to shake, but... "I'm fine. He didn't hurt me."

Zane's thumb slips across my lower lip. "You're bleeding."

"He tried to kiss me, but he didn't—"

Zane spins around and kicks Carson. *Hard.*

I grab his shoulders to stop him from doing more. "He didn't hurt me. I'm—"

"He touched you. That's bad enough."

There's a welt forming around my wrist from where he held me. I loop my hands around Zane's neck and pull him close, pressing my forehead to his. "I'm okay. I swear."

The door to the dining room opens and there are too many voices to keep track of. A few of Carson's friends drag him away. I think someone might be calling 911.

"What happened here?" Coach demands.

Zane opens his mouth, but I step in front of him. "Carson attacked me. He grabbed me and tried to—I'm lucky Zane got here when he did."

"That fucking coward," Jace spits, looking angrier than I've ever seen him. "He cornered you? He followed you out here?"

I hold up my wrist. "He dragged me, actually."

Something shifts in that moment—something Carson can't come back from.

Coach Popov's jaw shifts. He claps a hand on Zane's shoulder, his eyes narrowed down the hall at Carson's limp form. "You get out of here, Whitaker. Go celebrate."

Zane shakes his head. "But—"

"I'll take care of it." Coach tips his head towards the door. "Get your wife out of here and enjoy the rest of your night."

Jace and Rachelle give me a hug and then Zane takes my hand and leads me through the restaurant.

We walk silently, the happy night shattered by one stupid, drunken moment.

We make it all the way through the front doors and onto the sidewalk when I grab Zane's hand and pull him to a stop. "No."

He arches a brow. "No?"

"No," I repeat. "Carson does not get to ruin our night. *Your* night. You're captain of the Phoenix Angels!"

"I don't care about that, Mira. I care that someone tried to hurt you. I was in the other room celebrating while he—"

"I'm fine." I lift my arms over my head and spin in a slow circle, letting him examine every inch of me. "Carson was so drunk that I—"

"If you say you can take care of yourself..." A dangerous growl rumbles out of his chest as he reaches for me. His fist tightens in the skirt of my dress, dragging my hips against his. "Just don't say it."

"How about I say 'thank you' instead? Is that allowed?" I flatten my hands on his chest, smoothing them down the clean lines of his suit. "You look incredible. Have I told you that?"

Zane looks annoyingly good in everything, but there's something about him in a suit.

He smiles, and all at once, the night feels sparkly again. Light and buoyant.

"Gratitude and flattery. If I didn't know any better, I'd think you were trying to seduce me, Mira Whitaker."

The sound of my new name on his lips still sends the butterflies in my stomach into a tizzy. "A woman never reveals her secrets."

"Lucky for you, a man does." He reaches into his pocket and pulls out a card.

It takes me a second to read the embossed logo on the side. And to follow the slight tilt of his head towards the glittering hotel across the street.

"But Daniel and Taylor—"

"Packed overnight bags in their car," he interrupts, curling my hair behind my ear. "I wanted it to be a surprise. I can't take you on a honeymoon right now, but I can give you this. Tonight. If you want it."

I slide out of Zane's arms and move to the curb. There's a valet at the entrance and brass streetlights around the block. The building is like something plucked out of the 1920s— sleek and classy and perfect.

But I wouldn't care if it was the rundown motel he found me in months ago; I'd still want it.

I'll always want him.

I look over my shoulder and hold a hand back to my husband. "Lead the way, captain."

50

MIRA

I'm not sure when I'll stop being gobsmacked by the luxury Zane has access to, but it isn't tonight.

I throw my purse on the bed and walk to the balcony doors in a trance, my mouth hanging open. "This is all ours? It's private?"

"Were you hoping to invite our neighbors for a swim?" Zane's arms circle around my waist from behind. I can see our fuzzy reflection against the sliding glass door, but the blue glow of the pool beyond still has most of my attention. "Because we don't have any neighbors. I rented out every room with access to this balcony."

"Good. I want it all to myself." I turn in his arms, my hands flat on his chest. "I want *you* all to myself."

Zane's expression sharpens. His fingers curl up my sides and stroke down my arms. He kisses my neck and sucks on the swell of my breasts, pushing the neckline of my dress lower with every sweep of his tongue. I close my eyes and sink back against the glass, happy to let him explore. Then his hands wrap around my wrists, and I wince.

In a second, the warmth of him is gone. He cradles my arm, turning my wrist over in his hand to examine it.

"It's okay." I try to pull my arm back, but he doesn't let go.

"We should get it looked at."

"Zane, I'm okay."

"You're hurt," he growls. "I don't want to make it worse if it's broken."

"It's not broken. I've had enough broken bones to know what they feel like." As soon as the words are out of my mouth, I know it was the wrong thing to say.

Zane's jaw flexes. The heat building between us ten seconds ago is chilly.

"I'm sorry," I groan.

"For what?" he grits out.

I gesture at the air between us. "For ruining your night! This is supposed to be a celebration, and I messed everything up. I shouldn't have let Carson—"

"You didn't *let* Carson do anything, Mira. That wasn't your fault. And nothing is ruined."

"Tell that to the very hot foreplay that just fizzled out."

Note to self: reflections on childhood abuse aren't good ways to stoke the fires.

He arches a brow. "'Very hot'?"

I bite my lower lip. "I thought so. What do you think?"

Zane closes the distance between us, his hands wrapping around my sides again. But this time, he finds the zipper at the back of my dress. He slides it down my spine slowly. His eyes go black as the material slips around my waist and then to the floor.

"You failed to mention you have nothing on under that dress." He stares at every bare inch of me, drinking it all in.

I shrug. "You didn't ask."

"We wouldn't have even left the house if I'd known."

I bite back a smile. "What's your plan now?"

He slips out of his jacket and starts unbuttoning his shirt. "I think you need to get in that pool. Now."

"It's cold out there," I argue weakly.

"It's heated."

"I don't have a swimsuit."

He unbuttons his pants and drops them, along with his boxers, to his ankles. My mouth goes dry. It wouldn't matter if that pool was swimming with piranhas—I'd get in right now if he asked me to.

"You won't need one." His voice is a desperate rumble as he reaches around me to open the door, gently guiding me backwards onto the balcony.

Steam is rising off of the surface of the water. The air bites into my exposed skin, but Zane leads me into the warm water and I sink happily below the surface.

The traffic sounds seem so far away. Even the city lights are fuzzy through the frosted privacy glass around the balcony.

"It feels like we're in our own world up here," I whisper.

"Because we are." Zane kisses my neck and my jaw. His lips whisper over my skin like a secret. "Nothing else matters right now except for you and me."

Questions sprout on the tip of my tongue. *Do you know where Dante is? Is Evan monitoring the house tonight? What security protocols are in place?*

But Zane seems to know what I'm thinking and he sets to work making sure I'm thoroughly distracted.

He corners me against the edge of the pool and works a hand between our bodies. He strokes one finger over me, dragging toe-curling friction against exactly where I want him.

"My one truth today is that I want to pretend we're two normal people on a normal honeymoon." His finger slips inside of me, stealing my breath away. "I want you to feel safe."

"I always feel safe with you."

Because of the security system and the bodyguards, yes, but also when we're under the blankets in our bed and he's crawling over me. When the shower door opens and he steps under the spray with me. When I wake up crying from a dream and he tucks a strong arm around my waist.

I trust Zane on a level I've never trusted another person in my life—with my past and my present, my heart and my soul.

"You know what I mean."

I know what he means, but *he* doesn't know what *I* mean.

"I do, but you—" He adds a second finger, and my head rolls back. The thoughts in my brain scatter.

He bites my lower lip, tugging on it while he fucks me with his fingers. "I love the way you look when I'm inside of you."

Suddenly, the water almost seems too hot. My body is on fire.

I fumble around between us until I can wrap my hand around his length. He hisses. "I'm so fucking hard, Mira. Have been since the party. Since before we even got to the party." He laughs. "I didn't even want to be there. The entire time, I was thinking about you."

Maybe we're supposed to take this slow, but every word out of his mouth zips through my veins. I'm vibrating, and I need him right now.

I think I say that out loud, but I'm not sure. All I know is Zane slides his fingers out of me and immediately fills me again. His hips press into me, and we both moan with how good it feels.

He wraps an arm around my lower back to protect me from the rough edge of the pool even as he's driving into me, panting against my mouth between sloppy kisses.

And I realize how much I don't want to know another version of Zane.

I don't want to wish away any single thing from his life that made him the person he is, that brought him to me.

His fingers dig into my ass as his hips snap against mine again and again. "Mira," he breathes. "God, I could come right now. Fuck."

"Me, too." And I could. But I'm not sure... "Wait, wait." I press a hand to his chest. "Wait a second."

Zane stops immediately, but his neck is red. I can see his pulse thundering in his throat. "Did I hurt you?"

"No. Never. I just… I think I want everything else to still matter."

He frowns, his chest heaving. "What?"

"I don't want another version of our relationship. I don't wish we were different people who met in a different way. I don't—" He twitches inside of me, and I hate myself a little bit for stopping us. "I want everything in our lives to matter. Because it *does* matter."

His lips linger along my jaw. Goosebumps zip down my neck. "I know it does. But not right now."

"Yes, right now. Always. It all matters. If everything had been perfect—my childhood, your past—we still could have found each other, but I think—" I adjust myself on the side of the pool, accidentally drawing him deeper inside of me. "It means so much more that we found each other despite everything."

I grab his face, forcing his eyes to mine. "I want you to know right now that I don't have any regrets, Zane. About anything. I'm glad we decided loving each other was more important than anything else. *My* one truth is that I'm so happy that we got married and are trying to make a baby and are building our life together, even while someone else is threatening to tear it down."

His eyes are locked on mine, wide and clear, and finally, he knows exactly what I mean. I see it in the flare of his pupils, the slight curve of his lips.

He presses into me again, and I sink against him. It's a slow push and pull. We're moving so carefully that the surface of the water stays still. The night is quiet. It's just our breathing and the press of our bodies and his eyes looking into mine, and it's all so fucking perfect that I snap.

My orgasm builds and swells until I'm clinging to Zane with both arms.

Until I drop my head to his shoulder and take a bite out of his neck to keep from crying out.

Only when I'm trembling from the comedown does Zane pick up the pace. Finally, he lifts my legs higher around his hips and drives into me. We crash together under the water again and again until he suddenly spins us around and sits on the bench that runs around the edge of the pool so I'm straddling him.

I sink all the way against him, and Zane is gone.

He buries his face against my chest while he spills into me.

I curl my fingers through the damp hair at the back of his neck as we both sigh and settle down. "I hope this is it," I murmur.

His eyes are glazed when he lifts his head. "What?"

"I hope we just made a baby."

He's still inside of me, and he rocks our bodies together. "Keep talking like that and I'll make sure it happens tonight."

"I don't know what time it is, but I'm not tired at all," I admit. "I want to enjoy every second of tonight with you."

His thumb brushes along my jawline. "Every second of tonight and every other night, it matters. They all matter. *You* matter, Mira. Always."

51

MIRA

When the door at the end of the hall squeaks open, I pause the TV.

Ten seconds later, there are shuffling steps behind me. I spin around to look over the back of the couch, but there's no one there.

Still, I know exactly who it is.

"You shouldn't be here," I warn.

Finally, a little head pokes around the corner. When Aiden knows he's caught, he slumps out from his hiding spot. His pajamas are covered in wooly mammoths and dodo birds and dinosaurs. The shirt says, *"Going to bed extincts."*

Aiden hugs his stuffed Spiderman toy to his chest and juts his lower lip out. "But I want to see my daddy."

My heart tugs even as I get up to lead him back down the hall to bed.

"I know, bud. And I promise you will... in the morning. Daddy is going to get home too late tonight."

Honestly, it won't be much longer now. Aiden has been getting out of bed every thirty minutes or so since I laid him down three hours ago.

"Where is he again?"

It's been the same question every night for the last four nights. It's the longest either of us have been without Zane, so I can't even blame him.

"He was in New York. Remember the show we watched last night where Daddy was on the TV?" I ask. Aiden nods. "That was in New York."

As the new team captain, Zane is the face of the team on the ice and off. The last few days, that meant showing up for photoshoots and fulfilling brand endorsements in the offseason. He tried to get out of it, but I convinced him he should go. He worked hard to be captain and I don't want anything keeping him from living out that dream fully.

(Plus, he sent me some of the photo proofs, and him shirtless with a milk mustache is my new screensaver.)

The plan was for Zane to get on a red eye flight as soon as his sponsorship duties were over, but a freak storm shut down the airport, and I firmly forbade him from even attempting to bribe a pilot to bring him home.

"You'll end up in TSA jail!" I said.

"Maybe. Or, alternatively, I'll make it home and be buried inside of you before sunrise."

As tempting as that was, I held my ground, and Zane finally agreed to get a hotel. He texted me a few hours ago that his new flight was boarding, and Daniel is going to meet him at the airport to drive him home.

"Can I please stay up?" Aiden yawns as I pull the blankets up under his chin.

He's going to drop any second, which is why I make a deal with him. "How about this? You can stay awake if you want, but you have to stay in your bed. *If* you hear your dad come home, then you can come out and say hi. But only if you hear him. Okay?"

He gives me a sleepy smile. "Okay."

"Okay." I kiss his forehead. "I love you."

His lips move around the words, but almost no sound comes out. I slip out of his room quietly just as I hear my phone vibrate in the living room. I jog to answer it, hoping it's Zane. But it's just the security system.

Front Gate Alarm Activated.

I groan just as my phone buzzes again. This time, it's Evan. *I got a notification about the gate. Are you okay?*

I'm in the middle of telling him I'm fine when he calls.

"Mira?" He sounds groggy. "You okay?"

"Evan, please tell me that stupid alarm didn't wake you up."

"Are you okay?" he repeats.

I can picture him poised on the edge of his bed. The man probably sleeps in cargo pants and combat boots, *just in case*.

"I'm fine. You know this security system goes off every time the wind blows. Zane is going to get rid of it next month and go with a new company."

"Have you checked the cameras?" Nothing I'm saying is comforting him at all. I wouldn't be surprised if he's already in his car.

I put my phone on speaker and open the security app. I try to select the front drive cameras, but they aren't pulling up. Neither are the backyard cameras. Or the interior cameras.

The entire stupid system is down. *Again.*

Since we've gotten married, Zane has spent more quality time with Lance from the security company than with me, I swear. And yet, it's still a piece of garbage. A *very expensive* piece of garbage.

"The cameras all look good," I lie, wedging my phone between my shoulder and my ear. "And Zane will be home soon. I'll have him double-check everything when he gets here."

Actually, I won't. I plan to make sure Zane makes good on the promise he made me yesterday, and he can't do that if he's outside trying to fix the front gate alarm in the dark.

Evan makes me promise to text him the second Zane gets home, and I give him a solemn "cross my heart and hope to die." Then I drop back down on the couch. I'm about to hit play on the TV when I hear what sounds like shuffling from the front porch.

Like suitcase wheels rolling across the cement.

Zane's home.

I jump up and run to the front door. I don't even look through the peephole before I yank it open to greet my husband.

Except there's no one there. The porch is empty.

So is the front walk and the driveway.

I squint into the darkness, trying to understand what I heard, when it hits me—what's wrong with this picture.

The gate at the mouth of the driveway is wide open.

Fear slams into me. Adrenaline thrums through my veins as I slam the front door closed, bolt it, and whirl around to grab my phone from the couch. I hope Evan is even more paranoid than I think he is and he's already on his way.

I'm halfway across the living room, still five feet from my phone, when a shadow falls over me. I don't even have time to turn around to see who it is before a hand wraps around my throat and a voice I'll never forget purrs in my ear.

"Hello, little sister."

52

MIRA

I can almost convince myself this is happening in my head. I've cracked. Lost the plot. My grip on reality is gone and I'm freefalling into a hallucination.

I can't see Dante, after all.

But I can *feel* him. There's no denying that.

His hand is clammy around my throat. His breath is hot and angry against the back of my neck. Something tells me his heart is beating as hard as mine is, but for a very different reason.

"It's been a long time." He squeezes tighter and I wheeze. "I've missed you."

I've spent years dreading this moment—waiting for it without ever fully expecting it to come. Now, it's here. *He* is here.

And I have no idea what to do.

I'm frozen. Terrified. The same way I was as a little girl, cowering in my room, hoping my dad and Dante wouldn't find me. I'm the same girl who would crumble to the ground while my dad yelled and kicked and spit. I'd curl up like an armadillo and wait for him to tire himself out.

But Dante isn't here to beat me.

He's here to *kill* me.

If I wait, I'll die.

As if to punctuate that point, Dante squeezes even tighter, closing my windpipe.

Finally, I drive an elbow back into his chest and break away from him.

He stumbles back with a groan and I manage to spin around to face him before he grabs me again.

"Maybe all of those kickboxing lessons are paying off." His mouth turns into what should be a smile, but it sends a chill down my spine. "What was all that training for? Were you hoping to fight back? I thought broken bottles were more your speed."

It's so much worse being able to see my brother. The last seven years have aged him seventy. His face is creased and lined. His skin is sallow. He looks like... like...

Like our dad.

"You don't need to do this, Dante." I try to step away, but his fingers are fisted in the collar of my shirt. "We can—"

"We can do what? Hold hands and sing fucking *Kumbaya?*" He spits on the floor to show what he thinks of that idea.

I can't think about the anger in his eyes or the firm hold he has on me. All I can think about is Aiden.

I told him he could come out if he heard Zane come home. What if Dante wakes him up? What if Aiden hears us and comes out?

I can't let myself imagine what my brother might do to my son.

"You want to kill me." It's not a question, but Dante answers it anyway.

"Yes. To put you down like a rabid fucking dog," he snarls.

My blood runs cold, but I refuse to shrink in front of him. "I'm still your sister. Don't you want to hear my side of the story before I'm gone forever?"

"You think I give a single fuck what you have to say?" He lashes out with a cruel laugh that makes me jump. *Too loud. Too loud.* "I didn't care what you thought when we were growing up together—so why would I care now that you're nothing more than the bitch who killed my father?"

"Because you've been chasing me for seven years. You've dedicated most of your adult life to tracking me down. There's no way you want it to be over so fast."

I hardly know what I'm doing. My mind is whirling, barking orders at me faster than I can follow.

Punch him in the larynx.

Find a weapon.

Get to your phone.

But all of those options could lead to raised voices and Aiden coming out of his room. They're not worth the risk.

He hauls me up almost to my tiptoes, trying to prove how much stronger he is than me. *Just like old times.* "You've always overestimated your worth, Katerina."

"I was worth seven years of your life."

"Our *father* was worth seven years of my life!" he fires back, seething. "The only reason I've been chasing after you is because of him. Because of what you did to him. *You?* You are worthless to me."

Some part of me hoped that Dante wasn't a monster all the way to his core. Over the years, I tried to make excuses for him, but staring up into his black eyes now, I know there is no good in him.

Nothing redeemable.

Nothing worth saving.

Before I can react, Dante yanks me off the floor by the front of my shirt and slams me down on the coffee table.

The air doesn't just rush out of me—it straight-up disappears. My lungs implode. I wheeze through several useless inhales before I can suck anything in at all, and then Dante is on top of me. His hand clutches around my throat.

Black is already creeping into the edges of my vision when I use every last bit of strength in my body to haul my legs up to my chest. I kick out, my foot glancing off of my brother's shoulder. It's not much, but it's enough for his hand to loosen.

Enough for me to suck in one much-needed breath of air.

Which is then enough for me to draw my arm back and land one solid punch to the left side of his face.

The force ricochets down my arm. My elbow aches. But Dante stumbles back, and I have an opening. I push myself to standing and lunge for my phone.

Evan. Zane. 911. It doesn't matter. I'll take *anyone*.

I'm fumbling to unlock it with my shaking thumbprint when I hear the door at the end of the hall squeak open.

No.

Tiny shuffling footsteps.

No. Please, God, no.

"Daddy?" Aiden's voice is raspy. Half-asleep.

"Oh, my. Who do we have here?" Dante croons.

I forget about the phone and jolt to my feet, standing between Aiden and Dante. Aiden is wide-eyed now. His blonde hair is mussed and he looks so much like Zane that it makes my heart ache.

"Mommy?" Aiden whispers.

"Go back to bed, Aiden." My voice cracks on his name. "Go to bed."

"No, stay," Dante offers in a way that feels more like a threat. "This is even better than I planned. A twofer."

I whirl around to face my brother. There is no plan, no ulterior motive. Just raw, pulsing fear. "Please don't hurt him."

He feigns a frown. "But it would feel so *right*, wouldn't it? You can watch me take your family out the same way I watched you take—"

"Run, Aiden!" I scream, not waiting for my brother to finish his villain monologue. There isn't time. Not if I'm going to save my son. I dart past my brother and run for the front door. "Aiden, run! Hide!"

I tear open the front door and sprint into the darkness just like I did that night seven years ago. I don't have shoes or socks on and the cement shreds my feet, but I duck my head and push myself as hard as I can.

I have to get away from the house—away from Aiden. I need to put as much space between my brother and my son as I can. Maybe, while Dante goes for me, there will be time for Aiden to get himself help. Or maybe Zane will come home and find him before—

I can't let myself think about another possibility.

This will work. It has to.

I chance a look back over my shoulder and, unlike the night that started it all, Dante is chasing after me this time. He's carving a quick path across the grass to cut me off at the gate.

I won't make it. I know I won't. But I sprint with all I have anyway.

For Aiden.

For his future.

For Zane and his son.

If this is how I go, it'll be worth it if the two of them survive.

I'm breathing hard and my limbs feel heavy, but some small part of me starts to wonder if I'll make it. Maybe I'll make it through the gate and down the road. A passing car could help me. Could scare Dante off. I could get back to Aiden and hold him, promise him everything will be okay now.

No sooner than the picture forms in my head, Dante slams into the back of me.

I plummet face-first into the lawn. Pain explodes across the bridge of my nose and deep in the back of my head. I gasp, but there's dirt and grass in my mouth, and Dante's knee against my spine is only grinding me further into the ground.

He's burying me. He's going to bury me alive, and Zane will find me dead. This will wreck him. He'll never forgive himself. It'll be all my fault.

Suddenly, Dante rolls me over. I take a gulping breath of air before he pins my back to the ground and bands both hands around my throat.

He's sweating and red-faced as he sneers down at me. "Dad always said you thought you were better than us. Look at you now. Living in this fancy house. Married to your rich hockey player. It's fucking pathetic."

I try to respond, but he's holding me too tight. Foam bubbles across my lips.

Dante said he didn't care what I have to say, but he loosens his grip so I can speak. "Zane is the man you wish you were," I croak.

My brother lets out a cruel, bitter laugh, but fury flashes in his eyes.

It hits me all at once how right I am.

"You hate me because I left. You hate me because—" I cough, and whether he means to or not, he releases my neck slightly. "You're mad because I found a life for myself outside of that house. Like Mom. The way you and Dad never could."

Dante is a dark shadow over me, silhouetted by the moon and the midnight sky overhead. His breath is hot on my face as he leans in too close. "Mom was a bitch who abandoned the only man who could ever love her."

I snort, the sound coming out in a rasp. "Dad has been dead seven years and you're still quoting him. You should get some new material."

I shouldn't taunt him, but the longer he's here with me, the more time there is for someone else to save Aiden.

"He's dead because *you* killed him!" he spits, winding back and slapping me hard across the face.

Red explodes behind my eye. I can already feel it swelling. But even through the pain, I manage a smile. "Wanna know something? Killing him was even better than I imagined it would be."

Dante roars and both hands close around my neck.

I knew it was coming, but I still claw at his hands and his arms. My mouth opens, trying to draw in air even though I know none will come.

I'd love to face the end with stoicism. I want to look into my brother's eyes and let him know I'm not scared of death. Not anymore.

The day I ran from my childhood home, I was so terrified— of what was behind me, what was in front of me. My life had only ever been pain, and I thought that was all it would ever be.

Now, I've seen the beauty.

Zane and Aiden and the little world we shared belonged to me for longer than I deserved, albeit nowhere nearly as long as I would have kept them if I had a choice. I knew I wouldn't get forever—but a taste of it was so, so beautiful.

As Dante leans over me, face red, lips pulled back in a snarl I can't hear over the ringing in my ears and the dying beats of my heart, all I see is Aiden and Zane.

And a bright white light.

I'm ready to walk towards it—but then Dante turns towards it, too.

He squints into it, actually.

I don't understand what's happening until a dark shadow charges at him, shoving my brother off of me.

I'm still on the ground. Still staring up at the sky. Then, like something out of a dream, Zane appears over me.

I wonder if I'm dead and this is my afterlife—but if so, Zane looks awfully terrified for someone in heaven. His blue eyes are wider than the sky, his skin deathly pale.

Maybe I got sent down south. I suppose that's not uncalled for.

"Mira!" His lips move around words I can barely hear. "Mira, are you okay? You have to get up!"

He's here with me, but he needs to be getting Aiden. Someone needs to help Aiden.

"Aiden," I wheeze. "Help Aiden."

Zane barks something over his shoulder and the white light disappears. Car lights.

Daniel. Daniel picked Zane up from the airport.

Daniel is going to help Aiden.

Aiden will be safe.

Nothing else has mattered to me since the moment I saw Dante. It was the only reason I fought, the only reason I ran.

I'm so relieved that I forget this isn't over until Dante screams from only a few feet away.

Zane turns, and I try to tell him to run. To save himself. But my throat is still raw, useless. I used whatever was left of my voice to warn them about Aiden. Now, it's completely gone.

And Zane doesn't run. He shields me.

The two men collide and roll into the grass.

Zane is bigger than Dante. Stronger. I've seen him hold his own on the ice and with Carson. He can take my brother, but I need to do something to make sure he wins.

I shove myself up to my hands and knees and crawl towards the driveway and the gate. I can see tire marks in the grass where Daniel must have swerved off of the drive so his headlights could illuminate our struggle in the grass. And a few feet from the tire marks, I see a long stick spilling out of a duffel bag.

A hockey stick.

My thoughts are still fuzzy, my body weak, but I want to help if I can.

I pick up the hockey stick and stand on shaky legs. I turn just in time to see Zane fall.

Dante stands over him and reaches for his waist. In the dim moonlight, there's a flash of silver.

A knife.

I silently scream into the night as he bends down and plunges it into Zane's torso.

I dig deep and run at my brother, finding energy reserves I didn't know I had. I lift the hockey stick over my head, mouth open in a battle cry my brother can't hear. One he doesn't know is coming.

He looks up at me just as I swing the hockey stick at his head.

Something sickening cracks.

Dante curses as he spins sideways. I swing the stick again and again. Bloody gashes open up on his face and his neck. He throws his hands up to defend himself, and I realize they're empty. The knife is gone.

It's lying on the ground next to my husband. Covered in his blood.

I push the thought from my mind as I throw the stick to the side and lunge for the knife.

Dante starts to sit up, but he's dazed and wounded. He isn't moving fast enough to stop me as I whirl around and stab the knife into the side of his neck.

53

ZANE

I don't even feel it.

I mean, I know what happened. I saw the blade disappear in my stomach. I watched Mira's brother pull it out, twisting to cause as much damage as possible.

But I don't feel a thing.

Adrenaline is pounding through me the same way it does before a big game. The stakes tonight are a little higher than gold and glory, though.

Mira comes out of nowhere with a hockey stick. She swings it again and again, taking Dante to the ground. As soon as he's down, she lunges over me, and pain shoots up my spine.

I feel that.

She's pushing on my wound, but the pain is there and gone in a second because Mira spins away from me just as fast, the knife in her hand.

I don't see it, but I hear the squelch of the blade as it hits its mark—then the labored sounds of Dante's wheezing.

"I *am* better than you, Dante," Mira rasps, her voice more breath than sound. "I never would have turned my back on you. I never would have sided with Dad over you. And I never, ever would have treated me the way you did."

Dante falls back, and I can finally see the gaping wound in his neck. Blood pulses out of it to the rate of his slowing heart, puddling around him on the ground. So much of it. So much blood. His face is growing pale as he blinks up at his sister—the last face he'll ever see.

Good fucking riddance.

"You and Dad were cruel to me, but in the end, I win. In the end, I killed you both." Mira spits down at him as his eyes droop closed.

Hands press against my stomach. I look through bleary eyes to see her. "Your face…" I reach out and touch her swollen cheek. I can't even look at the bruises around her throat. They're dark and angry now; they'll be worse in the morning.

"He stabbed you. He stabbed—" Mira pulls her shirt off, leaving her in nothing but a sports bra, and presses it to my stomach. The thin material soaks up blood too fast, but there's so much more than it can handle. "We need an ambulance."

As soon as the words are out of her mouth, distant sirens cut through the night. Daniel must have called.

Mira glances over her shoulder at her brother, and I know exactly what she's thinking.

"Where's the knife?"

"I don't know. You're losing a lot of blood, Zane." I can barely hear her through her swollen throat. "The paramedics will be here soon."

The sirens are louder. It'll only be a minute or two now.

"Knife," I say evenly. "Find it."

I can tell she doesn't want to, but Mira releases the pressure on my stomach and searches the grass. When she comes back, the bloody knife is in her hands.

I take it from her gently. Sitting up hurts like a bitch, but I find a clean corner of my shirt and wipe the blade clean.

"What are you—"

"He came at me with the knife. I didn't react fast enough and he stabbed me." I hold the blade over the wound in my stomach, gripping the handle as tight as I can. "But I pulled the knife out."

She shakes her head. "No, he pulled it out. He was holding it when I—"

"*I* pulled the knife out and *I* charged at him." I hold Mira's gaze, letting the words sink in. "I am the one who stabbed him in the neck."

"No," she croaks. "Zane, no. It was me. I did this. It's okay."

The sirens are just down the street now. I think I see red and blue flashing against the trees.

"There will be questions, Mira. If they find out you killed them both, it'll look bad. Tell them I did it." I reach for her with my free hand, pressing a bloody handprint to her cheek. "I should have done it, anyway. I should've been the one to kill him for you. I wanted to, but I didn't know he had the knife."

Her face is wet with tears. "You did enough, Zane. You saved my life."

No—you saved mine.

"Aiden needs you," I tell her instead.

If only one of us makes it out of this, I want it to be her. I already took care of my will. Mira and Aiden will get everything, and I know she'll take care of him. She was being strangled to death and the first word out of her mouth was our son's name. What more promise could I ask for?

"Aiden needs you," I say again. "He loves you."

My eyes are heavy. I want to close them, but Mira shakes me awake. "Stay awake. Aiden loves you, too. He needs you, too, Zane. Zane. Zane!"

The sirens are deafening now. They're so loud they drown out Mira's broken voice.

Mira waves her arm over her head, trying to bring the first responders my way since she can't shout.

I'm tired all of the sudden. I'm so fucking tired.

"What happened?" An EMT runs over with a medical bag in his hand. He's already lifting my shirt, inspecting my wounds.

"It was me," I pant, my eyes fluttering closed. "I killed him."

54

ZANE

"You love finding new ways to make my job hell, don't you?"

I crack my eyes open to see Hollis is sitting next to my hospital bed, his face forever buried in his phone. He tilts the screen towards me to show me the paragraph he's drafting, but pulls it away before I can see anything.

"As far as press releases go, this is one of the wilder ones I've ever written. Not *the* wildest. That accomplishment belongs to the unnamed supermodel whose pet tiger ate one million dollars' worth of someone else's diamonds. But this is a close second."

I have no fucking idea what he's talking about. I barely even know where I am.

I look around the hospital room, but Mira isn't here. She was earlier. At least, I think she was.

I have snippets of memory. Little flashes of nurses moving around my bed, Mira holding my hand, Jace's voice.

"How did I get here?" I clear the frog from my throat and immediately regret it. My stomach aches, and I press a hand to a thick bandage over my midsection.

"You should hit the nurse's button and request more pain meds." Hollis points at my wound. "You should also be grateful for that wound. It's the reason you're in a hospital instead of a holding cell right now."

I swear he shakes his head and calls me an idiot under his breath.

Again, I have no clue what he's talking about.

"Where is Mira?" I ask instead.

"Talking to the police. Telling them what happened."

I jolt up and, again, have immediate and painful regrets.

Hollis finally looks up at me long enough to shove me back down into the bed. I must be weak if he can manhandle me with one finger. "I said, Mira is telling them what happened."

"I know," I grit out. "I need to stop her."

I know killing Dante was self-defense, but the facts as they stand don't look good. Mira killed her father, went on the run for years, changed her name, and has now killed her brother. Who is going to be sympathetic towards her? She doesn't have the benefit of the doubt anymore.

"She's telling them exactly what *you* said happened, dumbass," Hollis hisses under his breath. He shakes his head. "Fucking idiot that you are, you took the fall. It's why you're cuffed to this bed, and she's out there confirming the deathbed confession you gave to the responding paramedic."

It takes a few seconds for his words to bypass the haze of whatever drugs are pumping through my system. I look to my right hand and realize it's handcuffed to the plastic bed railing. I didn't even notice. "Mira told them I killed Dante?"

"She didn't want to," Hollis grumbles. "She fought like hell to take the blame, but I knew what you would want. In the end, so did she. Still, the only reason she agreed is because I swore to her I could get you off."

I rattle my handcuff against the bed. "How is that going so far?"

"Considering the two of you refused to go to the police and hired private investigators instead?" he snaps, eyebrow raised. "Pretty damn good. I just sent a folder of evidence your P.I. and Mira's bodyguard gathered on Dante's movements the last few months. It's a clear pattern of escalation. We don't have the security cameras at the house as evidence since Dante was screwing with them, but you, Mira, and Daniel are all spewing the same story. Even Aiden is an eyewitness."

I wince. I don't want Aiden involved in this at all. I don't even want to think about what he may have seen.

I shove it all aside and hold out my hand—IV and all—to Hollis. "Thank you, Hol."

He takes my hand, shaking lightly. "I accept 'thanks' in the form of expensive whiskey and large Christmas bonuses, just FYI."

Hollis leaves to perfect my press release. A doctor and a few nurses check on me, but the only person I want to see is Mira. I ask anyone who walks into my room where she is, but the answer is always the same.

She's still being interviewed.

After an hour, I'm seconds away from climbing out of this bed and marching down the hall with my IV pole and my ass exposed, when the door opens.

"Mira."

She looks like she's been to hell and back. Her hair is tangled, her face is swollen, and her neck…

"*Fuck*. Your neck." I reach for her, but when she stops at the side of my bed, she keeps her hands behind her back. I don't want to think about what injury she must be trying to hide from me if the ones I can see are this bad.

"I'm okay," she croaks. "How are you feeling?"

"I feel like I want to get out of here and take you home."

"I want that, too." She swallows and it looks painful. I know Dante is already dead, but the sight of Mira hurting because of him makes me want to bring him back to life and kill him all over again.

"Have you talked to Aiden?"

"Not yet. I didn't want him to hear me like—" She gestures to her throat, and it's self-explanatory. "Daniel and Taylor are with him. He knows someone tried to hurt us, but he also knows we're okay. Daniel said he keeps asking for you."

"Well, as soon as I'm uncuffed, I'm ready to get the fuck out of here."

"You need to stay and recover, Zane. Dante did a lot of damage. I thought you might not—" Her voice catches. She stops herself, blowing out a long breath. "I want you to rest and recover as long as you need to."

I hold out my hand for her again. I'm itching to touch her. But she doesn't reach for me. Doesn't move.

"Mira," I plead.

She looks towards the window, ignoring me. "I told the police what happened."

"Yeah, Hollis told me he had to talk you into it. He said he'll be able to get me off easily." I curl my fingers, urging her closer. "Come here. Touch me."

Again, she ignores me. "I told the police everything that Dante had been doing for the last few months. The stalking, the threats. I told them everything they needed to know to prove you're innocent. The officer I talked to said they'd come and uncuff you in a few minutes... once I'm gone."

"Gone? You're not going anywhere. They should come uncuff me now. Mostly so I can drag you into this bed with me," I growl. "Come here, Mira."

Her eyes land on me, and they're glassy. A tear rolls down her cheek. "I hope you're not mad, but I told my one truth for today to someone else."

I can't explain why, but my heart is slamming against my ribs. "Mira..."

"I told them what happened to my dad—what I did. I told them who I really am and how I killed him."

"Okay. Okay." I can practically hear the gears turning in my head, trying to process everything. "Hollis had a plan for this. He's sending evidence about Dante to the police, so he can send the stuff about your abuse by your father, too. He'll take care of everything."

She gives me a sad smile. "If you could tell him to hurry it up, that would be great."

There's something she isn't telling me. There's a piece of this puzzle I don't have, and I don't like it.

An officer steps into the doorway and clears his throat.

When Mira looks over her shoulder at him, she turns just enough that I see her hands behind her back for the first time.

There are shiny metal cuffs around her wrists.

The final puzzle piece snaps into place, and I lurch towards the door. "No fucking way!" I splutter as agony rips through my torso like a lightning bolt.

"It's okay, Zane. I'm fine."

"You're in cuffs!" I spit. "You're not 'okay.' You're being arrested for saving your own life. It was self-defense!" The officer in the doorway doesn't budge. I strain against the handcuff strapping me to the bed, and it doesn't budge, either. "This is bullshit, Mira!"

"This is what I should have done seven years ago." She takes one step away from me. And another. And another. "Call Hollis for me, will you?"

"Mira!" My own cuff rattles against the bed, leaving deep dents in the hard plastic, but I'm trapped. Stuck here while my wife is hauled away from me.

I confessed to killing Dante to avoid this. I was supposed to save her from this.

The officer in the door steps aside to let her into the hall and my heart rate monitor is beeping off-the-charts fast. A couple nurses come in, worried, but I don't give a shit about them or my heart or anything but the woman walking away from me.

I arch off the bed, ignoring the pain that sears through my midsection with every breath, every motion, every cry. But it doesn't stop me from shouting her name again and again, as little good as it does me.

"Mira! Mira! *Mira!*"

55

MIRA

I don't know how long I've been here.

My holding cell doesn't have a clock, but the sun is starting to come up now. I think it's been a few hours since they booked me. Long enough that the ice pack a nurse at the hospital gave me has gone warm.

My eye is throbbing, but my throat hurts even worse. It feels like I drank a razorblade smoothie. The nurse gave me strict orders to ice it every six hours, but that was before I confessed to my father's murder. I have a feeling I'm not going to get top-notch medical care in jail. None of the officers who have peeked in to check on me have said a word about how I'm doing or anything else.

It's fine. I'm not up for talking, anyway.

I used my one phone call to call Taylor. "What do I need to do?" she asked as soon as the line connected. "How can I help?"

"Nothing. I'm just keeping my promise."

"Holy shit, Mira. You sound awful." Then: "Wait—what promise?"

I smiled even though I wanted to cry. "You made me promise that if I ever got arrested, I'd call you first."

"Now is not the time for inside jokes, Mimi! What do you need from me?"

"Nothing." I twisted away from the phone to clear my throat, which was enough to bring tears to my eyes. "Zane is taking care of everything."

"You really sound horrible."

"I look horrible, too. In case you were wondering." A P.A. at the hospital found me a t-shirt in the Lost & Found, and I thought that was bad. But the jailhouse scrubs are worse.

"Do you want to talk to Aiden?"

"No!" I blurted, necessitating another agonizing throat clearing. "I don't want to scare him."

"Fair enough. But... he's already scared. Daniel and I are trying to keep him calm, but we don't know what to tell him."

My chin wobbled. "Tell him I love him and that Zane will be home soon."

"You'll be home soon, too," Taylor said. "Trust me. Daniel is on the phone with Zane right now. He's going to do absolutely everything to get you out."

That was a buoy of hope for the first few hours. But I underestimated how isolating a jail cell could be.

I have no connection to the outside. No connection to my family. It feels like the world has stopped turning.

I lie down on the thin mattress and think about sleeping, since actually sleeping is very much off the table, despite how many hours I've been awake.

I'm still lying there when a key slides into my cell door. I sit up just as an officer slides the metal grate open.

"Katerina Costa," he says flatly, "come with me."

"Where am I going?"

The man doesn't answer. He stands stoically outside of my cell, waiting.

Wherever he's taking me, it can't be worse than here. So I shove to my tired legs and follow him down the long hall.

Most of the other prisoners are sleeping in their cells. It's still the middle of the night by most people's standards. But a few lift their heads to watch me lumber past.

I'm probably going to another interrogation. I willingly confessed, but the detectives at the hospital kept asking me the same questions over and over again. I'm sure they were trying to find inconsistencies in my story, working to poke holes in my version of events. But I held true to what happened then, and I'll do it again now.

I push my shoulders back and lift my chin, ready to face whatever comes next. But the door at the end of the hall has a large, hard-to-miss yellow sign affixed to the window.

Secure Exit Door.

"Am I leaving?"

I don't dare hope for anything good on the other side of that door, but I can't exactly help it. *He came for me. Just like he said he would.*

Instead of answering me, the officer grabs a walkie from his hip. "I'm at the door with Katerina Costa. We're ready to be buzzed through."

"Where are we—"

The door buzzes, and before I can get the question out, the officer pushes the door open.

The room beyond is bright and it takes a few seconds for my eyes to adjust.

Then I see him, standing in the middle of the lobby, and it takes everything in me not to drop to my knees.

"Your bail has been posted," the officer says, urging me forward. "Clear the doorway."

I manage two stuttering steps forward—just enough for the officer to slam the door closed behind me—and then Zane is there. His arms around me, holding me up even though there's no way he should be able to do that yet.

"Your stomach," I sob, fisting his shirt in my hands, holding onto him the way I wanted to in the hospital room.

Zane kisses the top of my head. "I'm fine."

"Actually, he definitely is not fine." Daniel winks when I look over. "He should be in a hospital bed."

"I'm fine," Zane grits out again. "The doctor agreed to discharge me."

"After you bribed him," Daniel explains helpfully. "They warned you that your stitches could open and you could bleed out, but you said, and I quote, 'I bet five grand in your pocket will help you agree that those stitches will stay closed.'"

I look up at Zane. There are dark circles under his eyes. He's too pale. "You shouldn't be here."

"Neither should you," he whispers, stroking his thumb over the bruise on my left eye. "I had to make sure you got out. I couldn't leave you here."

"Which is why he also bribed a judge to get your bail set before the courthouse even opened," Daniel mutters from behind closed lips.

"Zane!"

Zane rolls his eyes at Daniel. "I didn't bribe him; I threatened him."

"Worse!" I snap. "You do see how that's worse, don't you?"

He kisses my temple again, his lips whispering against my skin as he says, "It's going to be fine."

"We're trying to get *out* of jail, not find new ways to get locked up!"

"Okay, then how about this: next time you decide to confess to a murder you committed under completely justifiable and legal means, maybe give me some warning. I'd love to never repeat the last six hours ever again." His hand spreads across my waist like he's trying to claim as much of me as he can. "I couldn't get to you and it was driving me mad."

All at once, every bit of worry and frustration and fear drops away, and I'm exhausted. Zane tightens an arm around me, and I let him hold some of my weight. I lean against him, my cheek pillowed on his warm chest.

I was so close to losing him tonight. But he's here.

We both are.

And there's only one thing I want now.

"Let's go home."

56

MIRA

The lawn is a wreck. There are deep tire tracks across the grass from Daniel's car and the first responders, and the police left bright orange evidence markers all over the lawn. One sits next to a dark, marshy patch of grass that I know is where Zane was bleeding out. I have to look away as we pass.

Taylor did her best to clean up the living room, but Dante cracked the coffee table when he slammed me down on it and Daniel almost ripped the frame off the door when he barreled inside to check on Aiden.

"We'll go shopping for a new one," Taylor reassures me. "A lot of this furniture belonged to Davis, anyway. You have to buy new stuff. Because of cooties."

I smile and hug her tight, pretending not to notice when she starts crying softly on my shoulder.

"Aiden was up most of the night," Daniel chimes in. "He'll probably be asleep for a while longer if the two of you want to—"

"You need a shower," Zane interrupts, reaching for my hand. "And a change of clothes."

I don't argue. I wouldn't have the energy even if I wanted to.

Zane walks slowly down the hallway. As I tug off my jailhouse outfit and bury it in the bottom of the bathroom trash, I notice Zane pop a pill from a bottle on his nightstand.

He glances up at me as he dry swallows it. "Owen is keeping track of my pain meds," he explains. "He knows how many are in the bottle and how long they should last me. He's texting me every couple hours. Just in case."

I hold out a hand for him. "I trust you."

I've never trusted anyone more. Probably never will again.

Zane assesses me silently, running his hands over the red rings around my wrists, brushing a thumb across the bruising on my throat. He leans forward and kisses my swollen eye, whispering apologies to every injury on my body.

He starts the shower for me, careful to stay out of the spray. "I can't shower for another two days, but I've been away from you more than enough lately. I want to stay close."

I want that, too.

I nod, but when I try to speak, my chin wobbles. My throat tightens, and it's like Dante's hands are there again. It's like I'm pressed into the ground, unable to breathe. I open my mouth to say something, *anything*, but a wrenching sob comes out instead.

In a second, Zane is there. He turns off the water and curls me against his chest.

"It wasn't y-your fault. I don't blame y-you. I c-couldn't." Every tear I've held in for the last twelve hours—the last seven years—drains out of me.

Zane doesn't let go. "I know, Mira."

"I love you," I sob. "I didn't want you to get hurt. Or to go to jail for me."

"That makes two of us. But somehow, only one of us got what we wanted." He grabs my chin, lifting my ruined face to kiss one cheek and then the other. "Please know, as repayment, I plan to get my way for the rest of eternity."

I drop my forehead to his chest. The bandage on his stomach is dotted with blood, and I close my eyes. "You sacrificed too much already. I couldn't let you do it anymore."

"I haven't sacrificed a thing."

I pull back. "What are you talking about? You could have lost your son because of me."

"I didn't."

"But you could have. And you had to move out of your condo for me."

He shrugs. "I never liked the place."

I frown. "You almost lost your spot on the team because I brought all of my chaos into your life. You might not have been captain!"

"It's a lot of responsibility, being captain," he muses. "Frankly, I think the whole thing is overrated."

"Zane, be serious. I turned everything upside down. You gave up so much to take care of me."

"And I'd do it all again in a heartbeat. I'd give up more, actually." He cradles my face gently in his hands, forcing my eyes to his. "I'd give up absolutely everything to take care of you, Mira, and I'm perfectly serious about that. Because that's how much you mean to me. It's not a sacrifice if the thing I'm desperate not to lose is *you*."

I don't have the words to explain what Zane means to me. To tell him the lengths I'd go to to make sure I never lose him.

So I do the next best thing: I cry on his chest until I run out of tears. Then I wash off the terrible day and let Zane bundle me up in a robe and lead me to our bed.

We lie there together, crying and dozing and whispering, until our door opens and a shock of blonde hair pokes through the crack.

"You can go in," Taylor urges from the hall. "Just be gentle with them. They have owies."

Hearing my best friend say the word *"owies"* warms my heart in a way I didn't know was possible. Then Aiden bursts through the door, half in tears before he can even make it to our bed, and my heart disintegrates.

It's eviscerated. It's dust in the wind.

I haul Aiden onto the bed, nestling him carefully between us so he can hug his dad without hurting him.

"Everything is okay," Zane murmurs again and again, smoothing Aiden's hair back. "We're all safe."

"Because you're here now?" Aiden whimpers.

Something breaks behind Zane's eyes, but he nods and kisses Aiden's forehead. "Exactly, buddy. You're safe because I'm here."

Because Zane is the kind of dad every kid deserves. The kind of husband any woman would be lucky to have—me, most of all.

I didn't think a life like this was possible for me, but now, it's here, and I am never going to let it go.

Aiden eventually drifts to sleep, and Zane and I watch each other over the top of his head. He needs to remind himself that this is real as much as I do.

"What are you thinking about?" I whisper after a long time.

"Europe."

I bite back my first real laugh in way too long. "What?"

"I was thinking about Europe," he continues. "Southern Italy, maybe. Or the Maldives. You'd make a cute ski bunny, but selfishly, I'd like you in a bikini as much as possible."

I shake my head, grinning. "I have absolutely no idea what you're talking about."

He reaches over Aiden and links our fingers together. "I'm talking about our honeymoon."

"Oh." I blink. *"Oh."*

"We said we'd talk about once everything was over, and—" He shrugs. "—everything is over."

"Yeah, I guess it is." Tears prick the backs of my eyes, but I blink them back. I don't want to cry anymore. "I never actually thought this would happen. I don't actually know what comes next."

Zane brings our hands to his mouth, kissing my knuckles. "Luckily for you, I have nothing but ideas."

EPILOGUE: MIRA
TWO MONTHS LATER

"There should be a circle of hell dedicated to children's birthday parties," Taylor grumbles as a train of children chug through the kitchen, loudly blowing party horns. Aiden is at the lead, grinning from ear to ear. Once they turn down the hall for Aiden's room, Taylor sags against the countertop. "No offense."

I toss a pile of cake-covered paper plates in the trash with a shrug. "Why would I be offended? You're just saying the party I planned for the last three weeks and executed perfectly belongs in Dante's *Inferno*. What's offensive about that?"

To be fair, this party could've been done in only a few days. Zane's new assistant offered to help by calling vendors, ordering the cake, and sourcing invitations, but I told Gavin I would handle it all myself.

Honestly, I needed the distraction.

It's been almost two months since the night everything happened, and we're all slowly getting back to form. I sleep a little more each night. Aiden asks fewer and fewer questions about bad guys breaking in. Zane isn't compulsively checking the security cameras quite as often.

We each still have our good days and bad days, but today is a good day.

"I'm sorry." Taylor wraps her arms around my shoulders, squishing her cheek against mine. "Your superhero party for six-year-olds is the event of the season. Coachella has nothing on this."

"That's not a compliment! You hated Coachella. You said it was an 'overpriced, under-hydrated desert where music goes to die.'"

Taylor cocks her ear towards the patio doors. "What was that? Oh, Daniel is calling for me."

"I'm officially taking offense!" I shout at her back as she skedaddles onto the patio, but not before blowing me a kiss through the open door.

I slide some dirty dishes into the soapy water in the sink and start trying to make sense of the trash that's collected on the countertop throughout the day, when another pair of arms slide around my middle. This time, it's a stubbly cheek against mine, Zane's voice deep and warm in my ear. "You should be enjoying the party."

"I am. I love dishes."

He nips at my neck. "I'll clean the kitchen later. Come back to the party."

I spin around in his arms, letting him cage me against the counter. He and Daniel have been golfing a few days every week in the offseason, so his skin is a rich golden brown and his blonde hair is lighter than I've ever seen it. I run my fingers through it because I can never seem to stop myself. "Are you trying to seduce me with chores?"

"Absolutely. If you don't succumb, I'll take out the trash next."

"I'm soaking wet." I dramatically bite my lower lip. "What else?"

"You know that pile of hockey gear in the back corner of my closet?" he teases in a breathy voice. "I'll *organize* it."

I hook a leg around his hip. "Take me now, Prince Charming."

"Don't tempt me." He kisses me, nipping at my lower lip in a way that has heat swirling low in my stomach.

Thankfully, before mistakes can be made, a chorus of party horns echo down the hallway. The partiers stomp through the kitchen and into the backyard. Zane and I follow them through the door, taking up the caboose.

Each boy grabs a slice of pizza as they pass the snack table and then they march for Aiden's clubhouse underneath the slide.

"Do we need to order *more* pizza?" Davis shuffles through the pile of empty pizza boxes. "Who knew kids could eat so much?"

"Everyone with a kid," Jace snorts. "Gallagher eats more than I do some days."

"We've also been here for lunch *and* dinner." Rachelle turns to me. "If you need to kick us out, Mira, please do. We're intruding."

I wave her off. "We don't mind. I think the men missed each other."

The hockey players in question all grumble and deny it, but they've been huddled in a circle, chatting and laughing, since the party started seven hours ago.

"It's true. You all gossip like a bunch of old ladies." Taylor elbows Daniel in the side.

"Talking about where Carson Deluth got traded is not gossip. It's business."

I roll my eyes. "Is it also *'business'* to cackle like hyenas about how he got traded back East to the worst team in the league?"

"Okay, you got us. That isn't business," Daniel says, lifting his chin in defiance. *"That,* my friends, is karma."

I can't argue with that. Not after the way Carson treated me at the award ceremony. Coach Popov put Carson on suspension the day after he attacked me. Apparently, he couldn't be let go from his contract, but within the month, he was traded for three second-round draft picks.

Zane jokes that Popov would've probably accepted a washing machine and an IOU if that's what it took to get rid of him. He might not be wrong.

The party goes on way too late. Gallagher falls asleep while the boys are playing hide-and-go-seek, so Jace has to crawl under Aiden's bed and drag him out by his legs. When they leave—a sleeping Gallagher in tow—Reeves and Jemma collect Jalen and decide to call it a night, too. Jemma kisses each of my cheeks and Jalen thanks me for "the best party ever."

As soon as they're gone, I nudge Taylor. "Did you hear that? I threw the best party ever. I don't think the best party ever would be one of the circles of hell, do you?"

She rolls her eyes. "You're so dramatic."

"And you're still here even though it's—" I check the time. "—after nine! Sounds like a pretty fun party to me if you hung around for nine hours."

"You're never going to let that go, are you?" she drones.

"Never," Zane agrees. "Mira knows how to hold a grudge."

"It runs in my family."

There are a few beats of tense, nervous silence before Taylor and I bust out laughing at the same time.

Daniel joins in after a second, but Zane just shakes his head and tugs me against his side.

"How can I make it up to you, Mimi?" Taylor prods cheekily. "What do I have to do to make sure you don't go homicidal on me?"

"That's fucked-up," Daniel mumbles.

"According to my therapist, dark humor can be a coping mechanism." I turn to Taylor. "Which is why you have to let me plan your next birthday party. There will be chocolate fountains—"

"No!" she gasps in horror. "Do you have any idea how much hair and dust get in those things?"

"—and a karaoke machine that only plays Whitney Houston."

"No one but her can hit those high notes!" she complains. "I don't know why people even try."

I laugh maniacally. "Put me in full control of your party, and I'll forgive you."

She considers it for a second. Then a very, very suspicious grin spreads across her face. "What if I let you be my wedding planning partner instead?"

My brain short-circuits. I look from Taylor to Daniel and back again, but it's only when Taylor pulls a ginormous diamond rock out of her pocket and slips it on her ring finger that I scream.

"You're engaged and you didn't tell me?!" I yank her into a hug and we're laughing and jumping and stumbling all over the place.

"It just happened last night. You're the first people we've told."

"Oh my God." I hold Taylor at arm's length. "I didn't think this day would come. No offense."

She squeezes out a laugh. "Offense taken, you bitch."

We send Taylor and Daniel away with hugs and congratulations and promises to get together and start wedding planning soon. Taylor is positive she's going to need at least two years to plan the perfect wedding. Zane and Daniel share a look that seems to say something along the lines of *God help us all.*

Then they're gone, and we're alone.

I scan the dirty kitchen and the streamers still hanging from the patio, wondering where to start first. Then I realize what we're missing.

"Where did Aiden go?"

"He walked Jalen out to his car, but I haven't seen him since." Zane pads down the hallway, calling his name.

I know Aiden is fine. He's here in the house somewhere. Still, I have to take slow, deep breaths to keep myself from falling off a mental ledge. My panic button is on a hairpin trigger these days. It doesn't take much to set me off.

By the time Zane comes back a minute later and waves for me to follow him down to Aiden's room, I'm almost completely back under control.

Aiden is sitting at the end of his bed, a folder in his hands. Zane is sitting next to him.

Both of them are looking at me.

Maybe I should've done a bit more deep breathing.

"What's going on, guys?"

"Aiden has something he wants to talk to you about." Zane loops an arm around Aiden, who I realize now is shaking with nerves.

My heart jolts, but I walk myself through the facts.

We're all together.

The house is safe.

No one is trying to hurt us.

I kneel in front of Aiden. "You can talk to me about anything, bud. What's wrong?"

"You and Daddy got married," he says slowly. "Because you loved each other."

I'm not sure if it's a question or not, but I nod. "Yes, we did. I love your dad very much. And you."

He blinks at me with wide, blue eyes. "But we can't get married."

"No," I chuckle. "We can't. I'm already married."

"So... we can't be a family."

I frown and glance at Zane, but he doesn't look like he's planning to jump in. He's just observing. Watching me flounder.

"Oh, um, well, that's not exactly—" I blow out a deep breath. "You and I *are* family, Aiden. When I married your dad, you and I became family, too."

"But you're not my mom."

I bite my lower lip. I knew conversations like this were coming, but I didn't think we'd be getting into this yet. He's only six. He doesn't understand how money works. He thinks the internet is the one fruit matching game I let him play on my phone. How do I explain what constitutes a family?

I take his little hand in mine. "No, I am not your mom. I didn't carry you in my tummy and I didn't know you as a baby, but I love you like you're mine. I'll be whoever you want me to be."

"I want you to be my mom," he says with no hesitation, thrusting the manila folder at me.

I stare down at it. "What's this?"

Aiden looks at Zane like I'm being silly. "You said you wanted to be my mom. Now, you can sign these and you will be."

I flip the folder open, my chest seizing when I see the word **ADOPTION** printed across the top of the complicated-looking documents.

"What...?" I breathe.

Zane flips the folder closed and takes my hand. "Aiden came up with this idea on his own. He said he wanted you to be his mom. He wanted to have a ceremony like you and I did to make it official."

"But the social workers..." I look nervously at Aiden. "They haven't—"

"He's officially mine as of two weeks ago." Zane can't hide the grin that stretches across his face. "Peter Morris signed off on my legal guardianship himself, to my utter shock. Aiden is mine—and, as soon as you sign these papers, he can be yours, too."

Any attempt at swallowing down my tears goes right out the window. I sob so hard that Aiden gets concerned.

"You don't have to if you don't want to," he gasps because I'm squeezing him so tight.

I kiss his soft cheek. "Of course I want to, Aiden! I'd be honored to be your mom."

He points to my wet face and asks, "Happy tears?"

I nod fervently. "The absolute happiest."

I try to pull myself together, but after I cry through the entire first bedtime book, Aiden politely suggests I leave so I don't interrupt his routine. I don't even blame him.

By the time Zane is done putting him to bed, I'm changed

into a night shirt and rinsing my puffy face with cold water in the bathroom.

He leans against the doorway, a smug smile on his face. "Sorry to spring that on you. I didn't think you'd cry so much."

"The sweetest boy in the world just told me he wanted me to be his mom." I get choked up even thinking about it. My chin dimples, and I have to stare at the ceiling to keep from crying again. "What else was I supposed to do?"

Zane pads across the bathroom floor and brushes tears from my cheeks. "I can't believe I used to think you were Wednesday Addams."

"I thought that was just because of the dark hair."

He twists the end of my hair around his finger. "No, it was because you never smiled at me and I thought you were a stone-cold bitch."

"You were right about one of those things." I grin up at him.

"So true. Everyone knows stone-cold bitches cry over adopting little boys they love... and about baby frogs on nature documentaries that get eaten by bigger frogs—"

My lower lip trembles. "I just don't understand how the species survives if they eat their young."

He smiles at me so adoringly, my stomach flips. No one has ever looked at me the way Zane does. "You really are a softy now."

"It's your fault!" I poke him in the chest.

He kisses my neck. "Because I broke down the walls of your heart and made you fall in love with me?"

I bend to give him better access, stroking my hand under the hem of his shirt and over the broad muscles of his back. "Yeah, that, too, I guess. But I was mainly thinking about how you got me pregnant and made me all hormonal."

Zane stiffens. He releases one startled breath against my neck.

Then he jerks back, holding me at arm's length while wide, blue eyes search every inch of my face. "How I got you *what?*"

Tears well in my eyes as I explain everything.

How I thought I missed a period because of the stress, and the pregnancy tests kept coming back negative, but then I missed *another* period, so I scheduled a doctor's appointment.

I turn to grab something from the top drawer, but Zane's hands are fisted so tight in the back of my shirt that I have to pry his fingers loose to pull out the sonogram.

Zane stares down at the black-and-white image for so long I think he's frozen.

"I'm almost twelve weeks," I explain softly. "But I've been taking prenatals since we decided to start trying, so that's good. The doctor said the baby looks healthy, and I—I'm sorry, did you want to be at the appointment? I didn't know they were going to do an ultrasound that day. I didn't think it was possible I was that far along, but—"

Zane silences me with a long, passionate kiss that steals every thought from my head except for *more* and *please* and *right now.*

He lifts me onto the counter and takes the sonogram from my hand. I don't know where he puts it because I'm too focused on the way he hooks his hands around my thighs and drags me to the very edge of the counter, opening me for him.

His thumb brushes over the thin material of my panties, and I whimper against his lips.

"Twelve weeks," he breathes, stroking me. "That would be—"

"The night at the hotel. In the pool."

He inhales sharply, and I know exactly what he's thinking. It's the same thoughts I had once I found out.

Dante threw me on the coffee table. He tackled me in the grass. I was in jail.

I thought the endless weeks of nausea were from the stress of talking to detectives and coordinating a defense strategy with Hollis and navigating the trauma of it all. I even had a couple glasses of wine with Taylor one night to celebrate the police dropping all of the charges. I threw it up within the hour, though.

"The baby is healthy." I press my hand to Zane's face, pulling his eyes to mine. "Our baby is okay."

His jaw flexes. "Are *you* okay?"

"'Okay'?" I laugh. "As soon as I know you aren't mad at me, this is going to be the best day of my entire life."

All at once, Zane picks me up and carries me into our bedroom. He gently lays me on the bed, shedding clothes as he crawls over me.

I stroke my hands down his chest. "Does this mean you aren't mad at me?"

He presses a hand between my legs, dragging devastating

friction over exactly where I want him. "Would I be doing this if I was mad?"

"It wouldn't be the first time," I pant, arching off the bed to get more. "We've had hate sex before."

Zane slides his hands over my body, peeling away my shirt and panties like they're nothing. He kisses his way up my thighs and over my hips. His stubble scrapes over my stomach and between my breasts. By the time his mouth is over mine, I'm clinging to his neck, practically begging him to touch me.

"I never hated you, Mira." Zane positions himself at my entrance, and we both sigh in relief when he slides home. His jaw clenches. "I hated how much I wanted you."

We've barely started, and I'm already halfway there. I'm writhing against him, lost to the feel of him sliding in and out of me.

Zane's mouth crashes over mine. He tilts my hips, taking me faster until I'm whimpering, crying out his name with every thrust. He groans when we're sealed together. "I hated that I thought you would never be mine."

"I'm yours." I roll my hips, taking every bit of him I can. "I want you and I'm yours and I love you and please, please, for God's sake, fuck me."

His eyes darken and his hips snap against mine until the sheets are a tangled mess in my fists and we're slick with sweat. He whispers beautiful, filthy things against my skin until I come so hard I'm seeing stars.

Zane spills into me and then collapses next to me on the bed, wrapping me up in his arms and his warmth and his wintergreen skin.

"If I wasn't already pregnant, that would've been it," I breathe. "Apparently, we'll have to be careful. I think we might be good at this."

"At fucking?" Zane asks, circling my breast with his finger. "Obviously."

"At making babies," I clarify. "It didn't take very long with the first one."

"Good. I want to make so many babies with you, Mira Whitaker."

I hum in thought. "How many are we talking here? A normal large family or we-have-our-own-show-on-network-television kinda large family?"

Zane laughs. "Well, Aiden and I have talked about it and—"

I sit up on my elbows. "You and Aiden have talked about how many babies we should have?"

He shushes me, easing me back down on the mattress like it's all perfectly normal and nothing to worry about. "Looking at it practically, we only have the space for about five more kids."

"Five *more?*" I gape.

Zane kneels between my legs, his hands stroking fire up my thighs. "But that's only if we stay in this house. We can always move."

"We'll have to move into an abandoned schoolhouse with how many kids you apparently want!"

"There's an idea." Zane takes me in—*all of me*—and smiles. "My one truth for today is that I've never been happier in my entire life, Mira. I want it all with you. Everything you'll give me."

My one truth is that there's absolutely nothing I wouldn't give this man. Including a busload of children.

I keep that truth to myself for now, though.

I'll let him do his damnedest to convince me.

BONUS EPILOGUE: MIRA
FOUR YEARS LATER

Download the Bonus Epilogue for a sweet and spicy glimpse four years into Zane and Mira's future! https://dl.bookfunnel.com/mfl42t27ut

ALSO BY MARIAH WOLFE

Los Angeles Firebirds Hockey

Red Line Ruin

Red Line Riot

Dallas Bulls Hockey

Blue Line Lust

Blue Line Love

Seattle Wave Hockey

Blindside Sinner

Blindside Saint

Blindside Devil (novella)

MAILING LIST

Sign up to my mailing list!
New subscribers receive a FREE spicy hockey romance.

Click the link below to join.
https://sendfox.com/mariahwolfe

Made in the USA
Columbia, SC
20 July 2024